ISLAND OF GOLD

AMY MARONEY

Artelan Press

Artelan Press

Portland, Oregon

ebook ISBN: 9781955973007

Paperback ISBN: 9781955973014

Cover design by Patrick Knowles.

Find more books by the author at www.amymaroney.com

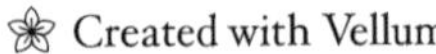

PROLOGUE

Languedoc, France
1435

Cédric offered the falcon a strip of rabbit meat. Ignoring the tidbit, she retracted her neck low into her shoulders, plumped her feathers, and fixed him with a baleful glare.

"Still off your feed?" he asked softly. "What ails you, my girl?"

A low growl of thunder startled him. He glanced through the open door to the courtyard, where rain pummeled the cobblestones. The scent of rotting straw hung in the air. If only sunshine would break through the clouds and give the land a chance to dry out.

Then a familiar figure filled the doorway, jolting him out of his thoughts.

"Philippe," he said in surprise. "But you're early—"

"It's your father," his sword master replied, breathing hard. "He's wounded."

Cédric dropped the pouch of rabbit meat and pushed past Philippe. He broke into a run when he glimpsed a guard and a servant across the courtyard, carrying his father through the front doors of the main house.

Inside the great hall, he cleared the broad oak table near the hearth with one sweep of his arm. Pewter and crockery smashed against the tile floor. Quickly, the men settled Papa on the table and removed his leather cuirass and chain-mail shirt. A deep wound gaped at his lower abdomen, leaking blood. His moans reverberated to the rafters.

Cédric yanked an embroidered flax runner off a nearby chest. It was one of the few reminders of his mother left in the house since her death on his twelfth name-day, nearly four years ago. With trembling hands, he wrapped it around his father's waist. The mingled aromas of sweat and blood filled his nostrils.

"It was the *écorcheurs,*" said the guard, removing his helmet and running a hand through his matted hair. "They surprised us on the road back from the seminary."

"They took my purse, my boots, my belt," Papa managed to croak. "The ring off my finger. And ran me through with my own sword."

"Those devils. I'll kill them!" The words exploded from Cédric's lips without warning. Philippe pressed a restraining hand on his shoulder. His heart thrummed crazily against his ribs all the same.

A servant hurried in with a jug of wine.

"Where is Yves?" Cédric demanded, tying the ends of the cloth together to bind his father's wound. The faint outlines of pink silk roses embroidered by his mother vanished under a relentless tide of scarlet blood. His eyes burned with tears at the sight.

"Your brother went to check on the mill this morning," Philippe said, accepting a cup of wine from the servant. "I've sent someone to fetch him. And the priest."

Cédric propped up his father's head and held the cup to his lips. He spluttered and coughed, then swallowed a bit of wine. A gust of wind and rain swept through the open doorway, the flames in the hearth dancing in response.

"These cursed rains," Papa muttered. "There will be no harvest this year."

Cédric stared at the fire, refusing to watch death tighten its grip on his father.

"And bandits circling like wolves." Philippe's voice was steady, but it held a trace of anger.

Papa sucked in a ragged breath. “My boy, look at me.”

Cédric dragged his gaze from the hearth with reluctance.

“Yves will take my place as viscount. Stéphane is safe at seminary, his path to priesthood is secure. But you—” His father struggled for air, grimacing. “God forgive me, I’ve not prepared you, Cédric. You care more for falcons than swordplay. You’re not ready to enter service for a *seigneur* . . .”

Philippe leaned closer. “I swear to you as a servant of the Knights Hospitaller that your son has the makings of a strong fighter. I’ll be sure his training is complete before he enters any lord’s household, my friend.”

Papa sought Cédric’s eyes again. “You can change your fate, but not if you spend your life bowing to the whims of other men, understand? One day you must make your own fortune.”

The worry and pain in his expression made Cédric’s heart twist.

“Vow it to me, son.”

“I vow it.” Cédric tried to swallow, but his throat felt dry as dust.

Papa’s face relaxed. His breath grew faint, his skin pale. “You will make your own way in the world,” he whispered. “But first you’ll learn to live by your sword—and stay alive.”

CHAPTER 1

Summer, 1439
Auvergne, France

THE THUDDING of dozens of hooves sounded on the road. Cédric put a hand in the air, motioning for silence. The men all exchanged somber glances. One of them crossed himself, then whispered to his horse in low tones. Cédric held his horse's bridle with one hand and clenched the hilt of his sword with the other. He glanced at the mule cart sitting in the shade of a hawthorn tree. It slowed their progress immeasurably. But there was no other choice. His entire future was bound up in that cart's cargo.

The riders began to pass by, shouting amongst themselves. The creak of leather, the metallic clank of swords, the snorting of horses filled the air. Cédric tightened his grip on his sword. He thanked God the weather had been dry this past week. The road here was hard-packed and dusty. Their presence would not be easily read in muddy furrows and hoofprints.

The approaching horses slowed.

Had the bandits seen something? Heard something?

God save us.

Then he distinctly heard one of them shout, "To the ferry!"

The hoofbeats quickened, the group sweeping down the roadway to the north, toward the river. He had bribed the ferryman to stay quiet about their passage when they'd crossed that river at dawn, but could only hope the man would keep his promise.

"We're nearly to the commandery," he told the men after a few tense moments of silence, climbing into the saddle again. "We'll arrive tonight, God willing."

"If we aren't skinned alive first," one of his companions retorted, fear still plain on his face.

"We've made it this far," Cédric said. "All the way from Bruges. We'll get there with our skins attached, fear not. And then you'll get your portion."

"How do we know we'll be safe there?" the man challenged him. "That band of rogues may have laid siege to the place this morning."

Cédric shot him a hard look. "The knights will not be bested by a pack of bandits, of that you can be sure. No more talk. Let's move out!"

As they rode back into the sun and headed south toward the rolling hills of central Auvergne, he hoped his claim was true. The commandery, like all possessions of the Knights Hospitaller, was strongly fortified and protected by skilled soldiers. But the *écorcheurs* were trained fighters as well, many of them mercenaries who had worked for powerful lords in the past.

A crow's raucous call in the woods to his left startled him back to the journey at hand. The lump of dread in his gut hardened with each turn of the cart wheels. Neither he nor any of his companions could resist glancing over their shoulders constantly as the day progressed, and they spurred their tired mounts forward with muttered promises of grain and hay.

They arrived at the commandery before nightfall, just as he'd hoped. Their exhausted horses plodded through the great iron-studded doors into the courtyard, where torches burned at intervals along the walls. A cloaked figure approached across the cobblestones.

"Cédric?"

In the wavering light, Cédric made out the familiar face of his father's dearest friend.

"Philippe!" Somehow he found the energy to spring down from his mount and embrace the sword master.

Stablehands emerged from the shadows as the other men dismounted.

The doors clanged shut behind them. For the first time in many days, Cédric drew a deep breath.

"I can't tell you how relieved I am to be here," he said to Philippe.

"Your cargo is sound?" Philippe nodded at the cart.

The mules pulling it looked ready to collapse.

"Fortune was kind on our journey," Cédric allowed.

Philippe turned to the other men. "Go inside. There's hot stew awaiting you, and we'll have water heated for baths."

"First I must take the falcons to the mews," Cédric said, though a hot meal and a bath sounded immeasurably better. Still, what was the point of transporting the birds all that way only to lose sight of them at the last?

Philippe nodded. "I'll come with you."

The other men collected their panniers and followed a servant through the commandery's inner doors.

Slinging an arm over Philippe's shoulders, Cédric smiled a little. "Why we're not dead on the roadside is a mystery."

"A mystery?" Philippe pointed at the heavens as they walked toward the stables and mews, a stablehand leading the mule cart behind them. "God was watching over you."

Cédric cast a glance at his surroundings, taking in the stone chapel and the other buildings that faced the central courtyard. An atmosphere of hushed prosperity and organization emanated from the carefully tended property.

"The knights live well," he observed. "How do you like your lot here?"

"Square meals, hot baths, quiet evenings. It can get a bit dull, to be honest. Nothing like my years working for the knights in Rhodes. But that was a young man's game."

"Dull sounds appealing at the moment," Cédric confessed. "I've longed for a quiet night since we left Bruges."

In the mews, Cédric and Philippe unloaded the wooden traveling cages and settled them in a secure, dry corner.

"Are their eyes seeled?" Philippe asked as Cédric withdrew the canvas coverings from the cages.

Cédric nodded. The hooded gyrfalcons, secured to their perches with leather jesses, barely stirred. "It was done in Norway before we left for the open seas."

He'd helped the Norwegian do the job, carefully stitching the falcons' eyelids shut with needle and thread. The stitches wouldn't be removed until the birds reached their final destination.

"Is there an under-falconer on duty here tonight?" he asked.

Philippe nodded, pointing at the dim figure of a man at the far end of the mews, who raised his hand in greeting. "He's seasoned, knows how to tend to these creatures."

"Are my father's birds healthy?" It was far too dark in here to get a good look at them now, Cédric realized.

"Just as they should be," Philippe assured him.

"You saved us, you know. If you hadn't persuaded the Order to buy Papa's falcons—"

"I only did what an old friend does for those he loves," Philippe said gruffly.

Together they walked out of the mews.

The other men had already eaten their fill in the refectory and retreated to the bathhouse. Cédric and Philippe sat at the end of a long table illuminated by several candles and the flames of a small fire in the hearth.

Cédric guzzled his wine and fell upon his bowl of mutton-and-barley stew as if he'd not eaten in days. Philippe ate nothing, just sipped from his own cup. Finally, when Cédric put down his spoon, he felt Philippe's eyes on him and glanced up.

"You must have a hundred questions." He poured himself another cup of wine.

"Not quite that many." Philippe's grizzled face twisted in a smile. "But a few, yes. You were gone longer than I imagined. I feared the worst. It was reckless of you, making this journey." He leaned forward, his expression hardening. "An enormous gamble."

"I was ready for it. Thanks to you."

"I had nothing to do with your survival. As I already said, you have God to thank for that."

"Not true," Cédric protested. "I never would have found a place in a *seigneur*'s household after Papa died without the blade skills you taught me. Surely, you can admit that."

"Swordplay always came naturally to you, even as a boy. And you've got courage. A bit too much of it, if we're honest." Philippe chuckled.

"Courage, maybe. But not luck. I chose the wrong man to work for in the end."

Philippe shook his head. "The *seigneur* died because of his own pride. He should have stayed within the keep of his castle rather than ride out to meet the *écorcheurs*. It was a tactical mistake."

"They were burning and raiding the villages on his lands! Wouldn't you have done the same?"

The sword master regarded Cédric thoughtfully for a moment. "When you consider what you came home to, perhaps fortune wasn't so unkind after all. Your family needed you."

Cédric fell silent, reflecting on his friend's words. He had retreated to the family lands after his employer's death with only the clothes on his back, a horse, and a sword. He had discovered his brother in debt, the mill providing much of their income rendered useless because of too many years without decent harvests.

"Perhaps you're right," he admitted.

"Indeed. You got your father's falcons safely here and kept the debtors at bay." Philippe pinned him with a glare. "Why you had to go chasing dreams in the North Sea is beyond me. Though I knew you had more chance of surviving the journey than most. Your time with the *seigneur* was exactly what you needed. There's a difference between swordplay and fighting for your life."

"Let's not forget who came up with the idea of big rewards for fulfilling a rich man's wishes," Cédric pointed out. "No one forced you to tell me the Count of Chambonac desired gyrfalcons."

"Just because a nobleman says he wants rare birds doesn't mean you should travel all the way to Norway to get them," Philippe said drily.

"Fair enough." Cédric shifted his weight on the bench. "What news of the count, anyway?"

Philippe put down his cup. "He snaps up castles like a wolf seizes deer in its jaws. Another one fell to him in the spring. But he is more merciful than some noblemen. He allowed the lady of the castle to bury her husband instead of putting his head on a pike. His new residence was completed not long ago, and the gossips say it's built entirely of pink stone."

"Will he honor his bid to pay handsomely for these falcons, do you think?"

"Nobles are an unpredictable bunch," Philippe said, shrugging. "One thing is certain, though. They all covet the falcons of the north. When you call upon the Count of Chambonac, whatever the outcome, I shall be at your side."

"But you're needed here," Cédric objected. "Trust me, I've survived enough violence for several lifetimes in the past few years. No matter what I encounter on the roads of Auvergne, I can fend for myself."

Cédric studied his old sword master in the flickering candlelight. His weathered skin was scored with fine cracks and lines, but he was still a formidably strong man. And the stubborn set of his jaw was all too familiar.

"Agreed," Philippe said, meeting his gaze. "But until those gyrfalcons are handed off properly, you can count on my sword just the same."

CHAPTER 2

Summer, 1439
Auvergne, France

THE AIR WAS COOL, signaling the coming change from summer to autumn. But the sun shone brightly over the eastern hills, and only a few wispy clouds marred the sky. It was an excellent day to travel. Cédric drew in a long breath, savoring the scent of oak leaves crushed under the horses' hooves.

Philippe rode beside him, sitting easily in the saddle. The long brown cloak he wore concealed his sword, fanning out over his horse's hindquarters. Behind them trundled the mule cart, its cargo hidden under oiled canvas. Two guards brought up the rear. The thought of relinquishing the gyrfalcons to the count both troubled and relieved Cédric. Would the man give him what had been promised?

You'll discover the truth soon enough, he counseled himself.

Overhead, a raptor soared, so high it was impossible to discern the color of its feathers. Just as he was about to point it out to Philippe, the sound of hooves striking the soil ahead of them made him stiffen.

A group of horsemen swept over a small rise in the road, headed straight for them. Cédric and Philippe stopped their horses, and the mule cart creaked to a halt. Cédric raised one hand in the air, signaling to the guards behind them to wait for his command.

The riders surged forward at a gallop, drawing up short at the last moment. There were a half-dozen of them, their metal helmets glinting in the sunlight. Over their chain mail, they wore black wool tunics embroidered with a coat of arms.

"The count's men," Philippe murmured, pulling his cloak aside to reveal his sword.

Cédric's horse shifted nervously underneath him, and he spoke to it in low, soothing tones until it quieted.

A man at the center of the group urged his horse forward a few steps.

"Identify yourselves!" he commanded, his eyes concealed by the visor of his polished helmet.

"I am Cédric de Montavon, lately come from Flanders—"

"What's in there?" the man interrupted, pointing at the cart.

"Cargo for the Count of Chambonac," Cédric said. "He expects our arrival today."

The raptor circling above them let out a piercing shriek.

"I know what it is you carry," the man said. "Falcons from the north. We shall unburden you of these creatures and take them to the mews at once."

He gestured to his fellow riders. Two of them advanced, heading for the cart.

Cédric drew his sword, his pulse quickening. "You shall not," he said. "We'll meet with the count ourselves and deliver the goods as promised."

The man let out a short laugh. He pushed up his visor and examined Cédric with cold dark eyes. "You're an insolent one. I'll have you know you're on the count's lands and under his power. As his steward, I speak for him. Move aside!"

His companions spurred their horses forward and drew their swords.

Cédric stayed motionless. "No. You'll not take these birds, not without a fight."

"Pity. It's a beautiful day, and I'd hate to mar it with bloodshed. But it appears I have no choice." The steward drew his own sword.

"Stop this." Philippe's rich baritone sliced through the tension. "I'm an agent of the Knights of St. John, tasked with seeing this cargo delivered. Cédric de Montavon owns these birds, and he will see them safely to their new owner."

The steward swiveled his gaze to Philippe. "No one but the most highly ranked nobleman may own a gyrfalcon, so I'm afraid what you've just said is a lie. This man should have his head on a pike for even possessing gyrfalcons."

Philippe regarded him steadily. "Those days are over, monsieur. Any falconer can purchase raptors and sell them again. Clearly, you are not acquainted with the matters of falcon trading, isolated as you are in the hills of Auvergne."

The steward's expression tightened. "How dare you!"

"If you take this cargo forcibly from us, the Order will know of it, and your master will lose favor with them. Is that what you wish? I know he has long cultivated a friendship with the Knights Hospitaller."

Philippe's calm words had the desired effect. The steward slammed his visor shut again.

"Follow my men," he said curtly. "And be quick about it."

The group turned their horses and cantered away.

Cédric exchanged a glance with Philippe as he sheathed his sword. "Let's hope the count is a bit friendlier than his steward."

Philippe shrugged. "No blood was spilled. And you've still got possession of your falcons. I'll call that a win."

A short time later, they crested a modest hill and were rewarded with a view of a shimmering lake surrounded by lush green meadows. On a flat-topped bluff beyond the meadows sat the rose-colored château, its roof gleaming in the sunlight. High stone walls encircled the bluff, protecting the château and the small village surrounding it.

"Your gossips did not lie. Pink stone and a slate roof. Perhaps you did really come all this way just to see the château," Cédric remarked.

"Don't be distracted by the beauty," Philippe cautioned. "Keep your wits about you."

"I will if you will," Cédric retorted, but he kept one hand on the hilt of his sword just the same, his ears pricked back for the reassuring sound of the cart wheels turning on their axles.

The count was waiting in the courtyard when they clattered over the drawbridge and through the arched gateway of the château. Surrounded by guards and valets, his hounds at his heels, he watched in silence as the group spilled through the gates. The steward leaped from his horse and ripped off his helmet, making straight for his master.

Cédric and Philippe dismounted. They approached the count and bowed to him.

"Rise, rise," he said, his voice unexpectedly pleasant. His angular face was arranged in a mild expression, but his dark eyes were cool and assessing. "Welcome. I'm most eager to see these falcons that have come to me all the way from the North Sea."

"Cédric de Montavon at your service, my lord." Cédric glanced at Philippe. "And let me introduce—"

The count cut him off. "I know your companion. Philippe, you look well. Life at the commandery must suit you."

Philippe bowed his head again. "I send greetings from my commander and much gratitude for your recent contribution to the Order, my lord."

"It was my pleasure," the count replied. "Now, let us inspect these birds."

Cédric strode to the cart and drew back the canvas, gripped by a rush of dread. What if they somehow had perished on this final leg of their journey and lay dead at the bottom of their cages? But his momentary fear was unfounded. The birds sat still as stone, their hoods in place, their talons gripping the perches. All was well.

The count approached, gazing at the falcons curiously. "Gray. I'd hoped for white, of course, as gifts for the king."

"They may well turn white, my lord," Cédric told him. "When they molt, they often change color."

The steward sidled forward. "My lord, shall we get the birds to the mews and send these men on their way?"

"There is no hurry," the count said dismissively. "Go about your business, man."

With a churlish look at Cédric, the steward turned on his heel and stalked off, dispensing orders to various guards and servants as he went.

"Now, tell me how you acquired these creatures." The count fixed Cédric with an expectant gaze.

"I sailed to Norway and procured them myself, with the help of a Norwegian ship captain."

"How did you acquaint yourself with a Norseman?"

"In Flanders. Norwegian ships voyage there each spring from the North Sea."

The count's expression grew thoughtful. "Do they?"

The truth was Cédric had spent a drunken evening aboard a Norwegian ship whose captain had a hospitable game table. He never meant to go to Norway, but then he lost a wager . . . obviously a story for another time.

He nodded. "There are far more buyers than birds to satisfy them, my lord. Many buyers travel to Bruges each year in search of falcons, and others go to Königsberg in Bavaria, for falcon traders gather there as well."

The count considered this. "Do you have some special skill with falcons? Surely, it takes more than luck to keep them alive on a long journey."

"I cared for my father's falcons and hawks as a boy," Cédric explained. "It's always been an interest of mine."

"And who is your father?"

"A viscount of Languedoc. He died some years ago."

The count tilted his head back, examining Cédric anew. "Viscount, eh? And you are the second son?"

"Third. My brother holds the title. I entered the service of a lord after my father died, but the *seigneur* I worked for met the same fate as he did."

"Which was?"

"Killed by *écorcheurs,*" Cédric said curtly. The interrogation was beginning to grate on his nerves.

"God rest their souls," the count replied, shaking his head. "But you've managed to evade the bandits yourself, an admirable feat." The nobleman clapped his hands, and two valets approached. "I shall take refreshment with my visitors, and then we'll tour the mews." He turned to Cédric again. "What say you to a bit of hawking this afternoon? There are partridges in my forests and meadows, ripe for the picking."

"As you wish, my lord."

❦

Later that day, they stood together near a copse of oaks in a meadow frothing with thigh-high grass, a group of attendants hovering nearby. A lanner falcon on his gloved wrist, Cédric ignored the steward's malevolent gaze as he waited for the "beaters"—local boys tasked with startling game birds into the air—to do their work. When a partridge rose from the earth, wings churning in panic, Cédric released the falcon and she cast off, neatly dispatching the bird in midair.

Her work done, she returned to Cédric's arm, accepting a tidbit of venison. An attendant trotted up with the dead partridge and displayed it to the count.

"Your ease with falcons is evident," the count said, looking at Cédric with new respect. "Would you consider a position as my master falconer?" He gestured back in the direction of the château. "I've a place for one. The position comes with a home and a generous salary. Of course, you must be willing to return to Bruges or go to Königsberg and buy more of these creatures for me from time to time."

Cédric stared at him in surprise. This was not at all what he'd expected the man to say. The thought of the journey he'd just endured made him hesitate. He shifted his weight from one leg to the other, contemplating the offer. The falcon retracted her neck into her shoulders and plumped up her feathers as if to shield herself from the emotion her handler was feeling. He glanced at Philippe, whose face reflected his own astonishment.

Before he could answer, the count spoke again.

"I need falcons to give as gifts to the king and others on his council, but the most valuable birds, the ones from the north, are nearly impossible to find." The count spoke more quickly now, warming to his idea. "You could change that for me. You would have to travel, but you would have the power of my purse and my guards behind you." He looked at Philippe. "Clearly, the Order finds this young man trustworthy, as you do."

Philippe held his gaze. "My lord, I've known Cédric since he was a boy. He is a man of honor, and I trust him to defend himself and his cargo."

"Excellent." The count turned back to Cédric. "What say you, then?"

Cédric's mind swam with the suddenness of it all. Fearing the count would see his composure crumble, he bent his head, fighting to calm his thoughts.

Answer the man, he ordered himself. *Only a fool would pass up this opportunity.*

"It would be my honor," he said.

CHAPTER 3

Autumn, 1439
Toulouse, France

SOPHIE TUCKED her arm through her maid's as they followed Papa and the others through the streets toward the marketplace. They were bundled in long wool cloaks, for the air had a crisp bite to it this morning.

The faint scent of roasting chestnuts drifted from an alleyway. She slowed her pace, savoring it. Perhaps they could stop and buy some. She swung her head around to call for Papa, but the men strode quickly ahead, hastening to the market square.

Sophie frowned. As usual, Papa and his notary were immersed in talk, their heads canted together. A manservant trotted behind them, his arms burdened with empty baskets waiting to be filled with goods.

A small boy tugging at a goat's lead blocked their way. The goat's flanks were loaded with baskets piled high with apples. The boy's father, leading a mule burdened with its own load of fruit, called to him repeatedly. But the goat planted its hooves on the cobblestones and balked.

"Poor thing," Sophie said finally. She darted forward, gave the goat a slap on the rump, and it moved.

The boy cast her a grateful glance. "Thank you, mademoiselle," he said, leading the animal after his father.

"You'd think he would have given me an apple for his trouble," Sophie said tartly when she returned to Christine's side.

"Your mother would not have liked you doing that," her maid retorted. "You're entirely too bold for a girl."

Sophie shrugged. "Maman isn't here, and you're just a maid—so who cares what you think?"

"Just a maid who was your wet nurse, young lady," Christine admonished her.

"Papa likes me as I am," Sophie asserted. "He says my boldness will serve me well one day."

They crossed the marketplace to the pastel stalls. The walls of Papa's stall were draped in velvet, the interior fitted with polished wooden display tables. Venetian glass oil lamps illuminated the rows of perfectly round cakes of vibrant blue pastel dye, laid out on lengths of silk.

Papa halted in front of his display. Well-dressed shoppers converged upon the stall as if it exuded the odor of freshly baked cream tarts. He studied the activity before him for a moment, then turned to his notary. Sophie drew up close enough to hear their conversation.

"Let us discuss with the other city aldermen the placement of my stall," Papa was saying. "I believe if it were a bit closer to the main street entering the square, more people would encounter it without a search. I want it to be the easiest to discover in the entire marketplace."

Sophie smiled. Her father was never satisfied, always fiddling with details, experimenting. But it seemed to work. His pastel business was growing. His attempts to recruit more wealthy men to the region had started bearing fruit. Last night at supper, they hosted three merchants who were all planning to move to Toulouse and build elaborate homes.

After supper, Papa had come to her and said one of the men inquired about her eligibility for marriage.

"What do you think, *ma chérie?*" he'd asked teasingly.

She'd made a face. "He was so old, Papa!"

"No older than your sisters' husbands."

"But you would miss me so if I were to wed. What would you do without me to make you laugh?"

"True enough," he'd rejoined, eyes twinkling. "I'd be bereft without my favorite daughter. Though you're getting old yourself. Nearly sixteen and unwed. It's practically scandalous."

She'd regarded him a moment, the smile fading from her face. "You'll let me choose my husband, won't you, Papa?"

"We shall see, Sophie, my pet."

She'd leaned close and kissed his cheek. "Thank you, Papa."

Sophie learned long ago that if she sweetened her demands with honeyed words and loving gestures, Papa was far more likely to acquiesce to her desires.

A well-dressed man hurried to her father's side, omitting the usual pleasantries and launching into a breathless monologue. Papa's expression tightened into a scowl as the man's words tumbled out.

"Another shipment of Cypriot fabrics lost to those blasted *écorcheurs*," he said bitterly.

"Your partners will have to be told, and quickly," the notary said in a low voice.

Papa let out an exasperated groan. "I convinced them to go in on it with me, to a man. If I want to keep them as partners, I suppose I'll have to reimburse them myself."

Sophie's skin tingled. Tales of the renegade groups of bandits roaming France were rife around the supper table, had always been. King Charles had begun stamping them out, that's what Papa said, but there were so many it would take ages to eradicate them for good. Until then, the entire kingdom was at their mercy. She edged forward again, absorbing every word.

Papa glanced at her. His troubled expression relaxed a little.

"*Chérie,* you are just the balm I need to take the sting out of this sordid news. Let's take a turn around the marketplace together and see what goods are on display today." He proffered an arm.

"Don't worry," she said, smiling up at him with tenderness. "One day the king will have an army, and the *écorcheurs* will be gone forever. Your fabrics will arrive intact from the sea, and your partners will be happy."

He chuckled and patted her hand as they began to stroll, Christine a few paces behind. "Nothing escapes your ears, does it? Too bad you were born a girl. I'd have dearly loved such interest in the world of commerce from your brother. I had to push him a little too hard in the proper direction. He'd much rather have been a Knight of St. John, if he'd the proper pedigree."

"Well, we can be grateful he didn't," she replied. "Then he'd be off on a ship to the East, and who knows if we would ever see him again. Mother would never allow it, anyway. He's the apple of her eye."

Papa glanced down at her. "True enough. It breaks her heart to have him living most of the year in Flanders as it is." His eyes narrowed. "Have you plucked your brows away again? Leave your beauty as God intended. Do not try to keep up with ridiculous fashions."

She tossed her head. "It's hardly ridiculous, Papa! All the noble-born women do it."

"You are not one of them," he pointed out. "Plucking your eyebrows won't change that. Nothing will."

Sophie shot him a challenging stare. "I must contradict you, Papa. That alderman's daughter who married the son of a *seigneur* a few years ago? She's a noblewoman."

"I thought the fellow she married was the second son, not the heir," Papa objected. "How could he get the title?"

"The first son died soon after the father did. It was the sweating sickness that got him, or so they say. The second son became the heir, and his common-born wife is now a fine lady."

Papa searched her face in suspicion. "How do you know such things?"

"Church," she said airily, turning away to look at a passing merchant and his wife, whose cloak was thrown open to reveal a gown of luminous sapphire blue. "All the news comes after church; you know that, Papa."

He snorted. "Your worldliness is truly astounding, my dear."

But as usual, his tone was indulgent. She smiled to herself. Papa's mood had gone from dark to light in the space of a few moments, thanks to her.

"Shall I throw open my cloak a bit, too?" She nodded in the direction of the merchant and his wife. "I wore my new blue gown today."

Papa's eyes lit up. "The silk brocade?"

Sophie smiled, loosening the ties of her cloak so her square-cut bodice and flowing skirts caught the light. "I think my gown is prettier than that woman's, Papa," she told him. "The color is exquisite. Your dye-house workers are more skilled than theirs, aren't they?"

He nodded, his mouth curving in a satisfied smile, and led her toward his market stall.

Her mind went again to the idea of him marrying her off to a dull merchant twice her age, as he had done with her two elder sisters. She set her lips into a firm line and tightened her grip on his arm. Papa would not do that to her.

No, if she were to marry one day, it would be to a man of her own choosing. With a little luck, it would even be a love match.

CHAPTER 4

Spring, 1440
Off the coast of France

A SALTY BREEZE struck Sophie's face. She pushed her hood back, wishing the sun would break through the clouds. But the sea reflected the sullen sky, a sheet of molten pewter stretching in every direction. To their right and left glided merchant galleys, smaller and more nimble versions of the vessel they themselves were on. Their white sails strained in the wind.

"So many ships so close together," she marveled.

"A merchant convoy is the best way to travel these waters," her father said. "It's a far better way to get to Flanders than taking those dangerous roads. We could hire a dozen guards for the journey north and it would not deter the bandits, not for a moment."

"Poor Maman, though," Sophie said, nodding toward the stairs leading to the cramped cabins below decks. "Her face is the color of ash."

"Yours is white as chalk," Papa said, examining her with concern. "Perhaps you should join her."

Sophie shook her head. "I prefer it up here with you. The voyage passes more quickly this way."

The truth was she felt desperately seasick. But the thought of being shut in the cabin with Maman and their maids, retching into buckets, made her feel worse. No, she would stand here with Papa and watch the waves churn.

When they'd left Bayonne, several Basque cod-fishing ships had passed them, heading out to sea. One of the ship's officers had told them the Basques were voyaging to a land locked in ice much of the year, where the waters were rich with codfish. The holds of those ships, he'd said, would be filled with barrels of cod packed in salt—if the vessels survived the return journey.

She turned to Papa, thinking of the man's words. "Codfish must be quite valuable for those ships to sail across the sea in search of them."

He shot her a surprised look. "Yes, indeed. I know some merchants who deal in codfish and are very wealthy men."

"Are codfish as valuable as cloth, then?"

"I suppose it's difficult to compare the two. Cod is cod. It's all the same, whereas there are many kinds of cloth, all valued differently. The silk damask of Bruges fetches much higher prices than the wool fabrics produced by drapers around Toulouse."

"But what about that special wool, the kind from over the mountains?"

"Merino?" He chuckled. "You don't miss anything, do you?"

After church last Sunday, he had been embroiled in a long discussion with several other merchants about the fine merino wool that had begun appearing in marketplaces near the Pyrenees mountains. Sophie found herself mesmerized by the conversation, mostly because the idea of the bears and wolves that roamed the mountains filled her with a strange combination of terror and fascination.

"Merino wool is costly," Papa went on. "But still, it doesn't touch the value of Syrian silks or Cypriot cloth of gold. We shall see fabrics from all over the world in Bruges, my dear. It will amaze you, I promise."

She slipped her arm through his and leaned closer, a thrill of anticipation running through her. "Thank you for bringing me along, Papa."

He patted her arm. "The true nature of your presence on this journey is to comfort your poor Maman, which as we've already discussed, you are failing to do at the moment."

His admonishment held no malice, as usual. He preferred her to be at his side, and she knew it. So she smiled sunnily up at him, secure in his affection.

"I shall return to her side as soon as we see a curious sight on the seas. A whale, a dolphin, a sea monster . . ."

Papa laughed outright. "A sea monster? Pray we do not glimpse one of those."

The wind picked up. An officer shouted a command. Several sailors dispersed across the decks, scaling the rigging as they prepared to adjust the sails.

One of the men paused and stared down at Sophie, a look of frank admiration on his face. She returned his stare with interest. A long, puckered scar ran down one of his cheeks. Perhaps that was the result of a sword fight with pirates, she mused. Papa reached out and tugged the hood of her cloak over her forehead.

"You should not display yourself like that," he scolded. "Enough of this. I'm taking you back below decks."

"Papa—" she began to protest.

"No, no, you'll go below and that is my last word on the subject." He pulled her away from the gunwales and led her toward the hold. They staggered a bit as the ship plowed through a large wave. "You have no idea what it does to a man, the sight of your face," he continued sternly. "You must be more modest, my dear. Especially when you are in the company of rough sailors."

"Yes, Papa."

They descended into the hold with caution. "When you get to the cabin, I want you to read to Maman. And do it the way she likes, with animation. Amuse her."

The thought of reading aloud by lamplight in the stifling cabin made Sophie grimace. "I am sure she's sleeping. She'll not want to be disturbed."

He harrumphed. "She hasn't slept more than a few winks a night since your sister died, Sophie."

Sophie felt a familiar tightness constrict her chest. Her youngest sister had been taken by a terrible fever over the winter, an illness that came on swiftly and blazed so hot it burned the life out of her in the space of a few days. She hated thinking of it. Every time her mother wept, she fought off tears of her own. It was not Sophie's place to sob and wail, Papa frequently told her. It was her duty to comfort Maman. Sometimes she cried quietly in the privacy of her own chamber at night, missing her sister's sweet, affectionate presence. They had shared a bed these past few years. The warmth of her sister's small body curled around hers was a comfort she would never know again.

But she kept her sorrow to herself. For Maman's sake.

"Yes, Papa," she said, dreading the afternoon ahead. "As you wish."

CHAPTER 5

Spring, 1440
Bruges, Flanders

CÉDRIC DESCENDED the steps of the inn with care, his head still pounding from last night's excesses. Mist clung to the rooftops, its cool dampness sending a chill through him. He had one more matter of urgent business before he returned to Auvergne. The sooner he could unburden himself of the gold coins in his purse, the better.

He crossed to the canal that lay opposite the inn. A family of ducks glided a stone's throw away, the ducklings paddling furiously to keep up with their mother. He smiled a little, grateful for a moment of peace, and began his trek to the harbor.

Just ahead of him, a city alderman and his entourage of notaries and servants entered the street from an adjoining lane, their dark caps bobbing like a flock of errant crows. Cédric quickened his stride, skirting past the group.

He passed a row of warehouses as the morning sun burned through the mist. A familiar figure exited one of the buildings, young cloth merchant Gregoire Portier of Toulouse, whom he'd met during his first stay in Bruges. They had shared a game table last night in a tavern not far from here. Portier was trailed by an older man in a fur-trimmed cap and a short black cape.

"How goes it, my friend?" Cédric called out, approaching the duo.

"Good morning!" Gregoire's bloodshot eyes were the only evidence of last night's revelry on his smiling face. He turned to his companion. "Papa, this is Cédric de Montavon, falconer to a count of Auvergne."

Cédric nodded to the elder Portier. "It's a pleasure to meet you, sir. Are you enjoying your visit to the north?"

"Exceedingly." The man inspected Cédric with interest. "Falconer, eh? You must have tales to tell."

"A few." The three men fell into step together. "Any more word of the Venetian fleet?" Cédric asked.

Last night at the tavern, before Grégoire had disappeared with a brightly painted courtesan on his arm, he'd passed along gossip that Venetian merchants were nearing Bruges.

"No," Grégoire said, squinting against the sun. "A new rumor came out of the cloth merchants' guild this morning. It seems the fleet was waylaid by pirates in the Bay of Biscay."

Cédric looked at him in dismay. "I pray the gossips are wrong. I'd hoped to be among the first to see their wares today."

"I know. We're eager to get our hands on Syrian silks, and the Venetian fleet can usually be relied upon for a good supply," Grégoire said. "What do the Venetians carry that you seek?"

"Items of silver," he answered vaguely, unwilling to share more details. He liked Grégoire, but the man had a wagging tongue. "Never fear, other merchants will come from the East. The Catalans can usually be counted on to show up with valuable goods at better prices."

"If you like your wares pirated," Grégoire said with a grin.

"For the right price, I don't care how their goods are sourced," Cédric replied. "The Venetians aren't above piracy either, though they'd never call it that."

The threesome arrived at the harbor's edge, where the alderman and his attendants stood discussing the missing fleet in worried tones. Cédric sighed. How long would his return to Auvergne be delayed?

"It seems my errand must wait." He shaded his eyes with a hand, pointing to a nearby barge. "If you're in no hurry, join me for a few rounds of cards. The captain of a Norwegian ship anchored down the river in Sluys has a hospitable game table. That barge makes the journey twice a day, for a reasonable price."

"Would it please you, Papa?" Grégoire put a solicitous hand on his father's shoulder.

"There's nothing I'd enjoy more," the elder Portier said.

At Sluys, dozens of ships were anchored in the harbor, their goods destined for barges returning to Bruges. The men followed Cédric aboard a battered-looking vessel that had plied the cold waters between Flanders and Norway many times. After greeting Cédric with an affectionate embrace, the captain welcomed the Portier men and escorted them all below decks into his quarters. On a table sat a stack of playing cards and a leather cup holding a pair of dice. The men settled on stools around the table while a sailor fetched wine and the captain shuffled and dealt the cards.

"A ship at anchor is far preferable to one at sea," Monsieur Portier remarked, arranging his cards in his hand. "Our journey here was far too stormy for my taste."

"The more time you spend at sea, the easier it gets." The captain looked at Cédric with a grin. "You'd better find your sea legs again. Fancy another scramble up some Norwegian cliffs? You proved an excellent nest robber the first time."

Gregoire glanced at Cédric in surprise. "You've been to Norway?"

"Yes." Cédric put a card in the discard pile and selected a new one. "I was lucky in my choice of companions. We netted two dozen raptors, half of them gyrfalcons, if I recall correctly." He looked at the Norwegian, shaking his head ruefully. "*Stol på meg*, Karl, I would return with you in a heartbeat if I could."

His friend laughed. "Those three words saved our hides more than once. They likely will again."

The Norwegian's laughter was interrupted by the clatter of boots descending from the upper decks. A man burst into the cabin, his short cape swirling around him.

"May I be of service?" the Norwegian asked, still speaking French. He put down his cards and rose from the table.

"Captain, forgive me for the interruption," the stranger said with a bow. His French was inflected with the rolling r's of Catalan. "But I was told on good faith that you carry a cargo of gyrfalcons. My employer has dispatched me to purchase some without delay."

Cédric's shoulders tensed. The hold contained several gyrfalcons and a peregrine falcon destined for his own employer's mews in Auvergne.

The captain's expression turned serious. "I'm afraid my gyrfalcons are already reserved."

The Catalan's eyes narrowed. "I've a letter to show you. It may convince you otherwise."

He withdrew a square of folded linen paper from a pocket and handed it to the Norwegian. From where Cédric was sitting, the seal looked like a star.

The captain broke the seal and studied the letter for a moment. His eyes widened a little as he scanned the lines of script.

"Tell me," the Catalan said when the captain met his gaze again. "How much did your other buyers pledge to pay? I'll double it."

Cédric scraped back his stool and stood. "You cannot buy falcons that are already spoken for, sir. Mine, for instance."

The Catalan turned. He was not much older than Cédric himself, with a taut, chiseled face and dark eyes. He gave Cédric a sweeping, dismissive glance.

"This is not your affair," he said sharply.

"I'm afraid it is," Cédric replied, stepping away from the game table.

The captain put up a mollifying hand. "My friend, there's no cause for you to worry."

"I disagree." Cédric took another step in the Catalan's direction, one hand gripping the hilt of his sword.

The Catalan widened his stance. "As I said before, my business is not with you, sir."

He slid his own sword from its scabbard with silent precision.

The Portier men looked at each other in alarm.

"Enough!" The Norwegian's tone grew hard. Two of his officers materialized in the doorway. "Aboard this ship, everyone is obliged to heed my command."

Cédric's chest grew tight. He sought the captain's eyes. "Answer me this. Will you honor our agreement or not?"

"*Stol på meg,* Cédric," the Norwegian replied in a low voice, his expression steady.

Clearing his throat, the Catalan retrieved a purse from his belt and shook it. The clink of metal resonated through the chamber.

"Perhaps you're new to the falcon trade, sir. Gyrfalcons are the most costly and rare of them all," Cédric said. "I doubt your purse holds enough gold for what you seek. Did you bring another?"

The Catalan shot Cédric a look of pure contempt and trained his gaze on the captain.

"Show me the birds, and I can pay you now, with my notary as witness." He called out something in rapid Catalan. Another man appeared in the doorway. "The deal will be quickly done, Captain, and you'll be a much richer man for it."

The notary drew a leather-bound book from a satchel slung over his shoulder. "With your permission," he murmured, spreading the book open in his hands. The seal of the city of Bruges was stamped on the first page.

The Norwegian nodded his approval. "Follow me," he told the Catalan and the notary.

The three men vanished, the officers close behind them, and the hard tap of their boots on the planks faded.

Cédric sat down, resisting a powerful urge to follow the men out the door. He refilled the mens' cups, took up his cards, and rearranged them in his hand.

"What's this?" Grégoire asked, his face twisting with bafflement. "You nearly ran that Catalan through with your sword a moment ago. Now you're ready to play at cards again?"

Cédric swallowed, willing himself to remain calm. He stared at his cards as if they were objects of supreme fascination.

"Those falcons are your livelihood," the elder Portier mused. "If I were you, I'd not let the Catalan anywhere near them."

The captain returned alone. He took his seat, picked up his cards, and drank deeply from his wine cup.

"That business was speedily done," Monsieur Portier observed wryly.

The Norwegian contemplated his cards with full attention. "Whose turn is it?" he asked finally, glancing up at the other players.

Grégoire threw his cards down on the table. "You can't be serious, sir. Did you sell my friend's falcons out from under him or not?"

"The truth is," the captain answered in a measured tone, "there are many like the Catalan who come aboard this ship. I've got a cargo more precious than any in the harbor. There are always new buyers crawling out from the woodwork, making me generous offers."

The elder Portier watched him with interest. "You might consider doubling your cargo, then. Think of the extra gold you would earn."

"Believe me," the Norwegian said casually, reorganizing his cards with care, "I've already thought of that."

Gregoire let out a cry. "Ah! You carry more birds than you let on, sir, for just such an occasion as this one!"

"No." The captain's eyes gleamed with amusement. "I don't. But a second Norwegian ship arrived last night in Sluys, you see. Its hold is full of falcons as well. I bade my officers accompany the Catalan aboard the vessel."

Relief flooded Cédric. He shook his head, unable to stifle a grin. "I'll admit, man, you had me worried for a moment there."

"Until the captain uttered those three mysterious words," Monsieur Portier said, fixing him with a shrewd gaze. "Then you stood down. What, by all the saints, does *stol på meg* mean?"

" 'Trust me.' " Cédric chuckled wryly. "One of the things I learned about this man on our journey—he loves a joke."

The captain threw back his head and let out a shout of laughter. "All in good fun," he said when he caught his breath.

"I've probably got my first gray hairs because of your 'good fun,' " Cédric said. "I'm glad I didn't run him through before he could tip his coins out. The seal on his letter looked like a star. Who was it from?"

"The Order of the Knights Hospitaller."

All three men looked at the Norwegian in surprise.

"The design was no star, then—it was an eight-pointed cross," Cédric said slowly. "The Order's mark. If the knights are involved, the falcons could be for a king, a sultan . . . even the pope."

"Whoever they're destined for, it was a deal I'd be a fool to refuse." The captain dipped his head at Cédric. "And thank you for pulling out your sword earlier. I doubt he'd have displayed his purse so quickly otherwise, nor promised to part with so much gold. How about I skim a little off the top for you, my friend?"

Picking up the pitcher, he refilled Cédric's cup with a flourish.

"I'll not refuse such a kindness," Cédric said, raising his cup in salute. "Now we know at least one Catalan's arrived in Bruges. Perhaps their merchant fleet is not far behind."

Monsieur Portier turned to his son with a raised brow. "Let's hope the fellow doesn't have an eye on anything we're after. He seems to have a bottomless purse and powerful friends."

Cédric shrugged. "He got what he wanted. I doubt we'll see him again."

CHAPTER 6

Spring, 1440
Bruges, Flanders

A SERVANT SPOONED a bit of brown gravy over the roasted capon breast in front of Sophie. She looked away, wishing she were hungry. The dark wood paneling on the wall opposite her gleamed in the firelight. Repressing a sigh, she studied the carved stone hearth, half-listening to her parents' conversation.

"Grégoire's friend accompanied us to the harbor today," Papa was saying to Maman. "The man is master falconer to a count."

"Is he noble-born?" Maman asked.

"I doubt a count would employ a master falconer who isn't, but I know nothing of the man's origins."

Papa mopped up a bit of sauce with a crust of bread. Maman picked delicately at a capon wing across the table from him, the ruby-and-gold ring on her middle finger catching the flickering candlelight.

"Tell you what, I'll make it my business to find out on the morrow." He popped the bread into his mouth.

"Tomorrow is Sunday," Maman reminded him gently. "We must go to church. There can be no cards or dice for you."

"Indeed, my dear," he agreed, patting the back of her hand. "I've no intention of gaming on a Sunday. No, the falconer will attend the same church as Gregoire. I invited him to sit with us."

At Papa's urging, Gregoire had become patron of a church in Bruges. He paid an annual sum to reserve a family pew. It had been carved with the Portier name.

"There are several other men I want to meet as well. Gregoire's promised me introductions. He's made new contracts with a cloth merchant from Amsterdam and another from London. And I inspected our warehouse. It's buttoned up tight, guarded just as it should be."

"What a relief, my dear," Maman said. "It was worth the investment after all."

"There are many who would give their eyeteeth to strip that warehouse bare. Fine woolens are precious enough, but pastel! Saints preserve us. It might as well be gold."

Sophie had heard Papa say this so many times she knew the phrase as well as she knew the psalms in her prayer book. Pastel, a blue dye made from the humble woad plant, was difficult to manufacture and therefore a costly product. For years now, Papa had paid farmers to transform the ugly green plants into cakes of luminous blue powder. How exactly the process worked was a mystery to Sophie, but the resulting product made Papa richer all the time.

"My belly aches," she complained, leaning back in her chair. She had forced down a few bites of supper and had no appetite for more.

Papa gave her a worried stare. "We'll soon remedy that. This is the finest inn of Bruges, after all. I've no doubt the cooks will be happy to make you a healing posset." He signaled to a servant who stood by the door. "Fetch my daughter a soothing draught from the kitchens with plenty of sugar. And white ginger, clove, cinnamon. Don't forget a dash of vinegar. And let it be warm, but not so warm it burns her tongue."

The young woman nodded and slipped out.

Maman turned a sharp gaze on Sophie, wiping her hands with a linen towel. "How many of those sugared almonds did you eat this afternoon?" she asked.

"Half a dozen," Sophie lied. In truth, she'd eaten handful after handful of the sweets Gregoire had purchased at the market yesterday.

"Perhaps you should stay abed tomorrow instead of accompanying us to church," Papa said.

She stiffened in her seat. "I am sure my bellyache will be gone by morning, Papa."

Although she was not eager to sit through Mass, she did want to mingle with Bruges society. After-church socializing was the ideal way to glimpse the wealthy citizens of the city.

"We shall see," Maman said darkly. "The last thing I could bear is another child ill, especially so far from home."

Sophie could tell by the set of her jaw, the narrowing of her eyes, that Maman would deny her the pleasure of an outing in a heartbeat.

Gregoire appeared in the doorway.

Papa flung his arms wide, eyes shining with delight. "My son! Come, join us. Are you hungry?"

Gregoire shook his head. "I supped at a tavern near the harbor."

Maman clucked her tongue. "I would not trust the food in such a place, nor the patrons. I hope you did not let any loose women near you. Though you often seem to forget it, you are a married man, my son."

"What are loose women?" Sophie asked.

Gregoire sank down in a chair next to Papa. "Never mind, *ma fillette*."

"Don't call me that," she said. "I'm not a little girl any longer."

He laughed. "Papa, when are you going to marry off this practically grown woman?"

Papa looked shocked. "Not yet, not yet. She is not ready."

Maman shifted in her seat. "Says who? Our elder daughters were already married at Sophie's age."

It was true. Sophie barely remembered the wedding of her oldest sister, Marie, to a merchant of Gascogne many years ago. She recalled Marguerite's nuptials, though. Her sister had been fifteen when she was married to a corpulent, swaggering merchant of Albi two summers ago. Sophie was sixteen now, yet her parents had not once broached the topic of marriage.

"Says me," Papa told her firmly.

"When I marry, it will be a love match," Sophie announced. "To a nobleman."

Gregoire burst out laughing.

"See what happens when you spoil a child?" Maman said in an accusatory tone.

"I have no quarrel with the idea," Papa declared. "At least one of my daughters should bring a noble line into the family. When noblemen wed common folk, the noble line is passed down to their children." He turned to Maman. "Imagine that, my dear. Grandparents to noble-born sons."

Maman's expression softened. A faraway look came into her eyes.

The maid appeared with the posset. She deposited the ceramic cup before Sophie and bobbed a shallow curtsy.

"What's this?" Gregoire asked. He picked up the cup and sniffed at it. "You spare no expense for Sophie, do you, Papa?" He set it down again. "I'm surprised you didn't ask the cook to add some saffron, too. Or gold dust."

"Why not?" Papa challenged him. "I'm a wealthy man. I can spend my money as I wish." He turned to Sophie. "Drink up, my girl. Drink it all before it cools."

She obeyed, nearly choking on the sweet, spicy concoction. The sourness of the vinegar warmed her chest.

Papa smiled in satisfaction. "That will bring peace to your innards. Tomorrow you'll be right as rain."

Maman's gaze came to rest on Gregoire again. "Who did you sup with, then?" she asked suspiciously.

"Cédric de Montavon, the falconer."

Sophie sat up straighter in her chair. "Satisfy our curiosity. Is he a nobleman or not?"

Gregoire eyed her in amusement. "His father was a viscount, but his older brother got the title and the lands."

"Imagine being a viscountess." Sophie fluttered her eyelashes at Maman. "Viscountess Portier, I'm enchanted to make your acquaintance."

Her mother chuckled.

"I found him a delightful fellow," Papa said. "I envied him a bit, to be truthful. Traveling about, buying falcons for a count. What a life."

The next morning, the Portier family entered the church one by one. The warm, stale air smelled faintly of beeswax. Sophie followed Papa, Maman, and Gregoire down the main aisle of the nave to their appointed spot, about three-quarters of the way back from the altar. Behind the altar a three-paneled painting of saints and angels was affixed to the stone wall. Above it, a round window made of colorful stained glass let in filtered sunlight. Sophie stared up at it, mesmerized by the beauty. Ensconced between her parents, she did not hear Cédric de Montavon slip into the pew. Her family's murmured greetings to him brought her back to the moment. She turned her head and met the falconer's eyes.

He nodded at her in silence as he took his seat. Flushing, she lowered her eyelids. When she raised them again, he was still looking her way, a faint expression of surprise on his face. She was accustomed to seeing that expression on a man's face when he first encountered her. Papa took great pride in the attention she attracted.

Like moths to a flame, he often said.

Usually, Sophie found the attention of men annoying. But this time, she felt a powerful tug of attraction. The heat in her throat and cheeks swept into her chest, then settled languidly just above her hips.

The priest began to speak. The familiar Latin words of Mass soon lulled her into a stupor. For a while she trained her eyes on the rosy light spilling forth from the stained glass window above the altar. Then she tried glimpsing Cédric de Montavon from the corner of her eye without turning her head.

She could see the falconer's fine black leather boots, the dark green hose he wore, his hands resting on his thighs. His slender, sun-browned fingers were a stark contrast to her father's plump white ones.

The priest droned on and on. She prayed for Mass to end.

Finally, it did. They all stood and filed back down the aisle through the tall doors of the church to the sunlit square beyond. It was a crisp spring day, with a gentle breeze that whispered over her cheeks. Sophie stood with Maman. They discussed the Flemish ladies' elaborate head coverings, the fine drape of their cloaks, the foreign sounds of their language drifting overhead. Gregoire and the falconer chatted with Papa about business matters, about trade and war and commerce and tariffs.

Several merchants joined them, their attention focused on Monsieur de Montavon. They peppered him with questions about falcons and his work for the count. Sophie watched him respond, admiring his confident manner, the strong line of his jaw, the hard angles of his cheekbones. She stared at his well-formed lips, at his short, carefully-trimmed beard.

"Sophie," Maman said. "Did you not hear Monsieur de Montavon?"

She scrambled to find her voice, feeling oddly shy.

"Forgive me, sir," she murmured. "What was your question?"

"How do you find Bruges, mademoiselle?" he asked. "Is it to your liking?"

His brown velvet doublet was criss-crossed with green silk thread embroidered in a diamond-shaped pattern. She was struck with an impulse to run her fingers across the raised ridges of the thread.

"I have lost my heart to Bruges," she admitted, favoring him with a smile. "I would like to come back every year. It's a beautiful city, not like Toulouse at all."

"And what is wrong with Toulouse?" Papa said, pretending to be hurt, but with a mocking gleam in his eyes.

While there were a few rich pastel merchants like him in Toulouse, the city of Sophie's birth was essentially an overgrown farm town riddled with abandoned and decaying buildings, still not entirely recovered from the plague that had ravaged the world a few generations ago.

"Papa," she laughed. "How can we compare the two? It is like comparing a stone with a pearl."

Papa grinned. "Too true, my child. There are treasures to be found here and nowhere else. Like gyrfalcons." He glanced meaningfully at Monsieur de Montavon.

"Indeed," the falconer replied.

"Gyrfalcons!" a merchant cried. "Why, aren't they the most costly birds on earth?"

Monsieur de Montavon shrugged. "It depends on the age of the bird, the color of its feathers, the condition of its health."

"What color feathers are best, monsieur?" Sophie asked.

"White gyrfalcons are the most coveted," the falconer responded. His eyes were brown, with flecks of green and gold that caught the light. "After the molt, of course, the feathers can change color. So a bird that begins gray can turn white. But one never knows if it will."

Grégoire pointed at the doors of the church. "Look there. Isn't that the Catalan we saw on the Norwegian's ship?"

Sophie watched a dark-haired man with a short beard emerge from church in the company of two other well-dressed gentlemen.

"Yes," Papa concurred. "One and the same."

Perhaps sensing the eyes upon him, the Catalan glanced their way. For the second time in one day, Sophie felt the curious prickling sensation of attraction under a man's scrutiny. He was nearly as handsome as the falconer, and more elegantly dressed.

"We were gaming on a Norwegian's ship and met that man, an agent of the Knights Hospitaller," Grégoire told the gathered men. "He was buying gyrfalcons for someone of great rank."

"Perhaps the King of Cyprus," mused Papa. "Imagine having a friend connected to the Cypriot court. The trade in camlets and cloth of gold would open up to us immediately."

"Cloth of gold has gotten harder and harder to find," one of the merchants complained. "The Genoese had a steady trade in it for a time, but pirates have made a mess of the shipping lanes in Greece. Sometimes Venetian merchants show up here with a few bolts, but the price!"

"Outrageous," Papa agreed. "I've a mind to hire a gold-beater or two, set up an atelier, and make the blasted stuff myself."

The men launched into a discussion about cloth prices and the perils of maritime shipping. Sophie had heard versions of this conversation too many times to count. Luckily, she stood directly opposite Monsieur de Montavon and had an unobstructed view of his face. He seemed distracted by the presence of the Catalan. He glanced at the man repeatedly. Then his expression tightened as the Catalan and his companions moved toward their group.

"We never had a chance to be properly introduced," the man said in French, sweeping into a polite bow. "Those business transactions leave little time for pleasantries." He looked straight at the falconer. "Your name, sir?"

The falconer gave a shallow bow. "Cédric de Montavon. And yours?"

"Nicolau Baldaia." The Catalan turned to Sophie's father expectantly.

"Henri Portier, at your service, sir," Papa said. "And my son, Grégoire."

The Catalan nodded at them both, then looked at Maman. "Madame Portier, I am honored to meet you," he said without waiting for an introduction. His eyes slid to Sophie. "And who is this?"

"Our daughter, Sophie," Maman said, hooking an arm around Sophie's waist. The gesture should have felt reassuring, but instead Sophie felt trapped. The Catalan's bold stare was oddly possessive, as if just with a look he had taken ownership of her. A fragment of fear penetrated her consciousness. She longed to escape the Catalan's inspection.

Fortunately, the merchants began to lob questions at him about his work for the knights, about news from Rhodes, about trade in far-off ports like Alexandria and Famagusta. Relieved, Sophie let her eyes drift back to the falconer just as he looked in her direction, his lips quirking in a slight smile.

Her heart thrashing like an eel in a basket, Sophie smiled in return.

CHAPTER 7

Spring, 1440
Bruges, Flanders

CÉDRIC HAD PROMISED to meet the Portier family at the belfry tower in the main square, and its relentless chiming drew him forward into the heart of the city.

Striding toward the tower, he spotted the merchant family standing in its shadow. The girl, Sophie, had one arm outstretched, pointing aloft. Her father tipped his head back, searching the heavens alongside his daughter. Cédric glanced up, too. A bird glided just above the tower, its wings dark against the blue sky.

"Greetings," he called out as he approached the family. They turned as one.

"Monsieur de Montavon," Sophie cried. "I believe there is a hawk circling the bell tower."

He came to their side and bowed. "Madame, Monsieur," he greeted the elder Portiers. "Grégoire. Mademoiselle."

"Good day to you, Monsieur de Montavon," said Sophie's father. "What say you? Is that a hawk or no?"

Cédric shook his head. "I'm afraid it's a gull, not a hawk."

"But gulls are white," the girl said with authority. "That bird is gray."

At church on Sunday, he'd found it difficult to drag his gaze away from her. Today was no different. He studied her features, struck anew by the elegant symmetry he saw there. It was her smile that had captivated him the other day, though. Her face had lit up with a blaze of joy that made the whole world fall away—the sight rendered him motionless, unable to speak. And best of all, it was a smile meant for him alone. At least, that's how it felt.

"Although I suppose it hasn't molted yet," she added thoughtfully. "Perhaps it will turn white in the end."

Cédric raised an eyebrow. She had been listening to the conversation after church, then. He was surprised a girl would take interest in the talk of men.

"The market stalls await," Gregoire said. "Let us be off."

Sophie took her brother's arm and tossed a glance over her shoulder at Cédric, smiling. His heart thudded faster.

"Did you find what you were looking for at the harbor?" Monsieur Portier asked him as they fell in behind the siblings.

The Catalan fleet had arrived two days prior. The set of silver falcon bells he'd purchased for the count had been made in Syria, if the merchant was speaking the truth. Whatever their origin, the craftsmanship was exquisite.

"Indeed I did. And did you find your silks?"

"All that I wished for, and some I didn't." Monsieur Portier gave his wife a fleeting frown.

She batted at her husband's arm. "I love the color pink, and so does Sophie."

"Between them, they bought enough silk to clothe a hundred women," her husband went on. "Perhaps I should think twice next time before bringing my wife and daughter along when a merchant fleet arrives."

Cédric chuckled. "How goes your quest to lure foreign cloth merchants to Toulouse?" he asked.

"Slowly, slowly. I'm just planting the seeds, you see. Toulouse is not as fair nor so blessed with riches as this place, but our pastel trade grows by the year."

Pastel dye was costly; few could afford to purchase it. Cédric doubted there would be enough demand to support a vast network of merchants in Toulouse. Then again, his understanding of how the merchant world worked was sketchy at best.

"Now, Monsieur de Montavon," said the merchant. "You must tell us about yourself. Gregoire says you are from Auvergne. I've heard it is a beautiful region, with mountains and valleys and vast oak forests."

Cédric nodded, his eyes fixed on the young woman ahead. Her black wool cloak twitched from side to side with each step she took. She bent close to her brother, murmuring something in his ear, and he let out a shout of laughter. For a moment, Cédric felt jealous, wondering what she had said.

"I live in Auvergne on the count's lands," he said, "but my own family is from farther south, near Albi."

"Is that so?" Monsieur Portier looked at him in surprise. "We've a house there, and we travel to Albi for the Christmas feasts each year."

"Why Albi?" Cédric asked.

"It's still the crown jewel of the pastel trade. To become a man of influence there, I was obliged to buy property and citizenship in the town. It is a splendid place, although Toulouse will one day surpass it in elegance, mark my words."

"My dear, let us hear Monsieur de Montavon's story," his wife chided him. "He's only just begun. How did you become a falconer, monsieur?"

"My own father had a respectable collection of falcons," Cédric said, "and I took interest in them from an early age. When my father died, I struck out on my own. After some time, I found employment with the count, thanks to my experience in the mews."

"Did an illness claim your father?"

He shook his head. *"Écorcheurs."*

"God in Heaven. My deepest sympathies."

"Your poor mother," Madame Portier chimed in, her eyes wet.

"My mother died when I was a boy," Cédric said.

"May God rest their souls. They would have been proud of you, monsieur. I imagine they would have wished to see you betrothed," Monsieur Portier said.

Cédric looked at him sideways, thrown off guard by the comment. His father had discussed negotiating a marriage for him before he died, but once he was gone, there had been no one to shepherd along the process, and Cédric was too busy for such matters.

"Death changes everything," he said simply.

"There must be many families hoping to forge an alliance with you. How many can say they are falconer to a count?" Monsieur Portier went on. "And a nobleman, too."

"Yes. Though my eldest brother inherited the title and the estate."

"Still, gentle birth is gentle birth." The merchant nodded in time with his words, the loose flesh on his jowls vibrating as he spoke. "There's value in that."

Cédric fought an urge to roll his eyes. The newly rich were so obsessed with rank it was laughable. Some wealthy merchants went so far as to buy titles from impoverished noblemen.

All the while, he kept one ear pricked forward, trying to catch bits of the lively conversation between brother and sister. It was being carried on in Occitan. Having grown up in the Languedoc region, where that language was spoken, Cédric was fluent in it himself.

Monsieur Portier pointed at a woman just ahead of them. The hem of her cloak was high enough to reveal the folds of a blue skirt.

"That wool was dyed with pastel," he said to his wife. "Do you not agree?"

"Yes, but the color is not as rich as it should be. Not like your fabrics, Henri. Nobody knows the secrets of pastel like you."

"Flattery will get you everywhere, *ma chérie*." He smiled down at her, then bussed her cheek.

Cédric observed the couple with a strange sensation of melancholy in his gut. He could recall few interactions between his own parents. His father had seemed to lead an entirely separate life from his wife. Cédric was certain, however, that he had never seen his parents jesting together the way the Portiers did.

Just ahead, Gregoire and Sophie had stopped to observe a puppet show. A crowd of small children and their minders stood rapt in front of the wooden caravan that served as a theater.

"Maman, Papa!" Sophie flapped an arm at her parents. "Come watch with us."

Monsieur Portier let out a low, indulgent chuckle. "Of course, my child, whatever you desire."

When they drew up by the siblings, Cédric found himself next to Sophie. He watched her from the corner of his eye as she dissolved in giggles. She smelled faintly of lavender.

One of the puppets, a princess, shrieked in distress as a pack of bandits approached her carriage. The unseen actor manipulating the puppet was clearly a man, his voice pitched unnaturally high. The princess produced a wooden club from beneath her skirts and proceeded to bash the attackers over the head with it. The children screeched in delight, and Sophie impulsively seized Cédric by the arm, gasping. The pressure of her fingers burned through his sleeve.

"Do you find it amusing, monsieur?" she asked.

Cédric smiled down at her. "Yes. Quite amusing."

Madame Portier looked over at her daughter. "Sophie!" she warned.

Quickly the girl removed her hand from his arm. Cédric caught her father's eye. Monsieur Portier assessed him with a long, shrewd gaze, then turned to regard the puppet show again.

Cédric inhaled her scent, savoring it. He eyed the curve of her rosy cheek, the delicate sweep of her profile. Her small, even teeth were like rows of gleaming white pearls. She tilted her head back, sought his gaze once more, deepened her smile.

Staring into her sapphire-blue eyes, he felt a curious weakness in his knees. The space between them seemed immense, though she was only a hand's breadth away. He longed to encircle her with his arm, draw her into his embrace, feel the soft curves of her body against his.

Taking a shaky breath, he tried to compose himself. The shouts and laughter of the crowd blended with the sonorous rhythm of the bells in the distance, but nothing could drown out the wild pounding of his own heart.

In that instant, Sophie's tantalizing promise of joy reeled him in like a falcon on a lure.

❦

That evening he supped with the Portier family. As the meal progressed, he noticed Madame Portier often lapsed into silence, a faraway expression on her face.

"Is your mother well?" he asked Sophie at one point, keeping his voice low.

Sophie whispered that her mother was in mourning for her sister, a girl who had lived to the age of five.

"You must miss your sister, too."

"Yes, of course." Sophie's tone betrayed no emotion, save a bit of impatience. She looked down for a moment. When she spoke again, there was a hint of sadness in her voice. "I have a heart, just as my mother does. But there is nothing we can do about what has already come to pass."

Cédric regarded Madame Portier across the table. She was listening intently to some story of Grégoire's about a stodgy Flemish merchant. Grégoire thrust out his lower lip and furrowed his brow in an impression of the man's dour expression, then launched into a monologue in droning Flemish.

"You're too cruel, my son," she scolded.

Grégoire winked at her, spooned up a bit of plum compote, and consumed it with an audible sigh of pleasure.

His mother laughed.

"I see how it is with you," Cédric whispered back to Sophie. "Grégoire is your mother's favorite, and you are your father's."

"Your eyes are as sharp as a falcon's. I thought *you* trained *them*—but is it the other way around?"

"Sometimes I'm not sure, to be truthful."

"Do you have a falcon of your own?" she asked, growing serious. "A pet you've trained?"

"I've had a few favorites over the years. As a boy, I had a sparrow hawk."

"I've heard they bring good luck."

"For some, perhaps," he replied. "Mine was given me as a gift when my mother died, but it perished not long after she did."

"I'm sorry." She studied him with a serious expression. "How dreadful."

He drank in her scent. The hair that peeked out from under her elaborate pink silk head wrap was like burnished gold, but her lashes were dark as night.

"Monsieur de Montavon," Monsieur Portier boomed from across the table. He hoisted his silver cup and took a swallow. "I've a proposition to make. What are your plans for Christmastime?"

With effort, Cédric forced his thoughts away from Sophie. "I have none."

"What say you to joining us in Albi? We would be honored to have you with us for the feast days," the merchant continued. "Our home in Albi is situated near the market square, and our cook outdoes himself every year with sweet and savory treats. The spun sugar concoctions he makes are truly a marvel."

Grégoire saluted Cédric with his cup. "What an excellent idea. You must come, my friend."

Cédric looked around the table, finally resting his gaze on Sophie. She was so tantalizingly close. Her rosy lips were parted, her skin shone in the candlelight.

"Thank you for the invitation," he said after a moment. "I confess I am tempted, but I must think on it."

Grégoire leaned forward. "Careful, my friend. If you think too long, the invitation might go to another."

"Oh?"

Monsieur Portier nodded. "When we went to visit the Catalan fleet, we ran into that fellow from the ship, the one who was after the gyrfalcons. He seemed to take a fancy to our Sophie, and she to him."

Cédric's muscles tensed. He tried not to show the surprise he felt.

"Papa, I was being polite," Sophie protested, her cheeks coloring. "He frightens me. Such a stern-faced man."

"But handsome," Grégoire said saucily. "You said so yourself."

Sophie's flush deepened.

By God, her beauty was distracting.

Her father leaned back in his chair. "The man has called upon us twice now."

"Is that so?" Cédric asked, attempting to keep his voice neutral.

Again that unfamiliar feeling of jealousy took hold of him. He pushed it away. In a few days, he would be on the road to Auvergne, the girl forgotten.

The elder Portier's eyes flicked back and forth between Sophie and Cédric, a satisfied smile on his face. "Pastel is not the only prize I've cultivated, you see."

CHAPTER 8

Spring, 1440
Bruges, Flanders

SOPHIE, Grégoire, and Cédric strolled along the canal and climbed the arc of the bridge straddling it. They stood admiring the reflection of the setting sun on the water. Rising above the rooftops was the bell tower of a church, the echo of its peals at the hour of vespers still reverberating through the cooling air. A cluster of dark clouds advanced from the west.

"A sea storm approaches, by the looks of it." The falconer tilted his head back, studying the sky.

"We'd best get you back to the inn before the rain starts." Grégoire aimed his words at Sophie, but she ignored him, instead watching a swift that had just plucked an insect from the water's surface and shot up again toward the bell tower.

"Do you think the swifts have a nest in that tower?" she asked, turning to Monsieur de Montavon.

There it was again, the twinge of excitement she felt every time she looked into his eyes. He held her gaze long enough to tell her without saying a word that he felt it, too.

"Surely, there are more peaceful spots to settle down." He grinned at her.

"But the view they must have!" she protested. "There are some advantages to their perch, surely."

Grégoire seemed bored by the conversation. "Maman and Papa will be looking for us," he said idly. "They've no doubt arrived at the inn by now and are thinking of supper. They'll soon start worrying."

Sophie watched another swift disappear under the peaked roof of the bell tower. "Start worrying?" she said. "They never stop."

"With a jewel as precious as you to fuss over, they've no choice," he retorted.

She saw the glance her brother exchanged with the falconer. Irritation rose within her. She was no child, and yet she was still treated as one.

"There was a vendor roasting chestnuts in the square near that church the other day," Monsieur de Montavon said. "Let's walk back to the inn that way."

The three of them descended the bridge and followed the canal toward the church, the amber streaks of the sunset rapidly becoming obliterated by a layer of clouds. Patches of golden torchlight illuminated the houses lining the canal. Sophie tucked her hand around Grégoire's elbow, though it was the falconer whom she longed to touch. His arm swung close to hers. If she stepped a fraction to the left, she might brush against it.

Just before they reached the church and the small square, the first few raindrops splattered against the cobblestones. There was no sight of a chestnut vendor. Sophie drew in a breath. She could swear the scent of roasting nuts lingered in the air. Or was it wafting from the vaulted stone arcades in the building across from the church?

"Ah, too late," the falconer said with regret.

"Perhaps he's over there," she said, pointing at the arcades. "Don't you smell chestnuts?"

Grégoire scoffed. "I smell nothing but the wind, and a deluge is coming. Let's return to the inn."

"Please, I want to see." She turned to the falconer. "You'll accompany me?"

A gust of wind tore Grégoire's cap from his head and sent it skittering across the cobblestones.

"Blast!" He scurried after it.

The falconer proffered his own arm, and she laid a hand there. Clinging to the crook of his elbow seemed too forward. But even this light touch made her heart jump nearly into her throat.

They stepped into the shadows of the vaulted arcades.

"So," Monsieur de Montavon said softly. "Does the scent of roasting chestnuts truly linger here?"

Hail began to drum against the stones in the square.

She smiled up at him. "Perhaps it was a fancy of my imagination."

They both fell silent for a moment.

"Kiss me," she whispered. The words tumbled from her lips before she could stop them.

The look of surprise in his eyes was quickly followed by one of enthusiasm.

"Is this something you do often?" he inquired teasingly. "Slip into the shadows with a stranger and demand to be kissed?"

"You are the first, to be perfectly honest." Peering around a stone column into the square, she laughed at the sight of her brother darting to and fro as his cap leaped in the wind. "I've never been alone with any man save my father and brothers."

"I find that hard to believe. You must have many suitors."

"None whom I wish to kiss." She tipped her face up to the falconer's.

His expression was serious now. He leaned close and fitted his lips to hers.

She kissed him back eagerly, resting both palms flat against the embroidered velvet of his doublet, feeling the warm resistance of his muscles through the fabric. He put one hand on her back and pulled her gently to him. His lips were soft against hers, inquisitive, sensitive. She forgot the rain, the hail, the illusion of roasting chestnuts, her brother. Everything around her disappeared. Everything but Cédric de Montavon.

"I should have known the two of you would take advantage of my runaway cap!" Grégoire's indignant voice sliced through the dreamy languor of the moment. Her brother's face was rosy with exertion. Bits of hail clung to his cloak.

Guiltily, she backed away from the falconer.

Monsieur de Montavon dipped his head at Grégoire in a semblance of a bow.

"Forgive me," he said. "I overstepped."

But Grégoire did not look angry. To the contrary, a playful smile quirked the corners of his mouth.

"No harm done," he said. "But now we well and truly must return."

His last words were meant for Sophie, and she had no intention of contradicting him. She slid the hood of her cloak over her head and took her brother's arm. The hail had turned to driving rain. The three of them hastened across the square, the wind at their backs. Sophie's lips still tingled from the falconer's touch. She pressed them together, willing the sensation to linger.

Striding next to her, Cédric de Montavon sought her eyes. She looked up, returned his gaze. And in his expression she saw reflected back at her exactly what she felt: a powerful, fierce longing—desire that would not be quenched with one kiss.

CHAPTER 9

Spring, 1440
Auvergne, France

WILDFLOWERS of every hue flecked the gently rolling meadows. A meandering stream gurgled along the roadside. Spring was at its glorious peak in the Auvergne countryside, but Cédric ignored the beauty all around him. He shifted in the saddle, cursing the slight rise that blocked his view of the road ahead.

Before leaving Bruges, he had lashed the cages to the frame of the cart and made sure its waxed-canvas cover was secured. He checked over his shoulder for the hundredth time today to assure himself all was well. Seeing him turn, the cart's driver waved. Two guards rode a few paces behind the cart on horses as large and well-muscled as his own.

His mount tossed its head and snorted softly, as if aware of Cédric's thoughts. He reached down and gave its glossy brown neck a pat. One of the many benefits of working for the count was access to his stables. Cédric had chosen this horse based on two qualities: speed and a calm temperament.

Because of the *écorcheurs*, he had no choice but to be vigilant on these journeys. At every village or inn, he inquired about any recent attacks or sightings of the well-armed gangs who swarmed over the landscape, stripping men bare of everything save the shirts on their backs. He had chosen a northerly route through Flanders and Bavaria, then cut down through the rough high country of outer Burgundy and Savoy before dropping into Auvergne. This slowed the journey substantially, but it allowed him to avoid the most perilous sections of France where the *écorcheurs* ruled the roads.

More than once they had been forced to hide deep in the woods, the cart disguised behind hastily cut willow boughs just off the road. He always took care to cover the wheel tracks and hoofmarks as well as their own footprints. So far his thoroughness had worked. But he knew his luck could not hold out forever.

They were about a day's ride away from the count's lands now. All of them were eager to be home, to finally put the worries of the road behind them. At Cédric's urging, they had set out from the inn where they'd lodged just as dawn broke, while cocks still crowed in the courtyard. With a quick pace, they would make it home by nightfall.

Behind him, the sound of the horses' hooves blended with the rhythm of the mules' steady clopping. A thunderstorm overnight had ensured muddy conditions today, and the cart jolted over deep grooves. Each time, Cédric winced, imagining the delicate workings of the gyrfalcons' innards. He cast an eye upward. The sun was hidden behind a bank of clouds.

Please, God, he prayed. *No more rain until we reach home.*

They passed a field that had been planted with barley. Tiny green shoots sprouted all over the rich soil. Cédric imagined a bowl of barley porridge doused with cream and honey, perhaps with a pinch of precious cinnamon sprinkled over the top. His stomach growled. All he'd eaten today was a dried crust of bread and a wizened sausage.

They passed into a copse of beeches on the crest of a low hill.

"Be on your guard," Cédric called out. He turned to check the position of the guards. They now flanked the mule cart tightly. "Drop back a bit," he ordered. "I'll pull ahead."

He urged his horse into a trot. But no threats emerged from the woods, and soon they were on a gentle downslope leading into another stretch of barley fields. They passed a tiny stone cottage that had long ago lost its roof. Its doorway gaped like a missing tooth. Inside the ruin, wild roses bloomed, a glorious froth of pale pink. The unexpected glimpse of beauty turned Cédric's mind to Sophie Portier.

Since he'd left his family's lands, he'd had little chance to mingle with women. They were often in his mind, though. Even though the inn he frequented in Bruges was no house of prostitution, there were women who discreetly plied their trade within its walls. They were a higher breed of whore than the ones in brothels—courtesans, really. Well dressed, well spoken. His encounters with them relieved the ache in his loins and made him forget his loneliness for a night.

But Sophie Portier sparked something different within him. Yes, he desired her with a familiar, primal urgency. But more than that, he wanted to listen to her talk, hear the infectious laughter bubbling from her lips, see the light dance in her sea-blue eyes. She made him feel there was joy to be had in this life, as if she'd opened a curtain and shown him what could be. He felt reckless, with her—in a strange, exhilarating way.

As they clattered over a bridge spanning a stream, Cédric shook the daydreams from his mind. Behind him, one of the guards let out a warning shout. A figure darted out from a stand of willows on the stream bank, a dagger in his outstretched hand. Two more men emerged from the willows in his footsteps. One rushed toward the guards. The other raced along the roadside toward Cédric himself, sword in hand.

"Bandits!" Cédric roared, turning his horse to face the advancing man. "Get the cart moving, quick!"

The driver cried out to the mules, urging them forward. But a bandit leaped aboard the cart and slashed at the driver with his blade. The driver screamed in pain and plummeted from the bench to the edge of the bridge, then rolled off and landed with a splash in the water below.

Cédric forced his attention to the most immediate threat, the man closing the space between them. Fearing injury to his horse, he pulled hard on the reins and dug his left heel into the animal's ribs. Backing and turning at the same time, the horse moved just enough to evade the man's blade. With the outstretched tip of his own sword, Cédric flicked the attacker's blade from his hand. Pulling a booted foot from his stirrup, he smashed it against the bandit's head, driving him to the ground.

The bandit who had control of the cart clutched the reins in his hands, bellowing orders at the mules. But they balked, spooked by the melee and the unfamiliar voice.

Cédric frantically spurred his horse toward the cart. He reached for the bridle of the nearest mule, lunging for the reins. With a savage yank, he jerked them out of the bandit's grasp. Slapping the rump of the mule, he startled it into motion. The mule team bolted forward.

As the cart rumbled by, he managed to catch hold of the bandit's cloak. The man toppled backward, and Cédric dragged him to the earth, nearly losing his seat in the process. His attacker sprang up again, slashing out with his blade. It came dangerously close to Cédric's thigh.

These are no common roadside bandits. These are écorcheurs, trained mercenaries.

Even as the thoughts pulsed through his mind, he raised his sword. Murmuring to his horse and applying steady pressure to the animal's sides, he lunged forward and ran the man through with his blade.

Cédric swiveled, eyeing the bridge. One of the guards was nowhere to be seen. He assumed the injured driver was still in the stream, prayed the missing guard was assisting him. The other guard was digging his heels into his horse's belly, bearing down on the *écorcheur* heading his way.

He turned back to track the cart. The mules had ambled to a stop a short distance away. And the man who a moment ago Cédric had left lying in the mud ran nimbly along the road to the cart as if he hadn't just sustained a massive blow to the head.

"Devil take you!" Cédric bent low over his mount's neck and urged the horse into a gallop. When he pulled abreast of the cart, the *écorcheur* was frantically pounding at a cage with the butt of his sword.

Cédric rode up behind him and plunged his sword into the man's back. One anguished cry and he crumpled to the ground face down. Cédric dismounted, leaped into the cart, and lashed a leather jess around the weakened cage frame. The falcons shivered on their perches, immersed in the darkness of their traveling hoods. Thank all the saints, no harm had come to them.

One of the guards cantered up, breathing hard. "The driver's hurt, but he'll live," he reported. "I killed one of the bastards." He glanced at the motionless bodies on the road. "You took care of the rest. And the falcons?"

Cédric's gut heaved. Reflexively, he put a hand to his neck, where the pouch containing the silver bells lay against his breastbone. He swayed a little, bracing himself against the cart for support. He was well paid, he worked with falcons, he had a chance to see the world, and he had a fine home, servants, a plentiful larder. But in the end, it all balanced on a knife point. If he displeased the count, his good fortune would vanish like a wisp of smoke.

You must make your own fortune. His father's dying words pounded in his brain.

The guard's voice cut into his thoughts. "Are you wounded?"

Cédric shook his head. "Just catching my breath. The falcons are unhurt."

"Saints be praised," the man said in relief. "I'd not want to return to the count's lands otherwise."

A fine mist began drifting down from the sky. Cédric glanced up, scowled at the gathering rainclouds, and straightened his shoulders.

"Whatever befalls us, we're bound to return," he said curtly. "Let's get back on the road."

CHAPTER 10

Summer, 1440
Auvergne, France

It was early evening, dusk. A sparrow hawk favored by the countess had been ill and off her feed lately. Though he usually relegated the daily care of the birds to the under-falconers, Cédric had taken to sleeping in the mews and administering healing remedies at intervals while the illness ran its course. For less valuable birds, he would have trusted his assistants to do the job, but with the countess's beloved hawk, it was a different story. This was the first time since the malady began that he had felt comfortable coming back to his home to eat and sleep.

When a servant answered the knock at the door, Cédric was in his parlor, sprawled in a chair near the hearth with his eyes closed. The clatter of crockery and kettles rose up from the kitchen. He breathed in the faint scent of roasting pigeon, looking forward to supper.

He stifled a groan when he heard the familiar voice of the count's steward at the door. Jamming his feet into the soft leather slippers he'd cast off when he flopped into the chair, he ambled to the entryway.

"I'm surprised to see you here, sir," he said by way of greeting.

The man wasted no breath on small talk. "You've not carried out your duties, have you? Not as promised."

"What are you getting at?" A slow burn of annoyance rose in Cédric's throat.

"Where are your record sheets, the tallies of salaries and expenditures for the mews?" he asked, pinning Cédric with a disparaging stare. "You told me I'd have them upon your return from Bruges, yet it's nearly midsummer now. And your expenses on the journey. Where is the record of those?"

"It's coming," Cédric told him. "I have little chance to write of an evening, with all my other duties. You'll have it all in two days."

"If you fail to do as promised, the count will be displeased. Despite your tardiness in completing this business, my lord insists that you be paid."

He removed a purse attached to his belt and thrust it out.

Cédric plucked the purse from the man's grasp. "My thanks to him."

"Another letter has come for you." The steward now waved a sealed square of paper at him. "The third one from Toulouse since spring. Is there a trade in falcons in that city these days?"

Cédric took the letter. "Not that I've heard. But perhaps whatever is in this letter will enlighten me on the matter."

"Your time is better spent writing than reading, in my view." Thin lips pressed together, the steward wheeled and snapped his fingers at the servant, who hastily opened the door.

Cédric watched the man stalk toward the château, still chafing with irritation. He kept a running tally of his expenditures in his head. It was all neatly tabulated in his mind. But the truth was he had never taken to the act of writing.

Oh, he had learned. Alongside his brothers, he had suffered the torture of practicing his letters. Even with welts on the backs of his hands from the tutor's switch striking him when he made an error, he never caught on as his brothers did. By God, he'd rather have chewed off his own arm than put a quill to parchment or paper in those days.

The steward receded into the half-light, the slap of his boots on the cobblestones fading. Cédric did not envy that man his position. The count's extravagant tastes and frequent entertaining meant the household was rarely at rest.

He returned to the parlor, sank down in his chair again, and broke the letter's seal by the light of the fire. The sight of Sophie's elaborate, looping script made his breath come a little faster.

He traced the words with a finger as he read. More than once he broke into a grin, even chuckled. Sophie's letters showed her to be not only entertaining but intelligent, with a wry wit. She offered amusing anecdotes about life in Toulouse, particularly her accounts of accompanying her father to the marketplace and to the drapers' guild, where he schemed to lure pastel merchants to his city. In one of Cédric's own letters, which were always quite brief in comparison to hers, he had asked her why she spent so much time with her father in the world of merchants. The answer came today:

Papa tells me I have a mind for business, and it's a shame I wasn't born a boy. But I believe the true reason he keeps me at his side is that he is displaying his wares. Maman has gowns dyed with pastel made for me each season. Everyone who looks upon me sees the quality of my father's products. He used to tease me and say I will find a husband this way. But since we returned from Bruges, I've told him I won't marry a merchant. I will marry for love. And you, master falconer? Do you intend to marry for love?

Cédric's heart thudded faster when he read those lines. He looked into the fire, mesmerized by the dancing flames.

Since we returned from Bruges.

Did that refer to him? Or to the Catalan? An image of the man's coldly handsome face arose in his mind. Cédric pushed away the thoughts and turned his gaze back to the letter.

He used to tease me and say I will find a husband this way.

Marriage. It was something Cédric had given little thought to. After his mother died, his father had slowly worked his way through planning the futures of each son. Yves, destined to take over the estate, had been matched with the daughter of a nearby *seigneur*; Stéphane had been conscripted to seminary and the life of a priest; and then Papa had died. There'd been no time to plan a future for Cédric.

His eyes fell to the linen paper in his hand again.

The last line was an entreaty to accept the Portier family's invitation to spend the Christmas feast days with them in Albi. There was no mention of the Catalan. Cédric took heart from this. Surely, if the man was still associating with the Portier family, Sophie would address it.

He sat up straighter. Traveling during the winter was never easy. Still, the idea of a holiday spent in the bosom of the Portier family was more and more attractive. Sophie Portier haunted his dreams—there was no denying it. He felt a fierce tug of longing every time she entered his thoughts. With this young woman, he could imagine a shared life. What would it be like to join her in a marriage bed each night? To father her children? His throat thickened with emotion at the idea.

If he were to court her, staying in Auvergne for Christmas was not an option.

The next day, he strode through a light mist to the château, intending to inquire at the door for his employer's attention. Luckily, the count was outside with an entourage of servants, taking his exercise in the gardens. The group stood in front of a fountain that spewed water from the mouths of gleaming marble fish.

"Master falconer!" the count called, waving him over. His neatly trimmed beard gleamed with oil, mimicking the fur lining of his cap and matching cape.

The steward glared at Cédric over the count's shoulder. Two other attendants eyed him with disdain. Like Cédric, these men were all noble-born—yet they regarded him with an air of contempt. Perhaps it was because he lived near the mews and the stables and worked with animals, but he suspected there was a different reason: they were jealous. He'd been in the count's favor since arriving here, but his victorious combat with the *écorcheurs* on the road home from Bruges had raised him even higher in the nobleman's estimation.

Cédric ignored the hostile gazes directed toward him and bowed. "My lord."

"What do you wish to discuss, master falconer?" The count's tone was, as always, polite and cool. His hooded brown eyes surveyed Cédric over a finely arched nose that was reminiscent of a hawk's beak.

"A merchant of pastel and his family have invited me to Albi for the Christmas feast days, my lord."

The people clustered behind the count began to whisper amongst themselves.

"A merchant of pastel, eh?" The count regarded him with bafflement. "How have you become acquainted with him?"

"In Bruges, my lord. At church." Cédric thought it prudent not to mention the card game that had brought him together with the elder Portier. "Might we speak privately?"

The count walked a few paces away from his attendants, and Cédric followed him. The steward let out an irritated sigh.

"To be perfectly frank, my lord," Cédric confided, "I am considering courting the merchant's daughter."

"I see. Naturally, you're free to marry. But to a merchant's daughter?" His expression betrayed his distaste for the idea.

"Without a title or an estate, I've little chance of marrying a noblewoman."

"And this girl's father probably has a fine dowry amassed. Well, I suppose I've no argument with it. But you shall have to continue your travels for me, as we agreed."

"Of course, my lord."

"Believe me, I am mindful of the dangers you encounter. You've shown great loyalty and courage, and there are not many who are your equal with a sword or a falcon. Mark my words, within a few years the *écorcheurs* will be a distant memory. The king makes great progress with his standing army, and the roads grow safer with each passing day." The count abruptly changed the subject. "Is my boy's falcon coming along well?"

Cédric was training a merlin he'd acquired from the Norwegian for the count's eldest son. She would eventually roost in the boy's chamber and accompany him everywhere he went, perched on a gloved wrist.

"She'll be fully trained in time for his name-day celebration," he said.

The steward approached, clearing his throat. "My lord, if you would, there is a matter regarding the fountains that requires your attention." He turned a haughty gaze on Cédric. "Have you brought the records I requested?"

"I told you yesterday you would have them in two days' time," Cédric reminded him. "So look for me tomorrow, sir." He bowed to the count. "Thank you, my lord."

Cédric turned away, his chest fizzing with excitement. That had gone better than he expected.

He would go to Albi. He would see Sophie again—and he would make his intentions known.

CHAPTER 11

Winter, 1440
Albi, France

Cédric's horse clattered over the bridge leading to the city walls of Albi. It was midmorning on the day before Christmas. The gray-blue waters of the River Albi glittered in the winter sunlight. His hands were stiff from holding the reins; his legs ached from all the days in the saddle. Still, a surge of anticipation rushed through him as the city guards admitted him through the gates.

Riding past the great church dominating the central square, he admired the soaring bell tower and stained glass windows. The structure was made of blush-colored stone, echoing the color of the houses that surrounded it. It was a brief ride to the Portier home in the cloth merchants' quarter. The pink brick structure rose three stories high. Its arched oak entry doors were large enough to admit a team of draft horses pulling an oxcart. Someone had seen him coming, apparently, for the doors opened before he could even announce his presence.

Inside, an expansive courtyard was laid with decorative stones in swirling patterns of black and white. Slim stone columns supported three levels of vaulted open-air corridors that wrapped around the space. Cédric spied the carved stone faces of a man and woman on the wall opposite him, and recognized them as Monsieur and Madame Portier.

Dismounting, he unbuckled his panniers and handed over his mount's reins to a stableboy, who led the gelding through another set of double doors. Then he heard a cry of excitement. On the second floor, a familiar face beamed down at him.

He had never seen Sophie's head uncovered before. Golden curls cascaded around her shoulders. She wore a red dress with a low, square neckline. By all the saints, she was lovely.

"Monsieur de Montavon!" she called, one arm raised in greeting. "Welcome!"

At her words, the house sprang into action. An interior door to his right creaked open and two footmen appeared, followed by Monsieur Portier. He flung his arms wide.

"Welcome, monsieur!" he boomed, face creased in a broad smile. "Your arrival has been greatly anticipated these past weeks."

Cédric made a little bow, weighed down by his leather panniers. He was suddenly aware of the dust coating his boots, his cloak, probably his face as well.

Madame Portier appeared behind her husband. She approached Cédric, trailed by the footmen. "Please allow the servants to take your panniers and show you to your chamber. No doubt you are ready to rinse off the dust of the road and rest a bit."

"You have read my mind, madame," he said gratefully. "It was a long journey, but uneventful."

"God watched over you," she replied. "We have been praying for your safe arrival."

At that moment, Sophie burst through the door behind her parents.

"Monsieur de Montavon, how good to see you." She drew up before him and curtsied with grace, her bosom heaving from the exertion of running down the stairs.

He smiled with pure pleasure at the sight of her. Those sky-blue eyes gleamed at him, alive with promise. She was as luminous as he recalled.

"I am happy to see you again, too, mademoiselle." He bowed.

"We have all sorts of entertainment in store for you," she said.

Her father came to her side. "My dear Sophie has talked of nothing but your visit these past few weeks. She wears your letters like sorcerers' charms."

"Papa," she protested, her cheeks coloring. "That is untrue. I simply carry them with me to keep them all in one place."

He winked at Cédric. "Yes, yes, my dear, very clever of you." Noting Cédric's disheveled state, he clucked his tongue. "Forgive us. Please let our footman show you the way. Your horse will be well tended to. We shall see you at supper. And tonight, we shall all attend Mass."

Sophie made to follow Cédric into the house.

"Sophie!" her mother said. "I have need of you."

Their voices faded as Cédric mounted the steps of an interior staircase to the second floor. The scent of evergreen trees was thick from all the festive garlands hanging on the walls. He spied several elaborate wreaths made of holly, too.

At the door to his chamber, he gazed around in astonishment. His ancestral home had been full of fine furnishings, but time and neglect made them decrepit. The tapestries bore moth-holes; the furnishings were battered by use. But this place looked as if it had been furnished yesterday, then doused with beeswax and linseed oil until every surface shone.

A great four-poster bed stood against one wall, and a fire burned merrily in a small hearth opposite it. The open shutters revealed glass windows made of fine diamond-shaped panes, each one polished and gleaming.

The footman placed the panniers on the floor near the bed.

Cédric nodded his thanks. When the door closed behind him, he removed his cap and ran a hand through his hair. A table near the bed held a pewter pitcher of water, a ceramic bowl, a linen towel, and a thick bar of soap. Castile soap, not tallow. The most costly kind.

This family was rich. Very, very rich.

And yet they were of common stock. The one thing people like them wanted most, nobility, was out of their grasp. Unless, of course,

Monsieur Portier bought his way into the noble ranks. Which he clearly could afford to do. Cédric was surprised he'd not yet managed it, in truth.

He sank down in a chair and removed his boots. The filth of the road was crusted on them. They would need a good cleaning and oiling before the return journey. In anticipation of this, he had brought a pair of soft pigskin shoes to wear during his visit. And a doublet of wine-red velvet embroidered with gold thread, and a pair of black wool hose he reserved for special occasions.

He closed his eyes, succumbing to the exhaustion of the journey. After a moment, he forced them open again. Sleeping through the feast of Christmas Eve and the Mass that followed it would not endear him to his hosts. Until he attended to the business occupying his mind and heart, he could not relax.

When he emerged from his chamber a short time later, he walked leisurely down the corridor and began descending the stairs, his shoes quiet on the stone treads.

"Monsieur," a voice said behind him.

He turned. Sophie stood in the half-light a few steps above him, her hair concealed now by an elaborate linen wrap.

"Mademoiselle Sophie." He repressed an urge to crush her against him and bury his face in her warm neck.

"Papa has my maid following on my heels," she whispered.

She descended another step. He listened for the sound of footfalls behind her, but no one followed.

"Where is your minder, then?" he asked. "You're alone."

"I'm cleverer than Christine. She thinks I'm downstairs." Sophie held out a hand.

He raised it to his lips.

She smiled at him, moving down one more step so she was a hair's breadth away, eye to eye with him. Now he felt her breath against his face.

"Kiss me," she said.

"Gladly." His voice was hoarse with desire. As their mouths met, a tingling sensation raced through his body. He placed a hand on the small of her back and drew her forward, losing himself in the soft, yielding pleasure of her warm lips.

Sophie gripped the back of his neck, pulling him closer, her mouth opening to let him kiss her more deeply. He traced a path with his fingertips to the hollow at the base of her throat, then down to the swelling curves of her breasts. She let out a moan of pleasure.

"Sophie!" a voice shrieked in the distance.

"I've been found out," she said, disentangling herself from him. "Don't worry, I've arranged for us to sup side by side. Papa promised me that."

"Does he ever say no to you?"

Sophie laughed. "Only on the rarest of occasions." She turned on her heel and darted up the steps.

He made his way to the great hall, where the Portier family and their guests were mingling. A trio of musicians played in one corner, and an enormous Yule log burned in the hearth. Sophie appeared a moment later and stood near her mother and several children, whom he assumed were her younger siblings. Her eyes found his, and they shared a conspiratorial look. Their gaze was broken when Grégoire Portier approached.

He greeted Cédric warmly, and they fell into conversation about the journey and the winter weather. Then he lowered his voice.

"Since you've come here, I assume you are planning to make your intentions known regarding my sister?"

Cédric nodded. "If your father will entertain the idea, yes."

Sophie's laugh resonated from the other side of the room, blending with the melody being plucked out by the lute player.

"She's convinced my father to give her a love match," Grégoire went on. "As far as I know he has no objection to you."

"And that Catalan is not a rival for her affections after all?" Cédric asked sharply.

Grégoire shook his head. "He seemed eager to pursue the attachment, but Sophie told our father she'd not have him. Besides, the Catalan isn't a nobleman. You may not have wealth, but you're well-born. Papa's quite impressed by your gentle birth. Just be warned, my friend, this is how she expects to live." He gestured around the great hall, at all the elegant furnishings and possessions on display. "She won't be happy otherwise."

An unsmiling woman advanced across the room toward them, staring fixedly at Grégoire.

"My wife," he muttered, looking stricken.

"Don't worry," Cédric told him. "If she asks, we've never been to a tavern together, only to church. And when you're parted from her, you assume the habits of a monk."

Cédric's last words were nearly drowned out by the beat of the drum. Monsieur Portier strode to the musicians and clapped his hands in time to the rhythm, then signaled to them to stop playing.

The merchant cried, "The feast of Christmas Eve is served! Let us all take our seats."

In the hubbub, Cédric lost sight of Grégoire and found himself seated on a bench next to Sophie, as promised.

They both plunged their fingers into the bowl of water on the table between them. Sophie laughed as their fingertips collided.

"Wait till you see what the cook has created for us," she said, her eyes on the long line of servants carrying dishes in from the kitchens. "He promised to outdo himself this year since we have a noble visitor."

"Oh? Who would that be?" Cédric teased.

"You, of course!"

He grinned at her. As he raised his wine cup along with everyone else at the table, he felt the warmth of her presence like a caress. Closing his eyes for a moment, he said a silent prayer of thanks to God for placing Sophie Portier in his path.

CHAPTER 12

Winter, 1440
Albi, France

CÉDRIC DESCENDED the staircase a few days later with purpose, his face and hands freshly scrubbed. Outside, the faint clang of church bells marked the hour of midmorning prayer.

"I would like to speak with you in private, if we may," Cédric told Monsieur Portier, intercepting him in the great hall.

"Of course." The only evidence of the previous evening's excesses on his host's face was a slight puffiness about the eyes.

Cédric followed Monsieur Portier into his study, a chamber off the great hall with lofty ceilings and a hearth framed with intricately carved stone. A wall tapestry featuring a hawking scene drew his eye at once. The falconer stood in the foreground, holding his lure, while the hawk hovered in midair, poised to attack a rabbit.

"That tapestry is finely made," Cédric said as they took their seats in front of the fire.

"Indeed it is. I bought it from a poor nobleman in Béarn who sold off all the family treasures in an attempt to keep his estate."

"Did he succeed?"

"Until a fever got him."

The merchant gazed into the fire with a thoughtful expression while a servant filled their wine cups. He dismissed the man, then turned to regard Cédric. "What did you wish to speak to me about?"

The ironic look in his eyes told Cédric the question was entirely unnecessary.

"It is about your daughter, sir." Cédric's throat felt dry. "I wish to discuss a betrothal with Sophie. I have not broached the topic with her, of course. Not yet."

The words hung in the air between them, which now felt uncomfortably thick with silence.

Monsieur Portier leaned back in his chair.

"I appreciate frank talk, and I shall respond in kind. Sophie has been smitten by you since we met in Bruges. I only gave her permission to correspond with you after she wore me down with her entreaties."

Cédric's mouth twisted in a slight smile at the thought.

"My other daughters were wed to men I chose for reasons of business," Monsieur Portier continued. "Sophie is my favorite; it's no secret. I want her to wed for love. I've heard nothing but favorable accounts of you, and I've been witness to your honorable conduct. But tell me this: Will my daughter be happy with a falconer who lives in the countryside? Yes, you work for a wealthy nobleman, but what are your living quarters like? She cannot abide shabby circumstances."

"I have a house near the count's residence," Cédric said. "It is not at all shabby, sir. As a man of noble birth, I live according to my station."

"I'm not saying this to offend, of course," the merchant said. "But I know my daughter. She is quite easily bored, I'm afraid. And she loves her little luxuries. She is rather . . . well, underprepared for the role of wife. And that's in no small part to my coddling of her. I fully admit it."

The merchant gave Cédric a rueful smile, then took a long pull of wine. "For this reason, I wish to assure you that her dowry will include a substantial gift of gold. So that you can accommodate Sophie's desires. It would go a long way toward ensuring a happy marriage, I believe."

Cédric shifted in his seat, a twinge of irritation rising within him. Every bride came with a dowry. But the man's tone rankled him. Monsieur Portier could not dictate the manner in which Cédric spent his gold.

"I assure you, I receive a generous salary from the count," he said. "Enough to meet all of my needs."

"I don't doubt it," the merchant said. "But your needs are an entirely different thing than Sophie's. And children—oh, once they start arriving, the expenses will become a river, then a flood. We will be eagerly awaiting those offspring, of course. Naturally, I have not ignored the fact in considering this match that your children will be noble-born, on account of you. Which will open up their opportunities in life considerably. Of course, a title would be even better, but one must start somewhere."

Cédric's jaw tightened. The more this man talked, the more vulgar his conversation became. Then he dispensed with his irritation. Once Monsieur Portier gave him the gold, he could do as he wished with it.

"I understand," he said coolly.

"And another thing. How secure is your position with the count? What will you do if he releases you from his service? I cannot abide my Sophie wandering from estate to estate with a traveling falconer, even if he is of noble birth."

Cédric sat up straighter, his fingers tightening around his cup. "The count considers me the finest falconer in Auvergne, perhaps in all of France. But I'm no fool. What he truly values in me are my contacts in the falcon trade and the fact that I can defend my cargo on the roads. Believe me, the man holds me in highest esteem. He is not inclined to release me from service."

"The count could die, of course," Monsieur Portier pointed out. "Then what? Your fates would be cast to the winds."

"Or I could die," Cédric said in exasperation. "We cannot foretell the future."

"No, but we can prepare for it," countered the merchant. "I know you are growing impatient with this discussion, but hear me out.

Perhaps we can engineer a place for you in the family business. You are a seasoned traveler. You speak Norwegian, and Grégoire told me you also speak some Genoese and Catalan."

Cédric raised an eyebrow. "Enough to barter, it's true."

"We could use a man of your talents as we grow our network of pastel merchants. I know Grégoire would jump at the chance to work at your side—"

"Forgive me, but that is not a possibility," Cédric interrupted. "I have no interest in the cloth trade nor the pastel industry."

"But surely you see how difficult it will be to continue your travels for the count once you're a married man with the responsibilities of fatherhood. You cannot think leaving Sophie on her own for extended periods of time will be possible, especially once she's with child."

"There is no safer place than the count's lands," Cédric retorted. "I have trusted servants in my home, and I assume you will send members of your own household with Sophie when she joins me in Auvergne."

The merchant's expression hardened. "My daughter will be taken care of, whether by you or by me. She will have her comforts. I am simply making clear to you how precious my girl is. If any harm comes to her, if any sorrow visits her, you shall answer to me."

Cédric resisted the urge to reply harshly. He imagined Sophie crossing the threshold of his home. Would the light drain from her eyes at the sight? It was almost impossible to fathom Sophie in a dark mood. He had rarely seen her face in repose. She always seemed to be smiling, laughing, bubbling with merriment. She radiated joy, sucked the very marrow out of each day, reminded him of the beauty in the world after too many difficult years.

"Any father worth his salt would say the same," he finally grated out.

"I am not like any father," Monsieur Portier replied. "Perhaps, if you are lucky, you will have a child whom you favor as I favor Sophie. Who lives in your heart the way she does mine. You cannot possibly understand until then. But hear this: if I give my daughter what she wants—you—I aim to be certain her choice is a happy one, that is all.

She is quite innocent, quite shielded from the evils in this world. If I can do anything to soften life's blows for her when they come, I will."

He stood abruptly. Cédric followed suit.

"Go to her now. But do not tell her what we've spoken of. I reserve that privilege for myself."

Cédric bowed and left the room, the tips of his ears burning. He had never been so relieved to quit a conversation.

CHAPTER 13

Winter, 1440
Albi, France

SOPHIE GAZED around the great hall in satisfaction. The holly and evergreen garlands draped along the walls gave off a festive scent. The musicians Papa had hired for the twelve days of Christmas played just as enthusiastically as they had on Christmas Eve, though the revelry had gone on for nearly a fortnight now. And today's feast, to celebrate the Epiphany, had surpassed all the rest. Trout, veal, goose, suckling pig, even a peacock roasted in its feathers. Then some *entremets*—delicate nibbles glazed with layers of sugar and honey. She had eaten a few too many of those, but she had no intention of passing up the highlight of the meal—*la fête des rois*, in which whoever got the hidden bean in their slice of cake would be king or queen of the feast. Sophie had never won this game, but she also never lost heart. Tonight, she was sure God had heard her prayers. She would win.

Next to her, Cédric leaned closer.

"I have never seen sweets loaded with so much sugar," he whispered to her, eyes twinkling.

"Well, I hope you've saved room for the *galette des rois*," she replied, gracing him with her most dazzling smile.

"Believe me, I would never pass up the chance to be king." He drained his cup of wine.

Sophie signaled to a servant. He scurried over and refilled the falconer's cup.

"You're taking good care of me," Cédric said, a look of amusement on his face.

"It is my duty. You are our honored guest. Papa bade me be certain all your needs are met."

He raised an eyebrow. Carefully, almost imperceptibly, she moved closer to him on the bench. Through the layers of her dress and underclothes, she felt the firm muscles of his thigh pressing against her own. He rested one hand on the table between them. She fiddled with her knife, grazing her little finger against his. The sensation of his skin on hers sent a thrill through her.

"The *galette des rois*," Papa boomed suddenly, standing with his arms spread wide.

Sophie looked at him, startled out of what had felt like a private moment. Her father's eyes bored into her, making her squirm.

Servants dispersed around the table, placing slices before each guest.

"Whoever finds the bean is king or queen for the night. I wish you all good luck." Papa raised his cup and saluted everyone, then settled back in his chair.

Shouts of disappointment and peals of laughter rang out as the revelers consumed their slices of cake.

Cédric ate his in a few quick bites and shook his head in dismay. "It's not meant to be. I won't be king tonight."

Sophie tore off a piece of her own slice and examined it closely. Excitement flared within her. Holding up her find overhead, she let out a cry of triumph. "I've got the bean! I'm queen of you all!"

Papa roared his approval and clapped his hands. The rest of the diners followed suit.

At Papa's signal, a troubadour performed a complicated series of trumpet blasts in Sophie's direction. Then another servant carried out a silver platter bearing a red velvet crown trimmed with cloth-of-gold. He bowed low before Sophie.

She plucked the crown off the platter and fitted it over her silk head covering. Slowly, she rose to her feet.

"My subjects."

Raising her chin, she sought the gaze of each family member and guest. Assuming what she imagined was a regal expression, she thrust her shoulders back. Papa had spared no expense on her blue silk dress, which matched the color of her eyes exactly. Surely, it was appropriate attire for a queen. All she lacked were jewels.

"Your Majesty!" they all shouted as one. More laughter rang out. Two servants appeared bearing pitchers of spiced wine.

"Why aren't true queens as beautiful as false ones?" Grégoire called from across the table, a mocking grin on his face.

"Silence!" Sophie ordered him, suppressing a giggle. "I *am* a true queen, sir. And just to prove it, I demand that you refill my cup at once."

Grégoire groaned. At a snail's pace, he rose from his seat, plucked a pitcher of wine from a servant's grasp, and trudged around the table. After filling her cup, he bent down in an exaggerated bow, inciting more laughter.

"What is your pleasure next, Queen Sophie?" Papa asked.

Next to him, Maman smiled, her cheeks rosy from the wine. "Do not delay," she advised. "Your subjects will get restless otherwise."

"I wish to play 'The Queen Who Does Not Lie,' " Sophie announced.

Excited murmuring swept around the table. The tambourine shaker rattled his instrument with flair.

"My first question is directed to my dining companion, our honored guest, Monsieur de Montavon." She turned to him and batted her eyelashes. "Sir. Answer truthfully, and you may ask a question in return. Who has stolen your heart?"

Silence fell. Her pulse thudded in her ears. It was audacious, reckless. But she was queen today. She would be forgiven for such boldness.

He stared at her for a moment without answering. Then he smiled a little. "Why, the queen, of course."

Applause broke out.

She glanced at her father, who bore an inscrutable expression.

"I see the truth in your eyes and hear it in your voice, sir," she replied, turning to the falconer. "Now you may ask a question of anyone you choose—and they must answer as truthfully as you have."

He hesitated, glancing at the expectant faces around the table. Then his gaze returned to her. "I wish to know," he said in a firm, clear voice, "who has stolen the queen's heart."

She felt an unaccustomed weakness in her knees. "It would not be seemly for the queen to share secrets of the heart."

Hisses and boos broke out, and the drummer pounded on his goatskin drum.

"Truth! Truth!" the crowd chanted.

Sophie held up a hand. "Very well. I will describe him with all discretion, then, as befits my rank. He is a man of gentle birth, for I only surround myself with noble-born companions. And he is well-traveled."

"And—let me guess—he's not a bad falcon tamer either," Grégoire shouted, his words blurred by wine.

Wild laughter rippled through the air.

Sophie glanced down at Cédric, who could not contain his own merriment. She raised her cup, pretending not to hear the hilarity.

"My lords and ladies," she began.

"There are no lords and ladies here," a cousin shouted from the far end of the table.

"Do you wish to lose your head?" she asked him icily. "I demand silence!"

The crowd quieted.

"My subjects, you are unruly. To show me your loyalty, you must obey me in this command: we shall all retire from the table and dance until the Yule log has burned to ash."

With that, she walked away from the table, winking at Cédric as she did so.

With good-natured groans and complaints, the rest of the revelers followed suit. Sophie gestured at the musicians and they struck up a festive melody.

Papa got to her first. “May I have this dance, Queen Sophie?” he asked.

“It would be my honor, Monsieur Portier.” She lowered her head in a regal nod.

They began circling each other, dipping and swaying in time to the music. Others joined them until a group of paired dancers had formed.

“You are by far too bold for a girl,” Papa said, the smile fading from his face.

“But I am not a girl, I am queen.”

“Tomorrow you will simply be my daughter again. And my favorite, as you so clearly know. But even the favorite can forget herself.”

“Papa, I am only playing the game,” she insisted. “It is not my fault I found the bean.”

“Do you think that was just luck, my girl?” he asked softly.

They faced each other, palm to palm. He bowed; she curtsied. The music swelled and the dancers drew close together in a tight knot, then dispersed.

“What do you mean?” she asked him.

“I made sure you got the bean, Queen Sophie. Good fortune is not often a matter of luck. It is a matter of influence.”

Disappointment shot through her chest. “Oh.”

“You’ve made it plain since we met Monsieur de Montavon that he has captured your attention. Today, you told the entire household and all of our guests that he has captured your heart as well. Was that true?”

“Yes, Papa, I’ve told you so many times, have I not?”

“So be it. Your good fortune continues, thanks to me. The falconer has asked me for your hand, and I’ve accepted.”

She stared at Papa, stunned. “But he has said nothing to me.”

“It is not his place to do so, but mine.”

“And he will take his place alongside you in the cloth trade? He will make a fine addition—”

"No, Sophie. He won't hear of it. If I were in his shoes, I wouldn't trade the life of a falconer for the life of a cloth merchant either."

"But, Papa, you often say there's no man on earth you can't convince to change his mind." Sophie used her most honeyed voice, sweetening it further with a pleading smile. "Perhaps you need a little more time . . . "

He pressed his lips together, his eyes darting to Maman and back again. "Your mother wanted you wed a year ago. I put her off. Said I wouldn't make a match for reasons of commerce and trade, as I did for your elder sisters. No, I wanted my favorite daughter to have the love match she desires."

A new refrain rose up from the musicians. Pulling her palm away from her father's, Sophie wove an intricate pattern of steps around him. Papa stood stock-still, the sober expression on his face a stark contrast to the jocular smile he had worn most of the day.

"I know you've been stalking him in the corridors," he hissed. "And twice the servants have seen you attempting to enter his chamber alone. Your behavior at the table with him verges on scandalous. You cannot flirt so openly with a man unless he is your betrothed. This is not a game, Sophie. I've indulged you to my detriment. But I won't have you compromise your virtue. No, you have made your choice. You will wed Cédric de Montavon on the day I ordain. If you do not comply, I will not entertain any further ideas of a love match. Do you understand?"

Tears burned in Sophie's eyes. She was queen, and yet her father shamed her on this day of all days when he should be granting her every wish. She forced down a sob. Caught Cédric's gaze across the room. The desire in his eyes made her breath catch in her throat.

"You're weeping!" her father said in alarm. "What is it?"

"I'm afraid, Papa," she admitted. "Afraid of leaving you, afraid of becoming a wife and mother. There's so much I do not know."

His expression relaxed. "My dear, we all fear what we do not know. I will always look after you, even when you're married and no longer by my side. But what matters to me is: Do you fear *him*? The falconer?"

She glanced at Cédric.

Again she felt that raw longing to be near him, to put her hands upon him. To press her body to his, to hear his heart pounding under her cheek.

The dance ended. Sophie lifted her chin and looked straight at her father.

“No, Papa,” she said with certainty. “I love him.”

CHAPTER 14

Spring, 1441
Albi, France

CÉDRIC MOUNTED the steps of the church, careful to shorten his strides so his bride could match his pace. He had never felt so acutely aware of public scrutiny. The square was filled with their guests, most of whom were the family and friends of the Portiers. Every pair of eyes was fixed upon them. Swifts circled the bell tower, their piercing cries the only sound he noticed save the thrumming of his own heart.

He glanced sideways, admiring the graceful lines of Sophie's profile, the sweep of her dark lashes, her rosy lips. Her blue silk dress was embroidered with hundreds of seed pearls that glowed in the sun. Her golden curls were hidden under the folds of her elaborate silken head wrap. She kept her eyes straight ahead, focused on the priest waiting at the open doors. It was the first time he had seen her so serious. She was likely as nervous as he.

They reached the top of the steps. The scent of incense wafted out from the cavernous church interior. Beeswax candles burned on the altar; wreaths of flowers and greenery adorned the pews.

Steady now, he counseled himself. *There's much to come before we enter these doors.*

The priest and his attendant stood in the open doorway, the priest's lavishly embroidered vestments nearly as spectacular as Sophie's dress. He blessed Cédric and Sophie in Latin, anointing them with holy water. At his signal, Sophie held out a pouch filled with golden coins. The priest's assistant made a show of counting them aloud. When he finished, the priest blessed the coins and thus the dowry Sophie would bring to the marriage. He turned slightly, directing an expectant gaze upon Cédric.

With trembling fingers, Cédric thrust out the small leather bag containing the ring. The priest removed it and held it up for all to see, blessing it before God. Then he placed it on Sophie's thumb.

"In nomine Patris," he intoned. He removed it and placed it on her index finger. *"Et filii."* Again he slipped it off, then placed it on her middle finger. *"Et Spiritus Sancti."*

A silence followed. Cédric took a long breath. It was his turn now. He took Sophie's hand in his and gently slid the ring from her middle finger to her ring finger.

Looking into her eyes, he said, "I marry you, Wife."

A ripple of satisfaction whispered through the crowd. Sophie gazed steadily back at him, her mouth curving up in a faint smile.

Then the priest stepped between them and took their hands, leading them down the aisle to the high altar, where the wedding Mass would take place.

Behind them, the guests climbed the steps to the church and filed through the doors. The high keening of the swifts followed them inside until the last guest entered and the great oak doors closed, shutting out the world.

The Mass began. The priest's words washed over Cédric with reassuring familiarity, but he could not make any sense of them, so fixated was he on the woman at his side.

His wife.

His love.

His Sophie.

At the supper feast, Sophie reveled in her position at the high table. She held court with her family and friends and led the dancing whenever the guests took a pause between courses.

Neither of Cédric's brothers were in attendance. The eldest, Yves, dared not leave home as his wife was with child and nearing the end of her confinement. And Stéphane had recently begun a stint as priest in a market town near Bavaria. He was not free to travel as he wished.

Cédric gazed around the room, searching for familiar faces. He caught sight of a young man who had served under the *seigneur* with him, raising his cup when their gazes met. Philippe was huddled across the room with a small knot of men who all had some connection to the Knights Hospitaller. Cédric smiled, grateful that his father's old friend had made the journey to Albi. For a searing moment, he longed for the presence of his parents.

An unending stream of guests approached to give him their congratulations. He saw the glint of envy in more than one pair of eyes. No man could drag his gaze away from his wife for long, and who could blame any of them? Sophie's beauty, merry laugh, and quick wit would have made her the center of attention even if she weren't the bride. Pride warmed his chest at the thought.

The gentle tones of harp and lute filled the great hall with music. During the dancing, guests trampled on the dried herbs and flowers that had been strewn on the polished tile floor, releasing the scents of rose and lavender into the air. Laughter and chatter sailed up to the rafters, dropping away whenever the servants paraded out from the kitchens with the next course.

During one of Sophie's many turns around the great hall while she mingled with guests and showed off her wedding finery, her brother, Grégoire, joined Cédric at the high table and plopped down on the bench next to him.

"You're a lucky man," he told Cédric, slurring a bit.

"I know it."

Grégoire raised his cup. "White wine, honeyed and spiced, is the best drink of all. I believe I've overindulged, but my favorite sister's wedding warrants some excess, does it not?"

Cédric smiled. "It certainly does."

He looked at the half-eaten portion of capon studded with pomegranate and sugar-coated flecks of anise on his trencher. If only he had the appetite to do justice to the food at his own wedding feast. But Cédric had little interest in food today. The enormity of what he and Sophie were embarking on had struck him in the gut when they ascended the steps of the church, and his nerves were still frayed.

He took a long draught from his own cup.

"Look at those lechers," Grégoire drawled, pointing out a group of well-fed merchants clustered near the dancers. "They were all vying for Sophie's hand, every one of them."

Cédric followed his friend's gaze. It was true; to a man, the group stared openly at his bride, clearly discussing her amongst themselves. He shifted uncomfortably in his seat, fighting an urge to put himself between his wife and the men.

Grégoire studied him. "You don't strike me as the jealous type. But perhaps you are. It will make your life miserable if that's the case. She'll attract the wrong kind of attention wherever she goes."

"Why would I be jealous?"

"She's a known flirt." Grégoire signaled to a servant for more spiced wine. "Between my parents and I, we've kept her in check. But now it'll be up to you." He chuckled. "I've come here for a reason. To tell you not to worry, for no matter how much she bats her eyelashes at other men, she wants you and you alone."

Cédric looked at him sideways. "And when did you become the authority on your sister's feelings?"

"In Bruges."

"Ah?"

"Yes. Remember when we went walking through the streets, the three of us, and I let you take her into that alcove for a private moment?"

Cédric's pulse quickened a little. That first embrace, that first kiss. The memory of it made him long for the feast to conclude so he could take Sophie to bed and finish what they started on that day.

"How could I forget?" he said drily. "Though I recall you chasing your cap at that moment, not chaperoning us."

"We followed the same route a few days after you left Bruges, Sophie and I. Only that time the Catalan was the third member of our little group."

"What?"

Grégoire nodded. In the flickering candlelight, his eyes were glassy with drink.

"She insisted. I suppose she wanted to find out if her heart belonged to you or him." He leaned a little closer. "She told me she was taken in by his looks, his fine clothes, the gold rings he flaunted. I suppose she can't be blamed for that."

Cédric's feeling of warm conviviality drained away. "What else did she say?"

"Oh, it wasn't what she said. It was what she did."

Cédric found his wife in the crowd. She was dancing with a group of girl cousins, all wearing wreaths of flowers in their hair. They wove circles around each other in time to the music, hands clasped, their faces alight with joy.

"What did she do?" he asked, keeping her in his sights.

"She let him put his arms around her, let him put his lips on hers, just as you did."

That arrogant Catalan placing his hands on Sophie, kissing her mouth. Possessing her, even for a moment. Anger flared within Cédric at the thought. He put down his cup with a thump.

"You waited until now to share this with me. I had believed you to be my friend."

Grégoire raised his hands in a gesture of protest. "You've not heard the whole story. Yes, she kissed the Catalan. But then she slipped from his grasp, couldn't return to my side fast enough. And she told me her heart belonged to you. To you! Does that not ease your mind? Other men may covet her, but you possess my sister's heart."

His last words were so blurred by wine Cédric could barely make them out. The music swelled again. Sophie and her cousins drew together tightly, like the inner petals of a rose, then stepped outward one by one, arching their arms over their heads.

"My wife," Grégoire groaned. "She is scowling at me from her seat. I've abandoned her for too long." He rose to his feet, steadying himself on the table for a moment, then saluted Cédric with his empty cup. "Welcome to the family," he said, staggering away.

Cédric watched him weave through the crowded hall. The words of a sopping-drunk man might hold a kernel of truth, but more often than not they were worth nothing. Grégoire was a born exaggerator anyway. He could spin a tale, knew how to keep an audience spellbound. And for better or worse, as the man had just reminded him, Grégoire was now part of Cédric's family.

The music ended. Sophie and her cousins collapsed together, laughing. The group of merchants observing them broke out in applause. Sophie curtsied to them, her smile inciting a ripple of admiring cheers. Cédric stiffened at the sight. She found his eyes over the crowd, and her smile deepened, exposing the dimples in her cheeks. The delight on her face could not quite vanquish the taint of Grégoire's drunken words.

He and Sophie had spent little time together since Bruges—a handful of days, really. Only now would he truly begin to understand who she was in her core, see parts of her that she had kept shrouded from him until this day.

He prayed he would not live to regret it.

CHAPTER 15

Spring, 1448
Auvergne, France

SOPHIE BRACED her lower back with one hand, shielding her eyes from the sun. She adjusted Mathieu's weight on her hip. Cédric and the two older children wandered in the meadow, little Estelle clinging to her father's hand. Etienne bent down to examine an insect or flower from time to time, his dark head disappearing below the tall grasses.

There had never been a more perfect spring day, Sophie was sure of it. The sky was vibrantly blue. A few wispy clouds sailed overhead. The oaks and beeches that edged the meadow wore a fresh mantle of green. She inhaled the mingled scents of sun-warmed earth and crushed grass, reveling in the gentle breeze that floated in from the north.

The baby let out a screech of joy in her ear.

"Happy boy," she murmured, brushing his soft cheek with her lips.

Mathieu had her blue eyes, her golden curls. Perhaps the life growing in her womb would be another miniature copy of her—a girl this time. Sophie put a hand to her swollen belly and sighed in satisfaction. She said a silent prayer, thanking God for their good fortune. Three healthy children and another on the way.

Though she felt fat and awkward in the final months, carrying a baby suited her. She never felt a moment's sickness, only fatigue. Being with child brightened her mood, made her more prone to laughter and good humor. And it made nights with Cédric even more enjoyable.

Once she had convinced him that it was safe for them to continue their marital relations through pregnancy, he was an enthusiastic partner, matching her nocturnal appetites with zeal. This was the part of marriage she had not accounted for—this longing for her husband's strong, warm body astride hers, this desire to lie naked with him, stroke his lithe, muscled limbs, propel him to the heights of pleasure.

"Maman! Maman!"

Her reverie was interrupted by the appearance of Etienne hurtling toward her with a handful of purple irises clutched in one hand.

She bent down, smiling, and sniffed the nosegay with exaggerated rapture. Etienne erupted in giggles. Mathieu lunged for the blooms and she let him take them, hoisting him high above her head while he babbled gleefully and waved the flowers in the air.

"Sophie," Cédric called from where he stood with Estelle in the grass. "Careful. He's getting heavy."

"I'll be fine," she dismissed him.

"But you're with child again."

"And has that ever slowed me down?"

His slow, rich laugh rumbled over the meadow. "You've got me there."

Scooping up their daughter, he closed the space between them.

She turned her face up to kiss him. "I wish you didn't have to leave tomorrow," she complained.

"I feel the same. But I'm bound to go. There's nothing I can do about it."

"You've worked so hard to train the under-falconers. They're trustworthy men, you've told me many times. And the roads are far safer now that the king's army has vanquished the *écorcheurs*."

"There are still bandits lurking on the roads, my love. None of the under-falconers are as skilled with a sword as I am. And I'm not going all the way to Bruges this year," he reminded her. "Königsberg is much closer."

Estelle reached up, stroking his beard with her small hands. The older children were so alike, Sophie thought. They both looked like their father.

As they walked back toward the house, the sun warmed the top of Sophie's head. The baby did feel heavy in her arms now, though she'd never admit it to Cédric. Carefully, she put him down, and he toddled ahead of them.

"I believe you like going on these journeys," she said. "You play at dice and cards, you stay up late drinking wine with traders and merchants, and God knows who else." Her throat tightened. She couldn't help the trace of accusation rising in her voice. "Even when you're here, your mind is on your work. You're always tied up with the mews, with training falcons, with organizing hunting trips for the count. In the evenings, you're inking numbers and notes in your record books. What about us? Your family needs you, too."

He looked at the sky and drew in a breath before responding. "What about the gifts I bring back from my journeys? You're always eager to accept those."

She glanced at him sideways. It was true. He sometimes brought back treasures for their own household, most recently an illustrated prayer book for her and carved wooden figures for Etienne and Estelle from Bavaria. But every time he was away, she sank into dark moods. There was no one else to talk to. The countess was far above her in station and would never deign to socialize with her. The village was full of simpletons. Even those who called themselves merchants were not much more than wealthy peasants, in Sophie's mind. She longed for the companionship of women like herself, but tucked away here in the Auvergne countryside, she would never have it.

"I have no one to talk to when you're away," she admitted. "No one besides Christine and the wet nurse, anyway."

Christine was a woman of few words, too old to be entertaining. And the wet nurse would be leaving them soon, as Mathieu seemed more interested lately in porridge and barley stew than suckling from a breast.

Thinking of it now, her mood began to plummet. Cédric stepped closer and draped his free arm around her.

"I shall bring you back a fine gift from Königsberg," he promised. "What would you like?"

She brightened a bit. "Venetian glass goblets, earrings made of beaten gold and sapphires, Castile soap . . ."

He threw back his head and laughed. "Not so fast, my love. I'll never remember all of that. Mind you, I'd not risk carrying Venetian glass nor jewels home. Soap, on the other hand, I can promise."

"You'll be carrying falcons for the count! What's more precious than that?" she asked. "Surely, a few baubles of gold tucked in your purse will make no difference. And besides, we have the money from Papa, gathering dust under the floorboards."

Cédric fell silent for a moment. He extricated Estelle's fingers from his beard.

"I'll take a few, buy you something of quality," he finally said in a sober voice. "But I've told you before, we'll have need of that money for more important things one day."

"Like what?" she challenged him, drawing to a halt. She planted her feet wide in the grass. "What's more important than making your wife happy?"

He turned to her, and for a moment he looked like a stranger. His expression was grave. The light, the tenderness that glowed in his brown eyes when he looked upon her had been extinguished.

Mathieu tripped and fell. His wail reverberated overhead, merging with the cry of a hawk that circled the oaks on the far side of the meadow.

Startled, Sophie hastened toward their son, the argument dying on her lips. She bent to comfort him, to kiss the tears from his round cheeks.

Bide your time, she told herself.

Tonight, in the marriage bed, she would convince Cédric his wife was worth more than a bar of Castile soap.

CHAPTER 16

Spring, 1448
Auvergne, France

THEY WERE HALF a day's journey north of the count's lands, riding through a sun-drenched landscape shimmering with the pale green leaves and grasses of springtime. The trek from Königsberg had been uneventful and dry. Cédric thanked God for that. He would much rather eat dust all day than navigate a muddy road, all things considered. And thanks to the pleasant weather, they had made great speed on the return journey. He glanced up, tracked the position of the sun. Good, it was not much past midday. They would arrive home well before twilight.

As they rounded a bend in the road, several riders bore down on them, all bearing the count's colors. He stiffened in the saddle, raising his arm to signal to his companions behind him to stop. The approaching horsemen drew to a halt in a billowing cloud of dust, their eyes to a man on Cédric.

"Praise God, you're nearly home. Your wife and child are ill," the rider in the lead shouted. "You'd best make haste. We'll accompany the cart back to the château."

At his words, Cédric spurred his tired horse on, a pit of anxiety burrowing into his gut. The sun was just beginning to sink in the west when he entered the count's lands. His horse could muster no more than a trot as they passed under the drooping branches of ancient oaks and pounded over the tender new grasses in the meadows. Flecks of foam beaded on the animal's neck and shoulders during the final climb up the bluff.

Arriving at his doorstep, Cédric slid from the saddle with a groan and tossed the reins to a stableboy. He ran to the door and burst through to see Christine descending the stairs. Her eyes looked swollen and bloodshot.

"Oh, sir, it's a terrible thing. Such a terrible thing—" She broke off, weeping.

Cédric pushed past her, took the stairs two at a time, and entered the bedchamber. Sophie lay in bed with the shutters closed against the sun, Mathieu curled next to her.

"Are you ill? Sophie, by God, what's wrong?"

He knelt at her side.

"The baby died in my womb," she said listlessly. "And Mathieu is ill. Feel his brow."

"You lost the baby?" Cédric asked, a fissure of pain opening up in his chest. "Oh, my love."

Mathieu's eyelids fluttered open, the trace of a smile emerged on his face at the sight of his father, and then he drifted into sleep again. The boy's hair was plastered to his skull with sweat. Cédric reached over Sophie and laid his palm over their son's forehead. It burned with heat.

"Has the doctor been here?" The boy was pale as milk.

"He left not long ago," Sophie said. "Christine does what she can with herbs and poultices, but the fever still swells."

Cédric took her hand. "Where are Etienne and Estelle? Whatever Mathieu has, we cannot let it pass to them."

"I've had Christine keep them away from us, to be safe."

He nodded, relieved. "Don't worry, *ma chérie*. Mathieu will improve in a day or two. You know how these fevers blaze so hot in children, then vanish."

"Yes," she whispered, her face so gaunt and wan it frightened him. Her eyes were ringed with dark shadows. "She was a girl, the baby we lost. Just a wisp of a thing, smaller than a newborn kitten."

He closed his eyes against the burn of tears and pressed his lips to her hand. "Did the priest—"

"He came," she said dully. "She'll have a proper burial. You'll see to it, won't you?"

"Of course, I vow it. You must eat," he said, rising. "I'll have the cook make you a broth of beef bones. You must find your strength again."

After overseeing the burial of their tiny daughter in the village church's cemetery, Cédric had no choice but to push aside his grief and attend to his work each day. He managed the other falconers, he purchased and administered remedies from apothecaries for the falcons' endless maladies. He planned hunting and hawking expeditions for the count and his associates. Sleep, if it came at all, was fleeting. He napped in the parlor when exhaustion overtook him, or snatched a few hours' rest in a cramped equipment room attached to the mews.

Mathieu's fever waxed and waned. Each time it improved, he awoke, ate, and drank, his eyes regaining their sparkle. And then, frustratingly, it would come on again, stronger than ever, and reduce him to a fragile, unconscious wraith. The doctor visited several times, and nothing he did cured Mathieu. In fact, Cédric thought he was bleeding the boy entirely too much. How much blood could such a tiny person afford to lose?

Cédric had more faith in the herbs and tinctures administered by Christine. After ingesting a tea containing pulverized bark of the willow, Mathieu's fever would drop and his spirits return for a time. But he was so thin and delicate, his skin nearly translucent. Sophie stayed at the boy's side, barely took her eyes off him. She whispered to him constantly, whether telling him stories or her own thoughts, Cédric was not sure.

One morning, after falling into fitful slumber in his oak chair by the hearth, he awoke with a start. Though it was just after dawn and the world outside was stirring, the house was quiet. He rose, stretched his stiff muscles, and padded upstairs to the bedchamber that once was a refuge promising joy and pleasure. Now, he approached it with trepidation. The shutters blocked the morning light, but he could just make out the forms of his wife and son on the bed.

Sophie stirred. "Good morning, my love," she said.

She turned to Mathieu at the same moment Cédric reached for the boy's forehead.

It was cool. Too cool.

"Mathieu?" he said, giving the boy a little shake. "Wake up, son."

The tiny body was immobile.

"No . . ." Sophie cried.

Cédric scrambled for the window and flung open the shutters.

In the light, he saw what had not been visible before: their son's blue lips, the ghastly pallor of his skin. He fell to his knees beside the bed, shaking. A roar of grief clawed at his throat. He somehow forced it back down into his chest, where it pressed against his heart like the sharp point of a blade. Sophie took Mathieu in her arms and curved her body around him.

"My angel," she sobbed. "My sweet boy."

Cédric stared bleakly at his wife and son. Dear God. Mathieu had been a copy of her, with golden curls and sea-blue eyes. He was her little treasure, she often said. Her perfect jewel.

And now he was dead.

Little changed in their home as spring gave way to summer. Sophie barely left their bedchamber. The sound of her weeping became the backdrop to their lives. Cédric thanked all the saints for Christine a dozen times a day. She fussed over Sophie, bringing her small treats, singing to her, coaxing her to bathe.

Cédric's own sorrow was cloistered deep within him, but his heart ached fiercely. In training sessions with a peregrine falcon he had brought back from Königsberg, he saw equal parts terror and rage in her eyes whenever he removed the hood from her head. She blazed with fright, flapping away from him with all her strength, the taut leather jesses and leash jerking her cruelly back to his meat-baited glove. Normally, he deployed the falconer's essential skill of watchful patience during such moments, emptied his mind, quieted his body, stilled himself so the falcon, too, could be still.

But not now. Not with Death looming over his shoulder, whispering in his ear. He looked at the stark fear in the falcon's eyes and understood exactly how that felt. A horrible feeling of failure consumed him during quiet moments; he simply could not bear the stillness that was required to tame a falcon. So he handed the peregrine over to an under-falconer and filled his days with other work, his two older children at his side.

Etienne and Estelle were eager apprentices both in the mews and in his study. Etienne was fascinated by the astrological charts he had brought to Auvergne from his own father's library. For her part, Estelle loved collecting falcons' feathers in the mews and watching him transform them into quills. She took to writing with enthusiasm. Her ability to sit quietly and make scratchings on a page astonished him.

One afternoon when he and the children returned from the mews, Cédric went to the bedchamber and knew he had to take action. The sheets stank of sweat. Christine was fastidious about housekeeping, washing their linens weekly and sprinkling them with rosewater while they dried on the line. But getting Sophie to emerge from the bedsheets long enough to change them was a tremendous challenge.

"It's time you get up," he said to Sophie. "Eat something."

Silence. His wife's face was to the wall. The faint movement of her shoulders under the sheet reassured him that she still breathed.

"You'll feel better when you get up." He sat on the edge of the bed, rested a hand on her hip. "At least drink a cup of warm broth."

Still nothing.

"The children miss you. Etienne and Estelle need their mother. The longer you stay in this bed, the worse you'll feel."

She sighed. "I'm not ready to face them, Cédric. To face the world."

One day soon he would have to leave his family again for another journey north. The thought of riding away from Sophie when she was so fragile and dispirited filled him with dread. His children needed their mother, and he needed his wife. Somehow he had to rekindle the light that grief had extinguished from his wife's eyes.

That evening, he took out quill and paper and wrote a letter to his father-in-law, pleading for help. Writing it was an admittance of his own failure as a husband, but he was too worried about his family to care. If he could not ignite the spark of joy in Sophie again, perhaps her father could.

CHAPTER 17

Summer, 1448
Auvergne, France

SOPHIE AND CHRISTINE passed beneath the drooping branches of an old oak and stood in the shade a moment. The meadow rolling away from them blazed with the colors of a thousand wildflowers. Once Sophie would have stopped and exclaimed over their beauty, but now she just marked the blooms with a listless gaze. A trace of morning mist still clung to the lake where Cédric often led hawking parties. On the far edge of the water, a family of swans paddled through the reeds.

"Look at the cygnets, madame," Christine said, pointing.

Sophie gave them a disinterested glance. The sight of small creatures under the watchful eye of their mother reminded her of Mathieu, as nearly everything did. She blinked back tears. When would her grief subside? It had wrung her out, turned her into a person she no longer recognized.

She knew Cédric longed for the wife he loved: a woman with a lively nature, a zest for life, someone who displayed wit and merriment. Slowly, agonizingly, her strength was coming back. She spent longer and longer periods outside, walking alongside Christine. Yet the joy her husband treasured in her stayed dormant. Even the pleasures of the marriage bed eluded Sophie. She submitted limply to Cédric's attentions and turned away as soon as he was spent. Her lust had once outpaced his own. Now, it was a distant memory.

Christine patted her arm. "Give it time. You'll feel joy again, you will."

"You don't know what it's like to feel this way."

Sophie regretted the harsh words as soon as they left her mouth. Christine had always been a comfort to her. And now the woman was her only link to the past, to the gilded childhood that she had never truly appreciated until she left it behind. How strange it was to one day be a coddled child and the next be a wife.

"I've grieved my share over the years," Christine said quietly. "I came to your family after I lost a baby and a husband both. That was why your father brought me on, to be your wet nurse."

Sophie's remorse deepened. "But you've never told me this before."

"It's not my place to tell you my troubles, madame."

A heron flapped over the lake, its ash-gray wings spread wide against the blue sky.

"Each day I awake hoping it will be better, but then I think of Mathieu and the baby . . ." Sophie began to weep uncontrollably.

A memory arose of her mother's grief after her youngest sister had died. For a fleeting moment, she yearned for her small sister's warmth under the coverlets, for the high sweet music of her laughter.

"You'll feel better. I vow it." Christine's voice penetrated her sorrow one soft word at a time. "Little by little, you will start to see the light in the world instead of the darkness."

The words were meant to soothe her. Sophie wanted them to be true. But she could not find a way out of this pit she'd fallen into. She was doomed to pace its cramped perimeter, peering up at the bright sunlight above, with no escape.

When they returned home, she saw the letter from her mother that she'd left on the oak chest in the entry hall. It had come last week, but its contents had not comforted her. Quite the contrary. It was not so much a letter as a tally of all the children Maman had lost herself. The unborn babies, the infants, the children who had lived long enough to walk, talk, run, laugh, even read and write. The sweet, sweet girl who had been Sophie's bedmate.

She picked it up, went to the parlor, and sat down by the hearth to read it again. Her eyes settled on the last few lines, the words that read like a chastisement when she first unfolded this letter. Maman wrote that despite all of her losses, she was a woman content with her life, with seven living children still, a husband who loved her, and a household that needed running. Sophie knew what her mother really meant: it was time to put her grief aside, to lock it in her heart and get on with her duties as a wife and mother.

She swallowed, pushing down the lump of sorrow in her throat. Her own mother had endured so much loss. Sophie had never truly understood until now what that could do to a person.

Leaning back in her chair, she let the letter slip to the floor and closed her eyes.

A pounding came at the door.

"Madame," Christine called from the entry hall. "You'll want to see this."

Sophie rose and walked to the front door. Outside sat a grand covered mule cart. It bore no banners, nor was a coat of arms painted on its wooden exterior. Two mounted guards accompanied it. They waited at a short distance while a man emerged from within.

The man was short and a bit stout in the chest, his cloak flung open to reveal a black wool doublet and sand-colored hose.

"Thierry?" Sophie said in amazement.

Her father's steward was the last person she expected to see in Auvergne.

"What a balm to the soul it is to see your lovely face again, madame." His face stretched into a broad grin. "I bear tidings from my master and goods for the household."

Another manservant clambered down from the cart, clutching a basket, and the driver descended from his perch.

"Might we stable the horses and mules? They've had a long journey," Thierry added. He gestured at the guards, then the four animals hitched to the cart.

Sophie took it all in, blinking. Her mind felt wrapped in fog.

"You've come a long way," she managed to respond.

Cédric and the children appeared from the direction of the mews.

"Maman, who are they?" Etienne's bright, clear voice rang out.

She saw Cédric's look of puzzlement transform into one of recognition.

"They're from your grandfather's household," he told the children.

"Did they bring sweets?" Estelle asked hopefully.

Thierry's smile deepened. "That we did, mademoiselle." He glanced at Cédric. "I bring my master's greetings to you, sir. And also a letter."

He handed a folded square of paper to Cédric.

"Bring it all in, stable the horses, and then take yourselves to the kitchen," Cédric told the men. "Our cook will find you refreshment."

The rest of the day passed in a whirl of excitement. They unpacked boxes of sugared almonds, marzipan, and candied fruit. Exquisitely crafted puppets for Etienne and Estelle, along with a set of miniature wooden farm animals. Bolts of fine black merino wool cloth and silk dyed in various shades of blue, ready to be made into clothing. Hand-cobbled shoes for the children made of the softest leather. A barrel of salted cod from Bayonne and another of wine from Bordeaux. In a tiny hand-carved mahogany box Sophie found a pair of beaten-gold earrings set with emeralds.

"Put them on," Cédric urged her, his eyes shining in the candlelight.

She acquiesced. The children clung to her skirts, telling her how beautiful she was. The sound of Thierry regaling Christine in the kitchen with tales of home filled her with gladness. The familiarity of her father's servants, the generosity of his gifts, brought tears to her eyes. At the sight of her weeping, Cédric's expression clouded a little. She knew he was reaching the end of his patience with her suffering. As she was.

"These are tears of joy, my love," she assured him, reaching out to take his hand. "I never thought I'd feel joy again, to be truthful."

He leaned in and kissed her.

"What does my father write?"

He smiled wryly. "You'll not be surprised by it, I'm sure. He told me to spare no expense, to distract you with treats and lovely things, and said you will soon find your way again."

The children turned to their toys. Sophie moved closer to her husband and pressed her body against his. He smelled of wool and woodsmoke and the forest. She breathed it all in, holding his scent in her lungs.

"That is my wish," she said. "To find my way."

CHAPTER 18

Summer, 1450
Auvergne

Locking eyes with Christine, Sophie drew in a long breath. The contraction rolled over her like a thunderous wave. She clenched her jaw, unable to suppress a groan.

"It's crowning, madame!" The midwife's voice was tinged with excitement.

Christine wiped the sweat from Sophie's brow with a flax cloth. The air in the room was hot and stale, despite the open window. Summer's heat was at full force this week and the evenings brought little respite.

"Quicumque vult salvus esse . . ." Christine whispered, chanting the familiar words of the Athanasian Creed in Sophie's ear. "Whosoever shall be saved . . ."

Gripping Christine's hand, she prepared to push again. This time, the pain nearly drowned her, but she gritted her teeth and managed to survive it.

"Nearly there," the midwife encouraged her. "Nearly done. Oh, infant, living or dead, come forth because Christ calls you to the light!"

Though the saying was traditional during labor, Sophie flinched at the words.

I beg all the saints, please let my baby live.

She closed her eyes and bore down with the last traces of strength left in her, convulsed by terrible, gripping pain. A few moments later, the baby was in her arms, clean and swaddled, his tiny face red from the exertion of his journey into the world, his mouth clamped onto her breast.

"He is well, truly?" Sophie demanded anxiously of the midwife, who was waiting for the afterbirth to appear, her brow knitted in a frown.

"Yes, yes, a fine boy. Healthy as an ox."

"Thank God," Sophie whispered.

Christine dipped the cloth in water and wiped Sophie's face and brow again, smoothing back her disheveled hair. She, too, bore a worried look until the afterbirth was delivered.

"Saints be praised," the midwife declared, beaming.

Sophie looked from one woman to the other, feeling a surge of joy despite her exhaustion.

"God has blessed us," she said, fitting her palm over her baby's soft cheek, marveling at the downy hair capping his head. "Christine, go tell my husband."

As the midwife busied herself with cleaning up, Sophie reflected on her good fortune. After Mathieu, after the loss of her precious baby girl, she had viewed pregnancy and childbirth with something verging on revulsion. But now, with another infant suckling at her breast, she felt the dread that had haunted her throughout the pregnancy begin to lift.

Be grateful, she counseled herself. *Seize joy when you can.*

Cédric's tread on the stairs startled her out of her reverie. The relief and tenderness in his expression made tears burn in her eyes.

He came to sit on the edge of the bed and tenderly cupped the back of the baby's head with his hand. "Thank the saints you're well. As is our son."

She smiled. "A boy in your image, my love. What will you name him?"

"It's been in my mind these last few days," he admitted. "I'd like to name him Jean-Philippe, after my father and my sword master."

"As you wish." She drowsed against the pillows, succumbing to a wave of fatigue. "Will you go to the château and the village to inquire about a wet nurse? I shall need one in a fortnight or so, and I did not want to make the plans until . . ." She broke off.

He nodded, the sympathy in his eyes conveying that he understood all too well why she had tarried. "It shall be done. Are you hungry?"

She shook her head. "Send Christine in, and she'll tend to me when I need something. And tell the children all is well. Tomorrow, they may see their brother."

Cédric leaned down and pressed his lips against her forehead. "I love you."

"And I you."

As soon as the sound of Christine's slippers on the stone floor penetrated her consciousness, she let sleep claim her.

Midsummer had passed and the heat had relented a bit when the sword master came for a visit. Sophie looked forward to it, as he always brought small gifts for the children and regaled them with tales of his exploits as a mercenary soldier for the Knights Hospitaller in his youth. They all sat in the parlor with the windows flung open to the summer air. After sharing some wine and celebratory sweets in honor of the new baby, Philippe rummaged in his pannier and approached Sophie with something clutched in his hand.

"It makes my heart glad to know there's a little boy in this household who carries my name, madame," he told her, thrusting out a brown linen sack tied with rough twine.

She looked at him in surprise. "For me? Surely, there is nothing in the knights' commandery appropriate for a woman."

He chuckled. "I've a few things in my possession that might surprise you."

Sophie untied the twine and drew out an object wrapped in soft, fine white cloth. "This is not linen, it's far too delicate." She glanced up at him. "Where did you find cotton of such quality? My father is always in search of it."

"From the East, perhaps Egypt. I got it on my travels with the Order."

She stroked the fabric with a fingertip. Then she unwrapped the object. It appeared to be a gold coin, albeit an ancient one, with the outline of a woman's countenance on its face. A small hole had been bored into the top, and a black leather cord was strung through it. It was certainly not a necklace she would wear, although the coin was quite attractive.

"Thank you," she said politely, turning it over in her hand.

"It is not meant for adornment," he said, his voice serious. "It was given to me by a Greek woman on the island of Rhodes, and she vowed to me it would bring good fortune. After all I've survived, I must say I believe her. I'd like you to have it. This little fellow," he nodded at Jean-Philippe, asleep in Christine's arms, "and his brother and sister—they all have a bright future ahead of them. A token of good fortune would serve them well."

She looked at him with gratitude. "This is kind of you, Master Philippe. I'll not forget it."

He stood. "I have some business at the château to take care of before I return here for supper."

Cédric rose as well. "I'll accompany you there."

But Philippe did not return for supper, and neither did Cédric. The count invited both men to sup with him. Sophie spent the evening attempting to cheer up her crestfallen children, who had anticipated an evening of entertainment in the company of their father's old friend.

Before Sophie went to bed, she wrapped the coin in its cotton covering and tucked it into the linen bag again. Then she placed it in the chest at the foot of their bed. Her thoughts lingered on the woman's face embossed into the gold. Where did she come from? Was she a queen? Who were her people?

Likely, she would never learn the answers to her questions, for the coin would stay where it was, as she would. Deep in the heart of the

Auvergne, in the quiet countryside, where nothing interesting ever happened to her.

She thought wistfully of Bruges, of Albi, of Toulouse. The bustle of city marketplaces, the chiming of church bells, the calls of street criers peddling their wares. All the mingled scents in the streets, some intriguing, some comforting, some repulsive.

The low hooting of an owl drifted through the open window. Sophie lifted her head, listening. In this life, in this place, the sounds of wild creatures had replaced the tolling of bells; the laughter and tears of children preoccupied her mind where once she had fixated on sweets and trinkets and the latest gossip shared in the social hour after church. The Auvergne smelled of earth, of sun-warmed grass, of stone washed by rain. Each season had its small pleasures, its own pure beauty. Yet the quiet could be maddening, too. It amplified her own loneliness when Cédric was away, pressed down on her like a suffocating cloak.

Crossing to the window, she stood looking out at the night, restless and melancholy, filled with a longing for something she could not name.

CHAPTER 19

Winter, 1452
Auvergne

Cédric hurried to the château, bending his head against the wind. A thin crust of snow covered the ground. It was late winter, and the cold burrowed into his bones as if it had been there his entire life. He could not remember what it felt like to sweat.

With stiff fingers, he patted the leather satchel under his long black wool cloak. At least it wasn't raining. God forbid the contents of that satchel might get wet.

Glancing up, he saw a row of sinister-looking icicles on the gargoyles fixed to the château's gutters. The stone figures looked even more macabre with those icy fangs jutting forth. He preferred them during spring rains, when water rushed through their gaping mouths to the gravel below.

A footman let him in and led him past elaborate wool tapestries and polished oak chests laid with silver plate to the hearth in the great hall. The crackle of logs echoed through the gloom, sending the scent of woodsmoke into Cédric's lungs. He shivered, rubbed his hands together for a moment to bring some movement back.

Two massive marble pillars carved with lacy, interconnected designs flanked the hearth. A frieze ran along the top of the mantel, sculpted with the figures of deer and falcons against a backdrop of oak trees. His examination of the craftsmanship was interrupted by the approach of another servant, who led him to the count's study.

His employer sat in one of two heavy oak armchairs placed in front of a hearth whose ornately carved stonework depicted winged lions and other fanciful beasts. The masons responsible for the mantels in this château were exceptionally skilled, Cédric thought as the count waved him into the other chair.

"Good day to you, *monsieur le fauconnier*," he said cordially. His slippered feet were nearly invisible, thrust into the thick bearskin rug on the floor. "Let us warm ourselves with some spiced wine." He waved a hand at the servant who had escorted Cédric into the chamber.

The man scurried away and returned a few moments later with a silver pitcher and two silver goblets. He placed a small wooden table between them, then poured their wine.

Count de Chambonac took a sip. "Ah—just the right level of heat. I prefer my spiced wine to be ripe with cardamom and cinnamon. And very little sugar."

The count's family crest, embroidered in blue and gold silk thread on his black velvet doublet, caught the firelight as he leaned back in his chair. Divided into quadrants, it depicted a pair of castle towers and a pair of crosses.

Cédric drank from his own cup. The liquid burned a fiery path down his throat, warming his innards. "Thank you, my lord. It is excellent. I've brought what you asked of me." He retrieved several folded sheets of linen paper from his satchel and handed them over.

The count put down his cup and took the papers. "The care and feeding of falcons," he read aloud. "A treatise for falconers." He continued to read in silence, then glanced up at Cédric. "Your skill with lettering is impressive."

"I am an adequate scribe," Cédric replied. "But I cannot take credit for these lines you read. My daughter, Estelle, has skills quite beyond my own."

The count looked at him in astonishment. "How old is the girl?"

"Next winter will be her tenth," Cédric said. "She and her brother Etienne learned to hold a quill when they were very small."

"And Etienne, how old is he?"

"A year older than Estelle, my lord. He helps me in the mews. He'll be a fine falconer one day."

The count tapped a finger against the pages. "This is to be a gift for the duke of Savoy. I've a mind to have these pages put into a book bound with leather."

Cédric nodded. "I saw a bookmaker's workshop in Königsberg last time I was there."

"Well then, you must take the pages with you on your next buying trip to Bavaria and have the book made for me." The count fell silent a moment, regarding Cédric thoughtfully. "And I've another idea as well. My wife suffers greatly in the cold weather from stiffness in her fingers. She cannot write at all as a result of it. She complains that her ladies aren't much help, and there are piles of unanswered letters that must be dealt with. Your daughter can come help her with this task each afternoon until they are all answered."

Cédric looked at his employer in amazement. His daughter writing the correspondence of a countess? He could not refuse, as much as he desired to. Though he tried not to think about it, moments like these reminded him all too starkly that he was the servant of this man.

You must make your own fortune.

His father's words penetrated his consciousness at the same time a knot of pitch exploded in the hearth. Neither he nor the count flinched at the sound.

Cédric met his employer's gaze, his mind racing. He may have bound himself to a powerful feudal lord, but one who was a just and honorable man. His daughter would be safe within these walls. And the truth was Estelle had the temperament for such a task.

"It would be her honor, my lord," he said.

That evening at supper, Cédric broached the topic with his family. Their astonishment mirrored his own, but as he'd had a few hours to digest the idea, he had warmed to it.

"Our child writing letters for a countess?" Sophie asked, her spoon clattering into her empty soup bowl. "Surely you jest."

Estelle sat watching him with wide eyes, her supper forgotten. Next to her, little Jean-Philippe banged his spoon on the table, a glint of mischief on his face.

"No, I speak the truth." Cédric laid a gentle hand on Jean-Philippe's, quieting him, then spooned up another mouthful of soup. Onions, barley, and beef all simmered together with a bit of wine and salt, just as he liked it. "The countess can't abide the cold, her husband told me. She can't even hold a quill during the winter months."

"It doesn't sit well with me." Sophie shook her head. "It's not safe for Estelle to be in the château without one of us in attendance, Cédric."

"Sophie, I know every member of the count's household. She will be fine."

His mind went to the steward for a moment. The man was hostile toward him, had always been. He was too obsessed with staying in the good graces of his employer to do anything cruel to Cédric or his family, though. There was a line he'd never cross—a line that only existed as long as Cédric himself was favored by the count.

His wife's expression hardened. "I don't like it."

He shifted in his seat, sensing an argument to come. "I have little choice in the matter, Sophie. What am I if not a servant to the count?"

"You're noble-born. You're the master falconer. You have the respect and esteem of all men."

"I work for the count. It's as plain as that. He commands; I obey."

Sophie drummed her fingers on the table. "Our daughter will get ideas in her head, consorting with the countess. She'll be impossible to live with."

Cédric sighed. So like Sophie to take another tack with her argument, probing for weakness in his resistance. "Estelle is not that kind of child. You know it; I know it. She will do as she's told, and no harm will come to her or us."

"The countess is carved of stone. I've never seen her smile. When we go to the château for feast days, she looks through me as if I'm nothing more than a wisp of fog."

"What do you expect? She's a noblewoman, after all—"

"And I am but a merchant's daughter," Sophie interrupted, her blue eyes glittering with anger. "Common-born. Thank you for reminding me."

"Sophie, it is the way of the world."

"That doesn't mean it's right. My father is a city alderman of Toulouse. He is one of the richest merchants in all of France. Surely, that means something!"

"Not as much as a title," he replied evenly. "Not to the countess, anyway."

Cédric glanced at Estelle, whose expression was stricken now. Whenever Sophie got into one of her moods, Estelle shrank into herself the way his falcons did when they were uneasy.

"Can I help, Papa?" Etienne asked. "Estelle and I could go together. I could help her. It would go faster that way."

Cédric ruffled his son's hair. "The count asked for your sister only. Besides, you don't enjoy writing. You'd rather be outside or in the mews with me, isn't that so?"

What he did not say was Etienne's lettering did not come close to his sister's in quality. There was no comparison.

He turned to his daughter again. "Estelle?"

She fiddled with her spoon. "I will do it, Papa."

He glanced at Sophie, but she would not meet his gaze. Her tight expression did not soften that night, and when he reached for her in the marriage bed, she turned away.

The next afternoon, Cédric and Estelle hastened through a light snowfall back to the château. They cut through the gardens instead of walking along the gravel drive to make their journey quicker. Just as they emerged from behind a row of tall hedges, something white and round hurtled in their direction and exploded against Estelle's face. She stumbled, her eyes welling with tears.

Childish laughter pierced the silence. A boy in a fur cloak and gleaming black boots careened around a shrub and ran toward the château.

"That's the count's youngest son, no doubt," Cédric said grimly, turning back to his daughter. He wiped snowflakes from her cheeks. "Are you hurt?"

She gulped back a sob. "No, Papa."

The misery in her eyes stabbed his heart. He knelt before her. "He didn't mean anything by it. Don't worry. Once you're inside with the countess, you'll see neither hide nor hair of the lad. I'm guessing he prefers it out here to in there." He jerked his head in the direction of the château.

Estelle followed his gaze. He watched her take in the turrets, the black slate roof, the drawbridge looming ahead of them. The children were convinced that monsters lurked in the moat's waters.

"Papa, I'm frightened," she admitted in a small voice.

"There is no reason to be." He stood and took her hand in his. "I'll bring you inside, and when it's time to come home, I'll bring you back again. You must write with a steady hand, be brave, and bring honor to our family, Estelle."

She nodded miserably. "Yes, Papa. I'll try."

The snow was falling harder now.

Hands entwined, they trudged forward.

CHAPTER 20

Summer, 1454
Auvergne, France

CÉDRIC SLIPPED OUT OF BED, trying not to wake Sophie. He fumbled for his clothing in the weak light seeping through the cracks in the shutters.

"Cédric," his wife murmured. "It's barely dawn. Why are you up?"

"The count wants a hawking expedition to the lake today. I must prepare."

She opened her eyes. "He has noble visitors to entertain?"

He shook his head, sliding his doublet over his head. "Not that I'm aware. No, he simply wants to take the measure of his falcons, I suppose. A peregrine I trained in the spring has proved a spectacular hunter. He wants to see her in action."

Sophie propped herself up on her elbows. "Why is she special?"

Cédric cinched his belt around his waist. "That peregrine was trained purely to take down herons. She is unmatched in the art. Nothing is certain with falcons, of course. But if Dame Fortune is kind, all should go as planned." He returned to her side and put a gentle hand on her belly. "How do you feel, *ma chérie?*"

"Never better," she reassured him, then sat all the way up. "When I was carrying Jean-Philippe, I was frightened. But this time is different."

He knew she was thinking of Matthieu and their lost baby girl, just as he was.

"Cédric, when are you going to ask him?" She swung her legs over the edge of the bed.

His good humor faded. Sophie had begun pestering him to ask for a raise when Jean-Philippe was born. All those dangerous journeys, all those precious birds he'd procured. Should he not be rewarded, she demanded? Besides, their expenses swelled with each passing year. It was true, there were many mouths to feed, visits from midwives and doctors, servants to pay. But the idea of asking the count for more money did not sit well with Cédric, so he'd kept silent on the matter.

He stood up and finished getting dressed. "When the right moment comes," he said, and hurried out the door.

The worries of his household could wait. This was an auspicious day, and he must have a clear mind to face it.

After inspecting the mews, the count mounted his black horse and led the hawking party from the château to the lake. Cédric rode at his side on the chestnut gelding he had taken to Königsberg last year. The hounds and kennel masters followed, ready for their part in the action. They halted a short distance from the water. Tall marsh grasses blurred the lake's edges, and graceful oak trees stood sentinel over its distant shore. Tendrils of mist rose from the shimmering surface in the morning sun.

The count's gloved arm bore his favorite falcon, a rare tartaret from Africa whose amber-tinted plumage glowed in the sunlight. Cédric carried the peregrine renowned for her ability to pluck a heron from the sky and send it spiraling to the earth, where a hound waited to complete the kill for her. If the bird should fall into the lake, two under-falconers who could swim were on hand to retrieve it.

One of the beaters approached Cédric and announced that a heron had been spotted in a field just beyond the lake. The party moved around its shores and readied for the hunt. At a signal from Cédric, the beater disappeared through the reeds in the direction of the field. A tense, anticipatory hush settled over the group. In the next instant, the dark form of the heron appeared, winging its way into the sky. Swiftly, Cédric unhooded his falcon and released her leash. She sighted the heron and cast off. He motioned at the kennel master holding the hound's lead, who freed the animal.

A collective gasp went up as the peregrine hurtled toward her prey, then smashed into it. Both birds tumbled from the sky, a writhing bundle of flesh and feathers. At the last moment, the peregrine extricated herself from the heron and reoriented herself toward the hawking party. Cédric felt the light weight of her landing on his wrist and fed her a morsel of boar's liver. Such a treat was reserved for rare moments like this, and she knew she had earned it.

The count smiled his approval as the hound trotted up with the heron in its jaws and dropped it on the grass before him.

"Well done." He turned in the saddle to regard Cédric. "You've proven your worth once again today, not that I was in doubt. And as for those who work in the mews—do you trust your under-falconers to a man?"

Cédric looked at him sharply, caught off guard by the question. "Of course, my lord. Because I'm often away, I've taken great pains to ensure the mews is in capable hands when I cannot be there."

The count gave a nod of satisfaction. He watched the hound being led off to receive a tidbit of meat as a reward for its efforts.

"And how is your young family these days?" he asked.

"Healthy and happy, my lord," Cédric replied, a bit bewildered by the abrupt change of subject.

"Excellent. I ask because I've a proposition for you that concerns them," he said. "Two, in fact. I assume you're aware Constantinople fell to the Turks last year?"

Cédric inclined his head. Philippe kept him abreast of the Hospitaller news, and though he had not fully grasped the implications of Constantinople's sacking by Mehmed II, Sultan of the Ottoman Turks, it was clear to him that all of Christendom had taken a tremendous blow with the loss of that great city.

"Since then, the Order has put out a call for more knights and more funds to shore up the fortifications at their headquarters in Rhodes. My cousin Jacques de Milly was elected Grand Master of the Order in May."

"What an honor, my lord."

"As we speak, he is en route to Rhodes. To show my support for him and indeed the entire Order, I want to send him a gift of falcons."

Cédric nodded. Now he could see where he fit into all of this. "I would be happy to arrange their transport—"

The count held up a hand. "My idea is a bit more complex. I propose that you and your family accompany the falcons to Rhodes. Jacques will need a master falconer of your skill and experience to oversee all the raptors in the Order's care and arrange for the purchase of birds when necessary—both for the knights' own use and as gifts for others. You've proven yourself a man of courage and loyalty many times over, and you understand falcon trading better than any man I've met. I want my cousin to profit from your presence as I have, for the benefit of the Order. I want to do what I can to assure his success. That is why I thought of you."

The idea of such an adventure sent Cédric's blood pumping. For a brief instant he imagined himself standing on the deck of a three-masted ship, speeding over the sea toward his future as master falconer of Rhodes.

Then he thought of Sophie and the children.

"My lord, this is a great honor. There is nothing I would like more. Yet the dangers of the journey, of living in Rhodes when the Turks may attack at any moment—"

"You and your family would be under the care of the knights. There are no greater warriors in the world."

"I've no doubt of it, my lord. But my wife—"

"I believe I understand the delicacy of the situation," the count interrupted again. "Let me propose an additional idea which might be of interest to your wife. The Grand Master of the Knights is elected for life. I pray my cousin will live to be an old man, of course, but I do not propose you stay in Rhodes indefinitely. No, I only want to lend you to Jacques for a time. And I've decided to grant you a piece of land

and a larger home, which you'll take possession of upon your return. Naturally, there is a title attached to the property. I believe that might help you smooth out any obstacles you encounter as you prepare to take on this endeavor."

Cédric could barely conceal his astonishment. A slight smile curved the count's mouth. His gaze flicked to the falcon on his wrist and then back to Cédric.

"You shall be a viscount, equal in rank to your brother and to your father before him—and your wife shall be a viscountess. If, that is, you agree to take on this position in Rhodes and fulfill your responsibilities there to my cousin's satisfaction."

"When would we be required to leave, my lord?" Cédric asked.

The count's smile faded. "As soon as possible."

Cédric imagined his wife's reaction to this news. Sophie hated her status as a common-born woman and made no secret of her loneliness in the Auvergne countryside. She would resist going to Rhodes, he was fairly sure, but she would succumb to the carrot being dangled by the count. As for the older children, Etienne would be beside himself with excitement at the prospect of sailing to an island ruled by Europe's greatest order of knights. Estelle would simply want to follow in her beloved brother's footsteps, as she had since the day she was born.

There was a splash in the lake, then a triumphant shout, followed by hysterical laughter. A boy at the shore had lobbed a dead partridge into the water, and a half-dozen hounds surged into the shallows in pursuit.

The count shaded his eyes with a hand. "My youngest son, no doubt. He has an irrepressible spirit. I dare not crush it. He will not be a boy much longer."

From the tender look in the count's eyes, Cédric guessed the boy would not be punished for whatever mischief he had made. He was thoroughly spoiled.

"And that brings me to my second proposition," the count said. "My middle son is betrothed to a daughter of the duke of Savoy, and will leave for Savoy in a fortnight. He needs pages in his retinue and your son Etienne is about the right age."

"Etienne?" Cédric repeated, sure he had misheard the man.

"Yes, yes. By all accounts, Etienne is an intelligent, strong boy. He will make a fine page. It will be a great honor for him to serve in the duke's household. I imagine it will improve his chances of a good marriage considerably."

The words rained down like physical blows.

No, Cédric wanted to retort. *Absolutely not.*

His firstborn. His eldest son. His heir. The idea of Etienne being torn away from the family and sent to a stranger's household was out of the question. He could never agree to such a scheme.

The count stared at him, waiting for a response.

The peregrine gripped Cédric's wrist tightly, sensing his inner turmoil. The pressure of her talons through the glove made him suck in a quick breath.

He forced his heart to stop thrashing in his chest, gathered his thoughts. This was the count's way of elevating his son's status in the world. Not many boys would have such an opportunity. He would be a fool to refuse such an honor. But he could not bring himself to utter the words. Not yet.

"Think on it," added the count. "Discuss the matter with your wife, and return to me tomorrow with your answer."

Reflexively, Cédric dropped his chin. "You honor us, my lord."

The count turned his horse and rode in the direction of the hawkers and hunters who waited nearby. If the business about Savoy hadn't come up, Cédric would have a light heart indeed. There was worry in his mind about the prospect of hauling his young family across the sea to the westernmost outpost of Christendom, on an island in the shadow of the land of the infidels. It was a dangerous undertaking, to be sure.

Yet a title, land, a bigger house . . . everything his wife dreamed of was within their grasp. It meant Etienne would be a viscount one day. Perhaps the boy would ascend the noble ranks even higher, depending upon what awaited him in Savoy. And most importantly of all, Cédric would be in possession of his own fortune.

You see, Papa? I will make my own way in the world yet.

A sense of buoyancy filled his body as he watched the count ride away. The rest of the day passed in a heady blur. Later, when he returned to the mews, he flew through his work with a foolish grin on his face. Through it all, he could not remember his feet touching the ground. But they must have.

For men, unlike falcons, have no wings.

CHAPTER 21

Summer, 1454
Narbonne, France

A SMALL COUGH woke Sophie in the night, jolting her awake. She stared into the dark, listening for another cough. But none came. Still, she could not drift back to sleep. They were all packed together in one room, she and Cédric and Jean-Philippe in one bed, Christine and Estelle in the other. It would be their last night on French soil for five years.

That fact alone was enough to keep sleep at bay. Excitement coupled with an undeniable tremor of fear had infused her very bones since the day Cédric told her of the opportunity to move to Rhodes. She had refused the idea at first, but when he revealed the count's plan to reward them with titles and land, her protestations had dwindled to silence. There was little to lose and much to gain by making this journey.

The hardest part about it was saying good-bye to Etienne. She knew he was lucky to go to Savoy. It was a chance few boys could hope to have. But she missed her eldest son's calm, kind presence. And

Estelle had been struck nearly dumb since he departed. Sophie had never realized the extent of their bond until Etienne left.

The sky outside lightened little by little. A cock crowed in the courtyard of the inn. Soon the sounds of buckets being filled at the fountain, of horses being led from the stables, would drift through the window and wake them all.

She reached over Jean-Philippe's sleeping body and found Cédric's hand.

Reassured, she ordered herself to make the excitement overpower the dread. Rhodes was unknown to her, but the island was under the command of the Knights Hospitaller. And it would be a far cry from the sleepy hillsides of Auvergne. Philippe had told her Western merchants and shipbuilders and their wives flocked to Rhodes to make their fortunes. It was a prosperous place, a sun-drenched island in a shimmering deep-blue sea. Of all the places he had seen on his travels with the knights, the island of Rhodes had been Philippe's favorite.

Weak morning light from the shuttered window washed over her husband, illuminating him in the gloom. She stared at the familiar contours of his lean, finely formed face. He was still as handsome as he'd been the day they met in Bruges. How had so many years passed since then? It sometimes seemed much of their life together had been spent apart. He'd traveled so often for the count, venturing to Bruges and Bavaria in search of rare falcons. But in the walled harbor city of Rhodes Town, he would work in the grand master's palace, a short walk from their future home.

The idea made hope and anticipation flutter in her chest. She imagined stepping out into Rhodian society as a couple, after being hidden away in the Auvergne countryside far too long. The idea of having women friends was almost too thrilling to contemplate. She would need new clothes, of course. So would the children. A procession of jewel-toned silks materialized in her mind's eye.

The cock crowed again. Jean-Philippe stirred. Cédric glanced at her and smiled.

"Memorizing my face, are you?" he whispered.

"I couldn't sleep," she confessed. "I'm a bit nervous. Very nervous, in truth."

"We all are," he said. "It'll be better once we're aboard the ship. I have trouble sleeping before a journey as well, but once I depart, there are too many distractions to be nervous."

He turned his head toward the wall, where a canvas-wrapped parcel stood an arm's length from the bed.

"It's still there, never fear," Sophie said. "Since we left Auvergne, that painting's become as precious to you as one of our children."

The count had given Cédric this portrait of St. John to deliver to the grand master upon their arrival. It apparently had hung in the château's chapel for many years. Sophie wouldn't know, as she'd not once been invited into the chapel herself.

Cédric nuzzled Jean-Philippe on the cheek. "Have you seen me kissing that painting? I don't think so."

Sophie couldn't repress a laugh. She sat up, pressing a hand to her belly. It struck her that her unborn child would emerge into the world across the sea in a foreign land. The lighthearted feeling in her heart faded as she got out of bed.

The morning passed in a rush. Sophie and Christine got the children ready while Cédric arranged for a mule cart and driver. Once they were outside, Sophie helped Christine and the children get settled on the cart's back bench, then she took her place next to Cédric and the driver. Cédric had promised she could hire Greek servants when they arrived on the island. When Sophie protested that she didn't know a word of Greek, he had assured her that many Rhodians spoke French. After all, French knights were a powerful influence on the island, and many of the grand masters had been of French origin.

She looked at him sideways as the mule cart rolled through the streets of Narbonne. His face did not betray any worry, and as they neared the wharf, he glanced back at Estelle and smiled. Sophie did not have to look back to know their daughter's smile was a perfect reflection of his own.

The cart jolted over a bump in the road, disrupting her thoughts, and she accidentally bit her tongue. The brittle, acrid taste of blood filled her mouth.

"We're here!" Estelle cried, pointing ahead.

Several merchant ships were anchored in the harbor. The docks bustled with activity. Sophie and Christine helped the children down from the cart while Cédric supervised the removal of their belongings.

"Look, Maman!"

Estelle was staring at a melee that had broken out down the quay. Several men were chasing someone through the crowd. There was a scream, a scuffle. After a few moments the hubbub quieted and the crowd dispersed, but a man lay facedown on the quay, unmoving.

"Is he dead?" Sophie gasped.

They watched another man approach the body and nudge it with his foot. The body splayed on the stone flinched, then curled in on itself.

A well-dressed merchant surrounded by servants saw Sophie's shocked expression as he walked by. "Careful on these wharves, madame," he warned. "Treacherous folk are about."

Sophie turned to Cédric, her throat dry as sand. "This does not bode well," she murmured, gathering the children to her skirts. "It's a bad sign, Cédric!"

"Calm yourself. The sooner we get on that ship, the better," he said.

As soon as they were aboard, the captain approached. "Welcome," he said with a smile.

Sophie was relieved at the sight of him. Her mind went immediately to memories of her voyage from Bayonne to Bruges with her parents so many years ago. She had reveled in the adventure and had spent as much time as possible above decks, breathing the sea air and watching the foamy waves roll away to the horizon.

When his gaze fell to the children, the smile faded from his face. "Sea voyages are dangerous, and there are many temptations for little ones above decks. For that reason, you must keep them confined to your cabin for the duration of the journey."

"But—" Sophie began, looking around at the calm, sparkling waters of Narbonne harbor. Surely, at least as they sailed away from France, they could watch their homeland disappear behind them.

"I have seen things happen to travelers at sea that I would not wish upon the devil himself," the captain continued, a note of warning in his voice.

"We will not allow them above decks, sir," Cédric promised. "Your ship, your rules."

The captain nodded. "You, sir, are welcome at my supper table in the evenings. You're a falconer, I gather? You should have some tales to tell. I've several servants of the Order aboard and merchants who've traveled the eastern seas extensively. You'll have much to talk about."

Cédric exchanged a smile with the man. "I look forward to it."

As they descended into the cramped, dark little cabin allotted to them, Sophie realized this journey would be nothing like the voyage to Bruges. For her, it would be an ordeal, not an adventure.

A gale struck late that afternoon. Soon everyone in the family was seasick. There was so much chaos in their little cabin that Sophie found herself doing the work of the lowliest scullery maid, wiping up vomit from the bedclothes and floorboards. Though she longed for fresh air and the children clamored to escape the bleak space, she now understood the captain's admonishment. Images of her children slipping overboard into the waves made her frantic with fear.

Cédric had stowed his work things in their cabin, for he worried sailors would rummage through his falconry supplies if they were loaded in the hold. So there they sat, wooden boxes full of leather straps and lures and tiny hoods, satchels packed with strange herbs and ointments. On top of the pile lay the painting of St. John in its protective canvas covering.

One morning Estelle moaned from her perch on the bed.

"What is it, Estelle?" Sophie asked. The poor girl had weathered the voyage mostly in quiet misery.

"I wish we could go with Papa," she said, arms clutched around her abdomen. "I wish we could meet all those travelers who sit at the captain's table. The tales they tell would pass the time."

The ship let out a deep, ominous creak as it plowed into a wave. Sophie sucked in her breath. Cédric did seem to be enjoying himself, supping at the captain's table each night. Men spinning tales, drinking wine, exchanging spirited conversation. Envy struck her. Her husband had the company of others to distract himself from the terrors of the sea, but the rest of them enjoyed no such advantage.

"You'd better get used to it," Sophie advised her daughter in a voice more bitter than she intended. “The captain’s table is the world of men. This”—she gestured around the tiny, cloying cabin—“is ours.”

Estelle’s golden-brown eyes were full of reproach, but she said nothing. For a moment, Sophie wished for her daughter’s sake that she had not been born a girl.

“Christine,” she said, rousing her maid with a gentle shake. “Tell Estelle a story. The one you used to tell me when I was a girl, about the honey seller who was chased by the bear.”

Christine drew Estelle into the crook of her arm and began to speak in the low, musical tones she’d once used to soothe Sophie to sleep.

The ship rolled deep into the trough of another wave. The painting slid off the pile of Cédric’s work things and tumbled onto the rough wooden planks.

Sophie knew she should pick up the painting and secure it, but instead she lay back on the bed and screwed her eyes shut, overcome with fury at the count for putting them in this position. Cradling her belly, she tried to calm herself by imagining the titles, lands, and larger home awaiting them at the end of this sojourn to Rhodes. But with the next lurch of the ship, she opened her eyes again, struck by a horrifying thought.

What good is a title if I sink to the bottom of the sea?

CHAPTER 22

Autumn, 1454
Rhodes, Greece

A NORTHWESTERLY WIND filled the sails of the merchant ship, propelling it briskly through the waves. Cédric gazed at the grape-blue water, confounded by the richness of the color. It looked different than the sea they had left behind. The Aegean was a deep, vibrant hue, darker than the cloudless sky. Sunlight glittered on small foam-capped waves in all directions. The crew had sighted Rhodes not long ago, and the energy on the ship had transformed. Other passengers—all men, mostly merchants, a few pilgrims, and agents of the knights—ranged alongside him, steadying themselves on the gunwales.

They passed the small islands of Nisyros, Symi, and Tilos, approaching the northern tip of Rhodes at a rapid clip. Soon, very soon, the harbor of Rhodes Town would appear in their sights, his companions assured him.

"See there," one man said to him, a notary who worked for the Order in Avignon. "That dark mass in the east?"

Cédric shaded his hand over his eyes, following the man's gaze.

"Turkey," the notary said. "Land of the infidels."

"It's that close to Rhodes?"

Another man leaned in. "Barely more than a stone's throw."

"That's where the sultan's army launched their convoy to attack Constantinople last year," the notary said. "One hundred thousand soldiers. How many vessels must that have been?"

"Hundreds," the other man said. "Maybe thousands. They had to carry cannons and weaponry, too. Food to keep the soldiers fed. All the trappings of war."

Cédric regarded the gray-gold outline of Turkey a moment longer, then tore his gaze away and fixed it resolutely on Rhodes. The fall of Constantinople had been nothing more than a story until today. Now, in the space of an instant, the vast scale of Sultan Mehmed's army had become tangible. War galleys could be launching at this very moment, their curved prows pushing silently through the waves.

His thoughts turned to Sophie and the children below decks in their cabin.

What have you done, man? What have you led your family into?

He pushed away the doubts, took in a deep breath of soft, salty air. "What happened to all the Christians of Constantinople when the city fell?" he asked the nearest man.

"Many fled to Venice, if they were lucky enough to find a way out. Some settled in Rhodes. Countless others are enslaved, captives to the infidels."

Another ship in their convoy drew abreast of them, its sails taut in the wind. It was a Hospitaller vessel, painted black, its banner emblazoned with the eight-pointed white cross of the Order of St. John. At the captain's table each night, there had been talk of the knights on that ship—men from France, Auvergne, Provence, even England and Bavaria, sworn to protect all Christendom from their headquarters in Rhodes. The thought comforted Cédric, he had to admit. His supper mates assured him that though the Turks had a vast army, their soldiers could not match the knights for their skill on the battlefield. And the knights' navy was impressive, the men claimed. They ruled the Aegean. Still, the thought of Constantinople's massive stone walls crumbling under the Turks' assault made him uneasy. How thick were the walls of Rhodes Town?

As if he knew Cédric's thoughts, the notary said, "The new grand master is tasked with strengthening the fortifications all over the island of Rhodes. I've heard the walls of Rhodes Town are already as thick as this ship is wide. But they'll be widened even more, moats will be dug, a new armory will be built—"

A cry went up as the ships rounded a promontory of land jutting into the sea. "The harbor! The harbor!"

Cédric's eye was caught by movement just off the prow of the vessel. Two gleaming dolphins leaped from the waves in tandem, then vanished under the water. Again they broke the water's surface and soared through the air as effortlessly as a pair of seabirds, then disappeared once more.

"Ah!" the man at his elbow said in delight. "Dolphins bring good fortune. What luck!"

The tension in Cédric's chest loosened a bit. He watched the harbor come into view, the pale dun-colored stone of walls and buildings rising up a bowl-shaped hill beyond the waterfront. The city seemed to flow down the hillside and embrace the harbor with its reassuringly massive seawalls. A row of wooden windmills stood along the easternmost seawall, their blades turning silently in the steady breeze.

"See that?" The man next to him gestured at what appeared to be an enormous iron chain stretching across the mouth of the harbor. Only the ends of the chain were visible, its center sagging out of sight underwater. "When there's a threat from the sea, that chain is stretched tight across the harbor, blocking entrance to the city."

Cédric was heartened by this news. The island did not seem quite so vulnerable now.

"They say that in the time of the ancients, a giant statue stood astride these seawalls. All ships had to pass under it to enter the harbor."

"But that can't be true," Cédric protested. "No statue could be that large."

"They called it the Colossus," the man said. "Made of bronze, it was. Who knows how they built it, how they rigged it into place."

"The ancients took their secrets to the grave with them, but they left their traces all over this island," another man put in. "You'll see.

Temples to their gods and goddesses, grottoes and sanctuaries where they prayed, theaters where they gathered. This island is littered with bits of the past."

There were already several ships anchored in the harbor. None of the banners rippling on their masts looked familiar to him. A merchant who had journeyed from France to Rhodes several times pointed at each and reeled off their origins.

"Catalan, Genoese, and Egyptian," he said.

"Egypt? But that's a land of Arabs," said Cédric in surprise.

"The knights have agreements with the infidels regarding matters of trade," the man said. "When you see what comes off a vessel from Alexandria, you'll understand."

"How so?"

"Sugar, pepper, silks . . . all at prices a fraction of what you'd pay in France."

"I once bought *manus Christi* from an Arab merchant," another man chimed in. "I paid a quarter of what I'd paid for it in Avignon."

Cédric looked at him, astonished. *Manus Christi,* a rose preserve, was effective in healing minor wounds as well as other ailments in both people and falcons. But it was rare and expensive to procure.

"There are many who've made their fortunes in Rhodes," one of the men declared. "With a little luck, I'll be next."

They were passing through the mouth of the harbor now. Armed guards stood at intervals along the seawall, staring at the ship and its passengers. Their polished helmets glittered in the sunlight.

Cédric closed his eyes and gave thanks to God for their safe passage to Rhodes.

Please, he prayed, *let our good fortune continue.*

CHAPTER 23

Autumn, 1454
Rhodes, Greece

When they arrived in Rhodes Harbor, the heat struck Sophie with physical force. Emerging above decks for the first time in weeks, she was nearly giddy with relief. She filled her lungs with long draughts of fresh air, squinting against the brightness, too fixated on keeping her children safe as they disembarked to get a good look at her surroundings.

Standing with Christine and the children on the stone quay while Cédric saw to their belongings, Sophie was overwhelmed by the harsh cries of seabirds, by the shouts of sailors on the many ships anchored in the harbor, by the stream of people passing them by in the fierce afternoon sunlight. She had never seen so many elaborate head coverings, so many draped and flowing garments in bright colors.

She turned her face upward. The sun burned hotter here than in France. And the sky seemed bigger. It was achingly blue, a vast canopy reflecting the sparkling sea.

Cédric shepherded them along the quay toward the high stone

walls encircling Rhodes Town. The harbor was crowded with merchants, with armed men whose swords swung at their sides, with people who spoke a bewildering array of languages. Faint with the remnants of seasickness, Sophie climbed wearily into a mule cart with the children in tow. Cédric helped the Greek driver, a servant of the knights, load their things into the cart bed and lash a canvas cover over the top. The cart's wheels creaked into motion as the driver pointed the mules toward the great wooden doors of the Sea Gate.

Seated next to Cédric and the driver, with the children and Christine packed together on a bench behind them, Sophie stared up at the guards patrolling the top of the city walls as they passed through the open doors. The helmeted men regarded them in silence, their red tunics bright against the pale yellow stone of the walls.

Everywhere she looked, she saw stone. This place was nothing like she'd imagined so far. Cédric had told her the island was a large one, with hills that bore pine and cypress forests in its center, and fishing villages spread along its shores. But here in Rhodes Town, there were no ponds where swans paddled and ducks skimmed over the water. There were no oak forests where deer stalked silently through the underbrush, where raptors glided over meadows eyeing rabbits in the grass.

Instead, the cart rolled along cobblestone streets past churches and busy markets. They passed donkeys pulling carts full of wine barrels and baskets of figs and ceramic canisters sloshing with liquid. A group of monks scurried in the opposite direction, followed by a cluster of women dressed like her in Western garb. Sophie turned her head at the sound of a woman scolding her servants in Greek, then spied a tall, bearded man with an elaborately draped turban and a crimson sash at the waist of his flowing cotton tunic.

Cédric touched her arm. "I just heard some French."

"I didn't hear it," Sophie replied. "It's so noisy here."

The chatter in the streets blended and layered in a babble of strange sounds. None of it made any sense to Sophie. But perhaps, in time, it would. Her queasiness began to fade. The more distance between them and the sea, the better she felt.

"They told me aboard the ship that Rhodes is a crossroads, but I did not understand what that meant until now," Cédric shouted over the noise of a braying donkey. "The pilgrims stream in without end, bringing with them their own private histories, the reasons that drove them to make their pilgrimages in the first place. The merchants and the traders flock to the harbor in their ships and galleys, their goods piling up on the quays, ready for the market."

"Market day—that is something to look forward to," Sophie said. "I want silks from the East and spices from Africa. To start. And soap flecked with rose petals and lavender oil and . . ."

They came to a small square with a fountain at its center. It was circled by half-timbered buildings that appeared to have living quarters on the second floors and shops and taverns at the ground level. Donkeys tied nose-to-tail clattered through the square ahead of them, and the cart driver halted the mules to give the donkeys space. People gathered in the street behind them, all waiting for the animals to pass.

A knight wearing a black tunic emblazoned with the eight-pointed cross of the Order of St. John appeared in front of a building nearby, stepping out from under a trellis shaded by grapevines. He was followed by a young boy who also wore the insignia of the knights. The knight caught Sophie's eye and bowed ever so slightly.

A smile took hold of her face. It felt strange, smiling. She'd nearly forgotten how on the journey.

"Children," she cried. "See the knight and his page?"

"Just like Etienne!" Estelle said.

Christine handed Jean-Philippe up to Sophie so he could see. He bounced on her lap, waving his arms frantically at the knight and his page.

"*Bonjour*!" he shouted in excitement. "*Bonjour!*"

When the objects of his attention both waved and responded in kind, Jean-Philippe clapped his hands and squealed.

"They're French!" Sophie said in surprise.

"From the 'tongue' of Auvergne, perhaps," Cédric told her.

"The tongue?"

He nodded, his eyes still on the knight and the page. "The knights are divided into tongues based on their origin. Each tongue has an inn where they lodge pilgrims and other travelers. There are three tongues from our kingdom—Auvergne, Provence, and Ile-de-France. Most of the grand masters have been French, Sophie. You'll see. There will be reminders of home everywhere."

The tension in her shoulders eased as he spoke. "The sight of them makes me feel safer, I'll admit."

Cédric slung an arm around her. "You'll feel even better when you see our new home. It's close to the 'Collachium', the knights' quarter. And these walls are truly impressive, don't you think? So tall and thick."

She nodded.

"Rhodes Town is a civilized place, a prosperous place," Cédric went on. "Ruled over and cared for by the Order. We've nothing to fear."

The driver urged the mules forward again, and soon they came to a stop in a quiet lane in front of a two-story marble-faced building that had a set of battered wooden doors.

"Here we are," Cédric announced, bounding down from the cart and reaching for Sophie's hand.

"No garden?" she said in disappointment, half-blinded by the sunlight reflecting off the house's stone facade.

"There's a courtyard inside, I'll warrant." Cédric went to pull back the canvas that covered their belongings and let out a cry of dismay.

"Where is the painting?" he demanded. "It was on top of our things. I put it there myself."

Sophie rushed to his side. Someone had used a blade to slit the canvas securing their belongings. The carefully-wrapped parcel they had shepherded across the sea was gone.

"It happened when we stopped in that square." Cédric's expression hardened. "We were all distracted by the knight and his page."

The surge of good spirits Sophie had experienced on the drive from the harbor vanished.

"When foreigners travel the streets, thieves follow," the driver said in heavily accented French. There was not a trace of apology in his voice.

Sophie wanted to slap the man for his insolence. But Jean-Philippe tumbled to the cobblestones at that instant and started screaming. She swept him up, her fatigue flooding back. It was an ill omen, the theft, just as that crime they'd witnessed in Narbonne had been.

But the distress on Cédric's face made her determined to conceal her feelings.

"Come." She held out a hand to Estelle, shifted Jean-Philippe's weight on her hip. "Our new home awaits."

CHAPTER 24

Autumn, 1454
Rhodes, Greece

Two Greek kitchen maids and a message from the grand master had been awaiting the family when they entered their new home yesterday. The maids spoke few words of French, much to Sophie's consternation. The note, emblazoned with the black wax seal of the knights, informed Cédric that Lord de Milly was touring the island and would call for him when he returned.

The news was a relief. Now Cédric had time to seek out the stolen painting he'd promised to hand-carry to the man. If he failed to find it, he had no idea what he'd do.

After a frustrating morning at the marketplace with Estelle and one of the Greek servants, followed by an afternoon of stupefied rest —they were all still recovering from the sea voyage—Cédric slipped out, muttering a vague excuse to his wife about sizing up their new surroundings.

But he was soon turned around by the labyrinthian streets. He flagged down a passerby, a man dressed like him in a doublet and hose, on the hope that he would understand French.

"Excuse me, monsieur," he began. Then, mimicking the shouted hellos between men he'd heard in the streets, he added in Greek, *"Kalimera,* kyrie."

The man paused. *"Oui?"*

"I'm in search of a reputable tavern to quench my thirst," he explained.

"That is easily remedied." The man, whose accent betrayed his Italian origins, pointed ahead. "Continue along this street, then turn there. You'll see the Georgillas tavern—there's a bunch of grapes fashioned of metal hanging over the door. It's Greek-owned, but many Latins patronize the place, too."

"Latins?"

"Yes, yes, men like you and me. French, Italian, Catalan, what have you—we're called Latins here."

When Cédric arrived at the tavern, he stood for a moment taking stock of the place. The whitewashed walls and ceiling were clean. Shutters were thrown open to let in light from a lushly planted interior courtyard.

The sounds of a half-dozen languages washed over him. The air held a strong odor of garlic and roasting lamb with a tantalizing hint of saffron woven through it. The thought of tipping back a cup of wine without a woman or child in sight filled him with anticipation.

The men here weren't soldiers or knights, as far as he could tell. As his gaze traveled around the room, Cédric noticed a clean-shaven man clad in a doublet at a nearby table. The man's bearded companions, a portly middle-aged fellow with silvering hair and a wiry young man on the cusp of adulthood, were dressed in the Greek style.

The clean-shaven man looked up and caught his eye. "Join us!" he called in Italian.

"Grazie." Cédric approached the table, grateful he had learned enough Italian over the years to bargain with Genoese and Venetian traders.

The man pulled another stool to the table and signaled for the barkeep. "You look thirsty."

His companions raised their cups in greeting. The tavern keeper bustled over with a cup and a fresh pitcher of wine.

"What brings you to Rhodes Town?" the man asked, pouring Cédric a cup.

"I'm Cédric de Montavon, the new master falconer for Lord de Milly."

There was a sudden charge in the atmosphere at the table. All three men eyed him with new interest.

"I'm Paolo Foscolo," said the clean-shaven man. He waved a hand at his companions. "This is my wife's cousin, Kyrie Neilos Georgillas, and his son Anteon. Their family owns this place. As well as most of the better taverns and vineyards on the island."

In the few words of Greek he'd learned, Cédric greeted the men politely. They responded in kind. The father and son both wore tunics with the same embroidered design around the neck, a repeating pattern of leaves and vines.

Cédric sipped cautiously from his cup. He sighed with pleasure as the wine coursed down his parched throat.

The elder Georgillas laughed. "You like Cretan wine?" he asked in thickly accented French.

"It's my first taste of the stuff, kyrie. But yes, so far I approve of it."

"Our family serves the best wine on the island," the young man asserted, with almost no trace of an accent.

"Is that so?" Cédric turned to him, one eyebrow raised. "Your French is quite good."

The Greek clapped his son on the shoulder. "Anteon speaks many languages," he said with pride.

"There's no other choice in Rhodes," Signor Foscolo pointed out. "We all speak a little of this and a little of that, though some of us are more gifted than others on that count." He sipped his wine and leveled his gaze at Cédric. "So you'll work for the new grand master. You've got quite a job ahead of you, I imagine."

"Did you know the previous master falconer?" Cédric asked him.

"Only by sight."

"They've been Latins for the most part lately," broke in the elder Georgillas. "Not since Agapitos Kassianos has there been a falconer worthy of the job."

Cédric took that in, trying to hide his surprise. "And he is . . . ?"

"Dead. He was a son of Rhodes but made a name for himself as falconer to the knights." The man's eyes shone as he warmed to his topic. "If he were alive today, how his pride would be bruised by the state of things now."

Signor Foscolo's mouth twitched. He was clearly holding back a smile. "The Greeks are proud of their countryman, as they should be."

"What is the state of things now?" Cédric asked.

"Each new grand master brings in his own people," the Venetian explained. "So loyalties are tested and jobs are lost with each transition, as I'm sure you can imagine."

Cédric nodded slowly, absorbing the man's words. A series of unsettling questions crowded his mind.

Who am I displacing? What awaits me at the palace?

The Greeks watched him, their dark eyes inscrutable.

The Venetian raised his cup. "But such matters are tedious. We've neglected to welcome you properly."

The other men followed his example, saluting Cédric with their cups. He returned the gesture and drank deeply.

"How do you find Rhodes Town so far?" the Venetian asked.

"Hot. And crowded."

"Ah. Well, there are seaside villages where you can cool off. I take my family to Archangelos from time to time. My girls splash in the waves there. The harbor is safe and small."

"How many children do you have?" Cédric asked.

"Just two who live. Both girls." The Venetian's expression sagged a little. "But there is still time for a son. And you?"

"Three who live. Two boys and a girl. But only two of them have come to Rhodes with us."

A stab of longing for Etienne burned in his chest. He didn't mention Sophie's pregnancy. It seemed cruel when the man clearly mourned his lost children and wished for more.

"How does your wife feel about moving to Rhodes from France?"

Cédric took a gulp of his wine. "She will adjust. The language difficulty is a problem for her. The servants sent by the Order speak no French."

The elder Georgillas snorted. "Don't bother trying to replace them, unless you have a bottomless purse. Greeks who speak French are in high demand on this island. Their skills would be wasted on domestic work."

"The children will learn Greek quickly," the Venetian reassured him. "You'll find a tutor soon enough."

"Estelle is the only one old enough for that," Cédric admitted. "She'll soon be twelve."

Signor Foscolo's expression turned thoughtful. "My daughter Anica is a bit older. She's good with languages, like Anteon here. She could teach your daughter both Greek and Italian; your daughter could teach Anica French. What say you?"

"Interesting idea. I'll think about it." Cédric sipped from his cup. "So your wife's family owns taverns. Are you in the family business as well?"

"He's an artist," Neilos Georgillas responded. "A painter. Very good, too."

Cédric looked at the Venetian. "Is that so?"

Signor Foscolo dipped his chin in a nod. "Trained by my uncle, a painter in Venice. I had the opportunity to move here a dozen years ago, try to make my fortune."

"And he married my cousin." The Greek grinned. "Now he's here for life."

The Venetian's eyes crinkled with amusement. "And what a life!"

The tavern door burst open. A man stumbled in, clutching his abdomen. Anteon sprang up from the table and ran to his side, followed by his father. The wounded man sank to his knees, pushing out a torrent of Greek between gasping breaths. Blood leaked from his midsection onto the plank floor.

"What happened?" Cédric asked Paolo, setting down his cup with a thump. He watched the open doorway, waiting for more men to appear.

"He says his sister was cast out from the house where she worked as a domestic and taken against her will into a brothel," the Venetian translated, rising from his seat as he strained to hear. "He traveled to Rhodes Town to free her from prostitution. The brothel owner refused to release her. When he left, he was followed by the man's servant, robbed, and attacked."

Cédric's eyes narrowed. For all its beauty, and despite the reassuring presence of the knights, Rhodes was no different than any other city in some respects.

"Which brothel?" Signor Foscolo called out, then grimaced at the response. "It's a place near the harbor called the Laughing Dove," he told Cédric. "Owned by Dragonetto Poulis."

"Who is he?" Cédric asked.

"He owns several brothels and he's a money lender, too. His father was an agent of the Order."

The tavern keeper cupped his hands around his mouth and shouted something in Greek at the patrons.

"Someone must fetch a doctor," the Venetian translated. "I'll go. Although I think it's too late."

"It doesn't hurt to try, even if he seems beyond saving," Cédric said. "I'll go with you."

They hurried out the door.

In the street, Cédric tipped back his head. The sky was a fiery amber, the air hot and close. Twilight was strange here. Where were the pale lavender skies he was accustomed to in France, the gentle, cooling transition from afternoon to evening? He fell into step with the Venetian as the man hastened through the streets.

"Do you take commissions?" he asked bluntly.

"Why?"

Cédric hesitated, wondering how much to share, and then let his trepidation pass. "I need a portrait of St. John."

Signor Foscolo looked at him. "Is that so? Someone tried to sell me such a portrait yesterday."

Cédric's pulse surged. "What? Did you—did you buy it?"

"No, because I knew it was stolen."

"How did you know that?" The words scraped against his throat, which had gone dry.

"The seller was one of Dragonetto's associates. Everyone knows he has a network of thieves working for him."

"If you tell me where I can find this Dragonetto, I'll seek him out tomorrow." Cédric's hand found its way to the hilt of his sword. He would get the painting back by whatever means necessary.

His companion eyed him soberly. "You're a foreigner. He might sell you back the painting, but at a price that will empty your purse many times over."

"I'll not pay anything. It was stolen from me." Cédric could not help the hard edge of anger that flared in his voice.

The Venetian's expression was sympathetic. "You'll make a powerful enemy on Rhodes before you've had time to make any friends. No, you need to entrust this to my wife's family. The Greeks have a system of their own for dealing with such things."

"How many ducats will I owe your Greek relatives afterward?" Cédric asked in suspicion. "Or will I have to make the payment in florins?"

The heavy gold coins, imprinted with the likeness of the grand master, were equal in value to Venetian ducats, but were minted by the Order's own treasury. Cédric had yet to hold one in the palm of his hand.

"When I was a newcomer here," Paolo said, "I had no friends and found myself in a difficult situation early on. Someone helped me without asking for anything in return. He had no reason for it, other than the fact that he had a big heart. He asked me simply to help another man when I was in the position to do so. For that reason, I am offering you aid now—as someone who remembers all too well what it was like to arrive on this island and wonder how in God's name to make a go of it here."

"But there will be a cost, surely."

The Venetian cast a sideways glance at Cédric. "There are other things on Rhodes just as valuable as money."

"Such as?"

Signor Foscolo gave him an enigmatic smile. "Save your ducats. Leave the matter of the painting to me."

As they headed downhill toward the Jewish Quarter along the city's eastern walls, a faint whisper of wind caressed Cédric's face. It was cool and smelled of the sea. From the corner of his eye, he took the measure of the man beside him.

He wanted to trust the Venetian, but part of him was wary of going along with the man's plan. On the other hand, what other choice was there? The painting was lost to him. Without the assistance of a local, he had little chance of getting it back.

Signor Foscolo was right on at least one count: Cédric was a stranger in a strange land, and he had no friends.

He would have to place his trust in the Venetian whether he liked it or not.

CHAPTER 25

Autumn, 1454
Rhodes, Greece

Cédric rolled over in bed and nuzzled his wife. She smiled drowsily, pressing her naked back to his chest. He had not told her about his conversation with Paolo Foscolo. Until the painting was in his possession again, it was better not to mention the matter. Though worries about this strange new life had kept him awake most of the night, he was determined to forget them for at least a little while. Sophie was the perfect distraction. He kissed her warm, soft shoulder and caressed her waist and haunches with a lazy hand.

Early on in their marriage he'd realized Sophie shared some of a falcon's worst traits: she was temperamental, prone to occasional fits of rage. When she felt wronged, she made no effort to hide her feelings. It was exhausting at times. But, like a falcon, she was also intelligent, courageous, brimming with barely contained energy. She'd mesmerized him since the first moment he clapped eyes upon her all those years ago in Bruges.

She let out a long sigh, turning to face him. "Well, good morning to you, my love."

He smiled wickedly and began trailing kisses over her neck, following a familiar trail along the creamy skin between her breasts, losing himself in the scent of her. She shivered with pleasure, opening herself up to him. Every care he had in the world vanished as she drew him deep within herself, her breath coming hard and fast with desire. One thing about Sophie—when she was with child, she was insatiable between the sheets.

After their midday meal, when the children were occupied with Christine, Cédric and Sophie wandered through their new home, inspecting each room and its furnishings together. Sophie had wrapped her hair tightly in a length of linen and covered her dress with an apron, but her cheeks still glowed from their lovemaking this morning, and her eyes held the merry light he so loved.

Like many homes in Rhodes Town, this house had been the property of a knight and had passed into the possession of the Order upon his death. It was not much to look at from the street, though it was faced with marble, but there was a certain beauty to the interior. Its best feature was the courtyard filled with potted fruit trees and rosebushes.

"See that wooden table in the shadows?" Sophie pointed to the opposite side of the courtyard now.

He nodded.

"I'll have the servants clean and polish it," she said. "If it stays this warm all year, we can sup outside every evening."

"They say it does get cold come wintertime. In the interior of the island, it even snows."

"We will be on top of each other inside these walls, then."

Her tone was just sharp enough to remind him of her disappointment with the home's size. The upper floor contained two bedchambers, each overlooking the courtyard, and two corridors connecting them; the lower floor had the kitchen, a modest servants' quarters adjoining it, a cramped study, and a larger room furnished with a table, benches, and two heavy armchairs by a hearth.

They left the courtyard and passed through the main room now. Cédric noticed a coat of arms carved into the backrests of the armchairs. He paused.

"The former owner was from Italy, of Genoese stock I'm told. A nobleman."

Sophie tossed her head. "He should have had finer possessions, then."

"Why do you say that? These are fine furnishings. Although I know your tastes. I'm not surprised you find them lacking."

She shot him a glare, but the twinkle in her eyes made him laugh out loud. When she was in the right mood, she could be teased. It was always a gamble, though. Today, it was well worth the risk.

They continued their tour, exiting the larger room into the study. It contained a slanted desk, a chair, and a cabinet lined with shelves.

"You've only just claimed this as your space, and yet it looks as if you've already lived here a year!" Sophie chided.

His papers and other belongings were scattered across the desk's surface, and various boxes of his things were strewn over the floor.

"Give me time, give me time," he said. "We're still moving in."

Sophie reached inside the small leather pouch at her waist. "I suppose we should see what's in the cellars," she said, rattling the house keys in her hand.

It was the only area of the home they'd not yet inspected. "Perhaps it's bursting with treasures," he said. "Chests of gold. Rubies. Pearls as fat as eggs."

She laughed. The warm, musical sound enveloped him. He savored it.

They went to the kitchen first, where the two servants sent to them by the Order were scrubbing the copper kettles with sea salt, chattering in Greek.

"Thank God for Christine," Sophie said, shaking her head. "If they were in the care of Greeks, the children would soon forget their French."

Sophie had decided to make Christine a governess of sorts, caring for the children by day to keep their French strong. She was not literate, but when Jean-Philippe was old enough for instruction in reading and writing, Estelle could take on the role of tutor. Cédric said a silent prayer of gratitude for his daughter's intelligence and steady nature. She was such a help, especially without Etienne on hand. He swept aside the thought with a quick exhale of breath. Why mar this day with longing for his absent son?

Sophie fetched a candle from a cabinet drawer in the kitchen and lit it from the embers that still glowed in the hearth. The Greek women fell silent for a moment, watching her move across the floor. As she and Cédric headed to the stairs leading down to the cellars, the sounds of the women's laughter followed them.

"They're mocking me," Sophie told him, her voice hard.

"Who's to say? Don't worry, Sophie. Estelle will pick up Greek quickly. And you will, too."

"How?" his wife challenged him. "I've no tutor, to start. And if we're paying servants, they should learn our language. Not the other way around."

With the candle clutched in one hand, Cédric led the way down the stairs.

"Careful on these steps," he cautioned his wife. He waited while she gathered her skirts in one hand.

The air was cool and earthy down here, holding a trace of moisture and a faint smell of moss. Sophie handed him the keys.

Two storerooms blocked off by floor-to-ceiling iron gates lay on either side of a narrow corridor. He went to the one on his left and tried the keys until he found one that worked. The gate swung open with an ominous creak.

"I'll have the servants oil that," Sophie said from behind him. "If I can figure out a way to tell them."

He held the candle up in the darkness. There wasn't much to see. A few casks, which, when he knocked his knuckles against them, echoed hollowly. Wooden cabinets against a wall contained dusty pitchers and uncorked jugs.

"We'll have to lay in a supply of goods for our own pantry," he said, thinking of his salary. How far would it take them this month? There were so many expenses involved in the move.

"We must get you some of that Cretan wine you love," Sophie told him. "And send a few casks to Papa as well."

He thrust the key ring at his wife. "Open the other gate. You'll likely be the one down here the most."

Sophie tried several keys. Finally, the gate swung open.

Casks were stacked two high nearly to the back of the space. Cédric edged through the narrow passageway between the stacks of casks. A few sloshed when he shook them. Perhaps they contained wine, but it was probably spoiled.

Reaching the back wall, he held the candle up. There was a depression in the wall at about chest height, a deep niche cut into the stone. A trickle of moisture darkened the wall beneath it, perhaps evidence of an underground spring. The trail of water was only a finger's breadth wide, like a tiny brook coursing over the stone.

His wife peered around his shoulder, then slid past him and put a hand on the damp stone.

"It reminds me of Auvergne. How the spring rains darken the trunks of oak trees near the house," she said wistfully.

There was a squeak, followed by a scratching sound.

"God protect us," Sophie muttered. "Please be mice, not rats."

"We'll get a cat," he promised. "I've seen a few prowling around the alley behind the house. Let's go back upstairs."

"Wait." Sophie moved deeper into the shadows. "I see something."

He followed her gaze. In the darkest corner at the back of the storeroom lay what looked like a crumpled length of canvas. Sophie bent down and jerked at the cloth. In the flickering candlelight, Cédric saw a face staring back at them, luminous as the moon.

Sophie bent down and touched the object. "It's a woman's head, made of stone. Marble, I think."

Cédric crouched and ran a hand over the nose, lips, and chin. The perfection of the stone-cutter's work was breathtaking. This must have belonged to the Italian knight. Whoever had cleared out his possessions hadn't cared enough to haul it up from the cellar. Or perhaps they'd not seen it.

"What should we do with it?" Sophie straightened. "Perhaps it's worth something."

Cédric arranged the canvas over the marble carving once more. "Keep this discovery to yourself, Sophie."

"Who would I tell?" she asked. "I know no one in Rhodes."

He ushered her out of the storeroom and locked the gate behind them.

"Before autumn turns to winter, you'll have a dozen new friends," he declared as they climbed the staircase.

"How can you be so sure?"

"You may have been tucked in the countryside for a long while, but don't think I've forgotten how it is with you." His mind flitted to the day of their wedding, to the sight of Sophie holding court with their guests, the covetous gazes of men staring hungrily at her, drinking in her beauty. Unbidden, the memory of her brother's drunken story about Sophie kissing the Catalan in Bruges rose up in his mind. "I'll keep you close at my side when we go to church. The men of Rhodes Town will flap about you like moths to a flame. I'd hate to see one of them try to kiss you—or worse, see you let him."

Whenever he brought up Grégoire's tale, Sophie brushed it off. Today was no different.

She shook her head. "Not that old story again, Cédric. I cared nothing for the Catalan! At any rate, I'm a matron now. Those moths you speak of will not concern themselves with me."

"Time has been kind to you, my love," he countered.

It was true. His wife's beauty had ripened since they met, not faded.

Hand in hand, they reached the top of the staircase. She leaned over and kissed him.

"I know you're trying to ease my entry into this strange place with your sweet words, Husband," she whispered. "And I must admit it's working."

Taking her hand, he led her toward the back door. "Now, let us find a cat for you in the alleyway. A fine mouser."

Sophie chuckled. "One that understands French."

CHAPTER 26

Autumn, 1454
Rhodes, Greece

CÉDRIC STOOD at the door waiting for Estelle to tie on her head wrap. Outside, the clatter of donkey hooves mingled with the distant blare of trumpeters at the grand master's palace and the sing-song calls of street criers peddling their wares. The constant noise was a stark change from the quiet Auvergne countryside, and he'd not grown used to it yet. Sophie studied their daughter with an anxious expression, arms crossed over her chest.

"I'm not sure I like this, you allowing Estelle to enter the home of a Greek stranger," she said.

"Paolo Foscolo is Venetian. He attends Mass at Santa Maria, where all the citizens of quality worship. His wife may be Greek, but her family is one of the wealthiest on the island. They are educated folk."

"Still, it makes me worry," she said. "These Greeks are full of treachery. I can feel it, see it in their eyes."

"Just because you can't speak their language doesn't mean they're cursing you in it," he said.

"You don't know that!" she retorted. "You only speak a few words yourself."

"Well, all the more reason to have Estelle learn it from a native speaker. Then she can teach all of us. You'll know exactly what the servants are saying. It will make your life easier."

Sophie's objections dwindled in the face of his reasoned answers. Her moods came on swiftly, but they usually vanished with haste as well. Over time, he'd learned it was often a matter of waiting out the storm.

Within a few moments, he and Estelle were descending the narrow lane toward the eastern quarter, where the Venetian's home lay. The sun glared down at them relentlessly.

"Is the sun bigger on Rhodes?" Estelle asked him. "It's so much hotter than the French one."

He laughed, glancing up at the cloudless sky. "There's only one sun, my girl."

Keeping careful hold of his daughter's hand, he navigated a stream of donkey carts laden with cypress logs, grapes, wine barrels, ceramic canisters of olive oil, and various other goods. The carts were all heading in the same direction—to the broad market street that cut a path from east to west through the heart of the city.

"Perhaps on the way back home, we'll pass through the marketplace after the crowds thin out," he told Estelle.

Crossing a small square, they stopped to admire a two-story building with an exterior balcony on the upper floor. A carved marble surround encased the entry door, and three water spouts in the shape of crocodiles jutted from the eves. This was the Kastellania, he'd learned, where the knights and their agents meted out justice regarding matters of commerce—and jailed wayward citizens. Nearby, a stone column mounted in the cobbled ground was outfitted with iron rings, its weathered surface streaked by rust-colored stains. Philippe had told him the knights held public floggings as a primary form of punishment. From the looks of it, the whipping post was frequently in use.

Estelle regarded the stone crocodiles with wide eyes. "I don't like the look of this place, Papa."

"It's where the knights keep the peace. After all, they rule the island."

"I thought Lord de Milly ruled Rhodes."

"He is like a king, I suppose," Cédric agreed. "Nothing important could happen at the Kastellania or any other place here without his permission."

They continued on and soon drew to a stop in front of Paolo Foscolo's house. It lay in shadow, situated near the city walls. A servant woman answered the door with a girl at her side. The girl was taller than Estelle, with honey-colored skin and large, expressive brown eyes.

"Welcome," she said in Italian, smiling. "I am Anica."

Mimicking the girl's accent, Estelle introduced herself in the same language. Cédric privately marveled at his daughter's ability to pick up languages. She sounded like a Venetian herself.

"Papa asked that you come in as well, monsieur," Anica said, looking at him without a trace of shyness. "He has something for you."

"Thank you," he replied.

The home was not as grand as he had imagined. It was much like their own, if a bit darker inside. From a room adjacent to the entry hall, Cédric caught a glimpse of small portraits arrayed along one wall, illuminated by the flames of oil lamps fixed below them.

The artist appeared in a doorway, beaming. "Welcome, *monsieur le fauconnier.*"

"Thank you." Cédric drew Estelle forward. "This is my daughter, Estelle, Signor Foscolo."

She curtsied to the man, murmuring a greeting in Italian. Cédric's throat tightened with pride. She was calm and brave, as always. So much like Etienne.

"Come with me," Anica said to Estelle. She pointed past her father toward the courtyard. "We can talk there."

Estelle looked at Cédric for permission.

"I'll be back when the churches ring four bells," Cédric told her. "Listen well to your lesson, especially the Greek. We're all relying on you to teach us what you learn."

As the girls disappeared through a doorway, Cédric followed Signor Foscolo through a dusky corridor and into a small chamber with a window that was open to the courtyard. There were wooden easels set up near the window, with a table between them holding various ceramic jugs and dishes. A neat row of paintbrushes lay on a square of tanned leather. Next to them was a dish containing two eggs.

"Eggs," he commented. "Not a sight I expected to see in an artist's studio."

"The whites are mixed with pigments to create the paints," Signor Foscolo explained.

Another table held a half-dozen paintings, most of them small portraits whose backgrounds glinted with gold leaf. Cédric drew closer, studying them, then glanced up at Signor Foscolo with a questioning look.

"There's a saying here, 'A house without an icon is like a man without an eye.' So for the most part, though I was trained in the Venetian style, I paint icons using the Byzantine style because my clients prefer it." Signor Foscolo crossed to a cabinet in the corner and unlatched it. Drawing out a canvas-wrapped object, he held it up. "Your missing painting."

"Praise all the saints!" Cédric hastily unwrapped the canvas and examined the painting. It looked in fine condition. For an instant, his knees wobbled. His fingers felt thick and clumsy as he wrapped up the portrait again. "The loss of this—it could have been very bad for me. Thank you, Signor Foscolo."

"Please call me Paolo."

"Then you must call me Cédric," he returned. "I hope there was no trouble retrieving it."

"My wife's family took care of the matter," the Venetian said. "As I told you, they have their ways of smoothing things over."

"I'm in your debt," Cédric said. "What can I do to repay you? You said you won't take money. But surely there is something else . . ."

The Venetian shook his head. "Not at the moment. I have everything I need."

At his words, a delicately built woman with glossy black hair peeking out from under a simple linen head wrap entered the room. She wore a loose-fitting green gown of Egyptian cotton.

"Everything?" she repeated in Italian, her eyes glinting with amusement.

"Cali." The painter's expression softened into a smile. "My dear, this is the falconer to the grand master, Monsieur de Montavon."

"Signora," Cédric said, bowing a little.

"Welcome to Rhodes, sir," she said, switching to deeply accented French. She trained enormous dark eyes on him. "Since my husband is too polite to do so, I shall tell you what he needs."

The Venetian's smile faded.

"It is simply the truth." She kept her gaze on Cédric, reverting to Italian. "My husband needs commissions from the knights. They have money; they have private chapels, villas outside the city walls. All they lack is art. Do you agree, Paolo, *amore*?"

He sighed. "It's true. But what can Monsieur de Montavon do about that?"

Signora Foscolo gave Cédric a pleading look. "You will be working in the palace, meeting with the grand master and the others. Surely you will have the opportunity . . . "

Cédric smiled at her. "Leave it to me, signora."

The Venetian put up a hand. "Now, please—"

Cédric waved away his words of protest, thinking back to their conversation in the streets. *There are other things as valuable as money in Rhodes.* Now, he was beginning to understand what the man had meant.

A trickle of laughter filtered in from the courtyard. Signora Foscolo went to the window. "The girls are already friends. Children do that with such ease." She turned back to face Cédric. "And how does your wife fare in Rhodes Town?"

"She is eager to visit the markets," he said. "Silks and spices are at the top of her list."

Signora Foscolo smiled. "Madame de Montavon will get her wish, for a fleet of merchants is due from Syria soon. I will look for your wife on the next market day."

"She will be pleased," Cédric said.

He left their home with the painting firmly tucked under one arm. The sooner he could unburden himself of the blasted thing, the better.

CHAPTER 27

Autumn, 1454
Rhodes, Greece

GRAND MASTER JACQUES DE MILLY returned from his journey around Rhodes on a Tuesday. On Wednesday, he held audiences all day with citizens who had business dealings with the Order or disputes that needed mediating. On Thursday, he met with high-ranking officials. So it wasn't until Friday that Cédric had the opportunity to meet his new employer face-to-face.

Hurrying up the Street of the Knights to the palace in the bright morning sun, Cédric barely noticed the exquisite craftsmanship of the knights' lodgings or the elaborate stonework of the Church of St. John near the entrance to the palace. On earlier explorations of this street, he had been dazzled by the elegant "inns" where each tongue housed both knights and travelers.

But today, he was focused solely on the coming interaction with Jacques de Milly. Though part of him dreaded it, another part was relieved. Now, he would begin the work he had come here to do. And the painting he carried would no longer be his responsibility.

Once inside the palace walls, Cédric followed a servant through a broad corridor and up a stone staircase that led to several formal chambers. When the doors to the receiving hall swung open and he stepped inside, Cédric was unprepared for the massive scale of the room, which exceeded even that of the count's great hall in Auvergne. Enormous wooden beams supported the ceiling. The floor was fitted with square marble pavers. Sumptuous tapestries worked in blue, red, and gold adorned the walls.

Lord de Milly sat on a dais surrounded by assistants, his rangy limbs seeming somehow too large for the oak chair he occupied. Like most of the men in the room, he wore a black velvet tunic emblazoned with the white eight-pointed cross of the Order.

At his signal, Cédric approached and bowed deeply.

"Welcome to Rhodes, Monsieur de Montavon," the grand master said. "I trust your journey here was uneventful?"

"Thank you, my lord. It was." Cédric straightened his shoulders.

"And you find your lodgings satisfactory?" Lord de Milly's face was dominated by a jutting narrow-bridged nose and a short, oiled beard.

"Indeed, my lord." Cédric pulled the parcel from under his arm. "I've brought you a gift, with the compliments of the count."

He approached the dais and handed up the portrait to one of the grand master's assistants without a word of its misadventures. The man unwrapped the painting and presented it to Lord de Milly, who inspected it silently.

"My cousin speaks highly of you," he said, waving the assistant away. "He promises that you are the ideal man for the job of procuring the finest raptors both for our own use and for friends of the Order."

"I will do my best to fulfill the count's promise, my lord." Cédric's throat was so dry he could barely push the words out.

"Your first such task is a gift for the King of Cyprus, who is of French descent and a close ally of the knights. You shall obtain a pair of gyrfalcons, white preferably."

Cédric's heart sank. Fulfilling this task so far away from Western Europe would be very difficult.

"I will make inquiries at once, Lord de Milly," he promised. "Though white gyrfalcons are exceedingly rare."

"I said white was preferable, but not required," the grand master replied tersely. "Also for the King of Cyprus, I wish you to find a noble-born falconer of French origin."

Cédric nodded, letting out his breath in a silent exhale. This order he felt reasonably certain he could fulfill. There had been a young Frenchman, of noble birth like him, whom he had met in Bruges several years ago and then again in Bavaria on his most recent buying trip there. Michel Pelestrine shared his love for raptors, was eager for adventure, and struck him as both intelligent and honorable.

"I believe I know the perfect candidate, Lord de Milly."

"You should know that I've seen all the mews on the island, and some improvements are in order. You'll tour the island and inspect them yourself, then supervise the necessary work."

Cédric nodded. "Of course, my lord."

The grand master shifted in his seat. "I expect to host many hawking expeditions during my time here. You'll be organizing the outings, naturally."

"As you command, my lord." Cédric's palms were clammy with sweat. The air in the room felt hot and close.

Leaning forward, Lord de Milly placed his hands on the armrests of his chair. "You and I both represent the tongue of Auvergne. That is our honor and our burden to uphold." He lowered his voice. "Though every servant of the knights and every citizen of Rhodes is sworn to respect and obey the Order, treachery lurks here in many guises. I reward loyalty, and I expect you to be a credit to me. If you fail, I'll hear of it—and the consequences will be unfortunate."

Cédric held his gaze. "I shall strive to bring honor to Auvergne, Lord de Milly."

"My secretary will assist you with the details of your post," the grand master said crisply. "I wish you good luck."

Cédric was led from the room by a young assistant. He was slight, with a narrow face and skin so pale he looked bloodless. They entered a chamber down the corridor from the receiving hall. It held a half-dozen desks and tables stacked with books, papers, and maps. Several other assistants were at work in the space.

The man unfurled a parchment map on a table near the window. "The Order's outposts are marked on this map of the island. Lord de Milly desires new falcons—sakers, peregrines, and merlins—for the mews in the palace and in his private villa beyond the city walls." The man pressed a finger on the parchment. "The grand master is particularly keen to visit the Rodini Valley during his hawking expeditions, just here. You will have to coordinate with the hunting masters at the kennels to plan these outings."

"It shall be done," Cédric replied, wishing for a draught of cool ale, honeyed wine, anything to moisten his throat. "But we are at a great distance from France, Bavaria, Flanders—every place where I know people who could help me fulfill this list of tasks. And I've no way of paying anyone from here. How does the Order conduct business from Rhodes?"

The man sighed. "No one has explained this to you yet?"

His tone was faintly accusatory, as if Cédric were lying.

"No. This is the first time I've been in the palace. I've had no dealings with any representatives of the Order regarding anything but my domestic arrangements."

"The Order has its own treasury," the secretary said. "We've a partnership with Florentine bankers that allows our agents to draw gold from banks in every important city of Europe. Our ships and riders transport correspondence to every kingdom in the West. When you have letters ready to send, come to the palace and find me or any of the grand master's other secretaries. We will assist you with the necessary arrangements for transfers of gold."

Cédric nodded, already drawing up a list in his mind of the contacts who could arrange transport of falcons to Rhodes. He was reminded of the Catalan who had appeared on the Norwegian's ship all those years ago. Never would he have suspected then that one day, he would source falcons for the Order himself. What had become of that man? Did he still sail the seas, spending the knights' gold?

"What about my personal correspondence, possessions, other goods?" he asked. "Can I send them that way too?"

"Of course, of course."

Cédric thought of something. "Will I have access to the Order's library?"

"Whatever for?"

"There might be records left by other falconers that could help me in my work."

"I shall have to get permission from the grand master." The man unhooked a leather pouch from his belt. "This is for you. Keys to the mews both here and elsewhere on the island. All the work you deem necessary will have to be approved and documented." The secretary deposited the pouch in Cédric's outstretched hand. "Come. I'll take you to the mews now."

They descended the staircase and exited through a door into the interior courtyard of the palace. Marble statues of male and female figures stood at intervals around the perimeter of the space.

"I've never seen anything like those statues," Cédric remarked as they crossed the courtyard and passed the arched doors of the stables. "Where did they come from?"

"The island is littered with such things," his guide said off-handedly. "The land is porous here, filled with limestone grottoes where candles still burn for the pagan gods. Such blasphemy is punishable by death, of course. Still, some Greeks cling to the old ways."

Cédric's mind flashed to the marble head in their cellar. Was it a representation of an unholy goddess? The thought made him uneasy. Perhaps he could find a way to sell the thing off quietly.

A guard stood at the door to the mews. Under the impatient eye of the secretary, Cédric fitted the key into the lock. The man swept through the doorway ahead of him, dispensing cursory introductions between Cédric and the Greek under-falconers, then hurried away again.

With the under-falconers trailing silently behind him, Cédric inspected the rows of hutches, peering inside each one, making mental notes to have Estelle transcribe later onto paper. The falcons sat on their perches, hooded, their muscled bodies relaxed under sleek feathers.

He paused in front of two birds that were dark gray in color and roughly the same size as gyrfalcons.

"Gyrfalcons?" he said aloud, perplexed. "I thought they were rare as snow here."

The old Greek drew abreast of him and shook his head vehemently.

"They are saker falcons," he said in French.

Cédric smiled in relief at the sound of his native language. "Ah, of course."

He knew of this breed, which originated in Asia, and he had seen a few juvenile birds in his day, but he'd had no idea how much the adults resembled gyrfalcons.

"Remove their hoods," he ordered the man.

The falcons eyed him with interest when freed of the hoods. Their feathers were in good condition, their legs and talons were unblemished, they looked frankly eager to spread their wings and get out hunting. For his part, he longed to do the same. Get a glove and a leash, a sack of rabbit meat, and put these magnificent creatures to the test.

When he spotted an underweight falcon with a white breast and lead-gray wings huddled miserably on her perch, her neck retracted into her shoulders, he paused. He glanced behind him at the old Greek.

"Her coloring marks her as a lanner falcon, but she's too small. What's wrong with her?"

"Yes, she is an *alfaneque*," the man replied. "From Africa. A good hunter. But very fragile." A mournful look gripped his wrinkled face. He muttered something unintelligible in Greek, but his last words sounded familiar.

"Agapitos Kassianos?" Cédric repeated uncertainly. "The falconer of Rhodes?"

A look of abject surprise, followed by pride, washed over the man's face, and he threw back his shoulders.

"The *best* falconer of Rhodes," the old man corrected. "He would know how to cure her, I promise you."

Cédric bent to fiddle with the broken latch on the door of an empty hutch, feeling the eyes of his new staff upon him. The old man's insinuation was clear: Cédric would work in the shadow of Agapitos Kassianos, and no Greek would let him forget it.

Treachery lurks here in many guises.

A powerful longing for Philippe's presence flooded him. What would his old friend's counsel be? If Philippe had witnessed the tug of loyalties within the Order, he'd never mentioned such things to Cédric.

A deep feeling of uneasiness settled in Cédric's bones. Would the under-falconers help him prove his worth to the grand master, or would they do everything in their power to show he was no Agapitos Kassianos? With his scant knowledge of Greek, he was at a serious disadvantage. He passed a hand over his face, realizing the enormity of the job before him.

Slowly, he turned back to face the men.

CHAPTER 28

Autumn, 1454
Rhodes, Greece

BANNERS OF JEWEL-TONED silks fluttered in the breeze. Merchants cried out to passing citizens, competing for the crowd's attention. A Greek matron paused, taken in by the shouted entreaties, then led her servants into one of the silk stalls. Sophie smiled. Merchants vying for customers—this was something she had grown up with in Toulouse, something she understood very well.

"Let's buy some silks," she told Estelle eagerly. Cédric had promised her a new silk cloak after she'd seen the fashions at church on Sunday, and she knew he would not refuse his daughter one, either.

"But we should wait for Papa," Estelle objected.

Cédric had gone in search of a leather craftsman known for making the tiny ornamented hoods worn by raptors.

"He'll be along soon," she replied. "Who knows how long these silks will be here? And we have her for help." Sophie jerked her head in the direction of the Greek servant they'd brought along. "We can get silk enough for two cloaks. Rose-pink for me. And you, *ma chérie*? You can choose whatever you like."

Estelle stood her ground. "Papa said we cannot spend too much. There are so many other things we need."

Sophie sighed in exasperation. "He wants us to buy silks. He told me so himself. And as I don't speak Greek, you must help me." She gestured at a vendor whose silks looked particularly tempting. A woman stood before him, bargaining loudly in French. Judging by the merchant's turban and long flowing tunic, Sophie supposed he was an infidel, perhaps a Syrian merchant.

"Let's go inside his stall. You must learn to bargain for the best price," she said firmly, pulling Estelle by the elbow. "It will be far easier to do it in French than Greek, won't it?" She listened intently to the merchant and his customer. Leaning closer to Estelle, she added, "We'll need two *bras* of fabric for each shawl. I don't intend to pay any more than that woman, and she's paying one ducat for four *bras.*"

Estelle gave her a quizzical look. "Four *bras?*"

Fabric was measured by the *bras,* or arm's length, something that had been pounded into Sophie's brain by endless repetition during her childhood. She'd gotten so caught up in her excitement that she'd forgotten Estelle's ignorance of this world. Commerce, business, the marketplace—it was all in Sophie's blood. But growing up in Auvergne, Estelle had never learned about such matters.

"That's how we measure fabric," Sophie explained, extending one arm to illustrate the concept.

When the merchant turned to them, Estelle selected the rose-pink silk for Sophie and a length of burnt-orange silk for herself, bargaining with the man until she secured the price Sophie had deemed acceptable. The merchant handed Sophie the wrapped fabrics and bowed his thanks.

"You did well," Sophie told her daughter as they moved on to the soap vendors. She slipped an arm around Estelle's shoulders. "You are a big help to me."

Estelle smiled up at her, glowing at the praise.

The sweet scent of Castile soap studded with lavender and rose petals filled Sophie's lungs. She directed Estelle to purchase more than they needed. She would send some home to Papa and Maman. How they would love it.

A male voice behind them made her jump.

"Sophie, Estelle," Cédric said. "What have you found?"

The merchant handed a large canvas sack to their servant, who hefted it in her arms with a frown.

"Did you buy soap made of solid gold?" Cédric asked.

Sophie tossed her head. "Of course not. We need to thank Papa for all of his help. What better way than sharing the bounty of this beautiful island with my family?"

Estelle tugged at her arm. "Look! There's Signora Foscolo." She pointed at a group of Greek women walking their way. "And Anica."

Sophie recognized Anica from church, but this was the first time she'd seen Signora Foscolo, an attractive woman with large dark eyes who wore a flowing, elaborately draped gown in the Greek style. The other two women were dressed in the simple garments of servants.

When they reached the Foscolo group, Cédric made introductions. The easy familiarity between the girls helped smooth over the awkwardness of the moment. Signora Foscolo's gaze settled on the swell of Sophie's belly for an instant, and her expression grew faintly wistful.

"Do you find what you are looking for in the marketplace?" Signora Foscolo asked in heavily accented French.

"Yes," Sophie said with a nod. "All I need now is honey, and an apothecary for bark of the willow."

"I can help," Signora Foscolo told her. "My apothecary is a trusted friend, and he shall be yours as well."

After buying ceramic jars of honey from an elderly honey purveyor, they turned down a quiet side street and Signora Foscolo pointed at a marble-fronted building on the corner that housed an apothecary.

But they had taken only a few steps along the street when Signora Foscolo paused at an alleyway. From the back of the group, Sophie craned her neck to see what was happening. A woman wearing a threadbare tunic lay huddled on the cobblestones, crying. Looming over her was a man dressed in the Greek style, gripping her by the arm.

Cédric stepped forward. But before he could act, Signora Foscolo spoke quickly to one of her servant women, who then stalked into the alleyway unleashing a barrage of angry words at the man. When he saw the rest of the group observing him, he released the weeping woman and drew himself up.

The young man was beardless, with a mop of dark, springy curls. He stood unmoving, an expression of hostile defiance on his face. Signora Foscolo advanced toward him a few steps, her arm held high. Sophie drew in a sharp breath when she saw the glitter of metal in the woman's outstretched hand.

Eyeing the weapon, the fellow backed away, sidling into the shadows.

Signora Foscolo's servant helped the woman up. At the sight of the woman's bruised, bloodied face, Sophie drew Estelle close.

"May God and all the saints protect us," she murmured.

She glanced down, saw Cédric's hand clenching the hilt of his sword.

Don't you dare go after that man, she pleaded silently.

In the space of a few moments, they had gone from sauntering through the autumn sunlight, purchasing silks and honey, to witnessing an episode of ugly violence. The delight she had taken in their long-awaited outing to the marketplace was ruined. A knot of dread lodged in her chest, making it difficult to breathe.

"What can I do?" Cédric asked Signora Foscolo.

"Stay with us, if you will. We shall take her to our home," Signora Foscolo replied.

"Who is she?" Sophie asked cautiously.

"A slave." Signora Foscolo's features tightened. "Her master is cruel, but her mistress is crueler."

"Signora Foscolo wielded her weapon like a man," Sophie whispered to Cédric as the group covered the last few strides to the apothecary. "She did not wait for you to draw your sword. Perhaps it's customary here for respectable women to carry blades. If that is the case, you should purchase a dagger for me."

Cédric did not answer. He stood aside to allow the women through the apothecary door.

Sophie glanced uneasily over her shoulder before she went inside. But the street was empty. The young man had vanished like a puff of smoke.

CHAPTER 29

Autumn, 1454
Rhodes, Greece

CÉDRIC ENTERED the mews at the grand master's private villa. Sun poured in from arched stone windows whose parchment coverings flapped in the wind. He shook his head at the sight. He was unsure about many things in Rhodes, but he did know falcons. They required calm, dusky, untroubled spaces. That was something he could create for them, at least.

Signaling to a young Greek under-falconer whose hazel eyes were startlingly light against the bronze skin of his face, Cédric pointed at the windows.

"This is a problem," he said in halting Greek.

Unfortunately, the Greek word for 'problem' had become all too familiar in his brief time on Rhodes.

"How can I help?" the young man replied in French.

"Praise the saints, you speak my language," Cédric said in relief. "You'll need to install restraints on the shades so their shifting does not disturb the birds. I'll find you the materials for the job."

The young man nodded. "It shall be done."

After finishing his inspection of the villa's mews, Cédric hurried back through lush irrigated gardens toward the city walls, barely noticing the beauty around him. He'd secured permission to visit the palace library yesterday, and was eager to search its volumes for any records left by previous falconers.

Once inside the library, he took stock of his surroundings in silence. Massive leather-bound volumes were locked in cabinets on the north wall. Perhaps those books contained the history of the knights. They might hold transcribed records of the various grand masters' rulings on matters of the Order. Or they might chronicle the disputes brought to the knights by Rhodian citizens.

He cast the thoughts aside and crossed to the south wall, where all the books were freely accessible. The afternoon passed quickly as he pulled out one book after another. Much of what he found was of no use to him—treatises on navigation, shipbuilding, astronomy, and mathematics. He used a ladder to retrieve books coated in dust from the highest shelf and thumbed through a medical treatise in French about remedies for various ailments, a Genoese portolan describing the safest route through the Aegean Sea, and a step-by-step instruction manual for fencers written in Provençal.

Then he pulled down a small volume with a gilt-edged brown leather cover. He opened it to the first page. An illustration confronted him—a falconer with a lure buckled at his waist, a raptor perched on his outstretched arm. The colors had faded, but the image came to life regardless. Every word on the page was Greek.

He leafed through several more pages. There were a few more illustrations of raptors, alongside notes that seemed to include measurements of various substances. These could be recipes, he realized. Healing recipes for raptor ailments, from a falconer of Rhodes. Cédric was used to the remedies French falconers relied upon. Surely, in this vastly different environment, there were ingredients better suited to the climate. At least he hoped that was the case.

With a heady feeling of anticipation, he slipped the book into his satchel and made for home.

After depositing his things in the study, Cédric washed his hands for supper and entered the courtyard. The waning light of day illuminated the olive-wood table in the center of the space. Jean-Philippe made a running leap into his arms, shrieking with delight. Cédric tossed his son into the air a few times, then settled him at the table. The Greek servants scurried back and forth from the kitchen, setting down platters of steaming food.

"I must say the markets are full of excellent fish. And rice—it is a rare treat at home, but here I can find it readily," Sophie bubbled as he took his seat. "The spices, too! Some I've never heard of, much less tasted . . . for far less than we'd pay in France. They say another merchant fleet arrives from Alexandria in a few days."

He drew in a deep breath, savoring the warm, citrus-infused air. Jean-Philippe and Estelle sat across from him, their faces round, rosy, and healthy. His gaze came to rest on Sophie's swelling belly. It would be a winter birth, something that normally filled him with trepidation, but perhaps he had no need to worry here with the mild weather.

"Rhodes Town is a marvel, isn't it?" Cédric spooned up a portion of saffron-scented fish stew, following it with a heaping spoonful of rice. "Just about anything can be purchased in the marketplace."

"I met a merchant's wife at church who told me about Cypriot fabric trimmed with gold thread," Sophie said. "You know how Papa is always in search of it. We should buy him a bolt or two of the stuff, then send it on a Hospitaller ship to France. How happy it would make him."

Cédric looked at her soberly. "We must wait until I get my next payment from the knights to spend money on costly gifts, my love. There's so much else we need."

"Once he sees the goods, Papa will make sure we have plenty of coin to purchase what we want."

"We don't know the full extent of the expenses we'll have as a result of this move, not for a while yet. It's best to be prudent, that's all."

Sophie smiled at him. Nothing could shake her good mood this evening, it seemed.

"All shall be well, Cédric," she murmured. "When Dame Fortune is smiling upon us, we must take advantage of her favor."

"True," he conceded, his thoughts turning to the falconry book. He looked at Estelle. "It's time you begin practicing your Greek letters," he told her. "I've found a book about falcons in the grand master's library. The only problem is I can't understand a word of it. You can help me by copying the words and bringing them to Anica for translation."

Estelle looked doubtful. "Translate a book in Greek? Papa, I've only just begun my studies."

"Anica is a good teacher. You've made excellent progress in a short period of time. Studying the written language will speed your mastery of it." He sipped from his cup, watching Estelle over the rim. "I need your help, Estelle. This is important to me—to the whole family."

"I don't see why Estelle must translate some ancient book for you, Cédric." Sophie's tone was sharp. "Surely her study of Greek should center on household words and phrases we'll need in the market. Things that will help us make sense of this place, make sure we're not being cheated. Some of the merchants speak French, but many do not."

"Trust me, Sophie," he said wearily. "What's in that book will help all of us."

Sophie's long sigh was meant for his ears, but he let it drift past him and float up through the open courtyard to the amber-tinted evening sky.

He'd not told her of his conversation with the grand master. She had enough worries of her own adjusting to life in this strange new world. But his success was the key to their future on this island. If Estelle's skill with languages could help him uncover the secrets of falcon care in Rhodes, by God, he would exploit it.

CHAPTER 30

Autumn, 1454
Rhodes, Greece

THE DAY ESTELLE returned from the Foscolo home with a page of text transcribed from Greek to French, Cédric's eyes were immediately drawn to the top of the sheet of linen paper, where two words stood out: Agapitos Kassianos. He grinned to himself, the back of his neck prickling with excitement. The legendary falconer of Rhodes had written a book—this book! He eagerly scanned the rest of the words on the page. One phrase was repeated often: *sang du dragon*. Dragon's blood was a legendary curative for animal and human ills alike, but it was costly and difficult to find in France.

Cédric could not help but draw the conclusion that the author used dragon's blood liberally in his work.

He did not tell Sophie his plan when he took Estelle out a few days later. All he said was he needed their daughter's help to negotiate a purchase. Since Sophie used that argument whenever she wanted to buy something, she had no quarrel with his announcement. Indeed, she was curled up like a cat in the shade of a potted lemon tree in the courtyard, watching Jean-Philippe chase a lizard across the stone floor under Christine's supervision. She waved at them off-handedly, both hands draped over her belly.

After quickly descending the streets of Rhodes Town and exiting through the Sea Gate, he and Estelle approached an Arab merchant's crew as they unloaded wooden boxes, ceramic jugs, and other mysterious cargo onto the quay. The scents of fragrant saffron, black pepper, ground ginger, cinnamon, and cloves assailed Cédric with a heady, rich aroma that mingled with the briny air of the sea.

The merchant caught sight of them and called a greeting. To Cédric's surprise, the man spoke excellent French. Cédric explained what he was after and the merchant rummaged through a box, producing a sack of *sang du dragon*—round, hard cakes of dried crimson powder.

"Here," he said, breaking off a small piece and gesturing to Estelle to hold out her hand. When she did, he crumbled a bit of the powder into her palm. She glanced up at Cédric, a smile spreading over her face.

"I can't sell it to you here," he went on. "Well, not officially, anyway. We're meant to sell it in the warehouses near the inner harbor or wait until market day." He lowered his voice. "But we could avoid the tariffs if we're quick and quiet about it."

A shout in Arabic from down the quay interrupted their conversation. A long, shuffling train of people was disembarking from a galley and being herded toward the slave market. They were mostly men, but a few women and young girls were among them.

The merchant glanced in the direction of the slaves. "That privateer is back with more booty, I see." He pointed at the vessel, which was still disgorging its human cargo. It was a low-slung galley whose red-and-white banner fluttered in the wind. "I pity the folk who find themselves in his path."

"It's not right," Cédric said. "Ordinary people should not be taken captive, nor bought and sold."

"It's the way of the world. And the knights would be lost without slaves." The merchant glanced at Estelle. "Do you like sugar?"

She nodded, wide-eyed.

"Well, you eat it thanks to Muslim slaves working on the knights' plantations here and in Cyprus." The merchant smiled, but a hard edge had crept into his voice.

Muslim slaves, Cédric had learned, did the most backbreaking and difficult work for the knights. Christian slaves tended to be relegated to households, where they were still at the mercy of their masters but fared better overall than their Muslim counterparts, as far as he could tell.

A trio of men appeared from behind a tall pile of wooden chests stacked on the quay nearby. At their center was a short, solidly built man dressed in hose and a fur-edged green silk tunic. His Latin-style black cap partially concealed a shiny, bald pate. His two companions wore the loose, long cotton tunics favored by locals. One had a full beard and a predatory look about him that matched his formidable physique. The other, Cédric realized with a start, was the young man who had threatened the slave woman near the apothecary.

He felt the stares of all three men upon him and Estelle as they walked by. Draping a protective arm around her shoulders, he returned their gaze with an unsmiling appraisal of his own.

But the group paused. The man in the black cap said, "What's this? A girl buying dragon's blood on the quay to avoid the tariff? No one would ever suspect. How clever. I'll have to find a girl to do my business dealings as well." He let out a mirthless laugh.

Estelle dropped her arm, and the dragon's blood scattered to the ground. She pressed against Cédric, her face downcast.

"You speak out of turn, sir," Cédric said coldly. "We had no such intention."

"My eyes did not deceive me," the man replied, affecting an air of innocence. "Once something is seen, it cannot be unseen. As much as we might wish otherwise." He glanced beyond them at the captives being led toward the slave market. "You are fortunate the knights' attention is focused elsewhere today. I pray for the sake of the girl that your luck holds."

Cédric's hand went to the hilt of his sword. Only the presence of his daughter kept him from advancing on the men, ready for a fight. Instead, he said nothing, wrestling with his anger as the group sauntered away, following the captives toward the slave market.

"Papa, are we in trouble with the knights?" Estelle asked quietly, her face pale.

"No," he replied. "We've done nothing wrong."

The merchant's face was twisted in a scowl as he stared after the men. "That one makes life miserable for anyone not on his payroll."

"What do you mean?" Cédric asked.

"Have you not heard of Dragonetto Poulis?" The merchant jabbed a finger in the direction of the bald man. "He's got his finger in just about every pot on this island. He owns"—the man glanced quickly at Estelle—"certain establishments that are quite popular."

"Yes, his name has come up once or twice," Cédric said, feigning disinterest.

"Come to the warehouses this afternoon. I'll give you a good deal on dragon's blood to make up for what happened just now," the merchant said.

Cédric nodded his thanks and guided Estelle along the quay toward the Sea Gate, each step putting a little more distance between them and the miserable people shuffling toward their fate in the slave market. Soon the gurgle of water in the harbor faded, replaced by the creak of cart wheels, the shouts of citizens greeting one another on the road, the distant trumpeting of the grand master's guards in his palace on the hill. The glare of the midday sun made Cédric long for shade.

"The other man, the young one, was the one we saw that day with the Foscolos," Estelle said, her forehead creased with anxiety. "Wasn't he?"

Cédric hated the worry in her eyes. She was too young to have such cares.

"Yes," he admitted.

"That injured woman lives with the Foscolos now," she confided. "She is with child."

He looked at her sideways, surprised. "Who is she?"

"A slave to a Florentine banker," Estelle said.

"But why was she bleeding on the streets?"

"Anica told me the banker's wife beat her and cast her out when she learned the slave was carrying his child. Now Signora Foscolo is nursing her back to health."

Cédric swallowed. As much as he hated his daughter being exposed to such ugliness, he was under no delusions that she would elude life's inevitable brutality. She might as well learn from the example of a compassionate family.

"The Foscolos are good people," he said, catching sight of a fruit vendor ahead. "Ah! That's just what we need. What do you say we quench our thirst with some grapes?"

She nodded eagerly, increasing her pace. After stopping at the fruit vendor, they entered the open gates of a small garden adjacent to a Greek church and stood in the shade of an orange tree, munching their grapes.

"When will we return to France?" Estelle asked in a small voice.

Cédric smiled. "You always ask me that when something upsets you."

Estelle dropped her chin. "Rhodes is a strange place, Papa. Mostly, I like it. But it frightens me, too."

"I know."

She raised her gaze to meet his. "I miss Etienne."

Cédric nodded. "We all do."

"Can't we go back, Papa?" she asked, her eyes wet with tears. "We belong in France."

With his thumb, he swiped at a tear on her cheek. "We cannot, *ma chérie.* Not yet. But it will get better, I promise you. As time goes on, you will find things to love about Rhodes. We all will."

The stubborn set of her jaw told him she disagreed, but she kept quiet.

He held out his hand. "Come. We'll take a different route and walk past another garden on the way home, a secret place filled with daffodils and golden lilies that only bloom in autumn. I saw a dragonfly there the other day, scarlet as a ruby. It's a beautiful spot, I promise you."

He felt the resistance that still coursed through her body, saw it in the tilt of her head. Estelle had none of her mother's mercurial temperament, but she was strong-willed in her own way. She would need that strength in the years to come. All too soon she would be a woman, and Cédric would not always be at her side to guide and protect her.

The thought made his own eyes prick with tears.

CHAPTER 31

Autumn, 1454
Rhodes, Greece

Cédric looked up from his work when his daughter entered the study.

"Estelle, I have a task for you." He gestured her forward. "I've learned of a source for saker falcons on the island of Crete. There's a Venetian gentleman there who may be able to help us. Will you help me write the letter to him?"

"Of course, Papa."

"Fetch a fresh sheet of paper and the quill and inkpot, and we'll begin."

After getting settled at the desk, Estelle hesitated, chewing her lip.

"What is it?" he asked.

"Papa, the Foscolos invited me to go to the women's bathhouse with them." She lowered her voice. "I would like to go."

"You know what your mother would say."

"We don't have to tell her." Estelle's golden-brown eyes pleaded with him.

"My obedient girl! That's not like you," Cédric mock-scolded her.

She sat up straighter. "Everyone does it here, Papa. You've told me yourself. The men and the women."

"You have a point," he conceded. "There are more bathed bodies in Rhodes than in all France, it seems."

He thought for a moment. What harm could it do to let Estelle experience the women's bathhouse? The Foscolos were trustworthy, a respected family. His daughter was a responsible, cautious girl. She would be in good hands with Madame Foscolo.

"Why not?" Cédric said finally. "I know I can rely on you to keep silent on the subject should it arise with your mother."

Estelle's face lit up in a smile. "Thank you, Papa!" She took up her quill and dipped its tip into the inkpot.

Sophie breezed through the door a few moments later, the rich fragrance of jasmine wafting into the room with her. Besotted by the scent of the Arabian jasmine vine planted in their courtyard, she had abandoned lavender oil soon after arriving in Rhodes Town.

"Are you writing to Etienne?" she asked.

They had all resolved to write him a letter a week since it was so easy to send correspondence on Hospitaller ships. Naturally, Estelle had been chosen as scribe.

"Not at the moment," Cédric replied. "Estelle is helping me with another matter."

"My dear, I've an idea." Sophie came to his side and kissed his cheek. "We should purchase a slave woman."

Cédric stared at his wife in astonishment. "I would never buy a slave," he said firmly.

"The finest people on this island own slaves," she asserted.

"Perhaps here on Rhodes things are different, but we're French."

"The grand master is French, too. And he owns slaves. How do you explain that?"

He shrugged. "The knights have their own rules, after all. Lord de Milly must abide by them."

"Buying a slave could rescue a woman from a terrible fate, from—" Sophie glanced at Estelle. "Horrible things can befall women who are captured. Like that poor wretch we saw in the street after the market."

"None of this is fit for our daughter's ears," he reminded her.

"Even Paolo Foscolo owns slaves," she persisted. "A respectable man. A man you admire."

"Just because I like a man doesn't mean I want to adopt his ways. And most slave owners are not like Paolo Foscolo." He tamped down his impatience. Sophie had been so even-tempered of late. He'd hoped it would last at least until the new baby came. "No more talk of slaves, Sophie. I've work to do."

Sophie put a hand on her hip, another retort clearly taking root in her mind. But before she spoke, Cédric crossed to the door and opened it for her.

Silently, she stalked out.

His wife would forget this ridiculous idea soon enough, he told himself. In the meantime, she'd reminded him of a debt that needed repaying.

The next morning, on his way to the palace, he paused on the Street of the Knights, studying the inns maintained by the various tongues of the organization. Though the knights were officially meant to live within their own ranks, he'd learned that many of them owned homes in other quarters of the city. Depending on their rank and their wealth, the men moved about at will, lived where they wished, and some of them even owned villas outside the city walls like the one belonging to the grand master. Even the three sacred rules of the Order seemed to be mere guidelines—except the one commanding obedience. As for poverty and chastity, Philippe had confided to him long ago that many knights flouted those rules.

The truth was, as long as the knights did their primary job of protecting the citizens of Rhodes from an infidel attack, Cédric did not much care how they spent their time.

He approached the Inn of the French. Greeting the steward of the place, he inquired after a knight whom he'd been told was the son of a neighboring noble in the region where Cédric had grown up. The man was in residence, and a messenger was sent for him.

They settled in the parlor together and exchanged stories from the old country. Cédric carried with him a longing for France that often felt like a stone slung against his heart. But today, his conversation with the young French knight lifted that weight. Their reminiscences about the landscape, the food, the changing seasons, the holiday feast days—it all infused him with a feeling of kinship he hadn't experienced since arriving in Rhodes.

It turned out that, like Cédric, this man was a younger son with no chance of inheriting the title or lands. His family had scraped together the funds to apply to the Order several years ago, and to their surprise he'd been accepted. Since arriving in Rhodes, he had taken part in raiding attacks by the knights on the western shore of Turkey, where many captives had been taken and sold into slavery.

"If the infidels attack Rhodes, I'm well prepared," he said, lowering his voice. "I've seen enough violence for a lifetime already, but I'd much rather fight in a battle than raid villages and take captives. If I had known how I'd be using my sword, I might not have been so eager to join the—"

His next words were drowned out by a group of French pilgrims who entered the parlor, chattering loudly about their visit to the marketplace.

"Let's take our conversation somewhere quieter," Cédric said. "The chapel, perhaps?"

"Yes, a good idea," the knight replied, rising from his seat. "Follow me."

The chapel was down a short flight of steps, but it felt far away from the communal spaces of the inn. It featured a simple altar and a few rows of hand-carved pews. Several beeswax candles illuminated the small room, giving off a pleasing scent.

The walls were nearly bare of adornment. There was one painting of St. John, as Cédric had expected, but no others.

"I was at the Inn of Provence," he said, "and the walls of their chapel were hung with a half-dozen paintings of saints, done in the same style as this one of St. John. I must say I'm surprised to only see one painting here."

The knight looked at him. "They must have been shipped from

Provence, I suppose, for one can't get such paintings in Rhodes. They're all done in the Greek style here."

"There's a Venetian-trained painter in Rhodes who paints in the Western style," Cédric asserted. "He's quite talented. And a quick study."

"Is that so? What's the fellow's name?"

"Paolo Foscolo. I've heard that knights sometimes pay for paintings and stonework and the like. So do pilgrims and merchants. The Venetian would do a fine job filling these walls with portraits of saints."

"I don't know if there's money set aside for such things," the knight said dismissively.

"The Aragonese chapel is adorned with portraits as well, I hear," Cédric remarked, stepping closer to the portrait of St. John.

"The Aragonese and the Catalans have got the coin for whatever they want. You can barely walk in this town without stumbling across a Spanish ship captain, merchant, or mercenary."

The knight turned away, clearly losing interest in the topic.

Just spit it out, man, Cédric told himself.

"Do you enjoy hawking?" he asked.

The man slowly spun around, one eyebrow raised. "Naturally."

"Put in a good word for Signor Foscolo with your superiors, and I'll see that there's a place for you on my next hawking expedition to the interior of the island."

The knight grinned at him, a gleam of anticipation in his eyes. "Now I understand what you've been getting at. I've not been hawking in a very long time, not since I left France."

Cédric smiled back. "What say you, then? Will you help Signor Foscolo get a commission from the French knights?"

"If hawking is my reward? Why not? I'll see what I can do for your Venetian."

CHAPTER 32

Autumn, 1454
Rhodes, Greece

THE PRIEST'S recitation of Mass echoed along the vaulted nave of the Church of Santa Maria. Sophie stifled a yawn and closed her eyes, imagining she was in Bruges the day she met Cédric for the first time. She smiled inwardly, remembering how taken she had been by the sight of him, the jolt of desire she'd felt in his presence. Perhaps she'd let herself nod off, just for a bit. She'd barely slept last night.

Her reverie was interrupted by the harsh cry of a gull. Sophie blinked, startled, and glimpsed the shadowy form of a bird flitting past one of the stained glass windows above the altar. The church abutted the city walls and was a stone's throw from the harbor. She sighed, impatient to trade the stale indoor air for an invigorating sea breeze.

When Mass ended, she followed Cédric down the main aisle and out the doors, handing a sleepy Jean-Philippe off to his sister as they entered the square at the base of the hill leading up to the grand master's palace. Cédric headed toward a cluster of ship captains visiting from far-flung ports.

Sophie watched the crowd gather in the sunshine to share gossip and discuss the news. The air above her head seethed with languages, and she listened hard for French as she searched for familiar faces. Finally spotting one, she waved at the wife of a Provençal merchant whom she'd met a few weeks prior. The woman smiled in recognition and approached with her companions.

Just as the women reached Sophie's side, a hush fell over the crowd. Heads turned as three men emerged from the church doors: the priest who had said Mass, the archbishop of Rhodes, and a short, barrel-chested man shrouded in a fur-edged silk tunic. A black cap adorned his bald head.

"Who is that bald gentleman?" Sophie asked Madame Taraval, the woman from Provence. "He seems to be a man of distinction."

Madame Taraval's expression hardened. "Distinction? There are some kinds of distinction that do not warrant respect. At least, not in Dragonetto's case."

The man bowed his head to the archbishop and the priest and turned on his heel, trailed by a servant.

"Dragonetto?" Sophie repeated, mesmerized by him now. "What an odd name."

His face was broad, the bridge of his nose lumpy, as if it had been struck with a heavy object and partially collapsed. He strode forward, occasionally murmuring a greeting as the crowd parted before him.

Madame Taraval nudged Sophie with her elbow, casting a meaningful glance at a group of Greek women and their servants walking through the square. Sophie followed her gaze, observing the soft drape of their gowns, the languid flutter of their cotton headpieces.

"I don't trust them," said the wife of a Genoese ship captain. "Not for one moment."

"Neither do I," said one of her companions. She placed both her hands on the stiff panel of her bodice as if to demonstrate the difference between her own garb and that of the Greek women. "They have such strange ways. They wail so frightfully at funerals that the knights had to pass a law prohibiting it. Many of them still worship the old gods, you know. If they're found out by the Church"—she glanced behind her at Santa Maria, whose doors gaped open still—"they'll be burned alive."

The Genoese woman looked dubious. "I don't know how many of them truly worship the ancients. You can't walk twenty paces without stumbling across bits and pieces of the old gods in Rhodes. My husband found a statue of a goddess buried in the mud under his shipsheds not long ago."

"What did he do with it?" Sophie asked, supporting her lower back with one hand and cradling her swollen belly with the other.

"He gave it to the knights, of course. That's what we're meant to do when we find such things."

Sophie bit her lip, thinking of the marble head in the cellar storeroom.

"I've just about given up with my Greek servants," she said, eager to change the subject. "They pretend they don't understand me, move like tortoises when I ask them to fetch me things. It would be easier to just do it myself."

"They're trying to frighten us, the Greeks," Madame Taraval asserted. "Ever since Constantinople, it's been worse. They gossip about the Turks attacking Rhodes Town and slaughtering us all. They say there aren't enough knights to protect us." She dropped her voice. "The truth is they want Rhodes back for themselves. One way or another, they want to scare us off the island."

Sophie watched her uneasily. "Slaughtering us?"

"Yes, yes. But Rhodes is so close to Turkey. If the infidels wanted to attack us, wouldn't they have done it by now? Besides, the grand master makes all sorts of agreements with them to keep us safe. Tribute payments and such."

A cold breeze flowed over the wall from the sea, raising goosebumps on Sophie's flesh. Not too long ago, she and Cédric had walked to the highest point in Rhodes Town. She'd clung to his arm, waddling and puffing like an ancient duck. The outing had been her idea. She'd wanted to see a house owned by a wealthy Genoese whose wife had been one of her first acquaintances at church. After reaching their destination and admiring the home, they'd turned and gazed east over the sea. A long smudge of land ran along the horizon, backed by shadowy mountains. She was shocked when Cédric told her they were looking at Turkey. It was much closer than she'd imagined.

But not until today had she contemplated how quickly the safe haven of these city walls could crumble into dust under a sultan's merciless attack. Rhodes Town was vulnerable—and so was her family. Just as the thought penetrated her mind, she heard the high, sweet voice of her son.

"Maman! Maman!" Jean-Philippe tugged on her skirts, demanding attention.

She spied Estelle a short distance away with Anica. Signora Foscolo was nowhere to be seen, as usual. Sophie felt relieved at that. It would be terribly awkward to bring a Greek woman into this circle.

"Estelle!" she called. "Come fetch your brother."

Jean-Philippe seemed to think they were beginning a marvelous game. He giggled and ran directly into the path of an oncoming man. To Sophie's consternation, she saw the advancing figure was none other than Dragonetto.

"Jean-Philippe!" she cried.

The man stopped, frowning, as she rushed forward and gathered her boy in her arms.

"Forgive him, sir," she said, straightening. "He got away from me."

Dragonetto ran his gaze up and down the length of her body with the expression of speculative lust she had seen in men's eyes since she was old enough to notice such things. She stiffened under his inspection.

"Any boy with such a charming mother is easily forgiven, madame." His French was thickly accented. "How can I have missed such a lovely addition to our little city?"

"You speak to my wife, sir."

Cédric stepped in front of her, partially blocking the man's view.

"Ah, is that so?" Dragonetto's cold dark eyes slid from Cédric to Sophie and back again. "You should keep better track of your children. These streets can be quite dangerous, I regret to say."

Cédric did not respond. Sophie put a hand on his arm, felt the coiled tension of his muscles.

"Your concern is noted," she said. "Good day to you."

Dragonetto nodded curtly and walked off without another word.

When they returned home from church, Sophie led the children into the courtyard and seated them at the table. She was so exhausted she wanted to escape to her bedchamber and rest, but a desire to see the children fed first won out. In Greek, Estelle asked one of the servants to fetch them bread, fruit, and cheese—all words Sophie recognized. Then she made another request to the woman that was completely unintelligible.

Cédric joined them just as the servant returned with the food and a pitcher of freshly pressed orange juice.

"Look," Estelle murmured to Jean-Philippe. "Orange juice, just as I promised you."

"Cédric," Sophie said. "Our daughter's Greek is so good now I mistake her for a native. Those language lessons with Anica Foscolo can end soon, don't you think?"

She saw a private glance between her husband and daughter. For some reason, it sparked a little flame of jealousy in her.

"As long as Rhodes is our home, we'll benefit from Estelle's visits with the Foscolos," her husband said. "There's more value in her time with them than just learning a language."

"Rhodes will never be home, Cédric," she retorted. "The language is impossible for me. And I don't trust the Greeks, not for a single moment."

"You'll get used to it. There's much to admire about this place. You've often said so yourself. Such delights in the marketplace. And the friends you've made at church, women just like yourself."

"You never told me how much danger we would be facing on this island." Heat rose in her cheeks, and her heart thudded against her ribs. "An attack could come from Turkey at any time."

Estelle shrank away from her, and Jean-Philippe stared in wide-eyed silence. Sophie pressed her fingers against her eyes, fighting tears as the dark mood sank its talons into her.

"Calm yourself. You're frightening the children." Cédric's voice was pitched very low. "We are well protected. The knights are stronger warriors than the Turks. And they have a fleet of warships that cannot be beaten. The simple fact is the Order rules the seas."

"We never should have come here." Her voice broke on a sob.

"You were as eager to move to Rhodes as I was." He put his lips to her ear, his tone infuriatingly calm. "A title? Lands of our own? Those rewards will only come to us if we stay on—and if I fulfill all the expectations of the grand master, which are many."

He leaned closer to her, his arm warm against her shoulders. She shrugged it away. She would not let him disarm her with tenderness, not this time.

Bracing both hands on the table, Sophie hauled herself up. She pressed her lips together, fighting off a torrent of angry words, and stormed inside. The climb upstairs to their bedchamber had never seemed so long. She flung herself on the bed, sobbing, and cradled her belly with shaking hands.

By all the saints, the moment those knights see war galleys coming from the east, I'm packing up our family and setting sail for France.

CHAPTER 33

Autumn, 1454
Rhodes, Greece

A FLEET of merchants had arrived in the outer harbor that morning. Eager to see the goods they carried, Cédric rushed through his duties at the palace and headed back down the Street of the Knights at midday. Approaching the Sea Gate, he saw a familiar figure just ahead.

"Paolo!" he called, hurrying to fall into step alongside the Venetian.

"Monsieur le fauconnier!" A grin creased the other man's face. "I'm headed to the harbor. You?"

Cédric nodded. "Can't miss the spectacle. You never know what those ships carry." He noticed the artist had exchanged the leather sandals he customarily wore for soft boots in concession to the cooling weather. He himself had thrown on a short cloak as he left the house.

"I've some news for you," the Venetian said as they passed through the doors of the gate, nodding at the helmeted guards. "I have a commission for two paintings of saints for the French knights' chapel —and you to thank for it."

"Is that so?" Cédric clapped a hand on Paolo's shoulder, relieved his efforts were beginning to bear fruit. “I’m pleased to hear it. Surely, more commissions will follow. You’re a man of talent.”

Paolo inclined his head in thanks. “How goes your work for the knights?”

“Busy. Communicating still has its difficulties. But it’s getting better. Lately, I’ve been organizing some hawking expeditions to the interior of the island.”

“I’ve been asked by the Georgillas family for you to consider doing them a favor,” Paolo said, his gaze turning serious. “Their kin would benefit from learning a few days in advance of such outings.”

“Why?”

“No one but knights and their favored lieges are allowed to hunt game,” Paolo explained. “Still, many Greeks flout the rules as a way to supplement their diets with a bit of extra meat. Who can blame them?”

“So they ask for a warning in order to conceal evidence of their hunting?”

The Venetian nodded.

“An outing to the Rodini Valley is planned in three days’ time. I hope that gives you enough time to get the word out,” Cédric said.

They had reached the warehouses along the harbor. Merchants and laborers hustled around, carrying goods from the harbor to their storerooms.

“What are you after today?” Cédric asked.

“First, minerals for pigments. Cinnabar and lapis lazuli, if I’m lucky. And then I’m off to the slave market.”

Cédric regarded Paolo a bit more coolly. “Oh?”

“I’m freeing a slave soon. Her seven years of service to me will end this winter. It’s time to replace her.”

“What will she do when you free her?”

“She’s marrying a man from Lindos who owns a fishing boat. I’ve put aside some ducats for her dowry. They will wed in the spring. Cali’s brother, a priest in Lindos, will conduct the ceremony.”

Cédric contemplated his friend’s words. Sophie had not been off the mark in her comments, then. A man could create a better life for a slave by purchasing her. Still, this fact was not enough to persuade him to do so.

"Ah! There's the merchant who sold me lapis powder in the spring." Paolo pointed at a man farther down the quay. "I'll find you after we've finished our errands."

A short time later, they met again near a warehouse jammed with sugar and honey merchants haggling with a crowd of customers three-deep. They walked along the perimeter of the harbor, then veered inland toward the busy shipyard that lay just beyond the small inner harbor where the knights kept their vessels.

Paolo pointed at one of the black-painted ships. "That one just arrived from the north with a hold full of captive Christians. Many townsfolk will be bidding on them."

"Including you?" Cédric asked.

The Venetian held his gaze a moment. "I know the practice of slavery doesn't sit well with you. It didn't with me either when I first arrived here. Come see the market. At least understand what you detest."

"Signor Foscolo!" a voice called from behind them.

Paolo stopped, turned his head. *"Buongiorno,"* he returned politely.

He and the man, a well-dressed, portly Italian accompanied by a male servant, exchanged a few pleasantries. The man was quickly distracted by the sight of another acquaintance and melted into the crowd. Paolo stared after him with narrowed eyes.

"Who was that?" asked Cédric. "You look pleased to see the back of him."

"A Florentine banker. He's fine to do business with, but his domestic troubles spill out from the walls of his household."

"How's that?"

"We took in one of his slave women not long ago. She was pregnant by him. His wife beat her half to death when she found out. Cali nursed her back to health."

"Of course." Cédric nodded. "We were with your wife when she found the woman in the streets. What happened to her, the slave?"

"She went back to the Florentine's home and had the baby. He owns her, after all."

They passed a building near the shipyard with a tavern on the ground floor and a brothel upstairs. A metal sign painted with the image of a dove hung over the doorway, swinging back and forth in the breeze. A trio of drunken Genoese sailors staggered up the stairs to the door. The sound of disconsolate weeping leaked out from the shutters of one of the upper rooms.

Cédric glanced up. “Someone’s not happy.”

“The Laughing Dove is badly named, for Dragonetto’s whores are not treated well,” Paolo commented. “No doubt he’ll be first in line for any young female captives. He’s probably threatening some poor woman up there, saying he’ll replace her with new flesh today.”

They entered the slave market and made their way through the shifting crowd. Citizens, shipmasters, and sailors milled about, their eyes fixed on the auctioneer. Cédric spotted the Florentine banker pushing forward until he was at the front of the crowd.

Soon the day’s first prospects were led onto the stone slave block. As the bidding began, Paolo and Cédric stood back a little, watching the action. Most of the male Muslim slaves were purchased by wealthy knights or people associated with them.

“They’ll be set to work fortifying the walls and towers of the city, I’d wager,” Paolo said.

Then the female captives were led to the auction block one by one. Cédric’s spine stiffened when a young girl was brought out. She was painfully thin, with matted brown hair and sores all over her arms and legs. The leather collar around her neck was several sizes too large. Her homespun shift was in rags.

“She’s nothing but a bag of bones,” muttered a Genoese ship captain next to him. “No value there.”

At that moment, Dragonetto muscled his way past Paolo. Cédric’s jaw tightened. Ever since the incidents at the harbor and the Church of Santa Maria, he had bristled at the sight of the man. Dragonetto was always in the same pew on Sundays, which seemed to be reserved for him and his associates. Even the most strident gossips fell silent as he exited the church each week.

Paolo entered the bidding for the girl at ten ducats, snapping

Cédric's attention back to the present moment. Dragonetto outbid him immediately, raising the price to twenty ducats. After a brief pause, Paolo made a counterbid, pushing the amount up to twenty-five ducats. The Florentine banker sidled toward Paolo.

"Why are you bidding on her?" the man asked. "She's not worth that. A healthy woman might fetch thirty or even forty ducats, but that girl looks like she has one foot in the grave."

Paolo ignored the banker as Dragonetto raised the bid again, to thirty-five ducats.

The captive girl marked Dragonetto's voice and tracked his position in the crowd. A look of abject fear came over her when she laid eyes on the man.

Cédric's body tensed. The girl couldn't have been much older than Estelle.

"I'm out," Paolo said. "I can't outbid Dragonetto. Forty ducats is far beyond my means."

"Yes, you can," Cédric ground out. "I'll cover the difference."

"What?" The Venetian looked at him in astonishment. "But then I'll owe you money I don't have."

"You'll pay it back one day."

Paolo stayed silent.

"Do I have any other bids?" the auctioneer asked.

A scuffle broke out at the edge of the crowd, followed by enraged shouts in Genoese. An agitated man rushed to Dragonetto's side. The pair bent their heads together, then Dragonetto followed him toward the harbor. Conversations rippled overhead as rumors flew about the source of the conflict.

Taking advantage of the diversion, Cédric thrust his own hand skyward.

The auctioneer pointed at him. "You wish to enter the bidding?"

Cédric glanced at Paolo, raised a questioning brow, and patted his purse.

After a brief hesitation, Paolo raised four fingers in the air. When the auctioneer asked for more bids, there was a resounding silence.

"Sold to the Venetian, for forty ducats," the auctioneer cried.

Cédric breathed a long sigh of relief.

The banker snorted. "Not a wise investment, I regret to say."

"We'll see," Paolo replied.

Cédric dug into his purse for a handful of gold ducats and handed them to his friend. When he looked up, he saw Dragonetto advancing toward them.

"Don't make yourself his target," Paolo muttered.

"I see *you* giving him a bold gaze," Cédric pointed out under his breath.

"I have the protection of Cali's family to keep me from harm's way."

"Well, I have the protection of the knights."

"Unfortunately, so does he."

Cédric watched while the Venetian wrote his name in a ledger next to the amount he had paid for the girl. According to the auctioneer, her name was Maria.

There was a tap on his shoulder. Cédric spun on his heel and looked directly into Dragonetto's eyes.

"Pleased with yourself?" the man hissed. "You cheated me of my purchase."

"I did not cheat you," Cédric replied. "I was simply helping out a friend."

"You're a stranger here," Dragonetto said. "This is not how business is done in Rhodes Town."

"It seems straightforward enough," Cédric said evenly. "The highest bidder wins. The man who stands down is the loser."

Dragonetto's eyes smoldered with anger. He took a step forward. "I did not stand down, as you well know."

Cédric's hand snaked toward the hilt of his sword. Then the light pressure of Paolo's hand on his arm made him pause.

"Our business here is done," the Venetian said, refusing the length of flax rope offered him by the auctioneer.

"If you don't rope her up, you'll regret it," Dragonetto snapped, turning away from them. "These captives are as slippery as eels."

Cédric had rarely been tested by so strong an urge to strike a man. He concentrated on Paolo and the slave girl, relieved at the Venetian's choice. There was no way he would lead a slave through the streets by a rope attached to her collar, and he wouldn't allow a companion to do so either. She was a human being after all, not an animal. And he felt partly responsible for her now.

"Come along, Maria," Paolo said to her. "I'll take you home to my wife."

The girl looked at him with frightened eyes, but followed close behind them. Retracing their steps past the Laughing Dove, they had to detour around the unconscious body of one of the Genoese sailors they'd seen earlier.

"He must have gotten in a fight with some other patron," Paolo remarked. "Or he was too rough on the women. That was the cause of all the noise."

A door slammed somewhere inside the Laughing Dove. Cédric saw the slave girl flinch. He slowed his pace, matching it to hers so his body would shield her from the sight of the place.

After they passed through the Sea Gate, she tripped and fell, scraping her knee badly against the cobblestones.

"Come now, get up," Paolo encouraged the girl. "You have a warm bath and a meal ahead of you, if you can just get moving again. My wife will bring you back to health, God willing."

The terror in her uncomprehending eyes drove a blade into Cédric's heart. He held out a hand to her. Ignoring it, she scrambled to her feet.

"Good luck," Cédric said, eager to escape her haunted expression. "I'm needed at the palace before I can head home."

"Now I'm even deeper in your debt," Paolo replied.

"You're a man of your word," Cédric told him. "The truth is I could not have stood by and watch her go to Dragonetto."

"When I told you not to become a target of his anger, I was serious." Paolo's face was grim. "Dragonetto has only attained power on Rhodes because the knights favor him. The influence of his Catalan father still runs strong on this island. The Catalan tongue is furious that another French grand master was elected—they want a grand master of their own kind to take the helm of the Order."

"Of course," Cédric said. "Every tongue wants that power. But how does it involve me?"

"The Catalans will seek ways to tarnish the reputation of Lord de Milly any way they can—and you are his representative. You've brought attention to yourself now," Paolo warned him. "Watch your back."

CHAPTER 34

Autumn, 1454
Rhodes, Greece

CÉDRIC HAD SPENT the better part of a fortnight preparing for the hawking and hunting trip with Lord de Milly and an assortment of guests into the forested interior of Rhodes. After much deliberation, he'd chosen the falcons for the expedition. In his initial training forays with various raptors, he had singled out several female saker falcons housed at the grand master's private villa just outside the city walls as the most reliable, accurate hunters in the Order's collection.

On the morning of the hunt, he hurried to the villa to oversee preparations for the outing.

As soon as he entered the mews, the sober look on the two under-falconers' faces set his stomach churning with dread.

"What is it?" he asked.

"Two of the sakers are dead, monsieur." The man who volunteered the information kept his head down, staring at Cédric's booted feet. He was the young Greek with light-colored eyes who spoke good French.

Without another word, Cédric went to the saker falcons. His heart sank when he saw the two birds motionless on the straw-covered floors of their hutches.

He turned back to the men. "These birds were fine when I was here two days ago. Why was I not told they were ill?"

"They were not ill," the young Greek replied. "Yesterday they fed as usual. Their eyes were bright. I swear it."

Cédric opened the hutches and removed the birds one at a time. There was no blood on their feathers, no evidence of violence on their bodies.

He regarded the under-falconers again. His foreignness was always between them, blinding him in ways he did not even understand. The men shuffled on their feet uneasily.

"A malady can strike quickly," the spokesman pointed out, a trace of defensiveness in his voice.

It was true. Cédric had seen it happen in France all too often. But the timing of these deaths couldn't be worse. He ran through the collection of other raptors in his mind. Which would most impress Lord de Milly?

"We'll bring the female saker remaining to us. And the peregrines," he said. "They've been reliable lately. Ready the traveling cages and gear. We'll use the jeweled hoods, not the everyday ones. Be sure the jesses are shining with oil."

The men nodded and turned away to do their tasks.

Cédric felt a knot of worry tighten in his chest as he went from hutch to hutch, checking on every bird. Taking one last look around the mews, he saw a dark form on the stone floor behind the hutches of the dead saker falcons. Approaching, he realized it was a rat. Well, dead rats were not uncommon. Making sure the under-falconers were not in view, he knelt and slit the rat's belly with his dagger. Strips of meat slid out, glistening in the weak light afforded by the parchment-covered window nearby. His eyes narrowed. Chopped rabbit and goat meat made up the bulk of the falcons' diet.

Carefully, he wrapped the contents of the rat's stomach in a bit of oiled canvas and slipped it into a leather sack. He placed the dead falcons in another sack, then locked everything in a small trunk. If this meat was poisoned, he would soon know for certain.

He could not shake the memory of Paolo's words.

Watch your back.

It was well past midday. After a morning of successful hawking at a lake in the Rodini Valley, Cédric accompanied the grand master and several knights and guards on an exploration of the pine forests in the surrounding hills. Lord de Milly rode up next to Cédric, his mount's muscular flanks glistening with sweat in the bright sunlight. Cédric's own horse was smaller than the grand master's, a biddable mare he found easy to maneuver in the dense forests.

Silently, Cédric gave thanks to God that the morning had gone so well. Two herons and several ducks had been bagged at the lake. From the bugling that now drifted over a hillside to the south, he presumed the hunters had brought down a deer as well.

"A fine start to the day," the grand master said, adjusting his position in the saddle. "Tarnished by the news that some of my best falcons have died. I had hoped that under your supervision the mews would be thriving. How do you explain their loss?" His tone was crisp and direct, but his eyes were sliding over the landscape, searching for movement in the trees.

Who told him about the saker falcons? Cédric's heart pounded faster. His horse felt the tension flooding his veins. She shifted beneath him, tossing her head.

"Falcons can die without warning, my lord. I've written to the Order's contacts on Crete and arranged for a dozen saker falcons to be shipped here this winter."

This wasn't entirely true. He had requested a dozen of the birds; how many would be sent and when they would arrive were mysteries. But those details were better left unsaid.

Lord de Milly fixed his gaze on Cédric. "I've had a letter from the King of Cyprus. Did you know he hunts with the aid of leopards and his falconers use camels for transport in addition to horses?"

Cédric shook his head, bracing himself for an order to come up with a menagerie to rival that of the King of Cyprus. The falcon trade was something he was well-versed in. Procuring exotic animals was something entirely different.

"The king is quite keen to welcome a French-born falconer to his court," the grand master added, tightening the leather gauntlet on one wrist. "What news do you have on that count?"

"I believe I've found the right man," Cédric told him. "French, a nobleman of honor, with an adventurous spirit. If the weather allows it, he will sail to Cyprus before the winter is over."

Lord de Milly looked at him with a trace of surprise. "That is excellent news. If it comes to pass as you describe, you'll be rewarded for your efforts."

Cédric's throat was dry as parchment. If his falconer friend Michel Pelestrine was indeed preparing to leave France for Cyprus, Cédric was still in the dark about it; no ships bearing a letter from the man had appeared since he sent off his missive to Michel in early autumn. Another worrying tidbit of information better ignored for the moment.

The grand master's mouth tightened. "But you had better keep a closer eye on the falcons in our possession. If I learn that those birds died due to neglect, I shall hold you responsible."

Cédric made a decision. He had no proof that the sakers had been poisoned, but he had to take steps to protect the other birds.

"My lord, would you permit me to make some staffing changes in the mews?" he asked. "Some of the men who work with the falcons may have . . . questionable loyalties."

The grand master looked sharply at Cédric. "Do you have proof of this?"

Cédric shook his head. "No. Not yet. But—"

Before he could finish speaking, an Aragonese knight approached, a highly ranked member of the Order whose lavish villa outside the city walls was a popular gathering spot for the island's most powerful men. His saddle was decorated with tooled leather tassels and silver filigree.

Lord de Milly waved at the man. Without taking his eyes off the knight, he said quietly, "This man's father is one of the Order's most generous donors. See that he brings down a heron or some such this afternoon when we return to the lake."

"It shall be done," Cédric promised.

The knight gestured at a hill sloping upward to the west. "There are grottoes over that hill filled with the ruins of the ancients," he said to the grand master. "Statuary and the like. And a temple with its columns still standing."

"Let us be off," Lord de Milly replied with enthusiasm. "There is much to learn from the ancients, I believe. They were truly masters of engineering." Before he turned his horse, he glanced back at Cédric. "Make the changes you see fit in the mews. I will expect to see results that please me."

The group spurred their horses toward the hill. Cédric saw an object fly off the grand master's saddle, landing in the underbrush near a dense copse of pine trees. He dismounted and led his horse toward the place where it had fallen. Crouching, he searched the ground for the item, finally spying a gleam of metal. It was a silver saddle ornament embossed with the eight-pointed cross of the Order. Something else caught his eye. In the shrubbery was a snare, cleverly concealed within a shallow depression in the ground. He rocked back on his heels.

Someone is setting traps in these woods.

Cédric rose and tucked the saddle ornament into his pannier. As he put one foot in a stirrup, he froze, feeling the weight of someone's stare. He lowered his foot to the ground again, looking around with a hand on the hilt of his sword.

A man stood in the shadow of a mature pine tree nearby. He was sinewy and slight, with a full beard. His brown eyes burned, enormous and somber, in a face twisted with worry.

"Kalimera," Cédric said.

The man did not move a muscle. *"Kalimera,"* he replied cautiously.

Cédric noticed a bulging satchel slung over the man's shoulder.

The Greek watched him with trepidation. He pulled on the satchel, trying to conceal it behind himself.

"I know you are hunting," Cédric said, the Greek words feeling clumsy on his tongue. His eyes fell to the man's neck. The same distinctive pattern of leaves and vines which he had seen on Neilos and Anteon Georgillas's clothing was embroidered on this man's tunic. The fellow must not have gotten Paolo's warning about the impending hunt. "You are a Georgillas?"

The Greek nodded. He looked even more fearful now.

"Go home," Cédric ordered him. "Now."

The man took a step backward, then paused.

"Go," Cédric repeated. He put a finger to his lips, unable to think of the Greek word for *quiet*.

The man ducked his head in a gesture of gratitude and slunk away.

Cédric mounted his horse. Those who did not adhere to the knights' rules faced severe consequences, as evidenced by the fresh blood that regularly doused the whipping post by the Kastellania after public floggings. He prayed this moment would not come back to haunt him.

Digging the heels of his boots into his horse's belly, he cantered forward, hoping that by evening the hawking party's game bags would be filled to bursting. The scents of pine and sun-baked earth filled his nostrils, but he found no peace in the beauty of the forest.

You'll be rewarded. Cédric turned the grand master's words over in his mind as he urged his horse on.

The count's promise to give him a title and land in Auvergne meant nothing if Jacques de Milly was not satisfied with Cédric's performance in Rhodes. The only thing that mattered now was making his new employer happy.

There was much to do before that day came.

CHAPTER 35

Winter, 1455
Rhodes, Greece

SOPHIE WAS NEARING the end of her pregnancy. The midwife her church friends had recommended visited every day now. Cédric had ordered the woman to do so; otherwise, Sophie would bustle around from dawn to dusk. Activity kept her mind busy, kept her from bemoaning the ponderous gait that made her waddle and sway like a crippled cow, kept her from worrying that her beauty would be stripped away entirely this time, that she would be transformed into a haggard matron. Such panicked thoughts only popped into her head during moments of leisure. Therefore, she was determined to keep moving.

She endured the enforced rest time only by bringing the children into bed with her and reading to them propped up by pillows. Papa had sent her an exquisite leather-bound book of hours created by the best illuminator in Toulouse, and the children never tired of poring over the bright colors of each page.

She was curled next to Jean-Philippe now, whispering to him from the book. He watched the track of her fingertip as she followed each inked word. Then the abrupt thud of the front door shutting startled them both.

"Letters from home!"

Cédric's cry traveled up the staircase. Sophie and Jean-Philippe locked eyes.

"Etienne?" he asked hopefully.

She pulled his small hand to her lips and kissed it. "I pray every day that we will get a letter from your brother. Perhaps today my prayers will be answered."

Cédric's footsteps pounded up the stairs. He burst into the room, trailed by Estelle. Jean-Philippe scrambled to his feet.

"Well?" Sophie asked her husband. "What news?"

He came to her side, planted a kiss on her lips, and reached for Jean-Philippe, who was now unabashedly jumping on the bed.

"Letters from your grandparents and your brother," he said to the children, swinging Jean-Philippe around in a circle, then planting him on the floor next to his sister. "And one from my friend Michel Pelestrine. He sails this way with a Genoese fleet. You'll all get to meet him, for the convoy stops in Rhodes on its way to Cyprus."

"What about the sword master?" Estelle asked. "He's only written to us once."

Sophie glanced at the oak chest that lay flush with the foot of the bed. The golden coin Philippe had given her lay inside the chest in its cotton wrapping, buried under their other possessions. She had not looked at it since they left France.

"Philippe doesn't care for letter-writing," Cédric said, tousling Jean-Philippe's hair. "He'll write when he has something important to tell us. Now. Which one first?"

His eyes gleamed with merriment. Sophie smiled, too, knowing full well what the children's answer would be.

"Etienne's!" they cried in unison.

"Are you certain?" Cédric asked doubtfully.

"Yes!" Jean-Philippe shouted, indignant.

He grinned, pulled the letters from his satchel, and handed them to Sophie. She held Etienne's letter to her nose, breathing in faint scents of leather, wax, and something mysterious she did not recognize.

Perhaps the Duchy of Savoy had its own distinctive aroma? Quickly, she cracked the seal and unfolded the letter. Her son's skill with lettering had never come close to Estelle's, but it was sturdy and serviceable. The sight of his writing made her eyes burn with tears. How she missed him. How they all did.

"Read, read!" Jean-Philippe demanded, tipping his head back for a better look. Cédric swept him up and balanced him on a hip. Estelle sat on the foot of the bed, fingers worrying the coverlet, eyes shining.

"He is well," Sophie reported. Cheers rang out from her family. "He has been welcomed into the bosom of the duke's family, he says. Each day he accompanies the duke's son to swordplay lessons, to his tutoring, to chapel." She looked up at Cédric. "Mass every day! Imagine."

"The house of Savoy must be quite devout," he observed. "It's good for him."

Sophie nodded. "I agree. Let's see, what else?" She scanned the words farther down the page. "They eat very well. Wild boar, partridge, other game. So much hunting and hawking! No wonder they have such feasts. He finishes by saying he misses all of us very much and wishes he could be with us for Christmas."

The children nodded, suddenly quiet. Jean-Philippe let out a shaky sob. "I miss Etienne," he said.

Cédric cleared his throat. "We must all be grateful and thank God in our prayers that Etienne is well and happy. Such news is nearly as good as having him with us for Christmas."

Neither of the children responded.

Sophie plucked the other letter from her lap. "Let's cheer ourselves by reading *Grand-Pére*'s letter," she said, cracking the seal.

The children looked at her expectantly, their sorrowful expressions lifting.

"Oh, I almost forgot." She glanced up at Cédric. "The servants found a dead rat in the cellar this morning, my love. We really must get a cat. Perhaps two."

His face registered surprise, and he hesitated a moment. "Yes, of course," he said slowly. "Ask your friends at church next Sunday if there are any kittens in their households."

She nodded.

"Maman!" Jean-Philippe pleaded, reaching for the letter.

"Yes, yes." She turned her attention to the sheet of linen paper covered with her father's script. "Everyone in the family is in good health," she said happily. "Grégoire has another son." She looked up again. "Cédric, we must send a gift to our new nephew on the next Hospitaller fleet sailing to France."

He nodded. "As you wish. The Order's treasurer told me no tariffs will be levied when goods we ship arrive in France. Another benefit of working for the knights."

"Really?" she asked, surprised. "From what I know of commerce, that's unlikely."

Cédric raised an eyebrow. "So you know more of the Order's inner workings than I do, my love?"

His tone was light, but there was something dismissive in it that prickled at her. Cédric himself knew very little about trade. He was the first to admit it. So why could he not concede that she, who had been steeped in commerce and industry from the time she could talk, had more expertise on the subject? She knew the answer to that question very well, of course. It was because she was a woman.

"More, more!" Jean-Philippe squirmed in Cédric's arms.

Sophie regarded the letter once more. The next line was not what she expected.

"It is a flood year," she said, frowning. "The rains were fierce all spring and summer, and they have not let up. The woad harvest is ruined in many places south of Toulouse. Papa's business is doing poorly because of it. The Christmas season will be modest for everyone. They will not even go to Albi for the feast days."

She raised her eyes to Cédric's. She could tell from his expression that he knew what she had chosen not to say. Papa usually sent them a large sum of money to make their Christmas feasts more merry and to buy clothing and gifts that they could not normally afford.

This year, there would be no such gift of gold.

CHAPTER 36

Winter, 1455
Rhodes, Greece

IT WAS the third week of January. The weather in Rhodes had grown steadily colder these past few weeks, and Cédric often woke to the soft patter of rain against the shutters.

Sophie was recovering well from childbirth, and a Genoese wet nurse had been hired. Their baby girl, Isabeau, was thriving. This was the first evening he'd felt comfortable leaving his wife and children since the baby's arrival. Now, finally, Cédric was headed for a long-awaited break from the household at his favorite tavern.

He left the house in the wool cloak he'd brought from France, its hood shielding his face from a light rain, and hurried to his destination. Meeting Paolo in the street just outside the tavern, he couldn't help throwing his arms around the Venetian.

"My congratulations, Cédric!" The genuine warmth in his friend's eyes filled Cédric with a jolt of gratitude. By God, Rhodes was not nearly as foreign when he was in the presence of this man.

"Monsieur de Montavon has a new daughter!" Paolo bellowed as soon as they were inside.

The room erupted with cheers. Men pounded Cédric on the back, offered to buy him wine, praised his wife for producing a healthy baby, even if it wasn't a boy. He was bombarded by well-wishes as the patrons cleared a path to the table of honor in a quiet alcove.

A carafe of the finest Cretan wine arrived. The two men raised their brimming cups.

"To your wife," Paolo said.

"I'll drink to that," Cédric said. "Wine for everyone, on me!" he called, feeling expansive and generous, even if his purse was lighter than it should be after all his recent expenditures in anticipation of the baby—plus the loan he'd given Paolo to help purchase the slave girl.

A roar of delight went up.

"To life!" the tavern keeper cried from behind the bar.

A trio of musicians entered the tavern and launched into a spirited Greek folk tune on their lyre, tambourine, and drum.

"What's this?" Cédric asked Paolo. He'd never seen musicians in the place before.

"A gift from Cali's family." Paolo raised his cup, beaming. "Such an occasion cannot pass without music, not in Rhodes Town."

Some of the men got up to dance, trying to outperform each other with flamboyant twirls and leaps. Shouts of laughter rang out.

Cédric and Paolo leaned close, trading stories about their travels, about France and Venice, lands that now seemed impossibly far away. As the evening wore on, Cédric reveled in the warmth of kinship he felt with Paolo. It was a feeling to savor. More than anything, it dampened the constant awareness that they were outsiders here—that, at their core, they were strangers navigating a foreign culture that could at any moment turn hostile.

All evening, he was approached by a constant stream of well-wishers, some of whom he recognized, some complete strangers. He was so used to the mixed origins of citizens in Rhodes Town now that the array of languages used in these interactions no longer seemed strange. Many of the men offered their sympathy for the fact that the baby was a girl. Though he accepted the comments politely, Cédric grew weary of the sentiment.

"If this girl proves to be the equal of her sister," he said to Paolo over the noise of the music and chatter, "I'll have no regrets on that count, I assure you. Estelle's intelligence matches that of any boy."

"I find your daughter's skill as a scribe remarkable," Paolo said. "She's quite young to have such a steady hand."

Cédric sipped from his cup. "She's helped me with my notes for some time. She has patience far beyond her years. To be honest, I'd never imagined a daughter being so useful in my work."

Paolo nodded. "Anica helps me in the studio, as a son would. I've yet to find an apprentice who is as quick to learn as she. But enough bragging about our girls. How goes your work for the knights?"

Cédric pitched his voice low. "Two saker falcons I'd trained specifically for the first outing I planned with the grand master died the day of the hunt. Neither of them had been ill. I found a dead rat near their cages and learned they were poisoned by tainted meat."

Paolo slowly put down his cup. "How can you be certain?"

"I fed the contents of their stomachs to the rodents infesting our cellar. Death followed quickly. It had to be poison. Perhaps it was the root of the monkshood plant—a creature in good health can die swiftly after ingesting it. But whatever was used, someone fed it to those raptors. I've no idea who."

Paolo balanced his elbows on the table. "It may be wise to hire new helpers to keep tabs on the others," he said. "People loyal to you—or to us."

"I have no other choice, it seems. And few friends in Rhodes. Will you recommend some names?"

Paolo gestured around the tavern. "Cali's family has plenty of candidates. Anteon Georgillas comes to mind. He speaks French, he's bright and hardworking. He travels from tavern to tavern all around the island overseeing things for the family. But his father is recovering from an illness now, and Anteon wants to stay in Rhodes Town until he is well."

"Again, I find myself in your debt." Cédric raised his cup in gratitude. "How goes your own work? Any new commissions?"

"The usual icons for Greek churches, thanks to Cali's family. Her brother is a priest in Lindos, so I've had an easy time finding work through him. And a commission came just before Christmas for a fresco in a Genoese merchant's home."

"No new commissions from knights, though?"

Paolo shook his head. "The French knights were pleased with my paintings for their chapel, though. That was good news."

"I'll find you more work," Cédric promised. "There is so much wealth in the Order; surely a bit more can trickle your way."

The wealthy Italian knight on the hunting expedition to the Rodini Valley had expressed interest in procuring more portraits of saints for the Italian tongue's chapel. Cédric had suggested Paolo for the work, but did not want to promise anything at the moment.

A shadow crossed Paolo's face. "Speaking of money, I've got half of what I owe you for Maria, and with God's good grace I shall have the other half soon. This new commission requires cinnabar and lapis lazuli pigments, which will lighten my purse considerably until I am paid." He rummaged at his waist and pulled out a small pouch bound with twine. "But take this in the meantime, with my gratitude."

"I pushed you to do it," Cédric replied, hesitating. "I hope it wasn't a mistake."

The Venetian handed the pouch over. "Maria will be a valuable addition to our household. Cali is pleased with her. Still, you've been most generous, and I hate leaving a debt unpaid."

"Pay me the rest when you can," Cédric said. "There's no hurry. "

Even as the words left his lips, his mind went to the letter from Sophie's father. He'd been counting on that annual gift to meet their own expenses, and things were getting a little tight on his salary from the knights. But as long as he could keep their household purchases limited to necessities—something his wife would never master, it seemed—they would be all right.

A long rumble of thunder sounded outside.

"Listen to that! I've yet to experience a thunderstorm on this island —" Cédric broke off when he saw a look of alarm pass over the Venetian's face.

The sound penetrated the walls of the tavern again, a deep, resonant growl. But this was no thunder, he realized with a shock. It was the bass-toned blare of the knights' alarm horns.

The door burst open. “The signal fires of Tilos and Symi have been lit!” a man shouted from the street.

In the scramble to get up, several stools crashed over. Men pushed past each other in their haste to exit the tavern.

“But what does it mean?” Cédric asked the Venetian as they donned their cloaks. “Are the infidels attacking?”

“Who knows?” Paolo’s face was ashen. “We must pray they are not.”

The lightheartedness that had buoyed Cédric’s spirits all afternoon was replaced by a crushing dread. He threw several coins on the counter for the tavern keeper as he hurried out.

“Has this happened before?” he asked Paolo, raising his voice over the shouts of passersby. He slipped and nearly fell on the slick cobblestones. Paolo reached out and steadied him.

“Every now and again. You have to remember the knights rule the seas. Their ships are even now being deployed all around the island. And there are turcopoles—mounted troops—stationed all along the coast.”

“But still the citizens panic.”

A donkey cart packed full of sobbing children clattered by, the driver whipping his terrified animal with a stout switch.

“Constantinople changed everything,” Paolo said. “Everyone believes Rhodes is next.”

At Cédric’s street, Paolo raised a hand in farewell. “Be safe, my friend. May God protect you all.”

“And you.” Cédric bent against the wind that blew in from the northwest as he covered the last few paces to his home.

He prayed that both their families would survive whatever lurked in the winter seas. Perhaps Sophie had been right. The dangers they faced in Rhodes were too great.

If that were true, he had only himself to blame.

CHAPTER 37

Winter, 1455
Rhodes, Greece

Cédric and his young companion, Anteon Georgillas, waited for the guards at the Sea Gate to wave them through. The many soldiers patrolling the city walls were evidence of heightened security in place since the signal fires of Tilos and Symi had blazed a month ago and the city erupted in panic.

Praise all the saints, the attack had been an isolated incident involving pirates and one unfortunate village on the eastern shores of the island of Kos, to the northwest of Rhodes. The Order had swiftly dispatched several war galleys in pursuit of the attackers, and they were slaughtered at sea, their captives rescued.

Ever since that night, however, people attempting to enter and exit the city were questioned and occasionally detained. In the days after the attack, Cédric had been given a black tunic embroidered with an eight-pointed cross identifying him as a servant of the Order. It eased his passage in and out of the city, but the queues formed by those who were not lucky enough to possess the mark of the Order were impossible to avoid.

Finally, it was their turn. The guards nodded at him.

"Any sign of the Genoese fleet yet?" Cédric asked them.

They shook their heads. One of them exchanged a greeting in Greek with Anteon.

"Is there anyone in Rhodes Town you don't know?" Cédric asked as they exited the gate.

Anteon grinned. "None come to mind."

As if to prove the point, he flagged down a boy whose father—a Genoese merchant Cédric recognized from church—was engrossed in conversation with a knot of other men nearby, all waiting for the fleet's arrival. The two young people began a conversation in Italian, heads bent together, their exchange punctuated by frequent bursts of laughter.

Cédric surveyed the activity around them, his body thrumming with nervous anticipation. The air resonated with the shouts of men, the clang of hammers on wood in the shipyard, the clatter of donkey hooves on the cobblestones near the warehouses abutting the harbor.

Movement down the quay caught his eye. Dragonetto's brothel was receiving its first patrons of the afternoon. It was Saturday, when coins burned in the purses of sailors everywhere, eager to be spent.

The number of brothels in Rhodes Town seemed to be matched only by the number of churches, Cédric mused. There were so many men with money to spend, so many sailors with idle time on their hands between voyages. Some brothels, like the Laughing Dove, were unabashedly public gathering spots. But others were within the city walls, cloaked as respectable-looking private homes. At night, their windows glowed with oil lamps to signal they were open for business.

He straightened his shoulders as a familiar figure emerged from the brothel doors. It was the Florentine banker whose slave woman had been taken in by the Foscolos after her beating. Cédric had seen him a few times at the Order's treasury when he retrieved his salary.

"Signor," he acknowledged the man when he drew close.

"*Monsieur le fauconnier*. What brings you to the harbor today?"

"I'm awaiting the merchant fleet," Cédric said. "And you?"

"I have a favorite there." The Florentine jerked his head toward the

Laughing Dove. "She once was mine and mine alone, but now I must share her."

"What happened?"

"The wench was carrying my child, which didn't sit well with my wife. Then she stole some bauble or other. I had to banish her from our household to keep the peace."

"What about the baby?" Cédric could barely keep the distaste from his voice. He remembered the terror on that woman's face when they had encountered her bleeding in the streets. It rankled him that once Cali Foscolo had nursed her back to health, she had been forced to return to her abusers.

The man looked at him as if he were stupid. "Of course I'll see to his education, make sure he's fed and clothed, and when the time comes, arrange a marriage for him." He glanced back at the brothel. "Obviously, I've arranged with Dragonetto to limit her visitors to men of my standing. No common sailor will touch her, I assure you."

The more this man spoke, the less respect Cédric had for him. What man would sell a woman away from her child? Slave or not, it was repugnant. Cédric followed the Florentine's gaze just in time to see a pair of men exit the brothel, heading toward the Order's private inner harbor. Even from this distance, he recognized Dragonetto by his squat, heavy-set frame, bald head, and fur-trimmed silk tunic.

"Dragonetto is well-regarded by the knights, I hear," he said. "I wonder how he has earned their favor. From what I gather, the Order believes Rhodes Town has entirely too many brothels."

The banker eyed him. "So you've been paying attention to more than the business of falconry."

"It would be foolish not to."

"His father was a wealthy Catalan with ties to the Order. Dragonetto Poulis is a bastard, though—his mother was Greek, some local girl he took for a mistress." The man pointed at a flurry of activity on the edge of the inner harbor, where slaves were busy constructing the foundation of a building. "See the weapons armory that Lord de Milly is having built? Partially funded by a low-interest loan from Dragonetto."

"The Order accepts loans from common folk?"

The Florentine smirked. “The knights don’t *accept* loans. They *demand* them. Merchants are obliged to prop up the Order with cash, but they’re rewarded for it. I’ve seen loans with interest rates as high as thirty percent. Dragonetto’s loan, on the other hand, had an interest rate less than half of that. He’s no fool. Each time a new grand master is elected, he makes sure they find reasons to favor him.”

“I see.” Cédric nodded slowly. “It all comes down to money.”

“Not just money. He helps keep order. The knights must focus on the threats that come from the sea. For the most part, they allow Dragonetto to, shall we say, keep the streets clean.”

The knights’ trumpeters sounded their horn blasts high on the hill above them, heralding the dispersal of street-sweepers through Rhodes Town.

The banker let out a short laugh. “Luckily, there is one kind of street cleaning the knights pay attention to. On Crete I hear the waste problem gets so bad they let bands of pigs roam the port towns eating the people’s filth.” He put a hand to his forehead, shading his eyes. “Ah, the merchant fleet arrives. I hope you find what you’re looking for.”

With a wave of farewell, the Florentine strode quickly toward the city walls, his cloak flapping in the wind.

In the hazy amber twilight, three merchant ships glided from the open sea toward the stone seawalls that framed Rhodes harbor. They were accompanied by four smaller war galleys, two of which flew Hospitaller banners. A moment later, Anteon appeared at Cédric’s side.

“My friend’s father sells the best honey in Rhodes,” he said, displaying a small ceramic jug.

“Ah? How much does it cost?” Cédric asked, tapping one foot impatiently against the cobblestones, arms crossed over his chest. A cloaked man emerged on the deck of one of the merchant ships as it neared the harbor. There was something in his stance that was familiar. Cédric squinted, trying to discern his features in the gathering dusk.

“I’ve no idea. Our family trades in wine more than gold,” Anteon told him. “Wine for honey, wine for sugar, wine for just about everything.”

Cédric knew this was no exaggeration. In addition to importing fine wines from Crete and other places, the Georgillas clan owned vineyards all over the island—some of them within the walls of Rhodes Town itself.

"I'm surprised any of you carry coin, then." He nodded at the bulging purse tucked into Anteon's belt. "It looks like you must use ducats for something."

Anteon grinned. "Ducats?" He rummaged in his purse and retrieved a handful of small silver coins. "Ha! I carry nothing but aspers."

The asper coins, struck with the likeness of the previous Grand Master Jean de Lastic's face, were worth a small fraction of a ducat.

"For now," Cédric replied. "You'll soon possess some ducats or florins—if all goes well with your work for the Order."

Anteon had agreed to sleep in the palace mews this week to watch over a newly arrived peregrine falcon which Cédric was training for the grand master. There was no way to keep each bird on the island from danger, but at least the most favored and valuable raptors could be afforded an extra measure of protection. Cédric could see the young man rising in the ranks of the Order, with his language skills, social connections, intelligence, and energy.

He turned to study the approaching ships, confident now he knew the man standing on the deck of the leading vessel.

"Michel!" The word tore from his lips before he realized he'd uttered it aloud.

He stuck an arm in the air and waved. When the man on the ship's deck caught sight of him, he returned the wave with both arms. Faintly, Cédric heard him calling out a greeting over the choppy waves.

He glanced at his companion, his spirits rising at the thought of a familiar face. "How would you like to sup with two French falconers tonight, Anteon?"

"As long as we go to my family's tavern. Otherwise, I won't hear the end of it."

"I wouldn't have it any other way."

Anteon frowned. "But look—your friend's ship is continuing south, along with two of the war galleys."

It was true. The lead vessel's bow was pointed south. The other merchant ships veered away from it and passed into the harbor. Michel waved again and bellowed something, but the wind smothered the sound of his voice.

"What the devil is going on?" Cédric asked, perplexed.

The clank of metal on stone startled him. The massive iron chain that formed a barrier between the harbor and the sea was being drawn up from the depths for the night. And the ship his friend sailed upon had vanished, obscured by the spinning arms of the windmills ranged along the eastern seawall.

Michel Pelestrine and his precious cargo were gone.

CHAPTER 38

Winter, 1455
Rhodes, Greece

As soon as the Genoese vessel anchored and the crew began unloading its wares, Cédric and Anteon flagged down one of the ship's officers.

"Why did the other merchant galley continue south?" Cédric asked him.

The man shook his head. "In Genoa, the captain got word that his son was killed by pirates in Famagusta. He wanted to make haste to Cyprus. I can't say I blame the fellow."

Cédric stared at him in shock, his heart heavy with sympathy. "I'm sorry to hear it. Pirates in Famagusta? I thought the Genoese had that city well under control."

A notary working for the knights had explained a bit about the history of Cyprus to him. Though the island belonged to kings of French descent, its port city of Famagusta was under Genoese rule.

"Apparently, a Basque pirate ship entered its harbor, and the captain greased the palms of the city guards with gold. His men swarmed the city, wreaking havoc everywhere. Much blood was shed."

The seaman's expression darkened. "The captain's son was killed protecting his father's warehouse near the waterfront."

Cédric took in the words with a growing sense of dismay. He had instigated Michel Pelestrine's journey. Was the young falconer now heading into danger? To his death? He imagined the merchant ship set upon by pirates, lit ablaze, the crew and passengers hacked to death and sent to a watery grave. With effort, he forced the gruesome thoughts away.

"My friend carried two valuable birds with him. Do you know if they've survived the voyage?"

The man shrugged. "I know nothing about the cargo on that ship."

He turned away to resume his duties.

After a quick supper at the Georgillas tavern—during which Cédric barely spoke, his mind a tangle of worries about the fate of his friend—he accompanied Anteon back to the palace. The sky was a flat black. Clouds blotted out the usual starlight, and a light mist softened the air. As they made their way down a quiet lane toward the Street of the Knights, Anteon tripped on a broken cobblestone.

"We're stumbling through ink here." Cédric helped the young man right himself.

The sleek form of a white cat darted across the cobblestones before them, its paws as silent as a raptor's wings piercing the dark.

"Saints above, I nearly stepped on that cat," Anteon said. "Someone forgot to light the torches on this—"

Anteon trailed off at the sound of boots scuffling against cobbles. Cédric whirled and saw two figures advancing upon them from a nearby doorway. One of them barreled into Anteon. As the young Greek tumbled to the ground with a shout, the honey jug slipped from his grasp and shattered.

The other man dove at Cédric. Spinning away from him, Cédric snatched his sword and struck at his attacker. The sword connected with the man's shoulder. He cried out and wheeled, a dagger held high in one outstretched hand. Cédric kicked him in the kneecap and he went down hard. Using the butt of his sword handle as a bludgeon, Cédric walloped him on the head. The man slumped to the cobblestones and lay unmoving.

The other attacker grappled with Anteon, who had scrambled to his feet again. Cédric darted forward to intervene just as the man shoved Anteon against the wall and took off running toward the harbor. The layers of his Greek-style tunic flowed behind him as he flew around the corner of the lane and disappeared into the night.

"He took my purse, the bastard!" Anteon swore. "And so much for my honey."

Cédric flipped the prone man over. He was still out cold. Anteon trotted down the alleyway and returned in a moment with a burning torch. He held it over their attacker, illuminating the man's face.

"I've seen this face too many times now," Cédric said with a jolt of recognition as he examined the youthful features, the mop of luxuriant black curls.

"He's hard to avoid." Anteon let out a sigh of disgust.

"Who is he?"

"Loppes Poulis. He's brother to Dragonetto. Does a lot of his dirty work for him."

"Well, blood does tell." Cédric shook his head, holding the torch closer to the wounded man's shoulder. A dark stain bloomed on the fabric of his tunic, glistening in the torchlight. "Speaking of blood, he's losing a lot of it. A dead thief can't receive his punishment. Help me take him to the hospital. It's on the way to the palace."

"Why should we give him aid?" Anteon asked. "He meant to hurt us. Maybe kill us."

"Believe me, helping him is the last thing I wish to do, but I don't want his death on my hands."

"As you wish." Anteon yanked the unconscious man's purse from his belt. "Look what we have here. Everything evens out in the end, doesn't it?"

"I'll pretend I didn't see that."

Together they carried the young Greek through the torchlit streets to the hospital, Anteon grumbling all the while about their decision to aid an enemy, especially such a heavy and unwieldy one. Finally they lugged their human cargo into the pool of torchlight at the hospital doorway. Cédric banged on the tall oak doors with his fist until a monk admitted them.

Cédric pointed out the man's shoulder wound. "He attacked us in the street just now. His companion stole my friend's purse."

The monk studied the wound for a moment, shaking his head. "Loppes again."

"Everyone but me seems to already be acquainted with the man," Cédric observed drily.

Two other monks appeared and carried the wounded man off to some interior room.

Then the monk who had opened the door turned back to Cédric. "He always lands on his feet. He'll be on the streets again before too long."

"Not if I can help it," Cédric said. "The knights will punish him and his companion, too, for what they've done."

The monk looked doubtful. "The knights have more important business to attend to."

"I work for the grand master," Cédric told him.

"I hope you find that helpful with the matter, then," the monk replied in a voice that conveyed he did not think it would make any difference.

He led them back to the front door and pulled it open for them. "Good night."

Trudging up the hill to the palace, Cédric eyed his young companion. "We should be able to get justice from the knights, regardless of what the monk thinks."

Anteon looked at him sideways. "Please don't involve the Order." He lowered his voice nearly to a whisper. "They make things worse, trust me. The honey was only a trifle, and I've got his purse. To be honest, it's heavier than mine was."

Cédric did not answer for a moment. He chewed over Anteon's words, reflecting once again on how little he understood the way things truly worked on this island. But he had placed his trust in Paolo Foscolo and his Greek wife's family and so far had seen no evidence that this had been a mistake.

So he reluctantly nodded. "I'll keep the matter to myself, then. For now."

CHAPTER 39

Winter, 1455
Rhodes, Greece

SOPHIE STOOD WITH HER FRIENDS, observing the churchgoers in their Sunday finery spilling out the doors of Santa Maria. She inhaled the cool, salt-tinged air, grateful for the chance to catch up on gossip with her friends, pleased that Estelle and Anica Foscolo were keeping Jean-Philippe entertained nearby. Isabeau was at home under the Genoese wet-nurse's care. Sophie would not bring the baby to church until she was a bit older and sturdier.

Just then two more people exited the church: an exquisitely clad young woman with skin the color of burnished bronze, and a beaming older man whose stance and dress exuded power.

"Who are they?" Sophie asked of her nearest companion, Madame Taraval.

Madame Taraval made a low humming noise in her throat. "You've not heard? He's admiral to the king of Aragón. She's Magdalena Macheda. A commoner. He got the knights to exempt her from the class of *marinaria*—and then he married the woman! He's just back from taking her to Aragón to meet his king and all the court."

Another woman leaned closer to Sophie. "Sailors paint a verse on the walls in the harbor: 'Oh, Magdalena, nothing like the saint you are, your love is like a razor, my heart is just a scar.' "

Sophie took all of this in, her eyes fixed on the couple. The young woman had an arresting face, with liquid dark eyes and plump red lips. "What are the *marinaria*?" she asked.

"Surely you've heard of them," Madame Taraval said. "They're Greeks who are bound by the knights to row their galleys. People born into the *marinaria* pass the burden on to their descendants. But Magdalena and her future offspring escaped that fate, all because the admiral fell in love with her."

"If anyone ever doubted love will make a man move mountains, those two are living proof that it's true," another woman asserted. "He's mad for her. I'm sure she's bewitched him somehow."

The admiral kept one arm possessively draped around his wife. He had spared no expense to clothe her in the finest fabrics. Her velvet gown was a deep scarlet that matched the color of her lips, and her white silk head wrap must have been edged with gold thread, for it glittered in the sunlight.

A stab of jealousy tore through Sophie. "What a lucky woman," she said, more to herself than to the others.

"In many ways," Madame Taraval replied. "Her husband has a swift armed galley ready to speed her away to Aragón should the infidels attack."

Sophie looked at the woman in surprise. "Does he?"

The woman nodded. "There are others making similar provisions. My husband has begun taking reservations on our biggest merchant ship for travelers wishing to plan ahead. We'll set sail for Provence should an attack come."

"How much does it cost to reserve a place for a family?" Sophie asked.

"One hundred gold Rhodian florins."

Sophie repressed a gasp. That was an enormous sum.

The admiral let out a shout of laughter at something his wife said. She pressed her body against his, gazing up at him with a coquettish smile.

"Magdalena carries herself as if she were a queen," another woman observed. "Look at the rings on her hands. Every finger is studded with gold and jewels."

"In her core, she'll always be a lowborn Greek," Madame Taraval said with a hint of malice. "Still, I must admit I admire her. She managed to change her fate and that of her children, too. Few women can say that. But then Rhodes can twist fortune in ways we could only dream of in the old country."

Sophie scanned the crowd for her husband. He stood talking with the Venetian near the steps of the church. She bit her lip. Paolo Foscolo was kind. He had done her husband a good turn when the painting had gone missing, had made all their lives easier by inviting Estelle into his home to learn Greek and Italian.

But what could he do to help them survive the coming siege? Ever since the attack at Kos, Jacques de Milly had increased the construction projects all over Rhodes Town. There was no escaping the constant presence of slave gangs toiling from dawn to dusk to reinforce the walls amid piles of cut stone and timber. Every hammer blow, each thud of a mallet on stone, sent a tremor of dread through her heart.

The sight of the admiral and his wife laughing in the winter sunlight gave her pause. They were not afraid. After all, they had a plan. Why couldn't she? Each time she brought up her fears, Cédric insisted the knights would protect them in the event of an attack. Perhaps she could sidestep her husband. Collect the money needed for their escape on her own. The goods from Asia and Africa that floated into the harbor on merchant fleets made many men rich. Why not a woman as well?

All those years at Papa's elbow, she had absorbed his knowledge about commerce and goods. One common theme in their household was Papa's despair at the limited access he had to Cypriot cloth and gold thread in France. Why could she not source such goods and divert them to her family, help them prosper—and put aside a stash of gold for their escape at the same time? She glanced at the *marinaria* woman in her glowing silks and glittering jewels again. Perhaps Sophie could clothe herself in such finery without waiting for her husband to do it.

Sophie bent her head toward Madame Taraval's. "I shall never tire of the silks on display in Rhodes. I've not told you that I'm the daughter of a cloth merchant in France. I learned much at his elbow about fine fabrics and dyes, especially pastel."

The woman's eyes glinted with interest. "In Avignon, there are so many wealthy folk in love with the color blue that the demand for pastel never ceases. The production time is a problem, of course. I've heard it takes nearly a year after harvesting woad to make the dye."

Sophie nodded. "Papa pays woad farmers around Toulouse to produce pastel. He's a city alderman there; he travels the region recruiting farmers and finding merchants to invest in the scheme."

Madame Taraval looked intrigued. "We've no contacts in Toulouse. I suspect my husband will want to learn more about this."

"Papa is always eager to expand his network of cloth merchants—and the goods in his inventory," Sophie went on. "He has a collection of Cypriot fabrics that he's quite proud of, but he's yet to find a reliable source for the stuff."

"You must come with me to the harbor when the Cypriot merchant fleet arrives," Madame Taraval exclaimed. "To the wholesale warehouse. The goods are absolutely exquisite. And the prices are a fraction of what you would pay at home."

Sophie gave Madame Taraval her most dazzling smile. "There's nothing I would like more."

Over her companion's shoulder, she saw Dragonetto and his associates emerging from the church. As they descended the steps, Dragonetto brushed against Cédric hard enough to jostle him. Her husband spun around and leveled a hard glare at the man, who ignored him and kept walking. Then Paolo Foscolo touched Cédric on the shoulder, murmured something in his ear. Her husband's stance relaxed a bit. As Dragonetto made his way through the crowd toward the Street of the Knights, he caught sight of Sophie.

"Good day to you, madame." His eyes roamed up and down her body as if she were an item of merchandise he was considering for purchase.

"Good day," she said in a clipped voice.

Before he could speak again, a merchant approached and engaged him about some business matter. They canted their heads together and drifted toward the Street of the Knights.

Relieved, Sophie looked away, her gaze instinctively going to Cédric. He watched Dragonetto's passage through the crowd, stone-faced. She studied her husband's hostile expression with a combination of bewilderment and uneasiness. The same cold mask of anger had gripped his face the first time Dragonetto had spoken to Sophie. At the time, it had not struck her as significant.

Yes, the man's attitude of aggressive superiority was off-putting. But surely Cédric had encountered many other men just as unpleasant. What on earth had Dragonetto done to incite Cédric's ire?

CHAPTER 40

Winter, 1455
Rhodes, Greece

AFTER SUPPER THAT EVENING, when the children were asleep, Sophie and Cédric retreated to their own chamber and sought comfort in the marriage bed. Cédric's lovemaking never failed to make her troubles vanish for a time. Ever since the alarms had sounded during the pirate attack on Kos, she had been haunted by nightmares about Cédric slaughtered by an Ottoman blade or disappearing across the sea in the hold of an infidel ship.

In bed, such horrors seemed impossible. She exulted in his warm skin against hers, knitting herself to him with abandon, thanking God her husband was alive and well. When she was in his arms, her nightmares were the stuff of shadow and ash, easily tossed aside.

Later, as they lay breathless and entwined in the dark, their heartbeats calming, their skin cooling, Sophie asked the questions that had been on her mind since church.

"Who is Dragonetto, truly? And why does he make you so furious?"

"He's a brothel owner and a moneylender with powerful friends," Cédric said. "More importantly, he's a scoundrel."

"How do you know him?"

"Dragonetto is hard to avoid in this city. The man seems to have a finger in every pie. I made the mistake of crossing him not long ago, over a business matter that seemed important at the time."

"What was that?"

"Just keep your distance from him," Cédric told her. "He has that covetous look in his eyes that strikes every man who encounters you. On him, it's especially disturbing."

"Believe me, I am in no hurry to speak to him again. And just because a man looks at me doesn't mean he desires me, Cédric."

He snorted. "Oh yes, it does. Since first we met, I've witnessed it too many times to count."

"What do you speak of?"

"Bruges. The merchants who buzzed around you like bees to honey. And that Catalan. Though his intentions were more serious."

"Well, mine weren't," she asserted. "I never encouraged him, as I've told you often enough. It was Papa and Grégoire who did."

"You had enough interest to kiss him, according to your brother."

"Not this again, Cédric! Grégoire nearly floated away on a river of spiced wine during our wedding feast. And yet you gave the words of a drunk man such weight that they've been slung around your neck all these years?"

Since they'd moved here, her husband had brought up their time in Bruges on several occasions when he was trying to impress upon her the dangers that lurked in their new city. Yes, she was unaccustomed to living amongst so many rough and foreign men—but she was no fool.

"Why would he lie?" Cédric retorted. "He saw what he saw."

Sophie let out a short laugh. "What he saw was a girl set upon by a man who took advantage of a quiet moment in the shadows. I did not invite the Catalan's embrace, did not seek his kiss. He pinned me to a wall. He forced his mouth upon mine. How many times must I tell you? I agreed to walk with him in the company of my brother. I never wanted to be left alone with him."

Cédric was silent and still next to her. "This argument is a waste of breath," he finally said.

"I couldn't agree more."

"I'm worried for your safety because I have to leave you soon to inspect the mews throughout the island," he confessed in a softer tone. "That's all."

"Why?" she asked, surprised. "Is something wrong?"

"I'm still working out arrangements with my new under-falconers," he said vaguely. "There are some improvements to be made here and there, some staffing matters I must address."

"There's something you're not telling me," she accused him. "I hear it in your voice."

He sighed. "My duties have some complications I had not foreseen, but it will all work out."

"What complications? Is this about the pirate attack?" she asked in alarm.

"How did you know about Famagusta?" he said quickly.

"I know nothing of Famagusta. I speak of the attack on Kos, after Isabeau was born."

"Ah. No, my tour of the island has nothing to do with that, *chérie.*"

"Should I be worried about Famagusta?" Her skin prickled with fear. "Cyprus is only a few days' sail from here. Whatever evil strikes that island might soon set upon us."

Cédric said nothing.

"There's a Provençal merchant offering places on a ship in case of a major attack, Cédric," she went on. "We must prepare for that day. Others are reserving their spots already."

"For how much?"

She hesitated. "One hundred florins."

"Surely, they can't be serious. We could buy a house for that."

"There may not be a place for us if we wait much longer," she retorted.

"The knights will protect us, Sophie. That is what they're trained to do. Besides, a merchant cannot hope to slip past an infidel army in those seas."

"Monsieur Taraval keeps a ship in a warehouse near a cove on the west side of the island. If there's an attack, we will go overland in a convoy and escape from there."

"Have others given them money to reserve places on the vessel?"

"Yes. There are many prepared to go at a moment's notice. Especially families who escaped Constantinople and settled here. They are ready to flee again if need be."

"Is this what you talk about with the other women after church? Escape?" he asked wryly. "I'll not hand over one hundred florins to a stranger, no matter how ingenious his plan. Besides, we have little to spare at the moment, let alone a sum that large. We were counting on your father's gift, and by no fault of his he wasn't able to send it this year."

"I may be able to raise the money for us," she said. "I've learned some valuable things about the cloth trade on this island."

"What's this? You intend to enter the world of commerce?"

Though it was dark, she knew he was smiling.

"It is no jest," Sophie insisted. "Camlet fabric, gold thread, silks—it's all available in Rhodes, much cheaper than one can find it in France. And by sending the goods on Hospitaller ships, we'll avoid tariffs on the other end in Narbonne. We pass those savings on to Papa, and he can make a profit on Cypriot cloth while still selling it for less than any other vendor. Of course, there are many things that can go wrong."

"Like what?" He sounded intrigued.

"Shipwreck, theft, piracy, any number of disasters could befall the goods between here and France," she said. "Still, there is an excellent chance we can make a large profit in a short period of time. Plenty for a place on a ship in the event of a siege, and more besides."

Sophie's confidence blossomed as she talked. She had been developing her plan during rare moments of peace these past few days. The idea was a good one, and with Cédric's help she could execute it swiftly. He must see that now, as he turned the concept over in his own mind.

And then Cédric laughed.

Sophie recoiled at the sound. Anger rose in her chest like a flame, threatening to scatter sparks with every breath she took. She resisted the urge to roll away from him and spring out of bed. Spewing rage at her husband would do nothing to advance her plans. She drew in a breath and let it out in a long, low whoosh.

Calm yourself, Sophie.

Though she sometimes could not control her wild moods, one thing had become all too apparent over the years with Cédric: fury did not get her what she wanted.

"My love," he whispered, nuzzling her neck. "You've always been as clever as you are amusing. But surely you see such a venture could never come to pass? I will never allow you to enter the cloth trade on this island."

"Why not?" she challenged him.

His voice turned sober. "There are more dangers within the walls of Rhodes Town than you know. Ruthless men lurk all around the city, Sophie. They would not hesitate to take advantage of you if given the opportunity. I cannot allow that to happen."

His lips found the hollow between her collarbones. She stilled herself, letting go of her anger, succumbing to the sweetness of his touch. It was better to lose herself in pleasure than continue this argument, especially since he would soon be absent from their bed. But she would not give up on her idea. All that stood between her family and a secure future was the gold needed for the deposit. Even without Cédric's support, she would find a way to solve this problem.

All their lives depended on it.

CHAPTER 41

Spring, 1455
Rhodes, Greece

CÉDRIC STALKED into the mews of the grand master's private villa without warning, his boots pounding the stone floor. Several of the birds fluffed their feathers, shifting on their perches at the sound.

There was just one under-falconer here today, the young Greek with the light-colored eyes. The man stood at a table under a window, preparing strips of rabbit meat to feed the birds. He turned at Cédric's approach.

"Good day, monsieur," he said in surprise. "I did not expect to see you here."

Cédric looked around the space, letting out a satisfied sigh. "The birds look well. And healthy. I'm pleased to see it. Are you always the one who feeds them?"

The man stood a little taller. "Yes, usually."

"Did you feed them the night before the sakers died?" he asked.

"I don't know." The Greek dropped his gaze. "I don't remember."

"But you usually feed them. So you probably did. Didn't you?" Cédric stepped closer, searching the man's face.

"As I said, I don't remember." The man refused to meet Cédric's eyes.

"Who gave you the poison?" Cédric asked softly. "Dragonetto? Loppes? Or some other whoreson?"

A look of fear gripped the man's face.

"How much do they pay you?" Cédric continued in a calm voice. "Whatever it is, I'll pay you more."

The Greek silently digested this, compressing his lips in a thin line. "How do I know you're to be trusted?"

Cédric rolled his eyes. "I know how things work here. They call Rhodes the island of gold." He patted his purse. "So I've adapted. My purse is heavy. I need things in the mews to go my way, and I'm willing to pay for loyalty."

The man stared at Cédric's purse. "I'll think about it. I doubt you can match what they give me. There are few who can."

Cédric's arm flashed out. He gripped the man by the shoulder, slamming him against the wall. "You devil," he breathed. "You stupid, stupid devil."

The Greek's face twisted with a combination of shock and terror. He opened his mouth to speak, but Cédric silenced him with a fierce look.

"Your work here is finished. I'll have a guard escort you back to your village, and there you'll stay. No more gifts of gold for you, I'm afraid."

The man struggled in his grasp. "Dragonetto will be angry. You'll pay with your life. Or your family's," he spat. "It's you who are stupid, not me."

Cédric hauled the man away from the wall and pushed him toward the door. When he got there, he gestured to a waiting guard, who took the under-falconer by the arm and pulled him toward a mule cart.

Cédric looked at his assistant, a cousin of Anteon's whom he'd personally trained over the winter to be a competent under-falconer.

"Ready to begin?" he asked the fellow, trying to ignore the diatribe being hurled his way by the Greek he'd just sacked. Luckily, the man had reverted to his native language for his outburst, most of which Cédric did not understand.

Anteon's cousin nodded, gathering up his belongings and approaching with a grin. "I like to work in a clean space," he said, jerking his head at the shouting man. "Thanks for clearing it out."

Cédric did not return the smile. "Remember your training. You and no one else will feed the falcons, understood? Any problems, send a messenger to me."

"You can rely on me," the young man said, his face serious now. "Good luck on your journey."

He turned and entered the mews, his slight form soon swallowed up by the shadows.

Cédric watched the mule cart roll away, his mind already on the next destination. Climbing into his horse's saddle, he signaled to the man leading the group.

"I'm ready."

He had not ridden much since arriving in Rhodes, and his body was already complaining. He swiveled around for one last look at the mews, then turned resolutely forward. He was in the company of several other newly trained under-falconers, along with four mounted soldiers known as turcopoles. They were not knights, but mercenaries and local men employed by the Order.

The riders would follow the western flank of Rhodes to its southern tip, then sweep north again past the rocky, windswept cliffs that overlooked the distant shores of Turkey. Along the way they would inspect the raptors housed in the Order's other outposts—and Cédric would root out Dragonetto's other associates using the same tactic he had just deployed.

Of course, this system relied heavily on bribery to ensure the loyalty of his new helpers. For now, he had no other choice but to use his own salary for such payments. He was reluctant to inform the grand master about the situation. Drawing attention to his troubles might darken Lord de Milly's view of him, which, after the death of the sakers, was not entirely favorable.

Spurring his horse forward, he found himself wishing for Philippe. Their ride from the commandery to the count's château in Auvergne was indelibly etched in his memory. How he missed Philippe's wisdom, his wry humor, his sword. What he wouldn't give for a trusted old friend at his side on this journey, too.

The sea breeze was their constant companion as they rode past trees bearing pale green new leaves and hillsides speckled with wildflowers. The silvery calls of songbirds accompanied them. Despite the beauty, after several hours in the saddle Cédric longed for a bath and a meal.

"Nearly there," one of the turcopoles called over his shoulder. "The barracks is just ahead, past that hill."

Cédric gave his horse a pat on the neck and its pace slowed a bit.

"Rest is not far off," he said softly.

The glowing sun melted into the western horizon, streaking the sky with amber and gold. Cédric watched its descent with awe. The sunsets here were a daily reminder of the different world he now inhabited. He missed the evening sky in France, the nearly imperceptible drift from pale blue to the soft, velvety black cloak of night.

His companions paused on the crest of a hill that looked out at sea toward the island of Tilos. Cédric joined them, trying to make out any distinguishing features on the tawny bulk of the island.

A turcopole pointed at the dark shapes of two galleys cutting swiftly through the waves from the west. One of them was clearly flying a Hospitaller banner. But the other was not. As the vessels approached, Cédric made out a pattern in red and white on the banner of the second galley.

"A Hospitaller patrol ship and . . . ?"

"A Catalan privateer," the turcopole replied. "His ships ply these waters constantly. There are more mercenary vessels than ever doing the work of the Order."

Cédric recollected the same red-and-white banner on a ship in the harbor the day he'd bought dragon's blood with Estelle.

"How many mercenaries does the Order employ these days?" he asked, charting the progress of the vessels. By God, they were swift. Small white whorls made by the unseen rowers' oars blazed and faded on the water's surface, leaving a lacy trail in their wake. The ships' sails strained at the riggings in the wind.

"Thousands," the man replied. "And three hundred knights."

"Three hundred knights," he repeated. "That's all?"

Before the winter attack on Kos, he would not have asked that question. Until that night, he'd not wavered in his belief that the knights would protect the island in case of siege. The attack on Kos had not been significant. No invaders had set foot on the shores of Rhodes itself. But the event awoke a seam of doubt in Cédric's mind, made deeper by his wife's constant harping about danger.

The turcopole looked at him. "The grand master put out the call for knights as soon as he arrived here, but there aren't many ships from the west that come in winter. Now it's spring, more knights will be arriving in a steady stream. The Western kingdoms will answer the call."

Cédric returned his gaze to Tilos again, imagining he could make out the stone signal tower on its southern shore, piled with dry branches awaiting the touch of a flame. A strong gust careened over the cliff without warning, striking him in the face.

"I pray to God you are right," he said, but his words were swallowed by the wind.

CHAPTER 42

Spring, 1455
Rhodes, Greece

Sophie and Estelle stood peering through the iron gates of the garden. Myrtle and oleander shrubs crowded the space. The remnants of a marble pillar lay half-hidden in the shadows.

"See, Maman?" Estelle pointed to a far corner, where a ruined marble statue protruded from a pile of rubble, vestiges of a draped gown still visible over a gently curving female torso. "Papa said it's one of the ancient goddesses."

"Did he?" Sophie squinted, trying to get a better look. Her mind turned to the stone head in their cellar.

"If only we had the key," said a voice behind them.

Sophie whirled to confront Madame Taraval, who had a young, humbly dressed woman in tow. This must be the couple's new slave, recently purchased by Monsieur Taraval at auction. The sight of her made Sophie annoyed all over again at Cédric for refusing to buy a slave for their own household.

"Such a pity it's not whole," Madame Taraval went on, inclining her head at the statue. "It would fetch thirty or forty florins, I wager, if it were unblemished. I've heard there's a trader in Rhodes Town who buys such things and ships them back to Italy."

Sophie looked at her in astonishment.

"I know, it sounds absurd. But the wealthy have to spend their money somehow." Madame Taraval chuckled at her own wit.

"Don't the knights own these antiquities?" Sophie asked. "Rhodes belongs to them after all."

"Officially, if such items are discovered on a person's property, one must report them to the knights immediately." Madame Taraval dropped her voice. "That's why it's better to be rid of them quietly, sell them off to someone like that trader. The Order disdains these things as unholy, but I've heard they're displayed all over the courtyard of the grand master's palace and in the gardens of the villas kept by knights outside the city walls."

"Yes, I've heard that, too," Sophie said. "How did you learn of the trader who buys such things?"

"Apparently, he is obsessed with antiquities and travels all around the region searching for them. When he is in Rhodes, he's a regular fixture at the market, especially the sugar stalls. Or so the gossips say."

Sophie resolved to seek out the man herself and determine whether there was any truth to this tale. Perhaps she could raise much of the gold for their escape with one simple transaction. Once she investigated the possibility of selling the marble head to an antiquities trader, she would broach the idea with Cédric.

"Maman," Estelle said, tugging at her elbow. "Anica will wonder where I am."

"Yes, we must be off. Good day, Madame Taraval." Sophie exchanged a nod of farewell with her friend and took her daughter's hand as they turned away.

In the entryway of the Foscolos' house, while they waited for Anica to appear, she eyed her surroundings. The floor was tiled with colorful, hand-painted squares of stone. Through a doorway, she spied paintings of what she presumed to be Greek saints adorning a wall, illuminated by oil lamps. The largest and most colorful one was of a woman with dark, lush eyes and the barest hint of a smile on her red lips. She resembled Signora Foscolo.

As soon as Sophie entertained the thought, the mistress of the house swept in, clad in a diaphanous white tunic. Gold-and-emerald earrings glittered on either side of her head. This was the first time Sophie had seen her hair uncovered. It was caught up in a gold fastener at her temples, and spilled in a dark, wavy mass down her back. Her brown eyes held warmth and welcome.

"I am glad to see you, Madame de Montavon," she said in Italian, smiling.

"Grazie," Sophie responded. Her Italian had improved quite a lot over their time here because so many of her church friends spoke it.

Anica appeared in a doorway. "Estelle!" she cried with obvious delight. The two girls embraced.

"Join us for a pressed lemon juice," Madame Foscolo invited Sophie.

The idea made Sophie's mouth water. She hesitated for only an instant, then dipped her head in a nod.

In the Foscolos' courtyard, they sat around a polished wooden table surrounded by potted fruit trees and shrubs. The sharp, pleasing scent of citrus filled Sophie's lungs.

With the girls helping, the two women conversed in French and Italian about the weather, market goods, and food prices. Signora Foscolo was composed and gentle, dispensing quiet orders to her servants. When the cups of fresh pressed lemon juice mixed with sugar arrived, they were carried on a tray by a girl who looked barely older than Estelle. She was quite attractive, Sophie thought, with almond-shaped gray eyes and hair the color of chestnuts. The skin on the back of her hands and arms was marred by what looked like healing bruises and cuts.

Signora Foscolo spoke to the girl in Greek so slow and simple that even Sophie understood most of it—an order to fetch something or someone. The girl nodded and turned away.

Sophie watched her pad quietly toward the corridor. "Estelle has told me about the girl. Where is she from?" she asked.

"We know she's from the north, for the ship she arrived on came from the Black Sea. And she is Christian," Anica put in. "She's to be our maid, Heleni's and mine."

“Heleni?” Sophie inquired.

There was a flurry of noise in the corridor, the distinct slap of leather sandals on stone. Another girl appeared in the courtyard, dressed in a white cotton tunic embroidered at the neckline with red thread. Grinning at Sophie and Estelle, she lowered her head and shoulders in a shallow bow. Her oval face, large brown eyes, and full lips hinted at the beauty she would one day become.

Catching sight of the ceramic cups on the table, Heleni bounded forward, snatched one, and downed the contents in several quick gulps. She looked at her mother slyly, a challenge in her eyes. Instead of scolding her, Signora Foscolo murmured something in Greek that may have been a reprimand but sounded like a term of endearment. Heleni slid an arm around her mother’s neck and leaned into her.

Sophie recognized the look on the woman’s face and felt a twinge of nostalgia. She had never fully appreciated being the favored child until she left her father’s home. She missed being coddled.

“Your daughter is beautiful,” she told Signora Foscolo, then turned to Estelle. “You never told me Heleni studied with you and Anica.”

Signora Foscolo shook her head. “Heleni does not like to sit and read and write.”

“I hate French,” Heleni volunteered in Italian, her tone brash and confident. “But Papa makes me practice it all the same. And he tries to make me go to the Latin church, but I won’t.”

Sophie’s eyes widened in surprise. Spoiling a child was one thing, but everyone had to attend church.

“Heleni and I go to the Greek church,” Signora Foscolo said, kissing her daughter’s forehead. “She is my little shadow.”

Not so very little, Sophie observed. She was probably about Estelle’s age, a few years younger than Anica.

Maria reappeared with a plate of cut fruit. Heleni intercepted her, demanding a portion. Without breaking her stride, the slave plucked a piece of orange from the plate and handed it to the girl.

“It was kind of Monsieur de Montavon to help my husband purchase Maria,” Signora Foscolo said, her eyes on the slave. “She’s healthy and strong now, and quite intelligent. Already learning Greek and Italian.”

Sophie regarded Signora Foscolo in confusion. She must have misunderstood the woman.

"I'm sorry?"

"Yes, there were many who thought my husband foolish to pay so much for a child in such terrible condition," Signora Foscolo went on, looking at Sophie soberly. "Your husband was the only man at the slave auction that day who thought otherwise."

Sophie turned to Estelle, her pulse quickening. "Do I understand her to say your father bought a slave?" she asked. "This slave?"

"Please, Maman," Estelle pleaded. "Don't be angry."

The slave girl stood meekly nearby, her expression blank. Sophie studied her with consternation. Who knew what she had seen in her short life—or what she had done.

A stark realization struck her in the gut. Cédric had refused to consider her plea to pay for a space on the Provençal merchant ship in the event of an attack. Yet he had blithely handed over money to a friend in order to purchase a slave—after swearing to her up and down that slavery was wrong. Her cheeks grew so hot she felt faint. What else had he concealed from her?

Sophie wanted to push back her chair, grab her daughter by the hand, and flee the house. She had the uncomfortable suspicion that behind her impassive gaze, Cali Foscolo was laughing at her. But Cédric would find it unforgivable if she made an enemy of this woman.

Forcing herself to lean forward in her chair and pick up her cup, Sophie steadied her breath. She gave a curt nod to her hostess. "Yes, signora," she said evenly. "It was very kind of him indeed."

CHAPTER 43

Spring, 1455
Rhodes, Greece

SOPHIE WOKE WITH THE DAWN. She rose and dressed in silence, then peeked into the children's bedchamber. Estelle and Jean-Philippe lay curled together in one bed. The other had recently been vacated by Christine and the wet nurse, who were both dressing in the half-light by the shuttered window. Isabeau slept in her woven basket lined with wool, which sat on a raised wooden stand pushed up against the women's bed frame. Rousing Estelle, Sophie bade her daughter get dressed.

Estelle followed her into the corridor. "Where are we going, Maman?" she asked, yawning.

"We're to meet a friend in the harbor," Sophie told her daughter as they descended the stairs. "Madame Taraval."

They wrapped up in light cloaks. The weather had been warming of late, but the wind would still cool their brows near the water. Sophie checked that her coin purse was secured tightly to her belt. Though she did not want to bring a servant along, she knew they would attract unwanted attention without one. So she ordered the younger of the two Greek women to accompany them. The servant dragged her feet as if she were headed to her own execution, mumbling something darkly to her countrywoman as they left the house.

"What did she say?" Sophie whispered to Estelle.

"I don't know." Estelle rubbed her eyes with the back of a hand.

Sophie let out an irritated sigh. "You must be my ears," she snapped, "for I am at a great disadvantage."

"Yes, Maman."

Estelle's compliance should have soothed Sophie, but instead it flooded her with guilt. Ever since she had learned of Cédric's deception, she'd been consumed with dark thoughts. It was not right to take out her anger on Estelle, but sometimes her sharp tongue got away from her.

As they neared the Sea Gate, the trumpeters blared with their signal that the street cleaners would soon disperse over the city with carts and brooms. That was one thing Sophie appreciated about this place—the knights made a great effort to keep the city clean.

The guards touched their hands to their helmets as the women passed through the gate to the harbor. A brisk wind whipped up small whitecaps in the water. The row of windmills along the eastern seawall caught Sophie's eye. Normally, she paid them no mind, but today their great wooden blades whirled at high speed. As if to drive home the message, a gust of wind tore her hood off her head. She yanked it back on and took Estelle's warm hand in hers. The servant shuffled alongside them, a black shawl tucked tightly over her own head.

The fleet of merchant vessels from Alexandria crowded the harbor, an array of hulking ships and low-slung galleys. One of the warehouses nearby had its doors flung open. A hive of activity bustled around it. Sailors pushing wheelbarrows of goods streamed from the docks to the warehouse. Merchants gathered outside the open doors and several women with servants at their elbows waited just beyond them.

Quickly, Sophie led Estelle along the quay. A seagull swooped low over their heads. She looked up into its cold yellow eyes, then wished she had not. Something about seabirds unnerved her.

Madame Taraval stood a short distance away with two servants in tow.

"Good morning, madame," Sophie said, drawing abreast of the woman. Hopefully, she would make good on her promise to help Sophie purchase cloth at wholesale prices.

"Ah, good morning to you." Madame Taraval eyed Estelle. "You've brought your young helper, I see. Such a pretty one, too."

Privately, Sophie thought her daughter's countenance too serious. It made her look unhappy, and the world wanted to see happy girls. That was something she'd learned early on.

She felt the weight of someone's gaze. When she saw an attractive man in Latin attire near the warehouse door regarding her with an air of surprise, she gave a start. He nodded slightly in greeting. He seemed to know her, though she could not think why.

A merchant at the doorway called out an announcement in Greek. The crowd surged forward.

"It's time," Madame Taraval said. "They're opening the bidding now."

Sophie tensed. "Come, Estelle," she murmured.

They stepped across the threshold of the warehouse hand in hand.

Inside, the air swirled with voices. Merchants peddled their wares, traders and customers converged at the more popular stalls. Madame Taraval plowed ahead, using her elbows to push through the crowd.

"The best cloth is this way," she tossed over her shoulder. "The Syrian merchants have the highest-quality goods, and there's one in particular I like."

Sophie admired her companion's nerve. She kept tight hold of Estelle's hand and hoped their servant hadn't been swallowed up by the throng.

The air at the back of the warehouse was warm and cloying, scented with male bodies, the oily aroma of wool, and a faint hint of cypress radiating from the storage chests lining the merchants' stalls.

Finally, they reached the merchant Madame Taraval had hoped to find. He was a bear-chested man clad in an elaborately wrapped turban and a voluminous sand-colored tunic. A wide blue sash adorned his waist. Sophie's courage ebbed a bit at the sight of him.

Madame Taraval leaned close. "He speaks French, never fear."

Sophie nodded. Next to her, Estelle looked steadily at the man, no fear on her face. A blaze of pride warmed Sophie's chest. Her daughter had a core of boldness that had only begun revealing itself since they came to Rhodes.

Her mind returned to the matter at hand. Papa had sent a letter listing the prices he paid for Cypriot cloth and gold thread. Madame Taraval said they would be able to get the goods for half of what her father was accustomed to paying. She would soon learn if the woman's claim was true.

Finally, it was their turn. At the merchant's urging, Sophie fingered a length of sky-blue camlet fabric. The combination of silk and wool was pleasingly soft against her skin.

"This was crafted with a fine reed," she said in admiration. "The density of the weave is impressive. Is it dyed with pastel?"

He shook his head. The ends of his black mustache were oiled to perfect points, as was the beard he wore.

"Indigo," he said, patting the bolt with a bronzed hand. "Forty *bras* of the finest camlet made in Cyprus, shipped from Limassol instead of Famagusta to avoid the Genoese tariffs—a savings which, of course, I shall pass along to you. There is no other source of camlet so highly regarded, I can assure you."

Her father would want this fabric, to see how the indigo dye compared to his own pastel-dyed blue fabrics. She eyed the bolt with skepticism, recalling one of Papa's favorite sayings: *When in doubt, roll it out*.

"This looks like thirty *bras* to me," she said. "Please unroll the bolt and measure it before my eyes."

The merchant puffed out his chest and muttered something in Arabic, but Sophie stood her ground until he did her bidding. Once the material had been unrolled and measured, she asked the price.

"Twelve ducats," he told her.

Madame Taraval had not exaggerated. This was less than half what Papa normally paid for a bolt of Cypriot cloth.

"I shall give you eight," she promptly countered.

His frown returned. "Twelve is already a bargain."

When she did not respond, he said, "Eleven."

She held his gaze. "Nine."

He let out a deep, dramatic sigh. "Ten, or no sale."

"I accept." Sophie's fingers closed around her purse. She had resisted the urge to spend on what Cédric called "fripperies" these past few months, ever since she'd begun saving for a place on the Taravals' ship. Digging deep into her purse, she purchased the blue camlet fabric and a half-dozen spools of gold thread.

After Madame Taraval made her purchases, the merchant wrapped their goods in cotton and secured them with twine, then bade the women farewell. Sophie found her servant standing an arm's length away and piled the parcels in her arms. Taking Estelle's hand, she kept Madame Taraval in sight, pushing against the tide of shoppers to the doorway. Then a figure in a short cape and velvet doublet blocked their way. He was the same Latin-dressed man who had caught her eye outside.

"Madame." He lowered his head and shoulders in a bow.

The faint scent of sandalwood struck her. As he raised his head, Sophie drew in a sharp breath. Of course. Somehow his name had stayed with her all these years. He was Nicolau Baldaia, the Catalan from Bruges. His face still had the same finely etched features, the short beard, the unreadable dark eyes. He was a bit broader in the chest than she remembered, his forehead furrowed by a few lines.

"I know we've met. But I can't think where," he said.

Madame Taraval and her servants had disappeared into the crowd.

Sophie tried to gather her composure. "Perhaps we have," she hedged, unwilling to admit she recalled his name.

He put a hand to his heart. "Nicolau Baldaia at your service."

Estelle squeezed her hand. "Maman, I can hardly breathe."

Sophie glanced down at her daughter. For a moment she'd forgotten Estelle was there.

"I—forgive me, sir. We must get outside."

"Of course." His gaze swept over the crowd. "Let me assist you. It is getting difficult to move in here."

He turned and strode ahead of them, sweeping people from his path as if he were thinning weak saplings in a forest. Several men turned in irritation, but when they saw his face they swallowed their protests.

He is a man of importance here.

The thought resonated in Sophie's mind as they breached the doorway and emerged on the quay into the crisp wind.

"Ah, that's better," he declared, turning to her with a smile.

She raised her head and returned his gaze, feeling light-headed.

"Yes, now I recall," he said. "Bruges—the merchant's daughter. Time has been kind to you, madame."

In his eyes, she saw admiration and raw desire. A memory of his arms around her swelled in her mind. One of her knees began to tremble. The strange combination of attraction and fear he'd inspired within her all those years ago came rushing back.

"Ah! There you are." Madame Taraval bustled toward them, waving an arm in the air.

The Catalan touched a hand to his black cap. Without another word, he wheeled and returned to the warehouse.

Sophie stared after him, feeling a little shaky.

"Maman, who was that man?" Estelle asked.

"Someone I met a long time ago," she said slowly. "In another life."

CHAPTER 44

Spring, 1455
Rhodes, Greece

WHEN THE RIDERS passed through St. Paul's Gate into Rhodes Town nearly a fortnight after they'd departed, Cédric could think of nothing but home, a bath, and bed. After the horses were stabled and he made a quick visit to the palace mews, he retrieved his correspondence from one of the grand master's secretaries. There was just one letter, and he hoped the sender was Michel Pelestrine. He knew the merchant fleet carrying his friend had made it safely to Cyprus, but what had unfolded since then was a mystery.

Dear God, may he be in good health, may the falcons thrive, and may he please the king.

But the letter he held bore the seal of the Order's commandery in Auvergne. A letter from Philippe was welcome, if unexpected. Like himself, the sword master disliked putting quill to paper. Cédric retreated to a quiet stairwell lit by a window facing the palace courtyard and broke the letter's seal.

Philippe's news was not good. He had been unwell all winter and had decided to take his retirement and live as a pensioner in the commandery. Though he did not go so far as to say he was dying, he reported that he had made a will. Cédric was to receive his sword and other personal things. Whatever money he had left at the time of his death would go to the Order.

Cédric's chest felt hollow as he folded the letter and slipped it into his satchel. A heavy feeling of sorrow and regret settled in his bones. There were very few men he trusted, and Philippe was one of them. He did not want to imagine a world without his oldest, dearest friend.

He exited the stairwell and was crossing the courtyard toward the palace doors when Anteon intercepted him.

"A mercenary ship arrived from Crete with the saker falcons you wanted," Anteon said, his eyes glowing with excitement. "Word just came from the harbor."

"That is excellent news indeed," Cédric replied. "I was on my way home, but I'd best see about those falcons first. Will you join me?"

"I'd like nothing more."

After fetching a donkey cart and driver, Cédric hurried down the Street of the Knights with Anteon at his side. They exited the city walls, heading to the knights' small inner harbor reserved for Hospitaller ships.

"What do you know of the mercenary?" he asked Anteon.

"They said the man's a Scot."

This piqued Cédric's interest. He'd never met a Scot before, though English knights were a familiar sight to him. The inn of the English tongue sat near the Church of Santa Maria, and English knights often passed by during the social hour after Mass.

They passed the construction site of the armory, where stonemasons chiseled away while an overseer dispensed orders to a group of slaves. Warehouses with their doors flung open emitted the sounds of merchants and traders discussing their goods.

The Scot's galley was low and sleek in the water. The sails were neatly stowed; the oars had been drawn back into their portholes. A cheerful whistle drifted up from the hold. The sound was soon followed by a man wearing a sweat-stained linen blouse, his tousled sandy-brown hair pulled back in a leather thong. He caught sight of Cédric and Anteon.

"Can I help you?" he called in Italian.

"I'm Cédric de Montavon, falconer to the grand master," Cédric said. "I've come for the saker falcons."

The man nodded. "Come aboard," he said, in French this time. "They're in the hold."

Cédric and Anteon clambered up the gangway. "You speak French as well as I do," Cédric told the Scot, who grinned at the comment. He was half a head taller than Cédric, with broad shoulders and long, powerful-looking limbs. "I must confess I'm surprised."

"Scots who don't learn French are at a disadvantage in life," the man replied. "At least that's what my father told me as a boy when I protested my lessons."

"He was a wise father, then. How did the falcons fare on the voyage?"

"I'll take you down to the hold and you can see for yourself."

The Scot picked up a lantern and lit their way to the back of the hold. He flung aside a canvas cloth that hung from a beam, serving as a makeshift curtain. The hooded birds sat hunched on their perches within the confines of their wooden cages. Cédric made a quick, silent count. Twelve. The promised number.

"You lost none on the journey." It was a compliment as well as an observation.

"We made haste. I was told in Crete that the grand master himself would be counting these birds on arrival. Wanted to make a good impression."

"Are you new to working for the Order?" Cédric asked.

"This is my third job for the knights out of Crete. I was in Genoa for many years before then. But I'd like to make Rhodes my base. The more I see of it, the more I realize the worth of the place."

Cédric nodded. "There are opportunities to be had here, that's certain."

"I'll have a few of my men help you get the birds ashore."

"My thanks to you," Cédric replied. "If you'll be in town a while, come to the Georgillas tavern for wine in the evenings. That's where I meet friends. They serve the best Cretan red I've found in Rhodes."

Anteon brightened at his words. "The best Cretan red *anyone* has found in Rhodes," he corrected.

"How can you be sure?" the Scot asked him. "Are you an expert on the subject of wine?"

Cédric shook his head. "His family owns the tavern."

"Ah. Lucky you," the Scot said to Anteon. "Come on, then, let's get these birds off my ship and into your care."

The emergence of the cages onto the quay attracted a group of onlookers. With the help of Anteon and the Scot, Cédric began loading the cages into the donkey cart. He barely noticed the group of three men advancing toward them from the far end of the stone quay. From the corner of his eye, he saw one of the passersby step into Anteon's path just as the young man finished loading a cage into the cart. Caught off balance as he tried to avoid the man, Anteon launched into the harbor with a splash.

Cédric leaped to the edge of the quay. "Anteon!"

Anteon's dark head broke the surface of the water.

The Scot snatched a rope off the donkey cart. He flung it at Anteon, who caught it with one hand, treading water as if he hadn't a care in the world.

Assured his helper would be safe, Cédric ran after the men who had just passed.

"You there!" he called, coming abreast of them. "You knocked my man into the water!"

The group turned as one. A shock of recognition tore through Cédric. He squared his shoulders, cursing himself for provoking a confrontation with these men.

Loppes, whom he had deposited unconscious with the monks not long ago, was flanked by Dragonetto on one side and a coldly handsome man in Latin dress on the other. Something about the third man tugged at Cédric's memory. He was not entirely unfamiliar. But why?

Cédric jerked his head at the Scot's ship, where Anteon was climbing up the rope back to the quay. "Watch your step. He could have drowned."

Dragonetto shrugged. "These quays are dangerous. He should be more careful."

Cédric looked at Loppes, who returned his gaze with sullen defiance. "How's your shoulder?" he asked with false concern.

Loppes took a step forward, reaching for his sword. "Dirty thief. I know it was you who stole my purse." Until this day, Cédric had been unaware the young man spoke French at all.

"Perhaps you should stop attacking men in dark alleyways," Cédric suggested, draping a hand over the hilt of his own sword.

Dragonetto muttered something in Greek to Loppes, whose aggressive posture relaxed.

"I'd heard the new grand master brought a falconer from France," the third man said in Catalan-accented French, studying the cages in the cart.

"A falconer who has been making unwelcome changes," Dragonetto put in sourly. "Thanks to you, good men have lost their jobs, men loyal to the Order who have done nothing wrong."

Cédric gave Dragonetto a hard stare. "Nothing wrong? Falcons don't fall from their perches dead of poison by accident."

"Now, now, Dragonetto, surely this is neither the time nor the place for such an argument," the stranger said in a smooth, conciliatory voice, looking Cédric in the eyes for the first time. "I am sure the French gentleman would agree."

Confronting the man full in the face, Cédric realized with a jolt of shock why the Catalan had struck him as familiar. In truth, he had not changed much since Bruges. He was a bit wider in the chest now, the hard angles of his jaw softened by time.

"Still an agent of the knights, are you?" Cédric asked, finding his voice.

The man nodded, waving one hand in the direction of a vessel at the far end of the harbor. The red-and-white banner hanging from its mast was the same one Cédric had seen on the ship passing by the cliffs a fortnight ago.

"As long as they'll have me," the Catalan returned with a disarming smile. He glanced at Dragonetto, who was watching the exchange with a guarded but curious expression. "I met this Frenchman years ago in Bruges," he explained. "We both vied for the attention of a merchant's daughter. Lovely thing, as I recall. I always wondered what happened to her." As he said it, his gaze settled on Cédric again, and his mouth quirked in a knowing little smile. "It was quite a shock—a pleasant one, I might add—to see her at the warehouses here in Rhodes Town. How she has preserved her beauty so well is a mystery. But women do have their secrets, don't they?"

"She is my wife." Cédric's chest swelled with a wave of possessiveness. "Be careful with your words, sir."

The Catalan raised an eyebrow. "Is that so? Lucky man." He glanced at Dragonetto. "I'm between wives at the moment. Widower. But that's not a problem when I'm in Rhodes. Dragonetto puts aside his best whores for me as soon as he sees my galley enter the harbor."

Dragonetto's expression hardened. "I hardly have a choice, do I?"

"Let's keep things civil, shall we?" The Catalan peered over Cédric's shoulder at Anteon, who was again loading the falcons into the cart. "All seems well. But for the young fellow's trouble, take this." He pulled a ducat from his coin purse and tossed it at Cédric. "And our apologies, too."

Cédric caught the coin and closed his fist around it, a sick feeling burning in his stomach.

CHAPTER 45

Spring, 1455
Rhodes, Greece

CÉDRIC SET OUT for home in the dusk of early evening. A current of uneasiness snaked through him as he relived snippets of the conversation he'd just had on the harbor. Thinking back over the day, he realized he'd not eaten anything since dawn. In truth, his spirit felt as empty as his stomach. The exertions of his journey, Philippe's letter, and the events of the afternoon weighed heavily on him. He longed for a quiet night.

Sophie met him at the door. The hard set of her jaw and the flinty look in her eyes told him the peaceful evening he'd hoped for would likely not unfold.

Jean-Philippe bounded past her and leaped into his arms.

"Papa! Papa!" he cried, his sturdy little arms circling Cédric's neck.

He smiled, kissed the top of his son's head. To his relief, Sophie smiled too. Estelle appeared behind her, the baby in her arms. For a moment, seeing his family safe and well, Cédric forgot his worries.

The children were a rapt audience at supper, drinking in his tales of the journey around the island, the forts and castles he had visited, the coastal villages clustered around sparkling little bays. Finally, Christine shooed them away to bed. Sophie poured him another cup of Cretan red. He savored the slow burn of the wine traveling down his throat.

"Did you do much marketing during my absence?" he asked. "I heard some cloth merchants sailed in from Cyprus."

She looked at him sharply. "Yes, I suppose they did. I purchased what was needed at the market, that's all."

"Any other news to share with me?" he asked, giving her another chance to explain herself.

"No," she said. "Except for the story of my own humiliation at the hands of Cali Foscolo."

"What does that mean?"

She shifted in her seat. "I know about the slave girl you helped purchase, Cédric. Signora Foscolo told me."

He groaned. "I should have known you two would put your heads together one day."

"Why did you not tell me?" Sophie demanded. "After chastising me for wanting a slave of our own? You made me look the fool. What else do you conceal from me, Husband?"

The bitterness in her voice stung. He put down his cup, leaned forward. "I'm not the only one who conceals things."

"What do you mean?" she asked, clearly taken aback.

"I speak of the Catalan."

Sophie's eyes widened ever so slightly. "Not this again, Cédric—"

"I am not referring to the tale your brother told at our wedding feast," Cédric interrupted. "The Catalan is here, in Rhodes Town, and you saw him. When you were purchasing cloth at the harbor against my wishes."

"Who told you that?" she asked, the color rising in her cheeks.

"He did. I encountered him myself today. He wasted no time telling me he had seen you."

"I was invited to the cloth sale at the warehouse by Madame Taraval, and you were gone. I thought to take advantage of an opportunity that might not come again."

Cédric cocked his head to one side. "I turn your own question back to you, Sophie. What else do you conceal from me, Wife?"

She looked down at her hands. "Forgive me. I should not have done what I did without your permission. I would have told you I'd seen him, but—"

"But then you would have had to tell me the truth about your outing," he finished.

Her flush deepened.

"There can be no more deceptions between us." He rubbed his forehead, closed his eyes. "Let's speak of other things."

"Cédric," Sophie said quietly after a moment. "Something else is troubling you. What is it?"

He opened his eyes. The tenderness in her expression was genuine.

When he hesitated, she took his hand. "If there are to be no more deceptions between us, let us begin now."

Her gentle tone softened his resolve to keep his worries out of their home. One by one, the words spilled out. About Philippe's troubling letter. About the saker falcons that had abruptly perished the day of the hawking expedition with Lord de Milly, about the poison, his decision to root out Dragonetto's associates and replace them with men trusted by Paolo Foscolo.

"So much of this comes down to the Foscolos," he admitted. "Cali Foscolo's family, the Georgillas clan, seem to know everyone on this island. I've put all my faith in them. I pray to God every day that I haven't made a terrible mistake."

"So far the Venetian has been true to his word," Sophie said. "Although I still don't trust his wife. I could have sworn she was laughing at me when she told me what you'd done."

"I never deliberately set out to humiliate you, Sophie. I helped Paolo buy the girl to keep her from falling into Dragonetto's hands. I don't agree with slavery, and my view on that will not change. But once I was at the slave market—" He broke off, shaking his head. "That girl is Estelle's age. She looked so frightened. I could not stand by and do nothing, knowing Dragonetto would make her a whore. The truth is, I embarrassed him in front of the city's most respected men, and now I'm paying for it."

She knelt at his side. "I'm glad you did what you did, Cédric. But I fear Dragonetto will not leave you alone, especially now that you've sacked men who were his associates."

"I had little choice in the matter," he replied. "I am responsible for the falcons on this island. If they suffer, I'll lose my position, and the grand master will send us back to France. In that case, there will be no title, no lands waiting for us. The count won't want me in his employ any longer either." He looked at her bleakly, his voice low and rough. "Everything I've worked for will be lost."

CHAPTER 46

Spring, 1455
Rhodes, Greece

On his way to the palace a few days later, Cédric caught sight of Paolo Foscolo near the Church of Santa Maria. The Venetian had a look of barely suppressed delight on his face.

"Paolo, how goes it?" he called out.

"Ah, Cédric!" Paolo embraced him heartily. "It is a good day. No, an excellent day."

"Tell me of your good fortune," Cédric said. "Come, let's stand in the shade of Santa Maria."

They walked to the church and stood with their backs to its arched doorway. The morning sun edged up over the city walls behind them, illuminating the half-built walls of the new hospital across the bustling square. The faint scent of the sea drifted in on a breeze.

"First, the best news. My wife is with child."

Cédric clapped his friend on the back. "Saints be praised, man! That is welcome news indeed."

The Venetian glanced behind them at the church doors and crossed himself. "With God's grace, all will be well." His chest caved a little as he spoke the words.

"All you can do is pray, in the end," Cédric said softly.

Paolo straightened his shoulders. "I have something else to share. I come from the Inn of the Italians. I've two commissions from them. One is for portraits of saints in their private chapel and the other is a fresco for the walls of a home owned by a wealthy knight. Is this all thanks to you?"

Cédric smiled. "Could be."

Paolo extracted a small canvas sack bound with twine from his purse. "Thanks to the Italians, I can repay you in full now for helping me buy Maria."

Cédric took the sack with a smile of thanks. The money couldn't have come at a better time. In addition to his new habit of bribing under-falconers, he had a long-overdue gift to buy.

A pair of English knights in black Hospitaller tunics strolled by, heads bent together in quiet conversation.

"For my part, I've some unwelcome news," he confided.

"What is it?"

"A Catalan who once was a rival for my wife's affections has appeared in Rhodes Town. A close associate of Dragonetto's, apparently."

"Which Catalan?" Paolo asked.

"Nicolau Baldaia."

"He is not just Dragonetto's associate," Paolo replied with a shake of his head. "He's his half brother."

"What?" Cédric stared at the Venetian, astonished.

"Their father was a mercenary favored by the Order. He plied the waters between here and Cyprus pirating Muslim ships. He grew wealthy from his plunder, provided a steady stream of slaves for the Order's sugar plantations both here and in Cyprus. Nicolau Baldaia's mother was a Catalan, like her husband. But Dragonetto and Loppes Poulis, they're sons of a Greek woman, their father's mistress. Dragonetto brings business to the harbor with his brothels and his money-lending, and Baldaia is a valuable connection to Cyprus and the

Catalan merchant network. Between them, they've brought much revenue to the knights."

A group of German pilgrims passed within an arm's length of them, led by a monk.

Paolo lowered his voice. "In the end, that's all the Order cares about—keeping gold flowing into their coffers so they can prepare for war. The knights are in no hurry to jeopardize the relationship."

The sounds of the city dwindled in Cédric's consciousness as he absorbed his friend's words. Finally, he composed himself enough to speak again. "What else do you know of Nicolau Baldaia?"

"He inherited lands on Cyprus when his father died. He's got a brood of children there and he's buried at least one wife. But he's got too much of the adventurer in his blood. He's still pirating, bringing in captives and goods for the knights when it suits him. And he helps his brothers, too. I heard the brothel by the harbor has four new young infidel girls who were smuggled into Rhodes by Baldaia and traded for Christian girls destined for an Arab's harem."

A wave of repulsion struck Cédric. "How can the knights tolerate that?"

"Because Baldaia gave the Order what they'd asked him for as well: several valuable captives, Arab merchants who will be traded for Christian soldiers and a knight being held in Alexandria."

Cédric's breath grew shallow. There were so many layers of favoritism, obligation, and scheming in this strange new world that he could scarcely keep them all straight in his mind.

"I must play the game or be played, is that it?"

Paolo looked at him with sympathy. "I understand. I felt the same as you when I realized how things work here. My lot is easier than yours because of my wife and her family."

The sun moved higher in the sky, dousing their shady refuge with golden light.

"Everything is temporary," Paolo went on, squinting against the brightness. "Even with the favor of the knights and the interventions of Nicolau Baldaia, Dragonetto has proven adept at gathering enemies with each passing year. He cannot avoid the inevitable."

"Which is?" A bead of sweat trickled down Cédric's spine.

"His downfall, of course. One day his protectors will turn on him or fortune will cast a dark shadow upon him. Until then, stay one step ahead of the scoundrel. And use all the means at your disposal to do so. Including me."

CHAPTER 47

Spring, 1455
Rhodes, Greece

SOPHIE AND ESTELLE, trailed by Christine, followed the buzzing crowd to the live animal stalls. The morning sun was hot on Sophie's face. She shaded her eyes, trying to catch a glimpse of whatever it was that so intrigued everyone in the marketplace.

"Good morning, madame," a male voice said beside her.

She looked into the eyes of Nicolau Baldaia. Her gut tightened at the sight of him. The man's stare was so intimate, so penetrating. As if he had seen her undressed. She tugged her silk cloak around herself to hide the flush on her neck.

"Good morning," she replied.

Estelle regarded the Catalan in silence.

"An Arab trader has come from Africa with parrots and monkeys," he told them. "I saw him bringing his cargo up from the harbor this morning."

"What are parrots?" Estelle asked.

"Such beautiful birds, child. Their feathers are blue as the sea; their eyes golden as the sun. But what's more marvelous about them is they can be trained to talk. They're quite intelligent."

"Maman!" Estelle exclaimed. "Can we see them?"

Sophie could not help smiling. "Of course, *ma chérie*." Estelle was normally so reserved; it was a pleasure to see her lively and bubbly, the way Sophie remembered herself at that age. "If we can get past all those people."

"Leave it to me," said the Catalan. Grumbling men and protesting boys peeled away from him as he forced his way through the crowd.

Sophie cast a glance at Christine. "Wait here," she told her maid.

She took hold of her daughter's hand and followed in the Catalan's wake.

Several wooden cages stood on display in the stall, each bearing a bird or small monkey. The parrots gazed out at the crowd with unblinking pale eyes, their colorful feathers gleaming. The monkeys were smaller and more delicate creatures than Sophie had imagined. They had long, curling tails and glittering dark eyes. Some of them trembled in the corners of their cages, terrified.

The merchant was tall and thin, garbed in an intricately wrapped turban and a tunic of loose cream-colored fabric. A red silk sash gleamed at his waist.

A man shouted at him in Genoese, "Can they talk, the birds?"

The merchant held out both hands, gesturing for silence. The crowd quieted. He went to the cage holding the largest parrot. Bending close to it, he uttered a few words of Arabic. The bird cocked its head, contemplating him. Then it responded in kind.

Gasps and murmurs broke out all around them.

"What did he say to it, Señor Baldaia?" Sophie asked the Catalan.

"He wished it good day, and the bird returned the greeting."

Estelle's mouth fell open. The Catalan glanced down at her, grinning. People jostled and lunged, craning for a view, and Sophie began to feel uncomfortably trapped. She tightened her grip on Estelle, fearing they would be separated.

"I think it's time we gave up our place here," Señor Baldaia told Sophie. "There's only so much I can do to hold them off, I'm afraid."

"Of course. You've been very kind. Come, Estelle."

Sophie and Estelle followed him away from the crowd, back to Christine. Estelle took Christine's hands in hers, regaling her with descriptions of the creatures.

"I must thank you," Sophie told the Catalan. "Twice now you have parted crowds for us."

He chuckled. "Your daughter is brave. Not all girls would have wanted to push through that pack of rogues."

"I am sure they're not all rogues," Sophie said, more relaxed now that they were out of the crush.

"Believe me, scoundrels come out on market day, though they walk among us as if they were citizens of utmost respect."

"Is that so? Point out a rogue or a scoundrel to me. It's only proper for a respectable woman to know if she's in danger."

"I remember that wit and boldness, madame. Your liveliness was one of the things I admired about you in Bruges. Along with your beauty, of course. Those eyes . . . the exact color of the sea."

His compliments held her spellbound for a moment. Then she grew nervous, drawing her cloak around her throat once more. Thank all the saints Cédric was at work. The last thing she needed was for her husband to encounter her in the presence of this man.

"We are off to the sugar stalls, sir. Thank you for your assistance," she said coolly.

He dipped his chin, an infuriating look of amusement on his face. "I was heading there myself when I caught sight of you. I'll accompany you there."

They walked side by side, Estelle and Christine a few paces behind them.

"Sugar is so costly in France; I was surprised when I found how cheap it is to obtain here," she said, trying to steer the conversation onto safe ground again.

"Yes," he agreed. "The knights' plantations on Rhodes and Cyprus make it more plentiful. One of my galleys is headed to Barcelona now with a hold full of sugar and spices."

"How many ships do you have, Señor Baldaia?"

"My family possesses a dozen ships. They ply the seas as commerce dictates. I've one about to embark to Alexandria; another to Sicily, in the Kingdom of Naples."

"What goods does your ship carry to Sicily?"

"The usual precious items that the wealthy desire. Fine fabrics, sugar, spices." He glanced around as if to ensure no prying ears were listening. "And the odd antiquity."

She gave a start. "Oh?"

He nodded. "There's a growing demand for ancient statues in Italy, the kind that litter the soil all over Rhodes."

"A friend told me there's a trader here who buys such things," she said, "someone who frequents the sugar stalls."

"Ah?" The Catalan looked surprised. "I've not heard that."

She nodded. "I was hoping to acquaint myself with the man today, in fact."

"Is that so?" He slowed his pace. "Why?"

"I found something that might be of interest to him."

Now the Catalan's expression was taut and focused. "What that might be?"

Sophie hesitated. What was the harm of telling him? She glanced over her shoulder. Estelle and Christine were hanging back, examining a display of painted ceramic tableware.

"I found something in our cellar, perhaps part of a statue, made of marble," she confided.

"And you thought to sell it to him?" the Catalan prompted, his deep voice honeyed with encouragement.

"Yes. You see, families can reserve spots on merchant ships as a means of escape in case the island is attacked." She paused. "But it's so costly."

His expression grew sympathetic. "It's difficult to assure one's safety in a place like this. Madame, I would be honored to reserve a place for you and your family on one of my ships, should there ever be a need. At no cost to you."

"Truly?" Relief struck her with palpable force.

"I vow it. Now erase that worry from your mind," he instructed. "Tell me more about this statue you found in your cellar."

"It's not exactly a statue," she began. "More a portion of one. A woman's head—"

A young man rushed up to the Catalan, talking in rapid Greek. This was the man who had threatened the slave woman near the apothecary, Sophie was sure of it.

Señor Baldaia spoke to him dismissively in Catalan, gesturing in Sophie's direction. The young man ignored her. His switched to Catalan, his words coming faster and louder. Sophie flinched and took a step backward.

The Catalan's expression turned to stone. He flung out an arm and slapped the young man hard across the face, unleashing a string of harsh Greek upon him. The man staggered, a hand to his cheek, and cast a look of pure, savage hatred at Señor Baldaia. Then he spun around and ran toward the harbor.

"Forgive me, but I'm afraid you just witnessed a rogue in action." The tight smile on the Catalan's face did nothing to disguise his anger. "I hope he did not frighten you. He's really quite harmless."

Sophie swallowed. A tiny current of fear swirled around her midsection, pushing up against her throat. She glanced her daughter's way. Luckily, Estelle and Christine had missed the altercation completely. They were still distracted by the ceramic merchant's goods.

"I've tarried too long in the marketplace, sir. It was kind of you to help us. Come, Estelle!" Her voice sounded thin and high-pitched.

"Good day to you, madame," he replied, the warmth returning to his eyes. "No doubt we will meet again before too long."

CHAPTER 48

Spring, 1455
Rhodes, Greece

CÉDRIC STOOD for a moment in the sunshine outside the goldsmith's shop, the earrings safe in his purse. He could not repress a smile, imagining Sophie's face when he unveiled his gift.

Though she dropped hints constantly about the jewelry she coveted, he had only purchased her a few such items since they wed, and none since they left France. Here in Rhodes, Sophie was a fish out of water. Yes, she had deceived him by going to the warehouses and entering the fabric trade against his wishes. But her intentions were good. Above all else, she wanted to keep their family safe. He could not fault her for that—in fact, he loved her all the more for it.

He set off for home with a spring in his step. When he rounded a corner and came to the intersection with the market street, he noticed it was more packed with shoppers than usual. Following a group of Latin merchants toward the crowds, he caught bits of their conversation. Something about birds. Not falcons, though. Parrots. Intrigued, he quickened his pace.

A crowd was gathered in front of a stall in the live animal section of the market. Conscious of the valuables he carried, he stayed at the edge of the throng and caught a glimpse of the Arab trader inside the stall. It would require some muscle to get closer. He decided not to chance it. He would unburden himself of the jewelry and then return.

He hurried past the fabric stalls and soap sellers, then entered a side lane that led directly to the sugar stalls. Halfway through the lane, the sight confronting him just ahead made him stop in his tracks.

His wife stood not twenty paces away, talking to a man. Cédric's eyes narrowed when he realized her companion was none other than Nicolau Baldaia. Estelle and the servant Christine stood nearby.

"Hey ho!" shouted a Greek man behind him leading a train of three donkeys. "Watch yourself!"

Startled, Cédric wedged himself against the lane's stone wall to let the animals pass. When the view opened up again, the Catalan had vanished.

"Sophie!" he called, striding forward. "Why were you—"

"Papa!" Estelle cried, her eyes lighting up at the sight of him. "We saw monkeys and parrots! Did you know parrots can talk?"

He could not tear his gaze from Sophie's face. She looked intensely uncomfortable.

"I've heard rumors," he said to his daughter.

"It's true." Estelle slipped her hand in his, unaware of the tension vibrating between her parents. "I heard one talk. It said 'Good day to you' in Arabic. That's what the man told us."

"What man?"

"Maman's friend."

"Not my friend," Sophie snapped. "An acquaintance."

"Estelle, you and Christine walk ahead of us," Cédric told his daughter, keeping his voice light. "There is something I need to discuss with Maman."

He saw a look of panic cross his wife's face. "Walk with me, Sophie," he said. "And explain."

"There is nothing to explain," she replied, her voice wavering a bit. "The Catalan offered to part the crowd so Estelle could see the animals. I accepted his help."

"You were nowhere near the animals just now," Cédric pointed out. "You were deep in conversation with him."

"I cannot pretend I don't remember the man," she protested. "As you reminded me the other night. He made quite an impression on us both all those years ago."

"Sophie, you must keep away from him. He's not what he seems."

"He's a wealthy and respected agent of the knights," she said. "He told me just now that he trades in silks, spices, fabrics . . . and antiquities."

"Antiquities?"

"Statues of ancient gods. There is a trade in such things," she said, sounding defensive now. "I've looked into the matter, Cédric."

"Why?" He stopped, looked her full in the face.

She would not meet his gaze.

He pulled her into the shade of an arched doorway and gripped her by the shoulders. "Tell me truthfully, by God. Is there something between you and the Catalan or not?"

"There is nothing between us and never has been," she said flatly, her blue eyes hard as glass. "How many times must I say it? We discussed a matter of business, in truth."

"Now this I must hear." His voice was gritty with barely suppressed anger.

"I wanted to reserve a place for us on the Taravals' ship in the event of an attack by the infidels," she said. "But you would not hear of it. Too costly, you told me. So I thought to raise the money myself by purchasing Cypriot fabrics and shipping them to France for my father to sell. But again you said no; you forbade me to get involved with the cloth trade."

"For good reason. As you'll recall."

She raised her chin. "When I learned those ancient statues have value, I decided to look into selling ours."

"Ours? We found the head in a house that we live in—a house owned by the Order. That does not make it ours."

"If the Italian knight's family wanted it, they would have taken it away when he died."

"From what I heard, he did not have family," Cédric said. "He was the last of his line."

"No one else wants it, then," she asserted. "We can do with it as we wish."

Cédric relaxed his grip on his wife, regarding her with a mixture of exasperation and pride. "Is this what you and your friends talk about after church, then?"

Sophie's expression grew defiant. "We discuss things other than the latest French fashions, servants, the prices of oranges and figs. What mother wouldn't, in our predicament? If I do nothing to prepare for the worst, I'll go mad, Cédric."

"And *this* is what you spoke of with the Catalan?"

She nodded. "I'd gone to the market to find a trader of antiquities, someone Madame Taraval told me about. But then I came across Señor Baldaia, and the subject arose."

"Truly?" Cédric could not keep the disbelief from his voice.

"Why won't you believe he means nothing to me?" Sophie asked impatiently. "Yes, he caught my eye when I was young and foolish. He flattered me with his attentions. I've told you the truth of what happened in Bruges. There is nothing to be jealous of!"

"I am not jealous, Sophie. I am protective. He is more dangerous than you know. And powerful in ways I'm only beginning to understand. For the sake of our family, avoid Nicolau Baldaia. Will you obey me in this matter, or must I confine you to our home to keep you safe?"

She bit her lip. The muscles in her jaw tightened. "I will turn the other way if I see the Catalan in the streets. You have my word."

Cédric wanted to believe his wife, but there was a gulf of doubt between them now. He remembered what he carried from the goldsmith's shop. He would tuck away the earrings for a while. Only when this crushing weight of uncertainty lifted from his chest would he offer Sophie the gift.

CHAPTER 49

Spring, 1455
Rhodes, Greece

AFTER A PERIOD of heavy spring rains, Neilos Georgillas took a turn for the worse and Anteon returned home to help care for him. Cédric slept in the mews several nights in a row during his absence, training the saker falcons from Crete. He spent his days alternating between the palace and the villa, guiding the new under-falconers as they developed the essential skills of handling the birds.

One morning he awoke to sunshine and news that he was wanted by the grand master.

Quickly, he splashed water on his face and rubbed the sleep from his eyes. He hurried behind the servant who had been called to fetch him, anxiety tightening around his midsection. Upstairs, they bypassed the great receiving hall, continuing down the corridor to a doorway flanked by a pair of guards. Inside the wood-paneled chamber, Lord de Milly sat at a desk piled high with documents and scrolls. A fire crackled in the hearth, giving off the aromatic scent of cypress. Two assistants hovered nearby.

"Come forward," the grand master commanded, flapping an arm in Cédric's direction.

Cédric approached and bowed. "My lord."

"I've received a letter from the King of Cyprus," Lord de Milly said, his features set in a smooth, unfathomable mask.

Cédric tensed. "Yes, my lord?"

"He is pleased with your friend Michel Pelestrine, and with the gyrfalcons. Very pleased." The grand master's expression softened into a smile. "Well done."

Cédric returned the smile, overcome with relief. "I am happy to hear it, my lord. That is good news indeed."

The grand master leaned forward in his chair and tossed a small coin purse to Cédric, who caught it in one hand.

"A portion for your troubles."

Cédric dipped his chin. "This is quite unexpected, my lord. Thank you."

"How goes it with our falcons?" Lord de Milly asked abruptly.

Cédric hesitated. He had kept quiet about the poisoning, about Dragonetto's bribery of various under-falconers, for the simple reason that he had not yet gained Lord de Milly's trust. This moment was not the time to spill out accusations about a man with a long and valued history with the Order, however. So he chose his words carefully.

"I have made necessary structural improvements to all the mews of Rhodes, and I've installed new under-falconers in some locations. In doing so, I discovered men with dubious intent have been allowed close contact with the birds. While I believe I've resolved the problem for now, it would be helpful if your guards could follow the lead of my trusted under-falconers concerning who is allowed contact with the birds."

Lord de Milly studied him in silence for a moment. Then he turned to an assistant. "Instruct the servants that no one is to enter the mews either here, at my villa, or anywhere else on the island without permission of Monsieur de Montavon's men. A list of these under-falconers' names will be distributed to all the outposts on the island. Anyone disobeying this order will be flogged." He drummed his fingers on the armrest of his chair, his eyes boring into Cédric's. "Dubious intent, you say. Well, it does not take long to discover the tangle of allegiances on this island. I would rather not hear the details, as you seem to have the matter under control. Do you have anything else you wish to discuss?"

Cédric nearly shook his head, then caught himself. If ever there was a moment to ask a favor, this was it.

"My lord, if you are ever in need of more paintings, perhaps portraits of saints for your private chapel, I know a Venetian-trained artist who specializes in such things."

The grand master's eyes widened a bit. "I must admit that's the last thing I imagined you would say." There was a trace of amusement in his voice.

Emboldened, Cédric added, "He paints frescoes as well. For the walls of private villas, my lord."

"Is that so? I will keep it in mind." Lord de Milly leaned back in his chair, a quizzical cast to his expression. "You seem a loyal friend."

"Only to those who've earned my trust, and as I've only recently arrived, there are not many here who qualify," Cédric admitted.

"I know the sentiment all too well. My thanks again for recommending Michel Pelestrine. King Jean and I have strengthened our bond thanks to your falconer friend."

Cédric stood and bowed to him. "I am glad to be of service, my lord."

Descending the Street of the Knights, he floated effortlessly through the warm spring air, reliving the conversation he'd just had with his employer. It felt as if a leaden shroud had been lifted from his shoulders. The sun blazed down from a cloudless blue sky, gilding the stone of the surrounding buildings with gold. Skirting along the city walls, he glanced through the open doors of the Sea Gate at the harbor below as he passed. A merchant ship carrying the banner of Genoa sailed in from the open sea, followed by a smaller galley.

Rhodes is truly a marvel, he thought as he hurried along. *Yes, it feels foreign and strange and will never be home. But it has its advantages and pleasures nonetheless.*

It was incredible how different he felt about his situation here, all because of one conversation with one man. But that man might as well be king. And Cédric was now firmly in Lord de Milly's favor. He imagined Sophie's face brightening at his news. Perhaps this heavy purse would assuage her worries about getting off the island in the event of disaster, would end her obsession with ways to find more income. There was nothing he wanted more than to repair the erosion of trust between them. Now, surely, it could be done.

Cédric turned up the lane leading to his home. An old Greek woman who often sat watching the world go by from her second-floor window stared down at him from her usual position.

"Kalimera!" he shouted, touching his cap.

For the first several months in Rhodes, he had cheerily called out a greeting every time their eyes met. And every time, the old woman scowled at the sight of him. Lately, perhaps due to the advent of spring, she'd begun gracing him with a brittle nod. Today, for the first time, she returned his greeting.

"Kalimera," she replied, the corners of her mouth lifting in a faint smile.

He could not help breaking out in an enormous grin. She gasped and averted her eyes as if he had just done something unacceptably grotesque.

Cédric chuckled. But the woman never heard his laughter. For at that moment, the deep, ominous horn blast of the city's gate guards blared. The old woman screamed in terror and slammed her shutter closed.

The city awoke with a start, as if it had been set aflame. Animals bleated and barked, women wailed, children shrieked. Men poured out of their houses, shouting above the noise. And underneath it all, the alarm horns thundered.

Cédric ran the last twenty paces home and fell upon his door, bursting through it with a wild surge of energy.

"Sophie? Where are you? Where are the children?" He ran from room to room, searching for his family, then bounded up the stairs two at a time.

"Cédric?" His wife stood framed in the doorway to their bedchamber, her eyes bright with tears. "War has come, hasn't it?"

"Sophie, Sophie," he soothed, coming to her side. "The knights will protect us, whatever comes this way. Perhaps it is only a warning, like last time. Remember, even if a single pirate ship attacks an outlying island, the signal fires are lit."

"Estelle is not here," his wife said shakily. "She went to the Foscolos'."

A stab of dread tingled in his gut. "I'll fetch her, don't worry."

Sophie took his hands. "Quickly, my love. Then return to us straightaway."

"Where is the key to the oak chest?" he asked.

She unhooked the iron keyring from her belt and handed it over. Going to the oak chest by their bed, he unlocked it. Carefully, he slipped the coin purse from Jacques de Milly beneath a fine velvet doublet and matching cap he reserved for special occasions. Then he retrieved another item and locked the chest again.

"Here." He thrust the jangling keys and a dagger in a fine leather scabbard out to his wife.

She eyed the dagger with distrust. "What is that?"

"The weapon you asked me to buy not long after we arrived here, after you saw Signora Foscolo wield one."

She gingerly took the scabbard in her hands. "I've no idea how to use the thing."

The alarm horns blared again. The blasts penetrated Cédric's flesh, resonating in his bones.

"You'll find a way if you need to. And let's pray you never will." He gathered her in his arms and kissed her. "Go to the children now, keep them calm, and I'll be back soon," he promised. "Bar the doors when I leave. And make sure the gate to the alleyway is latched."

"Cédric!" Panic gripped his wife's face. "What if you don't return? What will I do?"

"You cannot think that way, Sophie," he said, turning toward the stairs. "You must be strong for our children, whatever happens."

CHAPTER 50

Spring, 1455
Rhodes, Greece

CÉDRIC RACED THROUGH THE STREETS, dodging frantic citizens, abandoned donkey carts, toppled baskets, and broken crockery. Assuming the marketplace was complete chaos, he stuck to side alleys and narrow lanes.

His lungs burned from exertion as he rounded the last corner to the street where the Foscolo home lay, near the eastern walls of the city. Advancing on the front door, he raised an arm to bang on it. But it opened just as he did so. Paolo Foscolo rushed outside, strapping on his sword.

"Paolo," Cédric panted. "I've come for Estelle."

"She is not here," Paolo said, shutting the door behind him. "She and Anica went to the bathhouse with Cali and the slave Maria."

"What?" Cédric stared at him in apprehension.

"Come with me." Paolo descended the front steps into the street. "They were going to buy sugar and fruit on the way home. Cali mentioned the apothecary near the Gate of the Virgin, too."

Cédric's heart sank. The apothecary was close to the Foscolo home; the bathhouse was a short distance from the Sea Gate. The sugar stalls sat at the west end of the marketplace near the tower of St. George, up a steep hill.

"They could be anywhere, in other words." Cédric matched the Venetian's pace as he broke into a trot. "Where to first?"

"The apothecary, quick as we can," Paolo said.

The two men ran through the churning streets, horn blasts roiling overhead.

Groups of knights in their red battle tunics now marched through the streets, heading to their stations. The metallic clank of their armor, spears, and swords added to the cacophony of sounds. A young boy rushing to get out of the way of a group of Italian knights fell nearby and wailed in terror as the men bore down on him. Paolo darted forward and swept the boy up, admonishing him to run home using side streets.

The apothecary's door was barred, its windows shuttered. Cédric and Paolo exchanged a grim nod.

Setting into motion again, they pushed through crowds dispersing from the marketplace, where the mayhem Cédric had hoped to avoid was in full swing. A peacock screeched mournfully on the steps of a marble building behind the silk sellers' stalls, where men were frantically dismantling their displays. A donkey laden with grape-laden panniers cantered by. Groups of panicked shoppers darted about, screaming for missing companions.

Please, God, let Estelle be where she's supposed to be. At Signora Foscolo's side.

They penetrated farther into the panicked masses, shouting the girls' names, Paolo yelling for his wife. Cédric's throat grew sore. He followed his friend up the market street, raking his eyes over each female figure he passed. But no one looked familiar here. Estelle's steady gaze, her golden-brown eyes, never lit upon his own.

"Estelle! Estelle!" he roared.

They would never find their daughters this way, he thought in despair. They were succumbing to panic, just like all the other citizens of Rhodes.

"The sugar sellers are gone," Paolo said, bending over and resting his hands on his thighs as he caught his breath. "See?"

It was true. The vendors had dismantled their stalls and disappeared. The only sign of the men and their wares were a few haphazard mounds of white sugar on the ground, which two lean yellow dogs were devouring.

"The fruit vendors?" Cédric shaded his eyes as he looked around for their stalls.

One man was still loading apricots and plums into his donkey's panniers nearby, but there were no other purveyors of fruit to be seen.

"They've all left," Paolo said. "Cali and the girls must have taken a side street back to our house to avoid the crowds. That's what I've always counseled her to do in the event of something like this."

Regret swept over Cédric. Why did he not have a plan for his own family? He had been so dismissive of Sophie's fears. He had been consumed with finding favor with the Order, so eager to show his worth to the grand master that he'd neglected the safety of Sophie and their children.

What a fool you've been, he silently berated himself.

They were nearing the Sea Gate now. Just ahead rattled a procession of mule carts, their canvas covers flapping open to reveal women garbed in brightly colored silk cloaks.

"What's this?" Cédric asked.

"Those brothels by the shipyards and docks." Paolo's voice rasped from the strain of so much shouting. "They bring the prostitutes inside the walls when the alarm sounds."

One of the women stood. "Signor Foscolo!" she screamed, pointing at the Sea Gate.

"Who is she?" Cédric asked. "I've seen her before."

"The slave my wife helped all those months ago," Paolo said, his brow furrowing in a frown.

The woman continued shouting in Greek, gesticulating as if a madness had struck her, until her companions pulled the canvas flap shut and her voice was silenced.

"What did she say?" Cédric asked.

Paolo looked at him with an expression of bewilderment mixed with dread.

"To the harbor," he said, a thread of desperation audible in his voice. "Quickly."

CHAPTER 51

Spring, 1455
Rhodes, Greece

CLOSE ON HIS friend's heels, Cédric followed Paolo north, past the hospital under construction, past the barred doors of the Church of Santa Maria and the Inn of the English, all the way to the St. Paul Gate at the mouth of the knights' inner harbor. It was a beehive of activity, with knights and soldiers streaming in and out of the city walls, readying war galleys for launch and bringing supplies into the city from the outlying shipyard.

They slipped out unnoticed in the clamor, making for the long row of warehouses that faced the harbor. But before they got there, Paolo stopped in front of the Laughing Dove. Its doors were locked, its windows shuttered. Not a flicker of life seemed left within its walls.

"Why do you hesitate?" Cédric asked his friend, feeling impatient. They were wasting valuable time.

Paolo looked at him. "That woman said the girls are here."

"What?" Incredulity and nausea struck Cédric at the same time.

He eyed the wooden doors. They would be difficult to breach, but not impossible.

"Come on, then," he said grimly, starting toward the doorway.

Paolo put up a hand, then touched a finger to his lips. "Let's go around to the back."

They crept through the narrow alley on the north side of the building to a courtyard accessed through a gate. As they neared the gate, Cédric heard a muffled conversation. Then a high-pitched scream rose up. His heart twisted. Was that Estelle?

A man's voice rang out, imperious and cold. "To my brother's galley, and be quick."

Cédric clenched his jaw, struggled to keep his breath even. It was Dragonetto who had spoken, he was nearly certain. He drew his sword. From the corner of his eye, he saw Paolo do the same. They crept forward in silence. The wooden gate slowly creaked open. Cédric and Paolo retreated a few paces toward the harbor and pressed themselves into the shade of a nearby doorway.

A servant leading a canvas-covered donkey cart emerged, heading toward the harbor. The gate swung shut behind it. Cédric saw the canvas covering tremble with movement, heard ragged sobs coming from beneath the folds. As the cart rolled by, Cédric slid alongside it. He leaped up, yanked the driver off his seat, and dumped him face-down onto the ground. The man moaned and struggled to right himself, but Cédric silenced him with a blow to the back of the head and rolled his body against the wall.

Paolo was already pulling back the cart's canvas cover, revealing the three girls huddled together, their hands bound with rope, their heads covered with flax sacks. Together they pulled the sacks from the girls' heads and cut their bonds.

"Shhh. You'll be safe now," Cédric assured the girls quietly, leaning into the cart to kiss Estelle.

"Papa," she said shakily, clinging to his hand. "I'm so frightened."

Next to her, the slave Maria wept silently, her head bowed. Paolo reached out and touched Anica's cheek, which was a vivid scarlet. He whispered a few words of comfort, then straightened and glanced at Cédric.

"You take them back home, and I'll make sure Dragonetto and his men don't follow," Cédric told him in a low voice.

Paolo took the donkey's reins and hastened down the alleyway. Cédric waited until they rounded the corner, then headed in the opposite direction and slipped through the gate into the courtyard behind the brothel. Dragonetto and the burly manservant who seemed to accompany him everywhere stood under a trellis covered with grapevines. Another donkey cart waited nearby, loaded with trunks and satchels. Clearly, they were planning to make their escape from the island, perhaps on the same ship the girls had been destined for.

Dragonetto looked at Cédric, his heavy-lidded eyes wide with astonishment. "What do you mean by this? Brandishing your blade on my property—" Then comprehension dawned on his face and his expression hardened. "The girls. What have you done with them?"

He made a cutting gesture at his manservant, who drew his sword. A man emerged from the back door of the brothel, a small trunk in his arms. At a signal from Dragonetto, he dropped the trunk and rushed out the gate in pursuit of the cart.

"You devil!" Cédric squared his shoulders, facing Dragonetto. His chest felt ready to explode with fury. "You took our daughters captive. You meant to make them whores."

"Kill him!" Dragonetto screamed at his servant.

The man lumbered in Cédric's direction, brandishing his sword.

Cédric parried, twisting away lightly with each thrust of the servant's blade. This man had little more than size on his side. He wielded his sword like a hammer, and his reflexes were woefully slow. Cédric lunged, feinted, lunged again. Anger and confusion registered on his opponent's face. Then Cédric felt rather than saw Dragonetto sidling up behind him. He sprang to one side, evading the silent thrust of Dragonetto's sword.

He edged toward the gate, now facing two opponents. "I should have known you were a backstabber," he growled at Dragonetto, evading another flailing thrust of the giant manservant's blade. The man's forward momentum carried him off balance and he fell heavily onto one knee. Cédric brought down the hilt of his sword hard on his head. He bellowed in pain and sank to the ground, unconscious.

Cédric turned on Dragonetto. His palms were slick with sweat. "You dirty whoreson," he said. "You'll rot in hell for what you've done."

"I've done nothing. It was my brother," Dragonetto cried, gripping his sword with two hands as he backed toward the steps leading to the brothel. "He forced me to do it."

"Liar." Another wave of anger crashed against Cédric's ribs. He raised his sword and advanced on Dragonetto. He had only taken two steps when pain flared in his right shoulder. A cry escaped his lips when he realized a small, wickedly sharp dagger was buried in his flesh.

Staggering backward, he saw Loppes standing framed in an upstairs window of the brothel, one arm outstretched. His eyes were wild with triumph, his unkempt curls rising in a dark halo around his head. Cédric pulled the dagger from his shoulder, gasping at the pain that accompanied the motion.

"Looks like your sword arm has lost its power." Dragonetto's voice regained its hard edge. "I'll rip out your bowels, you worm."

Cédric glanced up at the window again. Loppes had disappeared from view. He would likely burst through the back doorway in a moment with another weapon.

Dragonetto darted forward and executed a savage thrust, aiming at Cédric's chest. But Cédric dropped into a crouch and the blade found only air. Spinning on his heel with surprising grace, Dragonetto brought his sword down hard on Cédric's. The blade clattered onto the cobblestones and skittered away. Dragonetto smiled thinly, shifting his weight from side to side.

"You've lost your sword," he said. "What a pity."

The sun was behind Dragonetto. Cédric squinted against the light, the pain in his shoulder screaming through him. He struggled to regain his footing. Dragonetto raised his sword, this time aiming a great blow at Cédric's neck. With a desperate cry, Cédric dove to the ground, rolled toward his opponent, and thrust Loppes's dagger up into the man's gut with his left hand.

Dragonetto's eyes registered surprise. He dropped his sword and crumpled to the ground, groaning in anguish. Loppes burst from the brothel's back door wielding a sword, but faltered at the sight of his fallen brother leaking blood on the cobblestones.

"Murderer!" he cried at Cédric. "You'll die like the pig-spawn you are for your crime, Frenchman."

"And what about your brother's crimes? Taking girls captive, selling them overseas." Cédric scrambled for his fallen sword. Snatching it up, he danced out of the man's way, ignoring the pain in his wounded shoulder.

Loppes let out a bitter laugh. "You fool. This wasn't Dragonetto's scheme. It was Nicolau's. As they all are."

The sound of booted feet pounded in the alleyway, accompanied by the clank of helmets and swords. Soldiers.

"Murder!" Loppes shrieked, the cords on his neck standing out with the strain. "Murder!"

Two soldiers appeared in the open gateway. "What's this?" one of them asked in Genoese, breathing hard.

"He killed my brother!" Loppes cried, pointing first at Cédric, then Dragonetto.

The soldiers crowded into the courtyard to get a better look at Dragonetto's lifeless body. Then the immobile servant's great bulk gave them pause.

"Did you kill him, too?" a soldier asked Cédric.

"See my shoulder?" Cédric's sleeve was dark with blood. He swallowed, pushing down a tide of bile. "I was defending myself against these rogues."

Another voice shouted for the soldiers in the alleyway, ordering them to follow. The soldiers looked at each another.

"We'll be whipped if we don't go now," one of them said.

"You'll be flogged if you don't arrest this man," Loppes shouted, closing the space between himself and the soldiers. "He's a murderer, I tell you."

"We're under attack. There will be no justice for anyone if we're all dead." Cédric turned on the soldiers, planting his feet wide. "Do your duty to the Order and to the citizens of Rhodes. Go protect the island!"

They moved toward the gate, but before they reached it, Loppes squeezed past them and vanished into the alley, heading toward the water. The soldiers and Cédric followed in the young man's footsteps. When they emerged at the end of the alley, the soldiers made for a waiting warship.

Cédric saw a flash of white beyond them. Loppes's mop of thick black curls bobbed up and down as he ran along the inner harbor toward a low-slung galley with a red-and-white banner.

"God's teeth," he swore, recognizing the ship as Nicolau Baldaia's. "That little bastard."

He turned his back on the harbor and made for the city walls. All he could think of now was Estelle. Did Paolo get the girls safely home? Had that servant of Dragonetto's intercepted them?

Mercenaries poured out from St. Paul's Gate, marching toward waiting Hospitaller vessels. Cédric stepped aside to let them pass. The sun's glare pounded him mercilessly. He swayed, his knees trembling. A passing commander in a red tunic and a polished metal helmet paused, eyeing Cédric's injured shoulder, then the eight-pointed white cross on his tunic.

"A servant of the Order, are you?"

"Yes." Cédric felt a strange buzzing in his ears. The man's voice seemed to come from a great distance. "Where are these ships off to, commander?"

"Archangelos is burning," the commander said. "The islands of Kos, Symi, and Nisyros are under attack. Get yourself to the hospital, then take shelter."

When Cédric hesitated, the commander turned to a soldier. "Accompany this man to the hospital, quickly!"

The soldier hurried him toward the city. When they reached St. Paul's Gate, a group of knights pressed through it, blocking their entry.

Cédric glanced over his shoulder at the harbor. What he saw made his chest tighten with anger once more. The galley with the red-and-white banner was cutting through the water, angling toward the open sea. And on the deck stood both Nicolau Baldaia and his half-brother Loppes, their faces turned toward the north.

"Those devils," he said through gritted teeth. "So much for avenging their brother's death. Saving their own skins is more like it."

A break came in the crowd and the soldier tugged him through the city gates. They stopped in front of the hospital.

"Get that wound cared for," the young man said, his face glistening with sweat.

Cédric nodded at the soldier. “Good luck to you, and may God protect you.”

The soldier wheeled and made for the gates. As soon as he was out of sight, Cédric ran toward the center of the city.

CHAPTER 52

Spring, 1455
Rhodes, Greece

CÉDRIC POUNDED on the door of the Foscolo home with the butt of his sword. A frightened voice asked his identity. Hoarsely, he spoke his name. The door swung open.

"Where is my daughter?" he demanded of the servant who opened it.

She gestured to him to come inside and barred the door. Quickly, she led him into the kitchens. The three girls sat on a bench by the hearth, Paolo kneeling before them.

"Estelle!" Joy flooded Cédric at the sight of his daughter.

"Papa!" She leaped into his arms, sobbing.

His own eyes burned with tears as he gathered her to him. "Are you hurt?" he asked, pulling back to examine her.

Estelle shook her head. "We were on our way back from the women's bathhouse when the horn blasts started. It seemed like everyone in the world was screaming." She took a long, shaky breath. "We lost sight of Signora Foscolo in the crowd. Then a woman helped us. She told us to follow her, that she would get us to safety. But that was a lie." Estelle fought back a sob.

Anica spoke up. "The woman took us around a corner, where a covered cart was waiting with a mule and driver. Two men helped her push us into the cart."

"It happened so fast, Papa. We could not stop them." Estelle sounded apologetic, as if she imagined three young girls could fend off a group of adults bent on evil. "But Anica tried to fight back. Then that woman struck her across the face."

"She was a procurer," Paolo said, his face taut with anger. "Working for Dragonetto."

Of course, Cédric thought with disgust. Women too old to prostitute themselves anymore, working for the brothel owners, luring vulnerable girls off the street with false promises of security, lodging, and food.

Outside the muffled clamor of people and animals continued to swirl. There was a distinct crash, then a shout. A jolt of urgency struck him.

"Come, Estelle. I've got to get you back to Maman."

Paolo walked them to the door.

"How are your wife and younger daughter?" Cédric asked. "Are they unhurt?"

"Heleni did not accompany the others to the bathhouse. But my wife—" he shook his head soberly. "She was separated from the girls when the alarm went up. She tried to avoid being hit by a donkey running loose in the streets, then slipped and fell."

Cédric looked at Paolo with concern. "Dear God."

"She says she is well," his friend said. "We will pray the baby is, too."

"God protect you all, my friend."

Cédric gripped Estelle's hand all the way home. To lose her again would be unforgivable. The streets had emptied a bit, but voices raised in panic and fear seeped from the blank façades of the homes they passed. The shouts of knights and soldiers from their positions on the city walls struck his gut like hammer blows.

When they entered their home, Sophie flung her arms around Estelle, weeping. "My girl! My girl! Praise all the saints, you're home."

Jean-Philippe scrambled into Cédric's arms. Pain flared in his wounded shoulder. Christine stood with the baby on her hip, eyes swollen with crying. The other servants hovered nearby, sobbing and praying aloud.

Finally, Cédric could stand it no more. "Quiet!" he shouted.

A fearful silence fell. Sophie pressed her lips against Estelle's forehead, gathering her composure. Jean-Philippe stared at him wide-eyed. The servants waited warily for his next words.

"Rhodes Town is safe for now. The knights are defending the places under attack. We don't know what will come next. But we can do our best to prepare. We may have to move to a different location, so we must be ready. Sophie and Christine, pack satchels with enough clothes and supplies for several days." He turned to the Greek maids and continued in rapid French, "Prepare your things in case we must leave. And fill two baskets with food."

They stared at him blankly.

Your mind is addled, man, he scolded himself. *Gather your wits.* But the world unraveling outside was making a mess of his own thoughts.

Estelle quickly translated what he'd said into Greek. The women scurried for the kitchen.

Jean-Philippe buried his face in Cédric's shoulder, sobbing anew. A groan escaped Cédric's lips.

Sophie reached out, touched his bloody shirt. "You're injured!"

"I'll be fine," he assured her. "It's not bad."

She turned to Christine. "Take Estelle and Jean-Philippe upstairs. I'll be there soon."

He watched his offspring ascend the staircase. All accounted for, he thought with relief. Sophie came to his side and examined his shoulder, her face tight with worry.

"I'll get you wine, and *manus Christi* for that wound. How did it happen?"

"It can wait," he said. "Go help the others pack."

"Then what?" she demanded. "Sit in the house until they come to slit our throats?"

"Rhodes Town is not under attack," he reminded her.

"Then why must we pack?"

"We will take shelter in the palace if necessary."

Sophie's lips trembled. "You have not given enough thought to our future, our safety. Well, I have. I told you nothing of this before, because you would not have listened. We've a place for us assured on Nicolau Baldaia's ship. You must find him. Perhaps he's in the harbor now, readying his vessel."

Cédric's anger surged back. "No, Sophie. We will not be traveling with Nicolau Baldaia."

"He gave me his word," she insisted. "I know you don't care for the man, but—"

"His word means nothing."

She frowned. "Why would you say such a thing? He is a respected man of trade, an agent of the knights."

"The man just fled the harbor for the open sea. He meant to carry Estelle on that voyage. Our girl was taken captive today, along with Anica and the slave Maria. It was Baldaia's plan to trade them to an Arab for Muslim girls, all destined to be concubines. He trades in the flesh of children, Sophie. He's an evil man."

Sophie paled. She reached for the wall, steadying herself on it. "But how could this happen?"

"Even the most charming gentleman is capable of the foulest deeds," Cédric said flatly. "Now go get Estelle settled. She needs your arms around her."

In his study, he surveyed the books and papers in his cabinet. His eyes fell on the book by Agapitos Kassianos. Anica Foscolo had translated nearly the entire thing for him, and Estelle had written the French version in her lovely script. He shook his head, thinking back to his first days in Rhodes Town. The troubles of his workplace seemed insignificant now, but they had loomed so large in his mind since his arrival here that he had neglected to plan for his family's safety. Had it truly been just this morning that the Grand Master tossed him the bag of gold coins? It seemed an age ago.

A short time later, Sophie walked in carrying a tray laden with a jug of wine, a cup, clean linens, and a small pot of *manus Christi.*

She set down the tray on his desk and helped him remove his doublet and ruined shirt. Wetting a square of linen with wine, she gently patted his wound with it. He winced and balled his hands into fists.

"Here." She poured him a cup of wine. "This will take the sting away."

He nodded gratefully, raising the cup to his lips, and drank. Sophie opened the pot of salve.

"Estelle is shaken to the core." She applied a thin layer of *manus Christi* to his injury with her fingers. "I had to dose her with milk of the poppy to stop her trembling. And your wound—it was made with a blade. Who did this to you?"

Cédric drained his cup. He was too exhausted to tell her anything but the whole truth. "Dragonetto and Loppes Poulis took the girls to a brothel," he said bluntly. "Paolo and I went after them, and I ended up with this." He gestured to his shoulder.

Sophie rocked back on her heels. "But how did they—" She fell silent a moment, her mind working. "I still don't understand. Estelle was with the Foscolos. Did those men break into their home?"

"No. They were near the women's bathhouse."

"What?" she asked incredulously. "Cali Foscolo took our daughter to the bathhouse without our permission, and the girls were attacked in broad daylight? Taken captive from under her nose? I've never trusted that woman, and now I know why."

"I gave Estelle permission to go to the baths with Signora Foscolo, Sophie. If anyone is to blame for her presence there, it's me." He shifted his weight in his seat, grimacing.

Her eyes flicked to his shoulder again. A fresh trickle of blood leaked down his arm. "This wound is so deep," she said with concern, unrolling a length of linen and wiping the blood away. "Thank God you came out of the fight alive."

"There was a price," he said. "I had to kill a man in the process. Let's hope I won't be punished for it."

"Punished? But you were defending Estelle's honor," she protested. "Her very life."

"I killed Dragonetto," he said hollowly. "He was useful to the knights and half-brother to Nicolau Baldaia. His death will not go unnoticed."

She dropped the linen, her face ashen now.

"I believe Jacques de Milly is a just man," he went on. "And for the moment, thanks to Michel Pelestrine and the King of Cyprus, I'm in the grand master's favor. That gives me hope."

Exhaustion rolled over him like a thunderhead, rumbling in his ears, pinning him to the earth.

She took his hand in hers, raised it to her lips. "You and Estelle are safe now. Nothing else matters."

CHAPTER 53

Spring, 1455
Rhodes, Greece

THE SKY BRIGHTENED ALMOST IMPERCEPTIBLY, sending pale light through the slats in the shutters. Cédric watched the coming of the new day with eyes burning from exhaustion. Did a massive army congregate on the shores of Turkey under the rising sun? Did war galleys cut swiftly through the deep blue waves, their curved prows pointing at Rhodes?

These questions had plagued him all night. As the hours dragged by, he and Sophie had stared into the dark, hands entwined, awaiting the dawn. Until they knew the city was truly secure, he doubted either of them would find refuge in sleep.

He slipped out of bed and dressed, cursing under his breath at the sudden sharp pain in his shoulder when he went to pull on his shirt and doublet.

"Where are you going?" Sophie's voice was rough with exhaustion.

"To the palace for news."

"Be careful," was all she said.

The streets were oddly quiet. When he turned up the Street of the

Knights, small groups of knights in their red war tunics hurried past him to their posts. Men who had spent the night standing sentry on the city walls trudged back to their residences in the other direction, fatigue evident in their slumped shoulders and glazed expressions.

At the palace gates, a tense crowd of townsfolk stood in the morning sunlight, awaiting news from the knights. Paolo Foscolo was among them.

"Paolo," he called. "How is Signora Foscolo?"

His friend turned, the weariness on his face mirroring Cédric's own. "She's kept to our bed, more for the baby's sake than her own. All seems to be well."

"Praise all the saints." Cédric clapped Paolo on the shoulder. "And Anica?"

"She is more concerned about Estelle and Maria than about herself." Paolo's expression brightened a little. "My daughter has a stout heart."

"What news of Archangelos?"

"It was sacked. Many lost their lives. Homes and crops were burned, and who knows how many taken captive."

"Why did the Turks choose to attack now?" Cédric asked.

A man nearby spoke up, a notary from Provence who often supped at the Georgillas tavern. "The Order's fleet is thin at the moment. The knights launched several galleys a few days ago, heading south. It was as if the Turkish admiral knew they had gone and chose his moment to attack sensing a weakness in the knights' defenses." The man glanced at the palace doors. "I came to Rhodes two years ago to seek my fortune. Island of gold, people called it. So many opportunities, they said. So much wealth." He looked at Cédric and Paolo with eyes full of resignation. "I arrived just before the siege of Constantinople. If I'd known what was in store, I never would have left Avignon."

A sharp stab of remorse stung Cédric's gut. He had known about Constantinople, and still he'd brought his family here. All to chase a title and property back in Auvergne. Yet had he any choice in the matter? There was a pretense of autonomy; the count had given him a day to mull the idea over—but they both knew Cédric would accept the challenge.

The great palace doors creaked open and a stream of men emerged. Knots of citizens picked off the knights and their associates like carrion, lobbing questions at them as they moved forward.

Cédric caught sight of a familiar face. He said to Paolo, "There's the young French knight who helped me find work for you."

"Sir!" he said, catching the man's eye. "What news from the Order?"

The man bent his neck to get a better look at Paolo. "Who's this?"

"My friend Signor Foscolo, the painter," Cédric said.

Paolo nodded at the knight. "I'm grateful to you, sir," he said. "I have you to thank, it seems, for my commissions of late."

"It's nothing." A wry smile took hold of the young man's face. "I've done more hawking in the past year than I had in the previous ten."

"What news of the attacks?" Cédric prompted him again.

"The Turks retreated over the sea. Our navy overpowered them and rescued the captives on their vessels."

"How can the knights be sure the attacks are over?" Paolo asked.

"We've gotten word that the Sultan of Turkey is gathering his forces for an attack on Belgrade. As long as his eye is fixed upon the north, we'll be spared the full might of his army. The garrison of Archangelos will be rebuilt, as will the fortress on the island of Symi and outposts on other islands. A war galley and forty knights will permanently guard the port of Rhodes."

"That's all?" Cédric asked in alarm. "Surely hundreds more knights are needed."

The Frenchman dropped his voice. "Fewer and fewer respond each time the call goes out for knights to defend Rhodes."

"So the port will be safer, but what about the city itself?" Paolo asked.

"The eastern walls near the Jewish quarter will be rebuilt. They're the thinnest, the point of weakness. Lord de Milly said houses along the wall will be demolished to make way for the project."

Paolo looked alarmed. The Foscolo home sat near the Jewish quarter, in the shadow of the city walls. It would likely be among the structures targeted for demolition.

"And there was some discussion of a brothel owner who was

murdered on the day of the attacks," the knight said off-handedly as they reached the Inn of the French. He paused by the door. "No one knows who committed the crime, but the dead man was known to have many enemies."

Cédric felt as if a great bellows had sucked the air from his lungs. He did not dare look Paolo's way.

"Good day to you both," the knight said. Looking at Cédric, he added, "Keep me in mind if you're organizing a day of hawking sometime soon."

"I will," Cédric said.

The knight climbed the steps to the inn. Cédric accompanied Paolo down the Street of the Knights, heading for home. Before he returned to work at the palace, Sophie needed to know they were safe. At the base of the hill they turned toward the Sea Gate. The sun streamed over the city walls with force now, signaling a warm day ahead.

"As soon as I share these tidings with my family, I'll request an audience with the grand master," he said to Paolo, keeping his voice low. "The longer I wait to explain about Dragonetto, the more it looks like I'm trying to conceal something."

"Going to the knights might complicate things. Perhaps you should simply let the matter rest," Paolo replied. "As the knight said, Dragonetto had many enemies. There are few who grieve his absence. His associates will run his businesses now, and that is all the knights care about."

Cédric chewed over his friend's words. "I'm not sure what the best course of action is. I do know Lord de Milly deserves to hear the truth." He sighed. "My thoughts have been tangled ever since those alarm horns started blaring yesterday."

"Best to recover your strength, then. Look to your family, to your work." Paolo slowed his pace a fraction. "What I'm worried about is the return of Nicolau Baldaia. He's the one who can—and will—make trouble for you."

"Then let us pray he meets his death on the seas," Cédric said.

CHAPTER 54

Summer, 1455
Rhodes, Greece

THE SLEEK GALLEY sailed into the harbor at dusk, cutting silently through the darkening waters to the knights' inner harbor, its red-and-white banner fluttering crisply in the breeze. Cédric had known it was coming. A Georgillas cousin saw Nicolau Baldaia's galley sailing north past the Bay of Malona earlier in the day, and word had reached Cédric by mid-afternoon.

In the shadow of a warehouse near the edge of the dockyard, he watched the ship anchor. The sky blazed with glorious streaks of copper and gold, but he did not pay the Rhodian sunset any mind this evening, so intent was he on his spying. Two guards wearing the uniform of the knights appeared with a donkey cart. Cédric watched the Catalan direct his sailors to unload various boxes and pack them into the cart. Then Nicolau Baldaia abandoned the rest of his unloading duties and strode abreast of the cart toward the city walls.

Cédric drew back as the cart rolled by, his heart pounding. He heard the Catalan engage the guards in talk about the attack and its aftermath. A scant month after the attacks, he had the audacity to sail back into the city he'd deserted at the first sign of distress? Under his confident and brash exterior, he was a coward. Once the cart was well out of sight, Cédric went to follow it. But the approach of another cart along the quay made him change his mind. He edged out of sight again.

This time, young Loppes led a donkey cart toward the city, followed by two heavily armed companions. A muffled cry came from under the cart's cover. Cédric nearly stepped forward, then caught himself. Squinting in the descending gloom, he watched the cart rattle over the cobblestones, pausing just before it reached the Laughing Dove. Two men emerged from the brothel and greeted Loppes. They followed the cart down the alleyway where Cédric and Paolo had discovered their daughters.

He longed to creep down that alley and free the captives in the cart. They were likely young girls, destined to the fate that had nearly wrenched his daughter away from him forever. But the odds were not in his favor. Confronting all those men in the dark would be the death of him. No, he had to find another way to help these girls. Keeping to the shadows, he hastened back through the city gates and headed for home, his mind swimming with worries.

He had followed Paolo's advice and kept quiet about his role in Dragonetto's death, wanting to wait until he had the ear of the grand master himself to explain. But the secretaries had denied him access to the grand master since the attacks. And the hawking trips he'd planned this past month had been canceled. The Order was consumed with shoring up its defenses, readying the island for the inevitable next attack, and Lord de Milly was at the heart of it all.

Now, with the return of the Catalan and his half-brother, the matter would surely come back to haunt him. He must bluff his way into an audience with Lord de Milly—but how? Finally, he hit upon an idea: the young peregrine falcon he'd been training would be his excuse. She'd been purchased for the grand master in the winter. For months, he'd been carrying her around the palace grounds on a gloved wrist, exposing her to new people, sounds, and smells each week. With a hood on and a little luck, she would stay calm and help Cédric penetrate the grand master's inner circle. Then, finally, he would tell Lord de Milly about his actions at the Laughing Dove on the day of the attack—and share what he had seen this evening.

He quickened his stride, deciding to say nothing of this to Sophie until the matter was resolved.

As soon as he arrived at the palace the next morning, Cédric made his rounds of the mews. Satisfied that all was well, he dispensed orders to his staff and began preparing the young peregrine for her outing. He selected polished leather jesses and a braided leash, then slipped on a deer-hide glove edged with silver filigree. When he transferred the falcon from her perch to his wrist, she shrieked. The tiny silver bells attached to her legs jangled softly. He spoke to her in a low, calm voice, readying a bejeweled hood made of soft goatskin. Trying to hood a falcon when one was agitated or emotional never worked. Cédric concentrated on his breath as he slipped the hood over her head and tightened the braces. She spread her wings taut, then folded them again.

"Good girl," he murmured, squaring his shoulders.

He crossed the vast courtyard with smooth, long strides. When he reached the guards on the opposite side, he told them Lord de Milly wanted to inspect the falcon. They waved him through the doors without question. He climbed the wide staircase to the upper chambers of the palace, concentrating on his breath and the bird. Thinking ahead would send his heart racing, and she would sense his anxiety immediately.

Finally, he was at the top of the stairs. The doors to the receiving hall were open. He approached, but the chamber was empty. Just ahead, a pair of secretaries exited the grand master's private study and turned in the opposite direction. Hoping the grand master was behind that door, he continued forward.

"What is your business, master falconer?" asked one of the guards posted by the door.

"Lord de Milly asked me to bring his new peregrine to him when she was ready. The time has come for him to inspect her."

The guards examined the bird with curiosity.

"We've been told nothing about this," the other man said doubtfully.

"Those were my orders," Cédric said with false confidence, nearly choking on the words.

The falcon shifted on his wrist and cried out, sensing his trepidation. The tinkle of the silver bells echoed down the corridor.

A voice called out from behind the door. "Enter."

It was Lord de Milly. Cédric raised an eyebrow, looking from one guard to the other.

"As the grand master commands," one of them said, and opened the door.

Inside, Lord de Milly was seated at his desk in front of the hearth. No fire burned there today, in concession to the warm weather.

"Approach." The grand master waved him over.

Cédric stood an arm's length away while his employer inspected the peregrine.

"Is she a good hunter?" he asked.

"She'll be a fine addition to your next hawking party, my lord. I can arrange an expedition soon, if it pleases you."

"There will be no hawking for me anytime soon, unfortunately." The grand master gestured to the desk that stood nearby, strewn with leather-bound books, parchment maps, and piles of correspondence. Then he turned back to Cédric, his expression tightening. "Nor for you. I've had a letter from Nicolau Baldaia this morning. He has leveled quite an accusation at you, monsieur. Said you murdered Dragonetto Poulis and attacked his manservants. He's found witnesses, Loppes Poulis and a pair of soldiers who say they saw you at the scene." He drew in a long breath, let it out slowly. "Before I have you transported to a cell in the Kastellania, I would hear your side of the story."

A dull weight burrowed into Cédric's chest. How much to tell? How much to leave out? Did it matter, in the end? Was his fate already sealed?

"My lord." The words stuck in his throat like sand. He tried again, forcing strength into his voice. "My daughter was taken captive by

Dragonetto and his brother Loppes on the day of the attack. Along with two other girls, she was carted to the Laughing Dove. Just as the girls were about to be loaded onto Baldaia's galley, I intercepted them. There was a fight. To save my daughter, I had to kill or be killed. There was no choice."

The grand master's mouth compressed into a hard line. The peregrine shifted on Cédric's wrist, setting off the bells. When they quieted, Cédric risked speaking again.

"They were to be traded to a rich Arab in return for Muslim girls, my lord. They were to be concubines in his harem. Nicolau Baldaia profits from a trade in flesh, Lord de Milly. Young, innocent girls, daughters of respectable men, captured and turned into whores for the wealthy. What would any other father have done in my shoes?"

"It has been a month since the man turned up dead," Lord de Milly pointed out. "You did not come to me at once with this news. Why?"

Cédric took a deep breath. "These events happened on the very day of the Turks' attack. I've tried to meet with you privately, but your secretaries put me off. Paolo Foscolo can verify what I've told you. His daughter and one of his household slaves were the other girls involved."

His voice was trembling now. The peregrine retracted her neck into her shoulders, then thrust it out again.

Steady, man. Get yourself under control.

"This was not an isolated incident, I fear," he dared to add. "I believe Baldaia brought another group of girls into Rhodes Harbor last night, hidden in a cart, as my daughter was."

The grand master glanced at the guards who stood flanking the door, then settled his gaze on Cédric again.

"The Catalan brought a different load of cargo into the city last night as well," he said quietly. "The single biggest gift of gold the Order has received outside of the priories of Western Europe in response to the recent attacks. It will go far to bolster our defenses."

Cédric's lungs deflated. He struggled for air. "I see," he managed to say.

"I do not doubt your story," Lord de Milly went on. "But you see my dilemma. Baldaia demands vengeance, and the Order is in his debt."

"So there is no hope for me, because the Catalan must get his due." Bitterness rose in Cédric's throat. "What will my fate be? Will I be hanged? Burned at the stake?"

The grand master's expression tightened. "With my intervention, you may get off with a public flogging. That is all I can hope to do for you. I wish it weren't so. Such are the constraints of my position." He signaled to the guards behind Cédric. The doors swung open. "You'll be taken to the Kastellania and held until further notice."

"But my family . . ." Cédric's words came out as a croak.

The grand master's frown deepened. He seemed to wrestle with his thoughts. Then he said, "If it is any consolation, I would have done the same in your stead, *monsieur le fauconnier*."

He signaled to his guards. "Take the falconer back to the mews, see that he returns this creature safely to her perch. Then transport him to the Kastellania."

As the guards marched him out of the chamber, Cédric's shock turned to panic. The peregrine screamed, her wings slicing the air, her tail feathers spread wide. She felt his distress as acutely as he did.

God in Heaven, he thought. *What have I done?*

CHAPTER 55

Summer, 1455
Rhodes, Greece

THE CRY of the soap seller drifted up from the back alleyway. He would reach their home in a few minutes.

"Christine," Sophie called from her bedchamber door. When her maid appeared, she reached into her purse and retrieved a handful of silver aspers. "Can you meet the soap man by the back gate? We're running low."

"Yes, madame."

A moment after Christine went downstairs, Sophie heard a rap at the front door. Had the soap man come around to the front? He'd never done so before. Curious, she descended the stairs to find Madame Taraval standing in the entry hall, one of the Greek servants shutting the door behind her.

"Madame Taraval, this is a surprise," Sophie said. "Can I offer you refreshment?"

"Heavens, no. I cannot tarry here." Madame Taraval lowered her voice. "I've some terrible news. It's about your husband."

Sophie sent the servant back to the kitchen. "What is it? Is he hurt?"

"God willing, no. But my husband saw him being locked away in the Kastellania this morning. He had gone there on a matter of business, some grievance brought by the cloth merchants' guild about tariffs or some such thing, and when he was leaving, he spied your husband in custody. Two guards were handing him off to the gaoler."

"How can this be?" Sophie's legs felt unsteady. "My husband has done nothing wrong."

Please, God. Let this not be about the matter of Dragonetto.

Madame Taraval looked doubtful. "To be locked in the Kastellania—it's because he has committed a crime, or been accused of one." She pursed her lips. "I must fly. We've much to do before the merchant fleet sails for France. Good day to you, madame, and I regret being the bearer of such ill news."

Sophie opened the door for her visitor and nodded in farewell, unable to muster even a word.

She shut the door and leaned against it, her pulse pounding in her ears. Her knees buckled and she collapsed in a pathetic little ball on the floor. It was as if the very foundation of her world had cracked. Cédric held them all up, kept them safe, loved them, protected them. He was their sun.

"This cannot be," she whispered. "It must be some mistake."

Estelle's voice floated in from the courtyard. Little Jean-Philippe let out a shout of delight, then erupted in giggles. At the sound of their voices, Sophie dragged herself upright, smoothed her skirts. She closed her eyes and drew in a few long breaths, trying to compose herself, and climbed the stairs to her bedchamber.

Unlocking the wooden storage chest, she fumbled for the dagger in its leather sheath. After the fright of the attacks had worn off, she'd stopped wearing the thing. Her eyes fell to Cédric's fine black velvet doublet. She stroked it gently, her eyes stinging with tears, and felt something hard against her palm. Under the doublet lay a small sack. She opened it and drew out a handful of gold florins imprinted with the likeness of Lord de Milly. Where had Cédric gotten this money?

Sophie stuffed them in the sack again. It didn't matter where they came from. They would serve her well in the days to come. She slid the sack into her own coin purse and tied it onto her belt, then buckled the sheath next to it.

She went downstairs to Cédric's study and wrote a few lines on a scrap of linen paper. While it dried, she found Christine bringing in the sack of soap flakes from the back gate.

"What is it, madame? Are you ill?" Christine's eyes widened in concern at the sight of her.

Sophie shook her head. No matter how hard she tried to conceal her emotions, Christine could never be fooled. It did not bother her. It was, in fact, a great comfort.

"My husband is in trouble. Pack a basket with bread, cheese, and a jug of wine. Put in a jar of ointment, too, and some linen bandages for his wound. I'm going out to help him."

Christine set her jaw. "Not without me, you're not."

Sophie put a hand on her maid's arm. "I need someone I trust to stay with the children."

As Christine began to protest, Sophie silenced her with a look.

"Fine," Christine said, "but you should not be alone in those streets."

Sophie patted the sheath at her waist. "I won't be."

"How you can jest at a time like this is beyond me, madame," Christine grumbled, turning toward the kitchen while Sophie tied on her cloak.

When she stepped outside, Sophie remembered that today was market day. The streets hummed with activity. Normally, she observed the passersby with interest, craning her neck to get a look inside donkeys' panniers and cart beds piled high with goods. But today, she saw nothing but the image of her husband being forced into a cell, locked away from the world.

Please, God, let this not be about the matter of Dragonetto.

The words played over and over in her mind, like a sickening tune.

She hurried through a small lane and emerged into the marketplace, directly into the path of Cali Foscolo and her entourage. Sophie stood frozen, heat rising in her cheeks. This woman was the reason her husband had gone out in search of the girls the day of the attack. She had taken them to the bathhouse, put them in the path of danger. Even as Sophie had these thoughts, she could not help admitting to herself that it was Cédric who had given Signora Foscolo permission to take her daughter there.

"Signora Foscolo," she said coolly. "Good day."

The Greek woman stepped away from her attendants, her face grave.

"I have just heard the news of your husband." Unexpectedly, Cali Foscolo reached for her hand. "I am sorry. Monsieur de Montavon has been so kind to us."

Sophie stiffened at the woman's touch, looked at her with narrowed eyes. She would prefer not to discuss that particular sore spot again.

But Signora Foscolo did not mention the slave Maria. "It is only with your husband's help that my husband works for the knights."

"What do you mean?"

"Paolo makes portraits for the knights' private chapels. Before the falconer arrived, my husband could not get work from the Order. This has changed our lives."

Sophie stared at their entwined hands. "I had no idea."

Why had Cédric kept so much from her? He had been trying to protect her, she supposed, but in doing so had left her even less able to comprehend the difficulties facing them. The truth was she had never asked him much about his work or the challenges he faced. She was too wrapped up in her own problems.

She met Signora Foscolo's gaze. "It has been so long since the attack; I thought Cédric was safe."

"A powerful man is trying to have your husband punished," Signora Foscolo said. "It is what we all feared."

"Nicolau Baldaia?" Sophie asked.

Signora Foscolo nodded. "He has returned to Rhodes."

"I am on my way to the Kastellania now," Sophie confessed. "I thought to bribe the guards, try to pass Cédric some food, a bit of wine. I don't know what else to do, in truth. But I must do something!"

The words poured from her, bitter, fierce. She was helpless. Powerless. It was a feeling she hated, one she rarely harbored because, truly, her life had been one of privilege.

Signora Foscolo squeezed her hand. "Do not give up hope. The Baldaias have influence with the Order, but my family has power on this island, too. We will do what we can to help your husband. I vow it."

Sophie's throat swelled with emotion. "I will place my trust in you," she said. "I have no other choice."

"Now, let us accompany you to the Kastellania," Signora Foscolo said briskly. "Your plan is sound, and with me at your side you may even get your wish."

That night, in the privacy of her bedchamber, Sophie removed the dagger from its sheath. Turning it over in her hands, she imagined running the blade through the Catalan's heart. The idea did not strike her with remorse or shame. Quite the contrary. It gave her a moment's relief from the torment coursing through her.

Cali Foscolo had been true to her word. She knew the gaoler's wife, knew how much to bribe the guards—twenty silver aspers each sufficed, Signora Foscolo assured her. Thank God Sophie had not pulled out Cédric's florins. Then the basket disappeared into the bowels of the Kastellania with the promise that it would be delivered straight to Cédric.

She pressed her face into her hands, fighting tears. After a moment, she went to the oak chest, searching under the layers of velvet, linen, and wool. Finally, her hand closed around the cotton-wrapped gold coin given to her by Philippe in Auvergne. She shook it out of its covering. The woman depicted on the face of the coin was a mystery, her features blurred with age. Was she an ancient goddess? Perhaps it was blasphemy to beseech her for aid. But Philippe had not been struck dead for wearing the talisman. To the contrary, it had brought him good fortune.

She slipped it over her head and tucked the coin deep into her bodice, smoothing the soft leather cord around her throat.

A wavering cry came from the children's room. Estelle had suffered from nightmares ever since the day she'd been taken captive. Sophie straightened up, squared her shoulders. Amidst all this heartache and fear, one thing was certain. Tonight, her daughter would sleep in the marriage bed, safe in the circle of her mother's arms.

CHAPTER 56

Summer, 1455
Rhodes, Greece

CÉDRIC'S STOMACH RUMBLED. His mouth was terribly dry. No light penetrated his cell. No window offered a breath of fresh air or a means of escape, no sliver of daylight gave him a glimpse of the outside world. He was surrounded by pure inky darkness, the stench of his piss bucket, the rustling of rodents. His straw-filled pallet stank of sweat and terror, just as he did.

The thing he'd feared most had happened. He was in this cell because of Dragonetto's death. Now all he could do was wait and worry. Why had he not prepared for this eventuality? He could have arranged for Sophie and the children to sail back to France and go to Toulouse. At the very least, he could have asked Paolo Foscolo to see them safely off the island if something happened to him.

The sound of voices made him freeze. He reached for his sword, then cursed. Of course it was not there. It was the first thing they'd taken. That and his purse.

A key rattled in the lock, and the door to the corridor swung open.

A man carrying a torch entered. He handed Cedric a covered willow basket.

"You'll not starve," he muttered. "We'll see to that."

Cédric blinked up at him, his eyes aching from the torchlight. "Who's 'we'?" He could not make out any discernible features in the man's face, and his voice was unfamiliar.

"Be quick," someone ordered gruffly from the corridor.

Without another word, the man backed out, dropping the torch on the floor as he went. The door thumped shut, the key turned in the lock. The faint sound of retreating footsteps faded.

Cédric stared at the flickering torchlight, blessing the man for his gesture of kindness. He drew the canvas off the basket, overcome with a flood of gratitude for what he confronted within it.

First, he unstoppered the jug and drank deeply. A fine Cretan red. So the Georgillas family had done him this favor. He dug into the basket and found a jar of ointment and bandages. Washing his hands in a bit of wine, he smeared some ointment on his shoulder wound. It ached, but the pain was no worse than yesterday.

Feeling hopeful for the first time since his arrest, he wolfed down some bread. He knew he should ration the food, but he feared it would be taken away or attract rats. So he consumed every morsel of the bread and cheese and drank the entire jug of wine, entreating the torch to keep the darkness at bay.

The circle of light on the damp stone floor dwindled as the wine burned a warm path into his stomach. He clung to the glow of the flame like a drowning man, begging it to stay a while longer, to illuminate the four walls of his prison, make it seem a little more expansive and a little less frightening.

Setting the empty jug back in the basket, his fingers brushed a slip of paper. He drew it out, unfolded it, and held it up to the dying light.

Cédric, my love, my heart—I will free you from that place, I swear it. May God keep you safe until then. S.

His chest caved. A great wrenching sob tore at his throat. He read the words over and over, committing them to memory, like a prayer. The Georgillas clan may have had a hand in getting the basket to him, but his wife had been responsible for filling it.

Too soon the torch gave a last shudder and guttered out.

He was alone in the dark again.

Cédric lay back carefully on his pallet, the slip of paper clutched in one hand, and tried to relax his muscles. He had not felt this frightened since he was a boy, waking in the dark after a nightmare. Though he had few memories of his mother, he recalled some details.

She was calm, patient, skilled with a needle. Her embroidery had adorned fabric everywhere in the house—bed linens, runners, tablecloths. Each spring, the servants laundered and pressed the flax and linen fabrics, then sprinkled them with rosewater. When he awoke quaking with fear in the night as a boy, he would gather his bedclothes around him and bury his face in the linens, breathing in his mother's scent. It never failed to calm him. Even now, when he smelled the scent of roses, he thought of her.

A scuttling in the dark near the door made him jump. He drew in a long breath, then regretted it. The air was so foul in here.

You must make your own fortune.

His father's dying words rang through his mind. All these years, Cédric had failed to heed them. His future was still bound up in the whims and plans of other men. Why had he not taken to heart his father's plea? He'd had ample opportunity to try. If he had entered the cloth industry as Monsieur Portier had urged him all those years ago, he would have amassed wealth without putting his family in mortal danger.

He shifted his weight, stiffening at the sound of tiny claws scratching on stone.

Every decision he'd made had been selfish, he realized. Falconers were men of importance, and he'd reveled in that. He had always looked down on merchants. They were common-born folk desperate to join the ranks of nobles. His attitude struck him as shameful now. He had chosen a path entirely unsuitable for a family. A life of adventure, of danger. And he had never bothered to plan for their future, always placing trust in his employers to take care of him. He'd mocked Sophie for her obsession with plotting their escape, when she had been right all along.

As the night passed, Cédric's self-flagellating thoughts churned on, a treacherous tide rising in his head.

He had put all his faith in the knights, had never imagined that he himself would become the target of their ire. Foolishly, he'd assumed that Lord de Milly would protect him because he was a member of the Count de Chambonac's household, a countryman from Auvergne. But the grand master was, by necessity, a practical man. The Order was beholden to its donors, and one of their most generous supporters was Cédric's enemy. It was Nicolau Baldaia's gold that put him in this cell in the end.

And now he would suffer. His family would suffer. Poor Estelle had already suffered. If he escaped this predicament, he *would* heed his father's words. He would find a way to seize control of his own fate, by God.

Somewhere down the corridor a door slammed and voices rose in argument. His whole body clenched in anticipation of another key in the lock, his balled fists grew clammy with dread.

Cédric stared wide-eyed into the darkness, praying for freedom.

CHAPTER 57

Summer, 1455
Rhodes, Greece

SOPHIE LAY next to her sleeping daughter, anticipating the new day with anxiety. Estelle's slumber was restless this night. The air in the bedchamber seemed stale and hotter than usual, and Estelle had kicked off the sheet in her sleep more than once. If only a breeze would drift in. Summer was in full force, and the cooling afternoon winds often vanished once darkness fell.

Since Cédric's arrest nearly a week ago, she had brought their daughter into the marriage bed each evening to offer comfort when a bad dream struck. In truth, Estelle's presence was a buffer against Sophie's own terrors as well.

Her mind seethed with worries about Cédric. She carried food and wine to the Kastellania each morning. Paolo Foscolo had visited their home to tell her he'd submitted testimony to the knights and the council of city leaders about the events surrounding Dragonetto's death.

Sophie had written letters to her father and to the Count of Chambonac asking for their assistance, but no ships were sailing to France for at least a fortnight. Any help she could procure from home was months away, and Cédric's life was in danger now. In two days' time, the grand master would receive the citizens of Rhodes, hearing their grievances and legal matters in his great receiving hall. By God, Sophie would be there that morning before the cocks crowed the dawn.

She heard a faint thump. Her eyes flew open. The bedchamber was cloaked in darkness, save the moonlight that pierced the cracks of the shutters.

She sat up and listened, gathering the bedcovers into knots with nervous fingers. There it was again. A distinct thud. Careful not to disturb Estelle, Sophie slipped quietly out of bed.

Her clothes lay where she'd flung them last night on the chest. She shrugged on a long blouse and underskirt. There was no point fiddling with a bodice in the dark. Creeping back to the bed, she felt for the dagger under her pillow. Thrusting the weapon into her waistband, Sophie made for the door.

She paused to listen at the children's door a moment, then continued to the staircase, her bare feet quiet on the cool stone. She wiped her hands on her skirt, trying to dry her sweaty palms.

A rattle of metal made her jump. It had come from the cellars, she was certain.

Downstairs, moonlight illuminated the floor in curving patterns, flooding in from the courtyard windows, which they never bothered to shutter unless there was a driving rain. She contemplated waking the Greek servants. But what good would that do? She could not communicate with the women past the most rudimentary conversation without Estelle at her side.

Sophie reached the cellar door and opened it, then hesitated at the top of the stairs. A faint breeze wafted up, smelling of wet stone and ancient earth. There was no exit from the cellars save these stairs. She sucked in a breath as a memory flooded back. She had been so exhausted last night after the servants had decanted two pitchers of wine from a cask that she'd forgotten to return to the cellar and lock up. The keys were still down there, dangling from one of the storeroom gates.

With utmost stealth, she crept down the stairs. The darkness enveloped her like a smothering cloak. She kept one hand on the stone wall to steady herself, the other on the hilt of the dagger.

Dear God, don't make me use this thing.

Sophie entered the narrow corridor between the two storerooms. Faintly, she made out a figure rummaging in the storeroom that contained the marble head. Her gut tightening, she ran her fingers across the iron bars of the open gate, feeling for the lock. The keys were there, but she did not dare pull them out.

As her eyes adjusted to the gloom, she watched the intruder make his way slowly to the back of the storeroom. In another moment, he would discover the marble head.

Sophie had only an instant to act before he saw her. There were two dusty ceramic pitchers on the floor just inside the gate of the storeroom. She'd placed them there herself, meaning to ask the servants to take them upstairs and wash them. Another thing she'd forgotten in her fog of weariness.

She carefully eased one of the pitchers up from the floor with a trembling hand. Her heart flailed crazily against her ribs.

The intruder was a step away from the back wall now. He would find the head by the time she took her next breath. By God, he would not steal it! How dare he break into their house? In that instant, her fear vanished and a savage current of anger surged through her body. She lifted the pitcher high, darted forward, and slammed him over the head with it.

The man toppled to the ground, the pitcher shattering on the stone floor. He let out a long, agonized groan, then fell silent.

Sophie looked around wildly. Now what? If he was dead, so be it. But if not, he was still a threat. Somehow she scrambled over the empty casks to the back of the storeroom and reached for the marble head. It was so heavy. There was no way she could hoist it over the man's body or the casks. She would have to drag him out of here into the other storeroom and lock him in there.

He moaned again.

She climbed back over the casks and grabbed him by one foot. Pulling with all her might, she managed to slide him a short distance across the floor.

"Maman?"

Estelle's soft voice penetrated the dark.

"Estelle, go back upstairs!" Sophie said in panic. "There's a thief down here."

"Let me help you." Estelle was closer now.

Sophie reconsidered. Estelle was strong. They could do it faster together.

"Fine, but hurry. Grab his other foot and pull."

Between the two of them, they moved the man into the corridor.

"We've got to get him through the other gate," Sophie said. "Use all your might."

They tugged harder. His body slithered partway through the opening.

"Nearly done," Sophie encouraged her daughter.

They yanked him all the way into the other storeroom.

"Now, out."

Estelle stepped carefully over him and exited into the passage. Sophie followed, but to her horror, something bony encircled her ankle. He had her in his grip.

She lunged desperately toward the gate. The man's hand tightened around her ankle. In a panic, she stomped on his most tender parts with her other foot. He shrieked with pain and released her.

With a final burst of energy, she fled through the gate and slammed it shut.

He was flopping like a fish now. She grabbed the keys dangling from the other gate's lock and ripped them out, only to drop them on the floor. A loud clank reverberated through the darkness.

Calm yourself, Sophie, calm yourself.

She picked them up again.

The man was making more noise now. Coming to his senses. He mumbled something in Greek.

"Maman, he said he'll kill us!" Estelle whispered.

"Not if I have anything to do with it." Sophie slipped a key into the lock. It did not turn.

He grabbed for the gate.

She flung her body against it. "Estelle, help me."

Estelle pressed her shoulder against the gate. "He's too strong, Maman," she cried.

Sophie fitted the correct key in the lock and turned it with one smooth motion. She gave the gate a sharp tug. It held fast.

She took Estelle's hand. "He can push as much as he wants. He's not going anywhere, the dog."

The man called out to them in Greek again, his angry words following them up the stairs.

"I recognize that voice," Estelle said shakily. "He was there the day we were captured. He's one of the men who pushed us into the cart and tied us up."

Sophie swept her daughter through the cellar door and banged it shut behind them.

CHAPTER 58

Summer, 1455
Rhodes, Greece

THE GREEK SERVANTS intercepted them in the corridor, terrified. Sophie made a big show of yanking on the cellar door's latch to show it was locked, but they were not appeased. The rattling of the storeroom gate grew louder, as did the captive man's enraged shouts. The women babbled at her in Greek until Sophie felt her head would explode. She ordered them back to the kitchen in exasperation.

Sophie led Estelle to her bedchamber and dressed in the pale light of dawn. As she tied the laces of her bodice, her hands still trembling, she dispensed instructions to her daughter. "Wake Christine. Explain to her what happened and tell her I've gone for help. He cannot escape, Estelle. The gate will hold."

"Where are you going, Maman?"

"To see Paolo Foscolo."

Estelle nodded. Tears glistened in her eyes and the flush of fear on her face still lingered, but she kept her composure. Sophie gathered the girl in her arms for a moment, kissed the top of her head.

"Keep Jean-Philippe upstairs," she murmured. "Have Christine bring him bread and cheese and fruit, and play games with him. Anything to keep him busy. I'll return soon."

Before leaving the house, Sophie checked the back door and the gate to the alleyway. The gate was still latched and the door showed no signs of forced entry. She examined the window facing the small cobbled yard between the house and the wall along the alleyway. One of the shutters hung slightly askew on its hinges and the interior latch had splintered in two. This was how the intruder had forced his way into their home. The wall had been no impediment to him, and the shutter had been easily breached.

The sight made her even more uneasy, but for now, there was nothing she could do about the shutter.

Outside, the streets were quiet, the sky stained pink and gold. Sophie hurried down the lane. A lump as big as a quail's egg swelled in her throat. With each step, she became more anxious about leaving her children behind. Breaking into a run, she hastened through the streets to the Foscolo home. She pounded on the door with her fist.

"It's Madame de Montavon," she cried, her lungs aching. "Cédric's wife. Please, open the door!"

Oh, where was the man?

The door creaked open. Paolo Foscolo peered over his servant's shoulder, eyes wide with surprise.

"What's wrong?" he asked, waving her inside.

Sophie stayed where she was.

"A thief broke into our home before dawn. Estelle said he's one of the men who attacked the girls. He's still there now, and our shutter's broken—" She stopped to take a breath, on the verge of tears.

"I'll have some men come with me, and we'll take him away," he assured her, looking troubled. "We'll fix your shutter, too."

"Where will you take him?" she asked.

"To the Kastellania."

"But Cédric is there!"

"He won't be put in the same cell as your husband," the Venetian said.

Sophie raised her chin. "I will follow you there. I won't sleep until I see that scoundrel locked up with my own eyes."

Her true desire was to get a glimpse of her husband, to assure herself he was well. Perhaps with a group of sympathetic men she would be more likely to get her way.

Signor Foscolo frowned a little. "If that is your wish, so be it."

Back in her home, he and his companions secured the shutter and checked the other entry points to the house to make sure they were not compromised. Then the men hauled up the intruder from the cellar. His matted black curls clung to his skull and bloodstains marred his white tunic. He struggled in his captors' grasp.

"I've seen him before," Sophie told the Venetian with a jolt of recognition.

"He's Dragonetto's brother," he said. "His name is Loppes."

She clenched her jaw. "I don't care what his name is or who he claims as brother. He is the devil's spawn as far as I'm concerned."

"You tried to kill me," the man said in French. He looked her in the eyes without a trace of remorse. "You will die for it, just as your husband will die for murdering my brother."

Sophie stood her ground, her anger flooding back. "Your threats don't frighten me. Get out of my house, you scoundrel."

She thought she saw Signor Foscolo's lips twitch, but his tone was serious when he said to his companions, "To the Kastellania with him."

The men pulled their protesting captive along the corridor, through the entry hall, and out the front door. Sophie and Signor Foscolo followed close on their heels.

At the Kastellania, Sophie tilted her head, studying her husband's prison. The three stone crocodile heads that funneled rainwater from the roof had never looked so sinister. How many times had they stopped to admire this building in their early days here? Now she regretted it. The elegant exterior was simply a false veneer of beauty concealing the ugliness within.

As a church bell tolled in the distance, the Venetian climbed the broad flight of steps and thumped on the door.

"I've a criminal for the knights to take into their custody," he shouted.

Two guards emerged and surveyed the square where the men stood with their captive.

"What's his crime?" asked one.

"Shall I list them all or simply the most recent incident?" Signor Foscolo asked, his voice sharpening. "Surely, you recognize this fellow. Loppes Poulis. Lately, he's been skulking around the Laughing Dove, by the harbor."

In the moment of silence that followed, another church bell began clanging. But instead of marking the time, the bell pealed without stopping, over and over.

A third man appeared in the Kastellania doorway. The white eight-pointed cross of the Order stood out vividly on his black tunic. He was of middle age, with a sizable girth. This must be the gaoler, Sophie realized.

More chimes rang out, closer this time. Now a discordant chorus of tolling bells resonated through the city.

"What is happening?" Sophie asked. "Why do the bells toll?"

A young man on a donkey careened into the square and drew up before the flogging post.

"Plague!" the rider yelled. "Plague!"

He spurred his donkey onward, screaming his news to all the world. Sophie's heart seized with terror. The fear she felt was reflected in the eyes of every man in the square.

The two men gripping Loppes's arms let go, their faces alight with panic. Loppes wheeled and ran toward the Sea Gate.

"No!" Sophie cried. "He's escaping!"

Signor Foscolo hurried down the Kastellania steps. The gaoler and guards retreated inside, news of the plague clearly taking precedence over the arrest of a thief. Sophie sucked in a breath. She had to act. There would be no other opportunity to get close to Cédric.

She gathered her skirts and rushed up the stairs just as the door began to shut.

"Please, sir." Her voice was barely audible over the noise of the bells. She put a restraining arm on the door.

The gaoler turned, fixed her with a dark look.

"My husband is being held in there," she said, louder now. "Cédric de Montavon. He is a good man, a loyal servant of the Order. He's done nothing wrong. Please tell me, what news of him? Is he in good health?"

"I wouldn't know," the man said. "He was taken to the palace by the bailiff this morning for an audience with the grand master."

Sophie staggered back in shock. "What? Why?"

The gaoler ignored her and turned away. The guards shut the door behind him.

On weak legs, she descended the steps. Signor Foscolo offered an arm for support.

"Cédric is at the palace," she said, dazed. "I don't know what to think."

"I knew the council was meeting this morning, but I'd no idea Cédric was involved. Let us pray for good news," he said. "If plague has indeed come to Rhodes, the safest place for us both is at home. I'll accompany you to your door. We can find a reliable man to guard your house this evening, if you wish."

She nodded in gratitude, unable to muster even a word. The walk home seemed interminable. Her eyes hurt, her brain hurt, every muscle in her body ached. She longed for a night of deepest slumber, curled up in her husband's embrace. Would such a thing ever come to pass again?

At her doorway, the Venetian held her gaze a moment. "Madame de Montavon, I've done my best to help your husband. It was my hope that the interventions of my wife's family would turn events in his favor. I will not stop coming to his aid, no matter what happens. And may God spare both our families from the plague."

Sophie drew in a shaky breath, gripped by a profound sense of foreboding. "Please, Signor Foscolo, should something happen to my husband and I both, will you look after our children? Help them make the return journey to France? I've no one else to turn to."

He nodded soberly. "You have my word."

CHAPTER 59

Summer, 1455
Rhodes, Greece

WHEN THE GUARDS hustled Cédric out the doors of the Kastellania and down the steps to the street this morning, he'd been sure the flogging post was their destination. His eyes ached in the morning sunlight. After so many days and nights of confinement in a dark cell, he'd almost forgotten what it was to feel the sun on his face.

"Dear God," he whispered as they advanced toward the stone pillar. "Protect me."

One of the guards looked at him with sympathy. "We're taking you to the palace," he muttered. "You'll not be whipped this morning."

A mule hitched to a covered cart waited beyond the flogging post. The brief ride up the hill to the palace passed in a blur. Once inside, the guards led him up the steps of the wide stone staircase, then escorted him to an antechamber where he stood, hands bound, waiting for his fate to unfold. With every passing moment, his uneasiness grew. A wild urge to hatch an escape plan struck him. He searched the room for another door, studied the impassive faces of the guards, tested the strength of the bonds around his wrists. As he realized the impossibility of the idea, his breath grew shallow.

Murmured voices and the patter of footsteps along the corridor outside the door told him a crowd was gathering. Cédric shifted nervously on his feet, his heart galloping. The despair that had haunted him since his arrest gripped his chest like an iron vise.

Gather your wits, Cédric de Montavon.

He sucked in a sip of air, then a long draught. What he needed now was composure—if nothing else, he had to get through this day with his dignity intact. At the thought, he raised his chin and straightened his spine.

Finally, the door opened.

The guards led him to the receiving hall, where dozens of men stood before the raised dais where Jacques de Milly sat. The grand master wore a long scarlet robe with the eight-pointed cross of the Order stitched in white on the left breast, his hands folded at his waist.

He caught sight of Cédric. For an instant, their eyes locked. Then Lord de Milly looked away, his expression impassive.

Breathe, man.

Two benches sat empty in front of the dais, separated by the length of a man's body. He was led to one of them. As he took his seat, the buzz of conversation throbbed in his ears.

Would the grand master be true to his word, see that Cédric was let off with a flogging? The guards in the Kastellania had told him it was customary in such cases to receive one hundred lashes with a bullwhip. Whether he could survive such a lashing was uncertain. He would at the very least bear ghastly scars for life. He pressed his lips together, fighting an image of Sophie and the children looking at his ruined body with pity and revulsion.

Then a man sank down on the other bench. Sandalwood and some other rich, spicy scent assailed Cédric's nostrils. He did not have to turn his head to know who the newcomer was.

"Come to order," a voice called. A man wearing sober robes of black velvet came to stand before the assembled group at the foot of the dais. "I, the bailiff of Rhodes, convene this trial of justice. Gathered in this room are many good men of the island—men the Order knows as 'the first ones,' representatives of families who have been loyal to the knights for generations. We convene to deliver justice and to ensure the safety and security of all citizens of Rhodes. Let us begin."

Cédric kept his eyes on the grand master's face as the bailiff recited the facts of the case. Whatever Jacques de Milly thought was locked behind those cool dark eyes. He did not react, did not raise a brow, did not move a muscle as the words rang out.

Nicolau Baldaia shifted on his bench, cleared his throat. Cédric steadfastly gazed ahead, trying to ignore him.

"We will first hear testimony from Señor Nicolau Baldaia," announced the bailiff.

There was a brief silence, then Baldaia stood.

"Lord de Milly, Bailiff, esteemed members of the court," he said in a smooth, confident voice. "I am counting on you to apply the rule of law to this man, this murderer, on my right. In broad daylight, he slaughtered my beloved brother Dragonetto Poulis and attacked two of Dragonetto's loyal servants. With no provocation whatsoever. He is a menace to Rhodian society and deserves nothing less than execution."

Cédric's ears burned. He slid to the edge of the bench, every muscle tensed, fighting the urge to spring up and refute Baldaia's lies.

The bailiff studied the Catalan a moment. "So you say. But the council has heard testimony from others that there was provocation. That the daughter of Cédric de Montavon and two other girls were taken captive by Dragonetto with the intention of trading them to an Arab in exchange for Muslim girls destined for Christian men."

One of the council members moved forward, leaning heavily on a companion's arm for support. "I would speak."

Cédric regarded the man with a jolt of surprise. Anteon's father had been poorly of late. But somehow he had mustered the strength to appear here today.

The bailiff nodded. "Neilos Georgillas, say your piece."

"My son, Anteon, works for Monsieur de Montavon as an under-falconer in the palace mews. Myself, my son, and all the other men of my family who are acquainted with Monsieur de Montavon can vouch for the Frenchman's character. I have gotten word from relatives all over the island—from Lindos, Archangelos, the Rodini Valley—who want the Order to know they stand with the falconer."

When he paused, several men on the perimeter of the room stepped forward. One after the next, they repeated the same words:

"I stand with the falconer."

Cédric could scarcely dare to breathe. For the first time since his arrest, he felt a slight loosening of the dread clamped around his chest.

"I have a personal interest in this matter, for one of the other girls taken captive was my niece, Anica Foscolo," Neilos Georgillas continued. "Dragonetto's procurer used the chaos and terror of that day to take advantage of young girls and try to turn them into concubines. To destroy their virtue and make them slaves. Nicolau Baldaia was behind it. His galley waited for them. While the knights were assembling their warships to defend our shores, Señor Baldaia had other plans—to smuggle innocent girls across the sea."

"These are outrageous lies," the Catalan protested, his hands balled into fists. "There is no proof of such a scheme. The falconer has spread this tale. It's the story of a desperate man who wants to save his own skin."

Neilos Georgillas glared at Baldaia. "No. There are many who have come forward over the years to complain about Dragonetto. Everyone knows you controlled his purse strings. He did nothing without your approval. This particular scheme was one of many like it."

Sounds of affirmation flowed around the chamber. Cédric stared at the Grand Master, whose impassive face told him nothing. What would Lord de Milly do? The Order was indebted to Baldaia, but clearly the citizenry had no such allegiance to the man.

The faint tolling of a church bell penetrated the windows as the bailiff turned his gaze to Cédric.

"Now we must hear from the accused man himself," he said. "Cédric de Montavon, it is your turn to speak."

The Catalan sat down, his gaze pinned to Cédric. As he stood, Cédric looked the man in the eyes. What he wouldn't give to strike out, slam a fist into that smirking mouth, knock the devil to the floor. But he forced himself to face the bailiff.

"Grand Master, Bailiff, members of the council. I only did what any father would have done. I defended my daughter. I defended Anica Foscolo. I defended the slave Maria. There is little more to say. The girls were taken captive with the intent to sell them across the sea as concubines. What other choice did I have but to prevent that from happening? I took no joy in killing Dragonetto, nor did I want to injure his servants. I was defending myself. I still have the wound in my shoulder from Loppes Poulis's blade."

He pulled the neck of his shirt open to display the injury.

"Lies," Baldaia scoffed. "You could have gotten that anywhere."

"Silence!" the bailiff commanded.

More bells began to toll outside. Hushed conversations broke out around the room. Cédric watched the grand master's face. Still no reaction at all. Did the man have a heart of iron?

The bailiff spread his arms wide, calling for order.

"Why was my brother Loppes not called as witness?" Baldaia asked, rising again. "He saw this man murder Dragonetto. And yet his testimony is not invited."

Another council member stood. "Loppes Baldaia is a known criminal. He only walks the streets today because of your interventions. You line the pockets of his victims with gold so that they turn the other cheek. Why would we bother to hear the testimony of such a man?"

Baldaia drew back his shoulders. "I'll have you know Loppes is now the owner of the Laughing Dove. He is a responsible man of business. Yes, he's had his troubles in the past. But that is all behind him. He is devastated by our brother's death."

The tolling of the bells swept up the hill to the palace. The sound was impossible to ignore now.

The door creaked open and a page entered. He whispered to a guard, who approached the dais and had a brief exchange with the grand master. Lord de Milly's face registered shock for a fleeting instant. Then he shot a look at the Catalan and his expression grew thoughtful.

The men in the room fell silent, watching this. An atmosphere of tension began to crackle.

What now? Cédric passed a hand over his face, praying this news had nothing to do with him.

Finally, Jacques de Milly spoke. "Where is your brother, Señor Baldaia?"

"At the brothel, of course, overseeing his duties. Shall I have him summoned at once so he may give testimony?"

Cédric's heart sank. But the grand master ignored the Catalan's question.

"And where have you been staying since you returned to Rhodes, Señor Baldaia?"

"In my villa, of course. And occasionally at the brothel, to instruct my brother in his duties, now that Dragonetto has been so cruelly taken from us by this man." The Catalan flung a murderous glance Cédric's way.

"Were you at the brothel last night, Señor Baldaia?"

"Yes. Why do you ask, my lord?"

"Plague has come to Rhodes," the grand master said flatly.

Anxious chatter rippled through the crowd. A few of the men moaned aloud.

"It reared its head at the Laughing Dove this morning," Lord de Milly went on. "Hear this, Señor Baldaia. Your brother and all the inhabitants of the brothel will be quarantined east of the city in the old monastery near the windmills beginning today. You yourself must either join them there or leave Rhodes immediately. I will have you escorted to your galley if that is your wish."

The Catalan's mouth fell open. "What?"

Lord de Milly's expression tightened. "What is your choice? Shall it be quarantine or departure?"

"But what of my generosity to the Order? Is this how you treat a friend to the cause?" Baldaia demanded.

The grand master rose to his feet. "The survival of the knights and the citizenry of Rhodes takes precedence over you and every other friend of the Order, I'm afraid. So what will it be?" His deep voice held a trace of menace.

Cédric felt Baldaia simmering beside him. He dared not turn his head. One more look at the scoundrel would spark his own fury. Whatever else happened here, he must appear calm.

"Departure," the man finally spat.

"As I thought," the grand master said, signaling to his guards. "Escort Señor Baldaia to his galley."

Two guards flanked Baldaia as he drew himself up. Astonished by what had just transpired, Cédric watched Baldaia's retreating back until he disappeared through the doorway. Nobody else seemed to notice the Catalan's departure. Their heads were canted together, their talk devoted to the news of plague. With each clang of the church bells, the distress in the crowd grew.

"All brothels are closed until further notice. All citizens of Rhodes Town will be quarantined beginning this evening," Lord de Milly said. "When you leave the palace, return to your households and await more instructions."

More nervous exclamations broke out. The grand master raised one arm, signaling for quiet.

"As for the matter of Cédric de Montavon—" His voice boomed over the noise of the crowd and the bells.

A hush fell throughout the room. The gathered men turned their attention to Lord de Milly and the bailiff. Cédric steeled himself for whatever was to come.

"In light of the testimony we have heard today, and considering the current turn of events, I recommend we drop this matter entirely. Cédric de Montavon has shown himself to be a man of honor. The defense of the island and its inhabitants has never been more important than it is now—and we need men like Monsieur de Montavon in Rhodes Town, men who put their own lives on the line to defend the innocent."

A murmur of assent rippled around the room.

At a signal from the grand master, the bailiff stepped forward again. "Cédric de Montavon," he intoned, "you are free to go."

CHAPTER 60

Summer, 1455
Rhodes, Greece

AMID THE TOLLING of the bells and the agitated chatter of men crowding toward the grand staircase, Cédric moved slowly, cautiously, as if in a dream. After another interminable wait in the antechamber, guards returned his sword and handed over his keys. His abrupt transformation from prisoner to respected servant of the knights happened without comment, without ceremony.

But he could not savor his freedom until he walked through the doorway of his home and embraced his wife. Following the crowd across the courtyard toward the palace gates, Cédric could almost feel her soft warmth pressed against him, could smell the jasmine oil behind her ears. He quickened his pace.

"Monsieur!"

Anteon's clear voice rang across the courtyard from the mews.

Cédric returned Anteon's wave. Despite his desire to rush home, he could not leave without a word to his loyal assistant. And there was something else he needed to do in his workplace, as well.

When he approached the mews, the shock in Anteon's eyes told Cédric that his appearance had suffered while he was locked away.

"Welcome back," the young man said. "My father told me the news —all of it."

"Thank you." Cédric glanced around at the falcons in their hutches.

"I've been watching over them for you," Anteon assured him.

Cédric nodded, moving to the hutch containing the young peregrine he'd taken to the grand master on the day of his arrest.

She cocked her head, examined him with liquid dark eyes.

"We're both still here," he said softly.

The falcon dipped her beak as if in agreement, then fluffed her feathers.

He turned back to Anteon. "Quarantine begins tonight. After I let my family know I'm safe, I'll take over here and you can go home."

"Forgive me, but you're in no shape for that," Anteon said, shaking his head. "Not yet."

Cédric opened his mouth to protest, then shut it.

"I've already told my father I'll stay in the mews for now," Anteon said. "I sleep here often enough, anyway."

"I will not forget this kindness." Wearily, Cédric made for the door.

Cédric stood in the entryway of his home, swarmed by his family and the servants, unable to muster more than a wan smile. Sophie clung to him, smiling and weeping at the same time. Jean-Philippe and Estelle rushed to embrace him. Wrapped in the loving arms of his family, he swayed and almost lost his balance.

"After I get out of these clothes and bathe, I'll have more strength for hugging and kissing," he told them. "You must wait just a little longer."

Jean-Philippe let out a howl of protest. Estelle bent to comfort him. The sweetness between them made Cédric's throat swell.

Your family's safe. And so are you.

"I still don't quite believe I'm home again," he admitted, his voice thick.

Sophie put a hand to his cheek, her brow furrowing. "You look pale."

She told the servants to fetch water for a bath and led him toward the stairs.

Over his shoulder, he said, "Estelle, there's a small velvet bag inside my desk drawer. Will you fetch it and bring it upstairs?"

"Me, too?" Jean-Philippe demanded.

Cédric chuckled. "Yes, my boy. You, too."

Upstairs, Sophie supported him through the doorway of their bedchamber, then helped him settle in the chair near the window.

"I . . ." So many words crowded his mind, but he could not push them out.

"Don't try to speak," she soothed him. "Save your breath for now."

He closed his eyes, promising himself he would not fall asleep. When he opened them again, Sophie was removing his boots and filthy clothes. Soon the servants arrived lugging buckets of water.

Once the bath was ready, Sophie helped him step into the copper tub. He sank into the water, unable to repress a long groan of relief.

Sophie bathed him tenderly, taking extra care with his healing shoulder. "Praise the saints, this hasn't festered."

He succumbed to her gentle touch with gratitude. She lathered his hair, then carefully rinsed it.

"You got me through that, Sophie," he said in a rough voice. "You made it tolerable."

"The baskets made it to you, then?"

He nodded. "And your notes. They gave me hope."

Before she could answer, Estelle poked her head through the door, Jean-Philippe at her side.

"Papa?" Jean-Philippe said hopefully.

Cédric smiled, overcome with relief and love at the sight of them. "Come on, then, join us."

Estelle held out the velvet bag to him with a broad smile, two spots of color on her cheeks.

"Not to me, to Maman," he said.

She handed it to her mother. Sophie looked at him with a raised eyebrow, then opened the bag and slid out the contents into her palm.

"Earrings," she said. "Are these for me?"

He laughed. "Who else would they be for, my love? Gold and sapphires the exact color of your eyes."

She stood very still, regarding him with a mixture of delight and surprise.

"Put them on," he suggested. "Or perhaps Estelle can do it for you."

Sophie pressed the earrings into their daughter's palm. Then she dropped to her knees, raised a hand to Estelle's cheek.

"You're so warm, *ma chérie,*" she said.

Estelle touched her face with her fingertips. "I've been hot since yesterday."

"You barely touched your supper last night." Sophie looked at Cédric, her eyes bright with tears. "God forbid. It cannot be—"

He rose dripping from the tub and threw a towel around himself.

"No," he said, low. He led her a few steps away from the children. "The only known case of plague is at Dragonetto's brothel on the waterfront. His brother, Loppes, and everyone else who has been in contact with the place is to quarantine in a monastery outside the city walls."

Sophie stiffened, drew in a shuddering breath.

"What is it?" He put a hand on her arm.

"Loppes broke into our home this morning," she said hollowly. "He was after that marble head in the cellar. Estelle helped me lock him up. We had no choice but to touch him."

Cédric felt the blood drain from his face. He hoisted Jean-Philippe into his arms, retreating toward the door. "Why did you not say anything before?"

"When would I have had the chance?" she countered. "You just returned from a terrible ordeal. I wanted to give you a bit of peace."

"God save us," he said, his eyes fixed on their daughter. "If that man has the plague, we are all doomed."

CHAPTER 61

Summer, 1455
Rhodes, Greece

CÉDRIC STOOD OUTLINED in the doorway of their bedchamber, his face pinched with worry.

"How is she?" His voice was raspy, sleep-starved.

Now that Estelle was ill, any chance of rest was dashed.

"She still burns with fever and she won't eat a thing. But she shows no signs of the plague. No swelling anywhere, no cough, no bleeding, no vomiting."

Sophie locked eyes with her husband. A memory of sweet Mathieu paralyzed her for a moment. They could not lose another child. Her heart would burst from sorrow.

She bit her lip, forcing the thoughts away.

"Shall we bring in a doctor?" Cédric asked.

A wave of misgiving rolled over her. Doctors themselves could carry the plague from house to house.

"Let us wait one more day," she said.

"What about the recipes for curatives made with dragon's blood, from the Greek falconer's book?" Cédric mused. "Anica and Estelle have nearly finished the translation. Some of the Greeks I've met swear by dragon's blood to lower fevers. You've used it for women's ills, and it's done you no harm."

Sophie contemplated his idea. Perhaps those remedies could help. It would be better than doing nothing. "As you wish."

"I've got to go out for food anyway, so I'll buy whatever we might need."

The grand master's quarantine on all citizens of Rhodes Town was strict. One member of each household could venture out, masked, to purchase essentials when needed. Guards patrolled the streets to ensure no citizens loitered or gathered during such outings. An eerie quiet had descended over the city. The clang of church bells now served as a grim reminder of the morning plague was discovered at the Laughing Dove.

Sophie's pulse raced at the idea of Cédric leaving the house. She wanted to protest, to attach herself to him like a burr. Yes, he had been freed. But his freedom was a gossamer thread, a fragile gift that could be snatched away at any moment. There was no choice, of course. Cédric would leave her side today and many days going forward—for all their sakes. She would have to learn to live with that.

"Be careful, my love," was all she said.

"I will," he replied, tying on his linen mask.

While he was gone, Sophie stayed at Estelle's side, marking the passage of the hours by the tolling of church bells. She wiped her daughter's hot skin with a flax cloth dipped in lavender water. After several frustrating attempts to feed her broth laced with powdered willow bark, Sophie gave up.

When Cédric returned, he had grim news.

"Ten have died in the monastery," he reported.

"Loppes?" she asked, terrified of the response.

"He was not among the dead."

She let out a long breath of relief. "I find it strange that instead of hoping God has struck our enemy down, I'm grateful for his good health."

"As am I," he said.

That afternoon, they studied the recipes. Each page represented hours of work by Estelle and Anica Foscolo. The sight of Estelle's graceful, confident lettering made Sophie's heart swell with pride.

Please, God, let her live to pick up her quill again.

Sophie took care not to lean too closely over the pages, afraid her tears would mar her daughter's work. She watched her husband measure out the dragon's blood, mix it with the other ingredients in the mortar. He ground it all together with care, scraping the pestle rhythmically against the marble.

"Add the egg white," he instructed.

She cracked an egg and separated the yolk, then let the thick clear liquid of the white escape into the mortar.

"Let's add some willow bark, too," she said.

Cédric hesitated. "It's not in the recipe."

"It will cool her fever," Sophie insisted.

"What if dragon's blood and willow bark don't mix? There could be danger in combining these things."

Sophie set her jaw. "We know willow bark eases fevers. If her fever doesn't break soon . . ." She broke off, thinking of Mattieu again.

He nodded, understanding, and watched her stir it in.

Finally, it was done. Sophie held Estelle's head up, cradling it in the crook of her arm, while Cédric eased her lips open and poured the concoction into her mouth. She swallowed it. Her eyes fluttered open for an instant, a fleeting look of revulsion passed over her face, then she sank into oblivion again.

Sophie gently laid Estelle back on the pillows, feeling weak with exhaustion herself.

"I'll see that supper gets on the table," Cédric told her, his voice full of concern. "You lie down, try to get some sleep."

She crawled into bed next to her daughter and pulled the bedclothes up to her chin. Drawing Philippe's gold coin from its hiding place in her bodice, she curled her fingers around it, descending into the soft cocoon of a deep, dreamless sleep.

The next morning, bright light roused Sophie from slumber. She blinked, saw sunlight streaming in through the slats of the shutters. Her body felt rested for the first time in ages. She had slept soundly, somehow, and much later than normal.

She turned her head and looked at her daughter. Estelle lay on her side an arm's length away, gazing back at her. Her brown eyes were clear and bright.

Hope stitched its way through the dread in Sophie's chest.

"Estelle?" she breathed, reaching a tentative hand out to her daughter.

"I'm hungry, Maman." Estelle yawned. "And thirsty, too."

Sophie burst into tears.

"Why do you weep?" Worry furrowed Estelle's brow.

"Because you are well, *ma chérie*." Sophie could barely string the words together between sobs. She gathered Estelle in her arms, kissed her over and over.

Cédric's heavy footsteps pounded up the stairs. "What's wrong?" he cried.

"She's better," Sophie said. "The fever broke."

"Praise all the saints." He came to the bedside and embraced them both.

Sophie pressed her forehead against his. "God has spared our girl," she whispered. "Fortune is smiling upon us."

The hard edge of the gold coin dug into her collarbone as Cédric tightened his arms around her.

Thank you, Philippe. Thank you, Agapitos Kassianos.

Sophie did not realize she had uttered the words aloud until Estelle spoke up.

"Do you know what Agapitos means?" she asked, squirming free of her parents' embrace. "Anica told me. It means 'beloved.' "

"A fitting name indeed," Cédric said, intertwining his fingers with Estelle's. "Now, let's find you something to eat. And as soon as you have the strength, you can finish the job you started the day of my return."

She frowned. "What was that?"

"Putting these in your mother's ears." He picked up the earrings that had sat forgotten on the bedside table since their daughter fell ill.

"You do it, Papa."

Cédric turned to Sophie. "May I?" he asked.

She bent her head slightly to let him attach the earrings.

"My wife, my love," he murmured.

She blinked away more tears. "Thank you, my Agapitos."

CHAPTER 62

Autumn, 1455
Rhodes, Greece

THEY STOOD at the highest point in Rhodes Town, near the palace, still breathing hard from their climb up the hill. Though winter was nearly upon them, the blazing sun carried the promise of a hot afternoon ahead. Cédric was grateful for the breeze that floated in from the sea, whispering over his face. A floral scent drifted from the gated garden to their left, its sweetness hinting at jasmine.

Sophie shaded her brow with a hand, surveying the sea. "The waves glitter like jewels, don't they?"

Cédric followed her gaze. "Yes, my love."

Three small galleys headed south through the churning whitecaps, sleek as dolphins. Their banners fluttered in the wind, too distant to reveal their colors.

"It feels good to walk outside again," she said. "Do you think the knights will open the marketplace to everyone soon? The children need to get outside, see some sights other than our courtyard and their bedchamber."

Estelle's illness was a distant memory now, thank God, and the rest of their household stayed healthy during the long period of isolation. Since no one in the monastery had died of plague in nearly a month, Lord de Milly had relaxed the quarantine restrictions just days ago. Cédric admired the man for what he had done to keep Rhodes Town safe. Thanks to his swift action, the plague did not infect the rest of the city.

Cédric slipped an arm around his wife's shoulder. "This city will come back to life with a roar, and when it does we might miss the quiet of these past few months." He hesitated, then spoke again. "I've some news to share. Yesterday at the palace, I heard Loppes was caught trying to escape from the monastery. He attacked the guards—and lost his life in the end."

"I'm happy he's gone," she admitted. "I hope Nicolau Baldaia has met his end somewhere out there, too." She gestured at the waves. "As long as that man lives, I'll fear for you."

"Paolo told me what you did the day of the trial," Cédric said, turning to her. "How you climbed the steps of the Kastellania and confronted the gaoler and guards. Why did you not tell me yourself?"

Sophie met his eyes. "There was no point. Once you returned to us, I had what I wanted—the love of my life."

"You showed tremendous courage. You and Estelle both. Loppes chose the wrong house to invade that morning."

"I put us in mortal danger." There was a trace of remorse in her voice. "Perhaps you should not be flattering me, but scolding me."

He laughed. "Your wit is as quick as ever, despite everything."

"Not despite everything." She smiled a little, the old sauciness flaring for an instant. "If I do not find the humor in the world, it all gets too dark."

"I'd do well to remember that. The more you jest, the more worried I should be."

She shook her head. "To think we've only been here a year."

"But what a year," he said wryly. "I pray the next four will be substantially less interesting."

"That is my wish as well." She leaned against him, fitting her body to his.

The comfort of her familiar curves made his eyes prick with tears.

Those days spent alone in a dark cell had forced the realization that everyone and everything he loved could all vanish in a moment. He would never take life—or Sophie—for granted again.

"How will we get through those years, Cédric?" Sophie's voice broke, revealing the fear that lurked in her heart. It roosted inside his own heart as well, sharp as a fragment of glass.

"Day by day. We've no other choice."

His eyes fell to the sheath at her waist. This morning, he had watched her strap it on in silence, feeling a strange combination of pride and regret.

She seemed to know his thoughts. "Lately, I've had no need for the thing. A dagger is useless against the plague."

He pointed to the dun-colored landscape of Turkey massed along the eastern horizon. "You fear the plague more than that?"

"I still believe we need a plan in the event of an attack. And a means of escape."

"I agree."

She looked skeptical. "Do you?"

He nodded. "I placed us in harm's way, put all my faith in the knights, to our detriment. Not just by bringing our family to Rhodes, but by insisting on the life of a falconer all these years."

Sophie eyed him thoughtfully but said nothing.

"When the girls were taken," he went on, "I'd never felt so powerless and uncertain in my life. If there is another attack, we can at least be ready."

Sophie searched his face, seeking something in his eyes. She seemed satisfied and turned her gaze back to the sea.

"Let's walk to Santa Maria, light a candle, and say our prayers together," he suggested. "And on the way there, you can tell me more about your scheme to export Cypriot cloth to France."

"Why?" She glanced at him warily.

"The day my father died, I promised him I'd make my own fortune. So far, I've failed to make good on that vow. It's only now I understand I can't do it alone, Sophie. We must make our own way in the world—together."

"Will we be trading in antiquities, then?" she asked, one eyebrow raised. “From what I hear, there is much more money in that than the cloth trade.”

Cédric grinned. “I’m not sure I want to wade into waters quite so murky. Fabric is a business you know well, and you’ve got contacts in France eager for goods from Cyprus. I see the wisdom in the venture now, but I’m too busy with my work to help much. No, I believe this is an endeavor you should lead.”

A radiant smile took hold of Sophie’s face, the two dimples on either side of her mouth deepening. Light flared in her eyes. Those searingly blue eyes. How many times had he been mesmerized by their luminous depths? The sight sent him back to their first days in Bruges, when he’d been drawn to her like a falcon on a lure.

“What is it?” he asked, catching both her hands in his.

“You once said you would never allow me to start my own enterprise on this island.” Her expression held a hint of a challenge, but he also saw tenderness there. “And yet, here we are.”

Cédric bent and kissed her. “Yes,” he said softly. “Here we are.”

HISTORICAL NOTES

Island of Gold is the first novel in the Sea and Stone Chronicles, a series of stand-alone books about ordinary people living in the shadow of the Knights Hospitaller in fifteenth-century Rhodes and Cyprus.

After publishing the Miramonde Series (the story of a Renaissance-era female artist and the modern-day scholar on her trail) I knew I wanted to keep digging into the fifteenth century.

I decided the Sea and Stone Chronicles would star strong, inspiring women and the men—fathers, husbands, brothers—who helped them thrive. The series distills my love of history, adventure, and romance into page-turning novels based on solid research.

Readers are always interested in what is real and what is imagined. The following will give you an idea of what I found in the historical record and what I created.

I visited Rhodes with my family ten years ago and fell in love with the island, its culture, and its history. I was fascinated to learn Rhodes is not only a crossroads of maritime trade going back to ancient times, but was also the seat of power for the Knights Hospitaller of the Order of St. John in the medieval and early Renaissance eras.

After initial successes in the early Crusades, the knights were gradually pushed out of the Middle East by Muslim forces over a period of centuries. By the early 1300s, they had set up shop on Cyprus. Within a few years, they transferred their headquarters to Rhodes and annexed all the nearby islands. Their rule of Rhodes would last two centuries.

When I started the research for this series, I struggled to find information in the historical record about people in Rhodes during that time. After all, it was six hundred years ago, when few people were literate. Records that did exist mostly vanished over the centuries.

I did find tantalizing glimpses of the Order of St. John in various books and academic papers. Many authors of these resources share my struggle over the lack of details available about the Order's time in Rhodes. When the knights were forced out after months of siege by the Ottoman Turks in 1522, not all of their documentation made it to Malta, where they took up residence for the next several centuries. My efforts to gain access to the library of the Knights Hospitaller have been unsuccessful so far (the Order of St. John still exists and has a headquarters in Rome now).

In the end, I found enough information about the Order for my purposes, because my series isn't really about the knights. It's about the people living in their shadow.

To that end, I learned about a thriving merchant class in Rhodes and a steady stream of pilgrims stopping there on their way to Jerusalem. I dug up evidence of a bustling medieval maritime economy: Rhodes Town was a major trade destination for merchants from Europe, Asia, and Africa. I also discovered traces of Western-trained artisans and artists who settled in Rhodes Town and created commissioned work for merchants and knights.

It was difficult to find information about people not associated with the knights—especially women. I found much more detail about women in Crete and Cyprus than in Rhodes. For example, I found fourteenth-century wills that showed women owned property and businesses, bought and sold goods, owned slaves, and traveled.

Slavery was a huge part of the economy in the medieval Mediterranean. The knights engaged in piracy, as did the Venetians, the Genoese, the Turks, the Mamluks (rulers of Egypt during this era;

more about them will be revealed in future books in the series), and pretty much anyone else with a few ships at their disposal.

Naval warfare was constant, and taking captives was part of the routine once a ship was boarded at sea. The knights used Muslim slaves for their sugar plantations and their endless fortifications of the defensive walls in Rhodes Town. Many of the slaves I found evidence of in Rhodes were Greek Christians. There were also slaves from as far away as the Black Sea, Armenia, and Russia. Manumission was possible for Christian slaves (several I read about were freed after seven years in Rhodes) but I found only one example of a Muslim slave being freed in Rhodes. Often the freed slaves continued to work for their former owners, and sometimes the owners put up dowries for slaves to get married.

Grand Master Jacques de Milly was a real historical figure and he ruled the Order from 1454 until 1461. Many of the Order's war galleys used both sails and oars to move across the seas. A class of Rhodians known as "*marinaria*" were forced to labor as rowers for the knights, and they passed down the obligation to their children. The practice was abolished some years after Jacques de Milly's tenure ended; this could be due to the fact that people often fled Rhodes to avoid being conscripted into service.

I learned a lot about the precious fabrics manufactured in Cyprus and sold all over Western Europe, down to the cost per bolt of camlet cloth in the 1450s. I studied currencies and found records of prices in the Mediterranean at the time for everything from livestock to oil to wine to slaves.

The Greek falconer Agapitos Kassianos (who is usually referred to by European historians as Ayme Cassein) was also a real historical figure who worked for the knights in Rhodes. To create my fictional hero Cédric de Montavon, I delved deep into falconry and the trade in falcons throughout Europe.

I had already done a lot of research about the fabric trade in France and Toulouse during this era. My new research revealed that French women of the day paid taxes, owned businesses, bought and sold goods, belonged to trade guilds, and worked in many fields including art illustration and book making. This helped me develop the complex character of Sophie Portier.

The fifteenth century saw the growth of a trade in antiquities from Rhodes to Italy. During the early Renaissance, wealthy nobles and merchants in Florence and Venice developed a taste for marble statues, of which there were plenty in Rhodes. Temples and grottoes dedicated to Greek gods and goddesses were part of the landscape during the Order's rule and served as constant reminders of paganism. The knights expressly forbade worship of the ancient gods and threatened to burn at the stake anyone who defied that rule. The knights did allow the Greek Orthodox church to exist alongside Catholicism in Rhodes, although there were occasional uprisings against the Order led by Greek Orthodox priests.

Continuing a practice I started with the Miramonde Series, I used names of real people for some of my supporting characters. For example, Dragonetto is named for a powerful landowner of Rhodes who was influential with the Order during the early fifteenth century. A Catalan pirate named Baldaia plied the Aegean Sea at that time, and the historical evidence shows him to be a villain worthy of the name.

The attacks on Kos, Archangelos, Symi, and other places all did take place as described, although my sources contradict each other regarding the exact dates of the attacks and the names of all the islands involved.

Little did I know when I began my research during the COVID crisis that my story would involve an epidemic. But Jacques de Milly's stint as grand master demanded that he preside over both military attacks and a public health emergency.

According to historians, Jacques de Milly's swift implementation of quarantine kept a plague from sweeping through the population. It is unclear if this was indeed the "Black Death" or some other similarly deadly illness. People did wear masks to prevent transmission of disease and quarantine was an accepted method of dealing with epidemics during the medieval and Renaissance eras.

For more details about my research, please visit my blog at www.amymaroney.com.

ACKNOWLEDGMENTS

One of the best things about writing historical fiction is getting to know other authors. During the research and writing of this book, I was lucky enough to find my ideal writing critique partners. Elizabeth St.John and Cryssa Bazos, your insights and suggestions pushed me to be a better writer, and your support kept me motivated through a difficult year. I'm so grateful to you both, *amigas*.

Jenny Quinlan, thank you for your excellent guidance both at the developmental and copyediting stages. Thank you to all the members of the Coffee Pot Tweet Group for encouragement and inspiration. Thank you, Patrick Knowles, for my beautiful cover.

My deep gratitude goes out to Diana Gilliland Wright and Patricia Riak, two academic professionals who graciously shared their research with me and pointed me toward invaluable resources that strengthened my story and deepened my characters.

I am indebted to the academic researchers whose work is available on Academia.edu, and I've been lucky enough to locate critical documents through Interlibrary Loan and through communication with individuals. I am particularly grateful for the work of Anthony Luttrell, Nicholas Coureas, and David Jacoby.

As ever, a heartfelt thank you to all my family and friends for cheering me on. Special thanks to Julie Cassin, soul sister and first reader. My daughters Dahlia and Nora are the reason I started writing historical fiction about strong women of the past, and they continue to inspire me every day. Finally, I have only gotten this far in my author journey thanks to my husband Jon's steadfast love and support.

MEET AMY MARONEY

Amy Maroney lives in Oregon with her family. She spent many years as a writer and editor of nonfiction before turning her hand to historical fiction. When she's not diving down research rabbit holes, she enjoys hiking, dancing, traveling, and reading. Amy is the author of the Miramonde Series, a trilogy about a Renaissance-era female artist and the modern-day scholar on her trail.

Join Amy's community of readers and get monthly updates about her research and next books (plus great deals on historical fiction) at www.amymaroney.com.

If you enjoyed this book, please take a moment to leave a review online or spread the word to family and friends.

facebook.com/amymaroneyauthor
twitter.com/wilaroney
instagram.com/amymaroneywrites
pinterest.com/amyloveshistory

ALSO BY AMY MARONEY

The Miramonde Series is the award-winning story of a Renaissance-era female artist and the modern-day scholar on her trail.

Book 1: The Girl from Oto

Book 2: Mira's Way

Book 3: A Place in the World

Download *The Promise*, a free prequel novella to the series, when you join Amy's community of readers at www.amymaroney.com.